D0283560

From high school politics to prison system prejudice, Rivers offers a spot-on commentary on what it means to turn a blind eye and the price we *all* pay when light doesn't shine on the shadows. *Complicit* is a rare powerhouse of a literary thriller with a profound moral compass.

— JOE CLIFFORD, AUTHOR OF *THE SHADOW PEOPLE* AND THE JAY PORTER THRILLER SERIES

The kickoff to the Legacy of Silence series combines suspense, deep relationships, and a compelling protagonist.

— *BOOKLIFE REVIEWS*

A haunting deep dive into the demons all women must face. A brilliant masterpiece.

— -REA FREY, AUTHOR OF *UNTIL I FIND YOU*

Two sisters grown apart over the years, haunted by secrets they don't want to share, are drawn together when young girls from their hometown start disappearing...and dying. *Complicit* is an excellent romantic mystery that reveals one small town's ugly side.

— PAT STOLTEY, AUTHOR OF *WISHING CASWELL DEAD*

COMPLICIT

A LEGACY OF SILENCE NOVEL

AMY RIVERS

Compathy Press, LLC

Copyright © 2021 by Amy Rivers

All rights reserved.

Cover design by Carl Graves

Printed in the United States of America

First printing, 2021

Print: 978-1-7345160-4-3

Ebook: 978-1-7345160-5-0

No part of this book may be reproduced in any form or by any electronic or mechanical means, including information storage and retrieval systems, without written permission from the author, except for the use of brief quotations in a book review.

Compathy Press, LLC
2770 Arapahoe Rd.
Ste 132-1128
Lafayette, CO 80026

This is a work of fiction. Names, characters, businesses, places, events, locales, and incidents are either the products of the author's imagination or used in a fictitious manner. Any resemblance to actual persons, living or dead, or actual events is purely coincidental.

For my sister Cam
Hermanas son los mejores amigos.
You are mine.

In memory of my beloved aunt
Tina Godby-Ware
Loving. Kind. Strong. Badass.
May we all strive to be so.

CHAPTER ONE

April 1996

Kate pushed past her scowling sister, ready to get out of the house and away from the drama of the night before. She loved her family dearly, but Tilly's propensity to get into screaming matches with their parents had Kate counting down the days until she left for college.

"I'm coming!" she yelled as she raced out of her house, letting the screen door slam behind her. She'd heard the familiar half-dead horn honking from her room and knew there was more where that came from. Kate pretended to be annoyed but Roman's enthusiasm was infectious, even from a distance.

"Princesa!"

"Sorry, Dad!" Kate shouted, but she kept her pace, yanking open the passenger-side door of Roman's beat-up old car and throwing her bag into the back seat as she slid in beside him.

"Impatient much?" she complained, buckling her seatbelt. A trickle of sweat was already sliding down her neck. In one deft move she gathered up her curly brown hair, forming a messy ponytail and pulling the scrunchie from her wrist to secure the hasty hairdo.

"What?" she asked, noticing Roman staring at her. "By the way, the honking? What the hell! My dad was pissed."

Roman smiled. "Nah, he's used to me. Besides, it's already hot and I want to get there before we miss out on the shade." He eased the car away from the curb. Kate hoped her dad wasn't watching them as they turned off her street. It would be pretty obvious that they weren't heading for school.

"What are we listening to?" Kate asked, cranking up the radio, the only part of Roman's car that was shiny and new. R.E.M. blared through the speakers. Kate started singing at the top of her lungs, and before long Roman joined her. They kept the windows rolled up to let the air conditioner do its job. It also muffled the racket they were making. As much as Kate loved ditching with Roman she hadn't been caught yet, and with a month left before graduation, she was hoping to keep it that way.

The song faded out in the middle of a verse. "God, this guy is terrible," Kate groaned, turning down the volume to drone out the boring banter from their least-favorite local D.J.

"Yeah he is," Roman agreed. "Would have been nice if *he'd* left town after high school, eh?" As the words left his mouth, a shadow settled over his features. Kate looked away, hoping they could avoid yet another argument about Kate's post-graduation plans.

Kate had stopped talking openly about her plans after their first big fight. Roman hadn't entirely settled on a direction for his life, but Kate had her mind set on attending an out-of-state college and leaving her dusty hometown far behind her. She knew she'd miss her best friend, but that didn't give him the right to keep her from pursuing her dreams.

Luckily, Roman didn't seem bent on picking a fight. He began to hum, and Kate felt the tension leave her shoulders.

When they reached the spot where the road crossed the

creek, they could already see other cars driving up the creek bed.

"They never learn, do they?" Roman said as he drove past, heading for a spot further up the road where they could park on the shoulder and hike down.

"Idiots," Kate muttered, remembering the last time they'd driven up the creek bed, barely escaping the truant officers who knew the creek was a favorite ditching spot. All they had to do was camp out at the entrance and it was like shooting fish in a barrel.

Roman parked near an outcropping of creosote bushes that nearly hid his car from view.

They both got out, slid on their backpacks, and walked toward the cliff overlooking the creek. Kate felt the red dirt shift underneath her feet as she neared the edge. "Must still be a little wet from the rain last week," she called back as Roman joined her.

"Want me to go first?" he asked playfully.

"Yeah, right," Kate said, smiling. She started down the steep bank, lead foot sideways to compensate for the sliding that happened as she moved down.

They hiked upstream to a place where the water pooled and the mesquite trees provided some shade. Sometimes the place was packed, but today only a few kids were hanging around.

Kate and Roman found a spot where some big rocks formed a natural seat at the water's edge. They took off their shoes and stuck their feet into the cool water, using their backpacks as chair backs.

Fluffy white clouds dotted the bright blue New Mexico sky. For a while they sat in silence, soaking up the sunshine.

"Tell me you're not going to miss this," Roman said quietly. Kate closed her eyes and tried to maintain a neutral tone.

"I will miss it," she said. "But there's so much I want to do, Roman. And I can't get the education I want here."

"I know," he said miserably. Kate wished she could make him understand. She was excited about her upcoming move, but also scared. And it would have been nice to have Roman as her ally rather than having to survive his moodiness.

"It's not like I'll never be back," Kate said. "Thanksgiving is just a few months away, and you know I'll be home for luminarias and your mom's posole at Christmas." She tried to infuse her words with positivity.

Roman didn't respond, so Kate opened her eyes again and resumed her study of the clouds. She was so relaxed that she started to feel drowsy.

"Hey," Roman said, shaking her shoulder. "Wake up, Kate. You're going to burn."

Kate sat up, stretching back muscles that had started to cramp against the hard rock surface. "Sorry, I must have dozed."

Roman laughed. "Slept is more like it. You've been out for, like, an hour. I didn't want to wake you, but your face is getting pink."

"I didn't sleep well last night." Kate reached up to rub her eye and winced at her tender skin. She wasn't prone to sunburns, but it was getting to that part of the day when the sun was most intense. Looking around, Kate noticed the other kids had all gone.

"Where is everybody?" she asked, a hint of panic creeping into her voice. She scanned the surrounding area for lurking truant officers—or worse, the police.

"Must have been your snoring," Roman teased, skipping a stone across the water.

"I don't snore!"

"How would you know? You weren't the one who had to listen to you."

Kate scooped up a handful of water and threw it at Roman. He shouted "Hey!" but his eyes were bright with mischief. It was a look Kate had grown to love over the years. A look that usually landed them both in trouble. Roman seemed to think most rules didn't apply to him until he got caught. He was the perfect balance for Kate's uptight nature.

Roman started jogging up the creek.

"Wait up!" Kate called, struggling to pull her socks and shoes on while Roman widened the gap between them. She left her backpack behind and sprinted in his direction. When she finally caught up, she was sweating again. "Dammit, Roman," she panted, wishing she'd grabbed a drink of water before chasing him.

"Aw, come on. Don't be mad," he said, bumping her arm. A playful jab between friends. Something he'd done a hundred times.

Except this time it didn't feel the same. There'd been a lot more awkward moments lately. Kate couldn't put her finger on what was different, but his touch made her shiver. His skin was warm and soft against hers. Roman looked as uneasy as Kate felt. He dropped his arm to his side and leaned away.

Kate's body felt heavy, keeping her frozen in place. She looked at Roman, wondering why she'd never noticed the green flecks in his hazel eyes. Or maybe she had, but they'd never seemed quite as lovely. Her heart began to race.

"Kate," Roman said, his voice raspy, barely a whisper.

Something akin to terror squeezed Kate's heart as she saw the determination in Roman's eyes. Suddenly, she knew exactly what he was going to say, and a part of her wanted him to. He reached out and entwined his fingers with hers. Needing time to think, Kate turned. "Let's walk," she managed to get out.

She began upstream again but kept her hand in Roman's, her mind a storm of feelings and thoughts. She didn't dare look back at him for fear her heart would melt her resolve. Despite the fluttering occurring in her at this moment, in less than two months she'd be leaving town. And she didn't want anything keeping her torn between her past and her future. It would be hard enough just to leave her best friend.

She'd almost found the courage to tell him when they rounded a bend and stopped dead in their tracks, their hands breaking apart.

There was a car.

It was much further up the creek than anyone dared drive, and Kate could see that the interior had been burned out. The license plate was missing and the windows had all been smashed in. But the thing that caught her attention, the thing that had Kate trembling where she stood, was the sight of a charred hand hanging through the open driver's side door.

CHAPTER TWO

Present Day

Kate had never seen a person so changed in such a short time. When they'd first met, Mandy Garcia had alternated between glaring at Kate and shooting murderous glances at her mother who'd requested the sessions, her ponytail swinging each time she moved her head, her glossed lips pressed tight with disdain.

Today the teen sat slumped in the chair near Kate's office door, hair hanging over one eye, baggy clothing hiding her figure. This was only their third appointment, and so far Mandy hadn't spoken to Kate—not even to say hello or goodbye. When Kate opened her office door Mandy oozed into the room, settling into the chair furthest from Kate's where she barely moved throughout the session.

The clock in Kate's office ticked loudly as she stared at the silent girl. Mandy's eyes never left the floor, like she was studying every fiber in the threadbare carpet, if she was looking at anything at all. Only the rise and fall of her shoulders indicated the teen was alive. Kate had waited patiently, but toward the end she had to stop herself from drumming her fingers on the desk. Time was almost up.

"Look, Mandy. We're down to our last few minutes. You might not believe this, but I want to help you. I care about the time we spend here, and I'm not blind or stupid. I can see that something is bothering you." Kate shocked herself by being so blunt, but she'd learned quickly that the high schoolers she counseled reacted more favorably to frankness than to being coddled.

Unfortunately, her plea seemed to die between them. Mandy didn't react at all. Kate would have been relieved to see her roll her eyes or even shrug, but Mandy stayed still and silent.

When the bell rang, signaling the end of a period, Kate shifted in her chair. She pulled out her notes with a heavy sigh. "I'll see you next week, then."

Mandy grabbed her backpack and was out the door almost before Kate had finished the sentence. A disappointing end to a stressful day.

Mandy was one of Kate's repeat clients but Kate had seen a steady stream of shell-shocked teens drifting in and out of her office all day, clearly needing to talk about their missing classmate, Gabby Greene, but never quite knowing what to say. Kate had done her best to calm them, to reassure them, but the disappearance had the whole school on edge. Even Kate was struggling to keep her emotions in check as the hours wore on.

For a moment Kate wondered if that was Mandy's problem too but her gut told her no. Everything about Mandy's appearance and demeanor screamed trauma. Kate knew that Mandy's parents' divorce was not amicable. She wondered if something had happened to the girl on her weekend visit with her dad. It wouldn't be the first time a child had gotten caught in the crossfire of their parents' anger and frustration.

The final hour of the school day dragged by, but Kate was grateful that she hadn't had any more unscheduled visits. She took advantage of the lull to try and soothe her own nerves, practicing her breathing techniques. When she finally got back to her paperwork, she felt calmer and proud of herself for keeping a cool head despite the chaos of the day.

Mandy's face smiled up at Kate from the folder on her desk. Kate liked to have a picture of her clients in their files. It served as a reminder that the circumstances under which a client sought help were not the sum total of that person. After finishing her notes and replacing Mandy's file in the cabinet Kate packed her bag and walked into the front office, closing the door softly behind her.

A couple of Kate's favorite teachers walked past, waving good night. As much as Kate grumbled about being back home, she'd always been scholastically inclined and the school held a lot of good memories. She was especially fond of the overworked but incredibly concerned and caring teachers. If only the administration showed as much concern.

"I'm done for the day. How're you holding up, Steph?"

Stephanie Kramer had worked the front desk at Centennial High School for more than a decade, but she'd never looked as harried as she did that day. Kate and Steph had graduated the same year, but while Kate had gone away to college Steph had stayed in their hometown of Alamogordo, New Mexico. Usually she was upbeat and snarky, but it seemed that Gabby's disappearance had everyone spooked.

"I wish we could just go home when the kids do. This last hour is torture."

Kate smiled. "I know what you mean. Did Mandy's mom fill out that packet I sent home?"

"Not yet," Steph said with a roll of her eyes. "Honestly, from what I hear she's spending most of her time with her new man these days. Not surprised Mandy's having such a hard time."

"I'll follow up with her on Monday," Kate said with a sigh. "Again."

On her way home, Kate tried to leave work behind, but she was still fuming over Mandy's mother. Having children had never been a priority for Kate and at thirty-five, her chances were becoming slimmer. That being said, she did love children—even the angsty adolescents she now worked with—and it made her furious when she thought about Mandy's mother, who'd pushed Mandy into counseling but seemed uninterested in whether or not it actually helped.

Kate thought back on her own teen years. She got good grades, helped around the house, and had a good relationship with her parents. She dated a bit, but mostly spent time with her friends. Well, one friend.

Her childhood home had been a peaceful place until her senior year, when her younger sister Tilly was a sophomore. Tilly had always had a more abrasive personality than Kate, but that year she became an absolute terror. Kate could remember many nights when her mother and sister could be heard yelling down the block. Kate had been more than ready to leave and get started on her own life by the time she reached graduation. She'd left town with no regrets—or at least only one. Which was a pretty good average, she figured.

Now, Kate lived in the same house she'd grown up in. Slept in the same bed she'd slept in as a child. Every morning, she woke with the bright desert sun shining through vertical blinds that needed to be replaced, and she grieved for the life she'd left behind. A life where she'd delved into the darkest depths of human behavior and shaped policy that, she hoped, made the world a better place. A life where she didn't spend every day listening to the problems of cranky adolescents and fighting with school administration over budgets.

She loved being with her father but being back home without her mother and sister felt empty. She longed to have her own space, and a social life, not that she'd ever made much of an effort to get out before moving home, a point that her lack of freedom seemed to punctuate.

Most of all, Kate missed her career. She'd busted her ass to become a highly-skilled forensic psychologist, and had finally landed her dream job in the prison system. She ached for the challenges of working with inmates, despite the looming threat of violence and the anguish that permeated every moment of the day. No matter how long she'd been at the high school, she considered it a hiatus from her real career.

And yet, she wouldn't go back. She couldn't. One horrific act of violence had ended everything, sent her home to her father broken, physically and emotionally. The anger and bitterness, the bone-deep disappointment, made every day a struggle.

"Kate?" Her father's voice startled her. She'd been standing in the doorway, lost in thought. "Close the door, mija."

Kate did as she was told and set her purse down by the front door. "Are you ready to go?"

"Just waiting on you," he teased. Kate watched her father walk from the living room to the kitchen, noticing how slowly he moved. In his younger years Frank Medina had been a ball of energy, a source of perpetual motion in their house. Since her mother's death, Kate's father had aged quickly. Kate knew that grief took its toll on people, but it had been five years and Frank was showing worsening signs of depression and fatigue.

"I'm going to go change and then we can head out," Kate said, walking back toward her bedroom. She was pulling her favorite sweatshirt over her head when her father knocked quietly at her door.

"Have you heard from your sister?" he asked when she let him in.

Kate groaned. "No, Dad. I texted her the name of the restaurant. Again. Hope she shows up this time," Kate grumbled, instantly regretting the jab. Her father wouldn't tolerate any negative remarks about Tilly. Kate had gotten used to biting her tongue around him, despite the fact that Tilly was notoriously late and regularly bailed on them even when they drove all the way to Albuquerque or Santa Fe to see her.

Frank seemed content to forgive Tilly just about anything. Kate was not. She braced herself for a rebuke, but Frank stayed silent. Instead, he looked down at the floor before turning and walking back to the living room. Why did he always look so guilty when he talked about Tilly?

Kate studied her father. They were seated across from one another working on their third basket of bread as they waited for Tilly to make an appearance. The shadows under his eyes confirmed what Kate already knew—her father wasn't sleeping. He'd been coughing for more than two weeks, especially at night. Kate had pushed him to go to urgent care. But he was stubborn, as always, and waved her off. In the ensuing chaos at work, Kate had forgotten to nag him.

"You feeling okay, Dad?" Kate asked. She glanced at her watch. They'd been sitting in the restaurant for nearly forty-five minutes. Tilly was late, as usual.

"Just tired, Princesa."

Kate cringed at the nickname. As the firstborn Kate had been her parents' pride and joy, but the nickname had followed her into adulthood, at least where her father was concerned. At times it felt like a curse. She was about to offer a snide response, when her father's face lit up and she knew she'd turn to find her sister walking toward them.

"Hi, Dad," Tilly said as she approached the table. "Kate."

She slung her purse over the back of her chair and sat down without giving her father a hug. She never gave their father a hug. And each time, Kate would feel a little jolt of pain in her heart as she watched her father try to hide his disappointment.

Kate knew her father would disapprove of any sarcastic remarks, but Kate's patience was at an all-time low.

"Nice of you to join us," she snapped at Tilly.

"I'm sorry, Kate. My job doesn't have *predictable* hours like yours." There was no venom in Tilly's voice, but her dig hit its mark nonetheless. Tilly had no way of knowing how Kate felt about her current job. She never asked, and Kate never told.

"You're at a conference, Tilly. That's not exactly an emergency situation."

"Girls," their father said wearily. "Can we please not bicker."

"Sorry, Dad." Tilly's voice held no hint of apology despite her words. Kate closed her eyes and counted to ten, swallowing five long years of resentment before rejoining the conversation.

"Did you guys order?" Tilly asked, tossing her menu casually on the table.

"Not yet," Frank piped up, summoning a server to the table with a quick flick of his wrist and a smile.

They chatted uncomfortably as they waited for their food. Following the usual pattern, the conversation mostly revolved around Tilly.

"When I took this position, I didn't realize how much I was going to miss working with patients," Tilly said. "I know that what I'm doing will help so many victims, but it's hard not to become cynical working with law enforcement all day. Their prejudices are so deeply ingrained into the culture."

Kate listened intently despite herself. She and Tilly had always shared a common interest in criminal justice and investigation. Kate had chosen a path that led her to psychology and working with people to discover the underlying roots of their behavioral and social issues. Tilly had taken a different path altogether, becoming one of the youngest forensic nurses to serve on the National Forensic Nursing Organization Board of Directors. She'd taken a new position working on policy and training for law enforcement handling violent crimes.

Kate was envious, though she would never admit it to her sister. When her mother died, Kate had taken a leave of absence from her career as a prison psychologist to help her father get his affairs in order. After a year Kate sent in her letter of resignation, citing the need to take care of her aging father as her reason for not going back. There was more to it than that, not that Kate had shared her personal problems with her family. Now Kate was working at her hometown high school, helping kids navigate the perils of adolescence. It wasn't the life she'd dreamed of living.

"How's school?" Tilly asked, as if reading her thoughts. Kate hated talking about her job with her sister. She could feel the judgment in Tilly's tone.

"Pretty stressful right now, actually. A girl disappeared a few weeks ago and the kids are all on edge. So is the staff. It's pretty awful."

"A runaway?" Tilly asked, her focus entirely on Kate for once. Kate couldn't help but bask in the momentary spotlight, fleeting though it may be.

"Maybe. Though she's not the type. Good student. Quiet. Kind of a loner, or at least she didn't have much of a social life. The official consensus seems to be that she left on her own, but her parents insist she would never do that." Kate couldn't hide the skepticism in her voice.

"Is Roman still working for police department?" Tilly asked.

Kate's face flushed before she could gain control of her emotions. "Yes."

"What does he think happened?"

"I wouldn't know, Tilly. Roman hasn't spoken more than two words to me since high school," Kate said. Despite her promises to return, Kate hadn't come home for holidays or breaks. After that day in the creek, Kate cut all ties and her friendship with Roman was the only casualty she regretted. A bitter taste crept into her mouth. "Of course you'd know that if you ever came home. Or called. Or asked."

Tilly gave an amused smile, but her tone remained serious. "Your choices are not my fault, Kate. If you're unhappy with your life, change it."

"If I want your advice, I'll ask for it," Kate snapped, her voice rising in pitch.

"Enough!" their father said loudly, causing a few heads to turn. He lowered his voice. "I'm not in the mood to hear you two go at it tonight." He turned to Kate, his eyes pleading. "Katie. I am grateful for the help you've given me these past few years. I don't know what I would have done without you. Matilda." He turned to Tilly, but hesitated. Kate looked over and saw fire in her sister's eyes. She'd been surprised to hear Tilly's full name being used. Her father stayed silent, and Kate wondered, not for the first time, what had happened between the two of them to create such tension in their relationship.

Thankfully, before anyone could say another word, the food arrived. They ate in silence, the tension thick between them. Finally Frank said, "Girls, I have something I need to talk to you about." His voice shook.

"What is it, Daddy?" Kate asked, wincing at her timid tone and the childish moniker that only slipped out of her mouth when she was stressed.

"I've been diagnosed with pancreatic cancer. Stage IV."

Kate felt like the air had been sucked out of the room. Tilly gasped, her face draining of all its color.

"What does that mean?" Kate asked weakly. Her father had certainly seemed more tired than usual lately, but she just thought he was fighting off a stubborn cold. She couldn't believe he would have kept such big news from her.

"It means I'm going to die," he said, very matter-of-fact. "I saw the doctor yesterday and he confirmed it. They can try radiation and chemotherapy, but the cancer has spread to my lymph nodes and the prognosis is not good." He paused, gazing at his daughters, tears welling in his eyes. "I would like to spend whatever time I have left in peace, and I don't think treatment will give me that." He raised his hands as both girls started to object. "I'd like you both to respect my wishes."

The silence that followed threatened to swallow them. Kate was the first to break it.

"I'll ask Pete if I can reduce my hours at work," she started. "And Tilly can come help take care of you, right?" Kate looked at her sister, expecting cooperation for once. Tilly looked small in her chair, her face awash with emotion. For the longest time they sat there, suspended in time.

Finally Tilly cleared her throat, and in a small voice she said, "I can't." She paused, then added, "I'm sorry" to no one in particular as she grabbed her bag and fled the restaurant.

CHAPTER THREE

"Bad weekend?" Steph asked when Kate staggered into work with only a few minutes to spare before her first appointment at eight o'clock. She followed Kate to her office and leaned against the doorframe, looking concerned.

Kate rubbed her forehead, trying to wipe away her exhaustion. "Yes, and I didn't sleep much."

Pete McIntyre, the principal, peeked around the corner.

"Sorry to interrupt. We've got a bit of a situation out here."

Steph excused herself and Pete ushered a middle-aged man toward the open chair in Kate's office.

"Kate, this is David Garcia. Mandy's father." Kate extended a hand to the visitor, but he simply stared at her. She stole a quick glance at Pete, whose expression was apologetic. "Mr. Garcia is concerned about his daughter. I hoped you could talk with him."

"Of course," Kate said, steeling herself for a confrontation. David Garcia and his wife were engaged in a vicious custody battle over Mandy and her younger sister Leah. So far the court was siding with Mandy's mother, awarding custodial rights until a final resolution could be reached. Visitation was very limited, but Kate didn't know the particulars. "Please have a seat," she said. Pete lingered awkwardly at the door. "We're all right, Pete," she said, noting the grateful look on his face as he closed the door behind him.

David Garcia did not sit. He stood precisely where he'd been standing, stone-faced, back and limbs rigid.

Kate groaned but put on her best warm smile. "How can I help you, Mr. Garcia?" She took a seat, leaning back in her chair. She hoped modeling calm would help the man in her office let go of his tense stance, though she felt neither calm nor particularly empathetic at that particular moment. She could feel how puffy her eyes were without having to touch them, and she begrudged the interruption.

"My daughter told me she meets with you. I'd like to see her file," he said quietly.

"Mr. Garcia, I try to keep student files confidential as long as there is no threat of harm to the student or anyone else, and in Mandy's case, there's no sign of that. It helps the kids feel more comfortable speaking with me."

Kate was hedging. Without a court order barring David Garcia from his daughter's records, she couldn't actually keep them from him. She was surprised that Mandy had even told her father she was seeing the school psychologist. The sessions weren't going well, and Kate was worried that anything she said to Mandy's father might impede any progress she'd made. Not that there seemed to have been any.

"I'm her father," his voice was barely audible, but Kate could see his hands balling into fists at his side. He looked like a ticking time-bomb, but the aggression seemed to be inwardly directed. Nonetheless, she felt nervous.

"I understand your frustration," Kate replied, trying to match his tone. She could feel the hairs on the back of her neck prickle. It reminded her of her prison job, where the threat of violence was ever-present. She was grateful for her training even if she rarely used it in her current position. "I know that your family is going through a rough patch, and I'd like to try and help by providing a safe place for Mandy to talk about her feelings. That can be really important during a divorce."

Kate counted slowly in her mind, her senses on high alert. She moved her chair back ever so slightly in case she needed to stand, but she worked hard to keep her outward demeanor as calm as possible. After a few tense moments, Mr. Garcia unclenched his fists and his whole body seemed to sag. He took a seat across from her.

"Please, Miss..." He looked around, searching for a name tag or placard.

"Medina."

"Ms. Medina. I don't know what to do. I'm only allowed to see my daughters once a week, and I know there's something wrong with Mandy. Her mother tells me she's angry with me, but there's more to it. She's not herself." Desperation rolled off him in waves, tugging at Kate's heart.

"I'm so sorry, Mr. Garcia. To be honest, Mandy really hasn't opened up to me yet. We've only had a few appointments, and it takes some time to develop a rapport. There isn't much to share at this point, but I'm determined to keep trying." Kate thought for a moment about the intake paperwork that Mandy's mom had yet to turn in despite requesting the appointments. Perhaps Mandy's father could fill in some of the gaps. "Has anything happened in Mandy's life lately—besides the divorce—that might be troubling her?"

David's eyes grew wide. "What do you mean?"

Seeing his overreaction to her question, Kate backtracked. "Trouble with friends, or a boy she's seeing?"

David relaxed the tiniest bit. "No. Not that I know of anyway. Mandy's pretty social, but she doesn't date much. She's always been too focused on school and cheerleading."

That had been Kate's assessment, too. Despite her

popularity, Mandy was one of the only girls in her social group not joined at the hip with a boy. "Has Mandy shared her feelings about the divorce?"

David sighed. "Yes. Some. She's been very angry with both me and her mother. But I thought we were keeping the lines of communication open. A couple of weeks ago she skipped a visit, and the next time I saw her she was wearing those baggy clothes the kids wear so you can't tell whether they're a girl or a boy. And she stopped talking, seemed to withdraw into herself. She doesn't even argue with me. I asked her what was wrong a number of times, but she hardly said a word to me. In fact, she hasn't really spoken to me in weeks."

Kate had seen the same shift. She'd tried reaching out to Mandy's mother, but so far hadn't received a return call.

"I'm sorry I can't be of more help. But I promise you I'll do my best to help Mandy work through whatever is bothering her." Kate tried to keep her tone professional but compassionate. She was more determined than ever to get to the bottom of Mandy's issues. She stood and escorted David Garcia to the door. As he walked out of her office, he turned.

"Please," he said. "Mandy isn't one of those brooding teenagers, Ms. Medina. She can have an attitude, but she's very outgoing, cheerful. Whatever is happening . . . it scares me." His head hung low as he walked away. Kate returned to her desk with a heavy heart. Divorce was hard, but now that she'd met David Garcia she was beginning to think that Mandy's problems ran deeper than the current family crisis.

When Kate got home that day, her dad had made dinner. It should have made her feel happy, even grateful, but instead the sight was unsettling.

"What's up, Dad?" Kate asked, setting down her bag and kicking off her shoes.

"Nothing, sweetie. I know the last few weeks have been rough. I hate having to add to your worry. I wanted you to know how much I appreciate you being here with me." He smiled, but Kate's mind immediately went to her sister and the mood shifted.

"You heard from Tilly?" she asked, aware that the question sounded like an accusation.

"She called today while you were at work," her dad replied. "She apologized for walking out on us Friday. She took the news pretty hard."

"Must be nice to be able to only check in when it's convenient."

"Your sister hasn't had an easy life. Don't be so hard on her," Frank chided.

"Are you kidding?!" Kate couldn't help how loud her voice had become. Every bit of anger and grief she'd been feeling was back at the surface. "She didn't even come to Mom's funeral. I don't understand how you can keep defending her!" Kate could feel the tears coming. She hoped her anger would hold them back until she was alone.

"Katie . . ." her dad began, but Kate wasn't finished.

"No. No you don't. Every time I say a word about Tilly, you come at me with 'Katie' or 'Princesa'. I've had it, Dad. I'm tired of putting my life on hold while she gets to live hers whatever way she pleases." As soon as the words left her mouth, Kate regretted them. She resented her sister but she didn't regret the time she'd spent with her dad, especially since his diagnosis. Family was more important to Kate. Her heart ached when she met her father's eyes.

"I'm sorry. I didn't mean that."

"It's okay, Kate. I know how much you've given up to be here with me. I probably should have made you go back, but it was such a comfort having you here after your mom died. More comfort than I deserved. It was just so sudden. I didn't know what to do. I've been selfish. I've even let myself believe that you were happier here, though I can see the toll it's taken on you."

Kate was startled by his earnest speech. Her father was a man of few words, though they'd developed a comfortable existence together. He'd become much more talkative in recent months as if he knew his time was limited.

"Actually, I enjoy working with the kids more than I thought I would. It's the administration that gives me the most trouble. And the parents." Her mind went back to the look on David Garcia's face.

"Interesting day?" her father asked, changing the subject.

Kate smiled at the familiar question, her anger dissipating. She loved that questions and the discussion that followed. Her dad always listened with rapt attention as she described the minutiae of her day. For a moment, Kate felt bad for her sister. She missed out on the sweetest part of family life by staying away.

"A parent of one of my regular students came in today," Kate said, taking a seat at the table. "He was a mess. Nasty divorce. His daughter has been acting strangely. Dressing weird. Reminds me a little bit of that phase Tilly went through in high school." Kate had been rattling facts off almost absentmindedly when she noticed her father's face had turned pale.

"What are you thinking about, Dad?" She reached across the table to take his hand, but his thoughts seemed far away. It took several minutes before he came back to the present.

"I'm sorry, Katie. I must have drifted off for a moment." He offered a weak smile, but returned to whatever place he'd been.

A half-formed question stuck just out reach of Kate's conscious mind. She shook her head to dislodge it, but it was gone.

"Let's talk about something else," Kate said with a sigh.

"We've both had enough stress lately. I'll clean up and then I'm putting on a movie. I need to get my mind off of everything. Join me?"

"Sure, sweetie," he said, but his expression remained strained.

Kate tossed and turned, falling in and out of sleep without any real commitment to either state. In her lucid moments, she thought about her father and her family. Her inability to move forward in her life, fear of the past, and desire to avoid pain and uncertainty. All those big questions churning in her restless mind.

She dreamt vividly. Images of her childhood. Happy times with her sister. Before adolescence took hold of Tilly's personality and wrapped it in a storm of angst, tearing her away from their family unit and sending her out into the world without a tether to her roots.

Inevitably, her dreams took on a dark, familiar theme. A man, strong and vicious, squeezing the air from her body. Clawing fingers. Ripping flesh. The snap of breaking bone. Pain.

She woke with a start. Her hands flew to her neck, grasping at something constricting, knowing that she wouldn't find it. The images in this dream were always vague and blurry, though his face was clear in her waking mind. The feelings, though— those were different. Violent and visceral.

Since Gabby Greene's disappearance, Kate's nightmares had returned full force. How foolish she'd been thinking they'd been banished forever. She lay back down again, hoping sleep would come but understanding the futility of that desire.

Kate dragged herself out of bed the next morning, feeling weary deep in her soul. She wondered how she would survive the death of her father. As much as she hated to admit it she'd begun putting down roots again in her hometown, something she never could have imagined before her mother died. Something she'd never wanted to do. She'd been perfectly content living her life at a distance. True, she missed her parents, but when she was on her own she could follow her own trajectory.

I guess Tilly isn't the only selfish sister.

People often commented on how wonderful it was for her to put her life on hold to be with her widowed father. And Kate let them heap praise on her, knowing that it wasn't entirely true. Yes, she'd come home to help her dad. But that wasn't the reason she stayed. Her mind flashed back to her nightmares, memories she pushed as far away from her as she could. She took a deep breath to remind herself that she could.

"Kate?" Her father's voice drifted down the hallway. When she and Tilly were children, her father's booming voice could reach them halfway down the street. Now his voice was weak, a whisper of the man he used to be.

"Hey, Dad. How are you this morning?" she said as she opened his bedroom door.

Frank lay propped on his pillows. Raising himself up a little, he gave Kate a smile. "I'm all right. A little bit tired. I don't think I feel like getting up, but I'm hungry. I heard you stirring and wondered if you might get me a package of crackers."

"Of course," Kate said. "You sure you don't want something more substantial? I can make some eggs. Won't take long."

"Maybe later," Frank said, wincing.

"Did you take your meds?"

"I did. But the pain seems a little bit worse today."

"Do you need me to call the doctor?"

Frank waved away her question. "No, mija. I just need rest."

Kate padded into the kitchen and took a package of saltines back to Frank's room, laying them on his bedside table.

"Want me to open them up?" Kate asked.

Her father smiled again, but his tone betrayed frustration. "I'm not that far gone, Kate. You can go get ready for your day. I'll be fine."

Kate left her father's door slightly ajar as she retreated to her room.

CHAPTER FOUR

The next day Kate felt better. Right up to the moment when she stepped into her office and found Detective Roman Aguilar waiting for her. Though they'd been inseparable in high school, the two rarely occupied the same space anymore. She knew it wasn't only time and distance, but she liked to think of it that way—made her feel less guilty. Being around him was unnerving, and it brought back too many memories.

As she walked toward her desk, their eyes met and she was the first to look away. There had been a time when Roman knew her better than anyone.

"Hello, Roman."

"Hi, Kate."

His voice was the same as it always had been. When Kate's mom was killed in a car accident, Roman had been there to offer his condolences. Though she'd been trying to hold herself together at the time the sound of his voice burst through her defenses, tearing at her heart. She cried, letting the sorrow of her mother's passing and the regret over how she'd left things with Roman flow through her. She felt lighter and heavier all at once.

Even then, there's been no bridging the gap between them. Roman remained formal and aloof, excusing himself as quickly as he'd appeared. Since that day, they'd settled into a pattern of avoidance. And when that wasn't possible, professional courtesy.

"What brings you here?" Kate asked as she put her purse in her desk drawer and logged into her computer. Her attempt to strike a casual tone missed the mark. She kept her eyes locked on her screen so she wouldn't have to look at him.

"I wanted to talk with you about Gabby Greene."

Kate stopped what she was doing. She shifted in her chair, finally lifting her eyes to his. "I already told you guys I had very little contact with Gabby." Alamogordo PD had interviewed each staff member at the school after Gabby's disappearance, as well as many of the students. "Gabby wasn't one of the students I worked with. And I've never even seen her outside of school, so I'm not sure what kind of help you think I might be able to give."

Roman looked tense and tired. "We found Gabby's body this morning."

Kate gasped, feeling the bile rise in her throat. "Where?"

"At the creek, about a quarter mile upstream from the falls." He paused. Kate didn't push for more details. She wasn't sure she wanted to know but she had a feeling he was going to tell her, so she relished the moments of silence. Once again, the past was knocking at her door.

Kate held up her hand for him to stop but Roman continued. "She was raped. Repeatedly. Brutally. The cause of death was asphyxiation, but she was beaten before she died."

"Oh God, no," Kate said, hugging her arms tight around her middle, trying to separate herself from the news she was hearing. Between her own memories, Roman standing in her office, and the image forming of Gabby Greene's face, bruised and beaten, Kate felt anxiety swelling within her. "Does her family know?"

"We notified them this morning." He paused. "Listen, I know you can't tell me anything the students say in here, but something about this homicide was . . . familiar. It may be gang-related. Have you heard anything that would indicate that?"

Kate hesitated. She had nothing to share with Roman, and she didn't want to give him the impression that she was a willing source of information. But she did want to help. She'd spoken to quite a few students about Gabby's disappearance, and had to be very careful about the fine line she was walking. It was always precarious, trying to shield these young people without the usual aid of patient privilege. She also knew why he'd come to talk to *her*, in particular. This wasn't the first body found in the creek.

"I'm sorry, Roman. I haven't heard anything that would be useful to you." She watched his face fall. She knew that expression well. "But I would encourage students to reach out to law enforcement if they ever did tell me something that I thought you ought to know. And of course, if I suspected any student might harm themselves or someone else, I have a duty to report it."

"Fine. I'll speak with Pete," he said rather gruffly, making his way to his feet. Kate felt his disappointment like a heavy cape draped around her shoulders, the weight of which she'd grown accustomed to. She bit her tongue as she watched him close the door behind him.

Kate sat back in her chair, taking deep breaths and pushing aside any feelings her interaction with Roman had stirred. She would help Pete plan the school's official response. When the news became public, it would cause a lot of confusion and anger in the student population. And for the rest of the town, it was sure to dredge up bad memories.

Students were released early, with communications sent out to parents and the community about grief resources and a plea for any information in solving Gabby Greene's murder. Kate had pulled a few of Gabby's friends out of class before the announcement was made. The girls were overwrought, huddling together as they sobbed uncontrollably. Kate had notified their parents ahead of time, and when they arrived she was relieved to see the girls' families enfold their daughters in love and comfort. Kate ached for all the students who didn't have that.

The staff met that afternoon to plan for the coming weeks, but it was hard to stay focused. So for a while, Kate facilitated an impromptu support group. Given how tearful and weary the staff was, Kate could only imagine how the parents would be feeling. Alamogordo had its share of crime, with gang violence and domestic disputes keeping the town's police force plenty occupied. But it was so much harder to process when the victim was someone so young.

By the time Kate returned to her office, she was dead on her feet. It was all too much. Her dad. Tilly. Now this. And the sudden appearance of Roman Aguilar had sent her into a tailspin. Their lack of contact over the years had allowed her to convince herself he didn't mean anything to her. That she didn't miss his friendship. *Why am I agonizing about things I can't change?*

As she settled back to work, Kate thought about how things could turn upside-down so quickly in life.

Only a week ago, Gabby Greene had walked the halls of this high school and Kate had hardly noticed her. Now, in just a few hours, Kate had learned so much about the teen. How her family was poor. How Gabby worked every night until midnight to help support her five siblings. How her greatest aspiration was to become a doctor—a goal she was well on her way to achieving, having received a hefty scholarship.

A week ago, Gabby Greene had been working toward her dreams one day at a time. And now she was gone.

Kate realized she was crying again. She wiped at her eyes with the sleeve of her shirt, glad that the school was nearly empty and the likelihood of someone walking in on her was slim. Even Steph had gone home, leaving Kate, Pete, and maybe a few of the janitors to finish up the day.

As if on cue, someone knocked on Kate's door.

"Come in," she said, wiping up the last of her tears. Pete stuck his head around the door, his eyes red-rimmed.

"Do you have a minute?" he asked. He looked haggard—his eyes puffy, his skin pale.

"Of course," Kate replied. Pete took a seat across from her.

"How are you holding up?"

Kate shook her head, not trusting herself to speak.

"Me, too." Pete rubbed his hands over his strained face. "I was talking with Roman earlier. I'm not sure we're ready to go through this again."

Kate nodded. "I remember what it was like—the fear, the mistrust, the gossip. I hadn't thought about it much. Now I can't stop thinking about it."

Pete looked as if he might have something more to add, but he stayed quiet, fidgeting where he stood. His discomfort was palpable.

"I'm going to lock up soon and you should head home. Tomorrow's going to be a hard day." Pete got up and walked out of the office, leaving the door ajar. Kate could hear him puttering around. For a moment, her thoughts lingered on Roman and that last day at the creek. The day that changed everything between them.

Kate bolted upright in bed, her hands flying to her throat the way they always did with nightmares these days. As her chest heaved, she reached for the water she kept by her bed and took small steady sips between gulps of air until her breathing began to calm. She counted her breaths, a meditation that might help her go back to sleep.

For almost a year, she'd slept peacefully at night. Finally. But Gabby Greene's disappearance had brought the nightmares back. In tonight's torments, Kate had watched as Gabby fled from the shadow that often chased after Kate. She hadn't escaped, and the horrible sounds were still fresh in Kate's mind. No amount of meditation was going to help.

It was still dark outside, her alarm clock reading 4:17 a.m. The sun would be coming up soon. Kate turned on her bedside lamp and sat up, fluffing the pillows behind her so she could at least rest for a while longer. She pushed aside thoughts of Gabby Greene in favor of another stressful line of thought.

Roman.

It had been seventeen years since she graduated from high school and left town. After that day in the creek—when they'd stumbled upon the dead body, the burned-out car—Kate and Roman had hardly spoken. It was easy to see now how traumatizing that incident had been, especially when the body was identified as one of their classmates. A girl who, in life, Kate had only known in passing, but in death she couldn't get out of her head.

Kate had left town a month early, ready to escape the whispers and rumors that lingered. The fear in the eyes of every student, teacher, and parent. She gave her parents tearful hugs goodbye, with only a small pang of sadness that her best friend wasn't there. But how could he have been? She hadn't told him she was leaving. A choice that she could never take back.

And from the looks Roman gave her, a choice he would never forgive.

Though it was still an hour from her usual wake up time Kate switched her alarm clock off, pulled on her bathrobe and headed to the bathroom, hoping her early shower wouldn't disturb her father. She made the water lukewarm and stepped in, relishing the shock of the cool water, praying it would erase the terrible images and memories from her mind.

CHAPTER FIVE

Following the news of Gabby Greene's murder, a hush fell over the community. The parade of students coming through Kate's office turned to a trickle, and then stopped altogether. Whispers floated like ghosts in the hallways. True, Gabby had not been a particularly popular girl, but she had had friends, all of whom had turned dry-eyed and tight-lipped during the school day, though Kate had still seen them huddling together when they thought no one was looking. Like all the other kids, their words were a quiet hum, barely audible over the prevailing silence.

It was eerily familiar.

Usually able to compartmentalize, Kate caught her mind wandering to her own high school days. She wondered, not for the first time, why every trip down memory lane was colored with regret. After all, she'd done exactly what she'd planned to do. Had the life she'd planned on having—at least until her mother died.

She'd been lost in thought when there was a faint knock on her door. It was time for Mandy's weekly check-in. Kate wasn't sure she was up for another uncomfortable impasse. Mandy walked into the office, letting the door close softly behind her.

She dropped her backpack near the door and took her usual position in the chair opposite Kate, but didn't assume her usual slouch. Instead Mandy sat upright, alert and wary, her eyes bloodshot and red-rimmed. Had she been crying?

Kate scooted her tissue box nearer to the teen as a lone tear slid down her cheek.

Mandy made eye contact with Kate for maybe the second or third time in their entire professional relationship and held Kate's gaze. Her lips twitched, words forming but not quite ready to make their way into the world. When she finally did speak, she whispered, "I'm scared."

It took Kate a moment to collect her thoughts. She knew next to nothing about Mandy. They hadn't had a single notable conversation, and her mother still hadn't filled out the intake packet that Kate needed. They hadn't had a chance to build rapport. Fear was definitely not the first feeling she thought they'd be discussing. "Scared of what?"

The silence stretched. Kate could see that Mandy was struggling and she didn't want to spook the girl.

"What happened to Gabby..." Mandy stopped short and reached for a tissue, her hand shaking. When it was clear that she wasn't going to finish her thought, Kate stepped in.

"What happened to Gabby was terrible. If you want to talk about it, this is a safe place. Nothing you say in our sessions goes further than this room."

Mandy's eyes bored into Kate's. "You can't tell anyone? Not even my mom?"

Kate felt uneasy, but she nodded. "Unless you intend to harm yourself or someone else, I am bound by patient confidentiality." Kate knew that this wasn't strictly true for minors in her care, but she was determined to keep her sessions private as much as possible and would do whatever she could to honor that promise.

Mandy continued to stare at Kate, weighing her words, but

her lips remained tightly pressed together. Kate was unnerved by Mandy's demeanor. On instinct, she asked, "Mandy, do you know something about what happened to Gabby?"

Every fleck of color drained from Mandy's face, the fear plain in her eyes. Kate knew she'd gone too far too fast. Crossed a line she hadn't had time to understand. She scrambled to backtrack. "I'm sorry, Mandy. I didn't mean to rush you. Please, take your time."

Mandy fidgeted with her sweatshirt. Then, as if she'd finally reached a decision, she grabbed her backpack and stood, inching toward the door. "I need to go back to class," she stammered.

"Our time isn't up yet." Kate stood and walked slowly toward Mandy, whose eyes had become round as saucers. As her backpack bumped the door, Mandy reached for the handle.

"I changed my mind. I don't want to talk right now."

"Mandy, please. I want to help you, but I can't do anything if you won't talk to me."

Mandy considered this for the briefest of seconds, then shook her head. "They'll know it was me," she whispered, then opened the door wide enough to slip out of the office and down the hall before Kate had a chance to react.

It took two days for Kate to settle her internal debate. She would do her best not to betray Mandy's confidence, but she couldn't keep this new information to herself. The school still felt muted, dulled by the same tension that blanketed the whole town. Conversations with her father had become shallow. It was worse with her coworkers, who seemed unable or unwilling to let go of their communal grief.

Kate knew the effects of trauma, so the response was understandable. Still, a greater threat loomed, and she recognized the way people were hiding from it, refusing to speak out of fear. So she worked up the gumption, walked into the police station, and asked to speak with Roman Aguilar.

Her insides twisted in knots as she waited. She could imagine how odd she must look, fidgeting with her purse strap and shifting from one foot to the other. Nervous, or guilty. No one seemed to pay her any mind. By the time Roman came into view, she'd been waiting nearly twenty minutes and her nerves were shot.

"Kate," Roman said, offering his hand. His tone was friendly but professional. His eyes were wary. "I'm surprised to see you here. Let's go to my office."

Kate followed him, noting how several pairs of eyes tracked their movement. She returned her focus to Roman as he led her down a series of stark hallways to an office in the rear of the second floor. When she walked in, she was surprised to find the office so fastidiously neat. He gestured toward a visitor's chair and took a seat behind the desk.

"What brings you here?" he asked the moment he settled. Kate wasn't sure why she was disappointed that he'd made no small talk, no conversation. Being around Roman felt familiar, but she had to remind herself they barely knew each other anymore. She tried to shake off all the competing emotions.

"It's about Gabby Greene." Kate's feelings were so jumbled that she wanted to tread carefully. "Well, sort of."

"Okay," he said.

"How's the investigation going?"

Roman sighed. "I can't discuss an ongoing investigation with you, Kate. I'm sure you know that."

"Of course. Just like you know I can't discuss my patients with you, and yet you were in my office a few days ago." Kate's voice came out more snappish than she'd intended. She didn't know where she stood with Roman. How receptive he might be to hearing what amounted to a theory, though an educated one. Just being in the same room with him made her agitated.

"Fair enough," Roman said, and Kate thought she saw his lip twitch upward. "What I'm about to tell you can't leave this room. We're still waiting on the lab. There was no evidence that the assault took place in her car, so we're still looking for the primary scene."

"Not surprising."

"Her body was burned post-mortem."

"To destroy evidence," Kate murmured, finishing Roman's sentence.

Roman looked Kate in the eye, but his face was still devoid of expression. "Her personal effects were found with her, though most were destroyed in the fire."

Kate nodded impatiently and she felt like Roman was toying with her. "Do you have any suspects?"

"No." Roman paused. It looked like he was considering his words very carefully. "Listen, Kate. If you've got something to tell me, now would be a great time. Progress in this investigation is slow. I'm having a hell of a time finding anyone willing to give me any information. I don't have the time or the energy to satisfy idle curiosity, if that's why you're here."

"You don't have to be rude," she said, bristling. "I might be able to help."

"Your background doesn't give you special privilege. You're not part of the investigative team. You're the high school psychologist and, if I recall correctly, you didn't have much contact with Gabby Greene. So I don't see how you can add anything." His cheeks were flushed, though his voice remained even. Kate's frustration grew, but she didn't want to engage him. There were more important things to deal with.

Kate was quiet for a moment as she calmed herself. "You're right. I don't know anything specific about Gabby Greene. But I wanted to talk to you about what's going on at the school.

Usually, when something bad happens, kids are streaming into my office. They need someone to talk to about things that have nothing to do with whatever happened, but somehow tragedy seems to open the floodgates. But that's not happening this time. Not since Gabby's body was found."

"What's your point?" he asked, sitting forward in his chair. Whatever feelings he'd been struggling with seemed to ebb as he refocused on his case. Kate admired his dedication, though his words were sharp, biting.

"It's like they've all agreed not to talk about it. You know, like a gag order over the whole school. Hell, the whole town. Even my father doesn't want to talk about it. We've hardly had a conversation all week. It's disturbing."

"It's always hard when a young person is killed. People need answers so they can feel safe."

"I get that," she interrupted. "But wouldn't it be easier to get those answers by helping out the people investigating the crime? You said yourself that you're not getting much help."

"That's true." He sighed. "But this doesn't change anything. You're here because no one is talking about it. How does that help either of us?"

Kate felt the irritation turning to anger inside her. She knew Roman wasn't trying to be difficult. She knew she was adding to the vagueness of the conversation by not being direct. She decided to go a different direction. "When you asked me the other day about gang activity . . . have you found any evidence that this is gang-related?"

Roman raised an eyebrow. "Why? What have you heard?"

"Nothing," Kate hedged. She was walking a tightrope and the strain was getting to her. "I don't know anything concrete. But I suspect . . ."

"You suspect?" he parroted.

"I suspect," she continued with a sigh, "that there is something more significant going on. The students are scared."

"Students?" Now Roman was sitting tall, his eyes fixed on her. "I thought you said the kids weren't talking."

She felt her cheeks flush. Roman didn't miss a thing. It was time to come clean as much as she could, or leave. "Look, you know I can't tell you the things told to me in confidence, but after talking with one of my students I think there's something bigger going on. Involving more than one person. So I started wondering why you thought it might be gang-related."

Roman leaned back in his chair, his face rigid as stone. Kate wondered if she'd made a mistake coming to him. She really had nothing to go on. Just a hunch. Mandy's last words—*they'll know it was me*—repeated in the back of her mind. She'd wanted to ask who. Who would know? How would they know? But Mandy had avoided her since that visit.

Kate wasn't naive. She'd worked in a closed system where violence was prevalent despite all the safeguards put into place. She'd often been amazed at how many criminal acts took place in prison, right under the noses of guards, wardens . . . security cameras. And, unfortunately, she had first-hand knowledge of how quickly things could go wrong.

Schools were another institution that, despite best efforts, didn't always have a handle on the response to and prevention of violence. And gangs had always been a problem in this part of the county. Gang rape as part of initiation wasn't even a new concept, but that didn't make the idea less abhorrent.

Gabby Greene had been a sweet girl. Quiet. Shy. She'd been a good student who spent most of her free time working or studying. She'd even found time to do an internship at the city, a position she'd been very proud to secure, according to her teachers.

"There's no evidence that Gabby's death was gang-related," Roman finally responded, a frown creasing his forehead.

"But isn't that what you were thinking? You said it looked ritualistic." Kate felt both relief and disappointment at this news. She searched Roman's face for any clue to his thoughts, but his expression held no answers. After a moment Kate stood up, slinging her purse over her shoulder. "I'd better be going."

"Wait," Roman said, standing. He walked around his desk toward her. She stood frozen in place, but her heartbeat sped up. When he was a foot away he stopped and looked at her, the musky scent of his cologne invading her senses. She was starting to sweat, waiting for him to say something, and she wanted to step away so she could clear her head.

In her first weeks back home Kate had stayed detached, reminding herself that there was no reason to reconnect with old friends, especially Roman. She'd be gone in no time. Then the months stretched into years. Roman had kept his distance, so Kate kept up the pretense of detachment even as old feelings began to resurface. For the last few days, the wall she'd built around her had begun to crumble.

"Let me walk you out." He brushed by her, opening the door and walking swiftly down the hall. She followed, assuming he'd stop at the lobby. When he held the front door for her, she slowed her pace. Was he escorting her out of the building? His face was tense, and she wondered what his colleagues must be thinking. As they neared her car she turned, nearly slamming into him.

"What are you doing?" she hissed, her heart thumping wildly in her neck.

"Where's your car?" he asked, looking ahead. She'd parked her maroon Camry on the street in front of the station. He didn't wait for her response but made a beeline for the vehicle, leaving her a few steps behind.

"Hey!" she barked, watching him stop at her driver's side door. "What the hell, Roman? You're making me feel like a criminal." Unsure what to do, she planted her feet on the ground and crossed her arms like a petulant child, glaring at her ex-best friend.

He leaned his hip against her car, mirroring her crossed arms but looking much more relaxed than she felt. The street was quiet, but he stole a quick glance from side to side before he said, "I want to tell you something, but you have to understand this is just between you and me. Okay?"

Kate didn't like his tone, but she inched closer so he could lower his voice. Roman had always been her easy-going, joke-cracking friend—right up until that fateful day at the creek. The serious man standing before her was intimidating.

"There's evidence that Gabby Greene had sexual contact with multiple men. We didn't find any defensive wounds. I suspect she was drugged. Waiting on toxicology." Roman furrowed his brow. "Do you remember that girl in high school?"

"Yes."

"Everything's the same. Same damage and injuries. Everything down to the burning of her car." Kate touched her neck reflexively before returning it self-consciously to her side.

"A copycat?" Kate murmured. She'd gravitated toward him as he spoke and was now within arm's reach.

Roman leaned in closer. "I think you're right—something bad is happening here."

Kate was distracted on her ride home. Roman's eyes had been haunted. Those last words he'd spoken were a plea for help. But he hadn't explicitly asked for help and she hadn't offered. She had too many things to worry about in her life. She'd learned to keep a professional distance in her career, and this was one situation where she had to maintain it no matter how her heart stirred.

Kate had taken the rest of the day off to join her father for his appointment with the oncologist. She was hoping to change his mind about treatment, though her father had always been a stubborn man. Kate was in a state of denial, and happy to be so. It had been only five years since her mother died. She often felt those years were the longest of her life, but now that her dad was sick she realized how precious those years had been. She wanted time to slow down.

She pulled into the driveway to find her dad sitting on the porch. *Stubborn, but punctual*, she thought.

He got into the car, smiling. "Let's do this." But when he looked over at Kate his brow furrowed in worry. "What happened?"

"It's nothing," she said, trying to sound like she meant it. "A lot going on these days. I just need to relax a little."

"I couldn't agree more," he teased. "What have you been up to this morning? You left early."

"Ran a few errands," she replied. She hadn't wanted to start another strained conversation with her dad, but her brain was still spinning over her visit with Roman. "Do you remember that girl who was killed when I was in high school? Laura something?"

"Laura Fuentes. Your mother fretted for months after she died. A real tragedy what happened to that girl."

Kate wanted to ask more questions, but a shadow had fallen over her father's face and she decided this wasn't the time to discuss such heavy matters. Especially when she wanted him to focus on the possibility of getting better. She was about to turn on the radio when he added, "That family had only been in the area for a few years. They moved away right after."

"I didn't know that," Kate said, trying to remember more details. She hadn't known the girl well at all. Couldn't even conjure up a memory of what she looked like. Every memory of that horrible day brought her back to Roman. It was infuriating.

Kate flipped on the radio and they spent the rest of the trip listening to one of the local DJ's string of terrible song choices with intermittent, boring banter. When they arrived at the doctor's office, Kate opined nostalgically, "They need to get that guy off the air."

"Didn't you go to school with him?" her dad asked.

"No, he was in Tilly's class. I went to school with his older sister, but I didn't know her very well."

"Right. Their father is one of the head honchos out at the hospital," he said absentmindedly. "Didn't he run for city council a few years ago?"

"No, Dad. You're thinking of someone else." Kate unbuckled. "We're here. Better get checked in." She'd worry about her father's failing memory another day.

They walked into the medical office building and headed to the fourth floor, checking in with the doctor's receptionist and taking a seat in the waiting area. Kate and her father were the only people waiting.

"Mr. Medina?" A nurse peeked her head around the doorframe. "We're ready for you."

Kate followed her father down the hallway. She was surprised when they were seated in an office instead of an exam room. A big, mahogany desk sat in the middle of the room and the large window offered a view of the nearby mountain range.

"He'll be with you in a moment," the nurse said, closing the door behind her as she left them. Kate looked around, noting the diplomas on the wall. She also noticed some framed photos on a bookcase. A man with gray at the temples stood laughing with two teenage girls who looked just like him. Kate thought she recognized one of them, and she was about to get up and take a closer look when the door swung open.

"Hello, Frank," the doctor said, shaking her father's hand. "You must be Kate. I'm Mark Nivens," he said, offering her his hand. She was immediately taken with his easy manner and the smile that reached his eyes. Kate felt herself blush.

They spent almost an hour going over her father's diagnosis and the treatment options available. Despite Kate's best attempts, her father was adamant about avoiding treatment. When her frustration brought tears to her eyes, Dr. Nivens offered her a tissue.

"I understand your distress, Kate," he said. "Your father and I spoke at great length about treatment during his last visit, and I know he's been worried about how you would react to his decision which is why he thought having me talk to you would help. The bottom line is, the cancer is very aggressive and we didn't catch it early enough to get ahead of it. Not that there would have been any guarantee even then."

"But he might get a few more years with chemo?" she asked, knowing they'd covered this ground already but unable to put the topic to bed yet.

"It's possible," the doctor replied. "But his quality of life would diminish significantly, and there's a good chance he'd have to spend a lot of time in the hospital."

Kate rubbed her palms against the armrest of the chair and focused on her breathing, trying to get her anxiety under control. She rose from her chair and walked to the window, letting her feet drag against the carpet to get grounded. Her father and the doctor seemed to sense that she needed some time to think, so they chatted quietly while she worked to regain her composure. She noticed a small frame sitting behind the others, hidden in the shadow of the doctor and his daughters. Kate reached back and pulled the photo out to take a look.

"That's my daughter Anna and her friend Mandy last month at the hospital award banquet." The girls were dressed in black slacks and blouses and were holding silver serving plates in their hands. Their smiles were radiant. Kate wondered if Mandy would ever smile like that again.

"I didn't realize the hospital hired high schoolers as wait staff," Kate said, mostly to herself.

"It's a fun night, and it gives the kids an opportunity to meet some of the leaders in town. Those connections can be a real help when it comes time for college, job applications, internships…that sort of thing."

Kate studied the picture a moment longer. "This was taken last month?"

"Yes," Dr. Nivens said. "It was Mandy's first big event. Her stepfather thought it would help her come out of her shell."

It was hard to reconcile the smiling girl in the picture with the terrified teen who'd run out of Kate's office only days ago. Kate's first instinct with Mandy had been to suspect something bad had happened to cause such a dramatic change in demeanor. Her mind sifted through the possibilities until her father cleared his throat, bringing her back to the present.

Kate placed the frame back on the shelf and returned to her seat. She took her father's hand, looked Dr. Nivens in the eye, and asked the question she couldn't avoid any longer. "So, what comes next?"

———

After his appointment, Frank rested. Kate used the quiet time to research hospice, though her mind wandered. How had she gotten to this point? She was pushing 36 and was facing the prospect—no, the inevitability—that she would soon be an orphan. She'd thought losing her mother was the worst thing that could happen to her.

She was wrong.

Losing her father seemed particularly cruel. For one selfish moment, she wondered what had been the point. She wasn't twenty anymore, and there were so many things she'd never gotten around to doing. Never married. Never had kids. Never traveled to Europe. She tried to offset this list with all the things she had accomplished, but her mind wasn't willing. She let sorrow swallow her whole. When her phone buzzed, she answered without checking the caller ID.

"Hey." The shock of hearing her sister's voice was enough to shake her out of her funk. Tilly never called.

"Hi," Kate said, hearing the weariness in her voice.

"Are you okay?" Tilly sounded uneasy. Kate usually would have had some sarcastic remark for her sister, but she didn't have the energy.

"Not really," she said. "Just got back from the doctor with Dad."

"What did he say?"

"Same thing he told us. The cancer is terminal. Treatment will only buy him a few years, and his quality of life will be shit. He has maybe six months. We need to look into hospice." Kate rattled off the list, trying to keep her voice steady. The line was quiet. "Tilly?"

"I'm here," Tilly said. Those two words were more than Kate's heart could take. She began to cry and the crying turned to sobbing.

"Oh, Til. What am I going to do?" Kate lamented once she'd caught her breath. "I can't do this on my own."

"You'll have help. Hospice is wonderful. The nurses are so kind, and they'll help you, too, Kate." Her sister sounded encouraging, but Kate could hear the shakiness as she spoke.

"Can you come?" Kate asked weakly, readying herself for rejection. "Just for a while?"

She could hear Tilly sigh loudly on the line. "Yes, I'll come. But I can't stay long. Not for more than a day or two. It's…" Tilly muttered something that Kate couldn't make out.

"What did you say?" Kate asked.

"I'll call you next week. I need to rearrange my schedule a bit." Tilly didn't say goodbye. The line just disconnected, leaving Kate feeling emptier than she ever had before.

CHAPTER SIX

Kate had signed up for the school district health fair before her life started falling apart, and no one seemed interested in letting her off the hook. She tried hard not to stomp around as she set up her table, but her heart wasn't in it. She'd been up all night with her father, whose health had declined dramatically. It was as if he'd known the end was coming soon and had waited until the last possible second to tell Kate and Tilly about what was about to happen. She'd been on the phone with hospice. The paperwork was complete. As soon as the doctor signed off they'd set up his initial appointment, and Kate prayed the nurse could help with the transition. She felt overwhelmed.

On the positive side, things had begun to return to normal around the school. It was Friday—the weekend was on its way. Kids were laughing and joking around in the halls. Kate caught herself relaxing at odd moments. But the thought of Gabby Greene, whose story was quickly becoming old news, kept nagging at her. And it wasn't just Gabby. Mandy had missed her last two appointments. Kate had called Mandy's mother twice. Nothing but radio silence.

"Hey, Ms. Medina!" Kate turned to find a couple of National

Honor Society girls smiling brightly at her. "Do you need any help setting up?"

"I would love that. Thank you."

It was hard to be a grouch in such pleasant company. Kate put her worries aside and handed the girls a box to unpack. They pulled out fliers and brochures on topics ranging from grief to good hygiene, arranging them neatly on the table, giggling as they worked. Kate longed for those carefree days, though she wasn't sure she'd ever qualified as carefree. Even in high school she'd been driven, her eyes on the future. Except when she was with Roman.

Kate couldn't allow herself to dwell too long without losing her composure. She's always though of herself as being an expert at leaving the past behind. It was her best coping skill, and the one that had gotten her over some of the biggest emotional hurdles of her life. Now she wondered if she'd been lying to herself.

"All done, Ms. M," one of the girls said, and they headed off to the next set of tables. Kate gathered up the empty crates and stacked them underneath, creating a neat row that peeked out from under the draping.

"Hi there, Ms. M," said a deep voice behind her, mimicking Kate's student helpers. She didn't have to look to know that Roman was standing behind her. When she did turn to face him, she saw he was wearing a health fair nametag on the lapel of his jacket. When they were younger, Kate hadn't given much thought to Roman's appearance. He'd always been a little shorter than other boys their age, a little scrawnier. But he'd filled out. He kept himself fit, and his hair was neatly trimmed. He exuded confidence like every other police officer she'd met, but without arrogance. Kate had never thought of Roman as handsome, but as she looked at him now she realized that he was. The room suddenly felt stuffy.

"Good afternoon, Detective Aguilar," she said, sounding

more like a stern teacher than she'd meant to. He laughed, and despite herself she grinned. "Wow, that was obnoxious."

"Who? Me or you?"

"Both, but I was mostly talking about me. You know, it's not nice to make fun of the smart girls," Kate chided him.

"Sounds like the kids love you." He gestured toward the bubbly teens who were now helping the high school nurse set up a display board with charts and graphs.

"Sure they do," she chuckled. "When they don't have to come see me. When I'm out here, they treat me like any other teacher. When I'm in my office, they become selective mutes."

"Well, I don't recall ever feeling the urge to spill my guts to our school counselor either," Roman replied with a grin.

After years of avoiding one another, it was strange to see how easy the conversation flowed when Kate let her down her guard.

"Detective Aguilar?" Principal McIntyre had approached from behind, along with several members of the school board. She jumped when he spoke. Roman's face turned grave and their moment of levity fizzled. "Let me show you where we're putting you."

Roman followed Pete without another word. She watched him go, feeling deflated. Why did she care? She and Roman had been artfully avoiding each other for five long years. The only time he spoke to her was when she was with her father. Frank still talked about Roman like he was a part of their daily lives.

After her mother's death Kate had been busy around her dad's house, not to mention dealing with her own grief which she'd kept to herself. When she made the decision to stay in Alamogordo long-term, it hadn't felt like coming home. In fact, moving to a foreign country might have been an easier transition. But she'd eventually created a new life for herself—made a few new friends, started a new career. It was only in these last few weeks that she'd begun to feel that old pang of regret about Roman.

Luckily, the first bell of the morning rang and the onslaught began. The morning was reserved for the elementary kids. Kate had prepared an activity where the kids thought of three adults they could trust and then drew a picture of one of them. Some of the kids gave minimal effort to receive a candy prize, but Kate loved to watch the look on the faces of the more serious kids as they pondered and prioritized. As the pile of portraits grew, Kate smiled more than she had in days.

Despite the constant flow of traffic, time trickled by. Kate had energetic conversations with the younger kids, who were too young to be self-conscious yet. The teens gave her table a wide berth until they noticed the huge bowl of chocolate candy bars tucked behind her. She waited to bring the full-sized bars out until after lunch, knowing she'd need a pretty hefty incentive to get the adolescents to give her the time of day. Which was ironic since they were the ones most in need of her help.

"Fill out a survey and get a candy bar," she called to a group of boys who were trying to avoid making eye contact. She waved a Snickers bar at them. Reluctantly they came to her table, filling out her survey as quickly as possible and then scattering like mice with a stolen piece of cheese. Kate grinned. Chocolate always did the trick.

In between batches of kids, there was a lull in foot traffic. Those times were the worst. They gave Kate far too much time to think. Her table was in direct line of sight with the police department group, and it seemed like every time she glanced in that direction Roman was staring back at her. To distract herself, Kate chatted with the school nurse, though she found the older woman exceedingly annoying. Anything to make the hours go by as quickly as possible.

As the nurse droned on and on about how little she was paid

and how unjustly she was treated by school administration, Kate wondered, not for the first time, why the woman didn't just retire. It was a universal fact that the school district paid its employees a pittance. The only reason Kate could afford her current job was the fact that she lived with her dad, drove his car, and had very few bills of her own. The thought was depressing.

At the end of the sixth hour, Kate's candy bars were all gone and there were almost no kids left in the common area. As the final bell rang, the last straggling kids sprinted to their lockers to pack up. Kate started packing up, too. She started sorting through the survey cards, which were strewn around the table haphazardly.

A few minutes to four she picked up the pace, hoping to make it home in time to follow up with the hospice nurse. She laid the neat pile of cards on her table and was putting the leftover brochures in boxes, when she noticed a survey that had gotten wedged between two of her crates.

She was about to add it to her stack when she saw, written lightly in pencil on the back of the card, words that made her heart go cold.

I know who killed Gabby.

Kate's heart was screaming in her chest as she scanned the room for Roman. He was immersed in a conversation with a group of his fellow police officers and deputies from the sheriff's office. She approached the group slowly, thankful to catch his eye before she had to interact. The look on her face must have done the trick. Roman excused himself from the conversation.

"Is everything all right? Is it your father?" Roman asked, his voice fraught with concern. For a moment, Kate was taken off-guard. She hadn't known that Roman knew about her dad's health problems. Then she remembered the piece of paper in her hand. She handed it to Roman without a word. His brow furrowed.

"Where did this come from?"

"I had the kids fill out a survey today at my table. I have no idea who it came from or even when it was filled out. I just noticed it. It had fallen between a few of my boxes."

"Show me," he said, walking so quickly toward her table that she nearly had to jog to keep up.

"I was cleaning up and it was wedged between these two crates," Kate said, indicating two egg crates she'd pushed under her table behind her display board. "Now that I think about it, I don't know how it got back there."

"I don't see how it could have landed there by accident," Roman said, scrutinizing the card again. "Someone placed it there so you'd find it."

"I was standing in front of the table. I guess anyone could have stuck it in there without me noticing." Kate thought back on all the kids she'd talked with during the day, but she didn't remember seeing anyone acting strangely or moving around behind her table. She felt her frustration grow.

"Can we look through the rest of the surveys?" Roman asked. When Kate hesitated, he added, "We can go through them together. I want to see if there are any others."

"I guess so," Kate replied. She reached into her bag to pull out the stack of survey cards, but Roman put his hand up. She let the papers slide back into her bag.

"Would it be possible to do it later this evening?" he asked, glancing back over his shoulder at the conversation still taking place across the room. "I need to finish something."

"Oh. Sure. Do you want me to come by the station?"

"Would you mind coming by my house instead? Around 5:30?"

"I need to get my dad some dinner and in bed for the night."
Kate shifted uneasily.

Roman must have noticed, because he offered her a
reassuring smile. "How about 7:00 then? I want to keep this
quiet until we know what we're dealing with."

Kate looked back over at the group of law enforcement,
many of whom were beginning to cast curious glances in their
direction.

"Yeah, okay. That'll work," Kate replied. "What's your
address?"

Kate sat in her car, staring at Roman's house. It was a
nondescript house on a nondescript block, in the middle of an
average middle-class neighborhood—one of the newer
subdivisions that hadn't existed when they were kids. The lights
inside shone warmly through the living room window. Kate
could see Roman working at his desk, his back to the outside
world. She'd been sitting watching him work for ten solid
minutes, immobilized by anxiety. It wasn't until he started to
turn that she grabbed her bag and got out of the car.

Roman opened the screen door as she stepped onto the front
porch, ushering her inside with a weary smile. "Hi, Kate.
Thanks for coming."

She stood inside the door, taking in the room. She wasn't
sure what she had been expecting—some kind of macho
policeman's bachelor pad. She should have known better.
Roman wasn't the type. His living room was sparse, but each
piece of furniture looked as though it had been chosen with care.

Above the desk hung a series of diplomas and certificates in
matching frames. Kate stepped forward to take a closer look
and was surprised to see that Roman had graduated from

college with honors and had gone on to get his master's degree in Criminal Justice. Standing in this room, looking at all his things, Kate realized she didn't know Roman at all. Not anymore. Her chest felt heavy.

"Let's sit down over here," he said from the couch. He'd cleared a space on the coffee table. "Can I get you something to drink?"

Kate's throat felt dry. "Some water, please."

As Roman walked down the hall Kate set down her bag and started sorting the survey cards, putting them in piles on the table. There were at least four hundred, and while some of them contained nonsense answers—the price you paid when offering teenagers chocolate in exchange for information—most had thoughtful, if brief, responses that made Kate feel good about her work.

Roman returned, setting a glass of water down on a coaster near Kate. "Find anything?"

"Not yet," she said, reaching for the glass. She took a sip and then added, "I'm skimming to make sure there are no names or other identifying information."

"Understood." He reached for one of her piles. "Can I start here?"

"Yes." They sorted and read in silence for about five minutes before Roman chuckled.

"What?" Kate asked.

"I was thinking that kids haven't changed much." He handed Kate a survey where DECLARE THE DAY AFTER HALLOWEEN A NATIONAL HOLIDAY! was written in all caps under the question *What would improve your school experience?*

Kate laughed. "I know who wrote that, too. The kids were passing around a petition a few days ago, demanding that day off. Seems the strain of the post-Halloween sugar hangover is impacting their mental health." She turned back to the stack of surveys in front of her. She was finally starting to relax. Roman's house was decidedly homey and it was easy to be with him, as long as she didn't think about it too much.

They'd been working for about half an hour when Kate realized that Roman wasn't moving. He sat beside her on the couch, staring at the card in his hand.

"What is it?" Kate asked, taking the paper from him as his frown deepened. Under "Do you feel safe at school?" someone had written: *What a joke. We've never been safe at school.*

"Not particularly helpful, is it?" Kate murmured. She flipped the card over and squinted to read what was written lightly in pencil near the bottom corner. *Just ask Gabby Greene.* "Oh God," Kate said, leaning back. "Did you see this?"

"I did." Roman sat stiffly on the edge of the couch, as if he might leap up at any moment. He handed her another card. "This one, too."

Kate looked at the new card. Another mention of Gabby. "They know something. So why give these to me?" Kate's hands shook as she reached for her water glass. It was one thing to know that something big was happening, but quite another to find yourself tossed into the middle of it. Kate hated the fear she felt.

The silence was oppressive. When Roman finally spoke again, his tone was almost frantic. "You're in a unique position, Kate. The kids trust you. And you have experience working in the criminal justice system."

Hadn't Kate said the same thing in Roman's office? Hadn't she wanted to help? The paper in her hands felt heavy with the weight of the words written there.

"You said it yourself, Roman. That's not me anymore. This is just a job. I have to focus on taking care of my father right now. I'm all he has."

"Come on, Kate. You were in my office two days ago asking about the investigation."

"A lot happened in those two days."

"I know I was an asshole, but we both know you're not going to be satisfied standing on the sidelines. What are you afraid of?"

He was right, of course. But then, having to accept that her father was going to die had changed her perspective pretty dramatically. She still wanted to help the police find the people who'd hurt Gabby, but she wasn't in a position to do so. And she didn't want to put herself in another dangerous situation. Not while she felt so vulnerable.

Kate scooped up the remaining surveys, shoved them into her bag, and got up off the couch. She walked to the door, pausing only briefly to say, "I'm sorry. I've got to go."

CHAPTER SEVEN

Kate stayed at home all weekend, feigning a cold. She only left her room to check on her dad who, thankfully, seemed to be having a couple of good days. She needed to hide out. Roman had called her repeatedly after she left his house Friday night. Kate powered her phone down, like the mere act of stopping his calls could shield her from the horrible things happening around her and her own unwillingness to get involved.

That, and she was wrestling with the complicated emotions that seeing Roman unleashed.

Kate had always been fascinated by true crime novels and police investigations. She'd become a forensic psychologist so that she could be a part of that system without actually having to carry a gun or do anything dangerous.

She'd been naive.

For nearly a decade Kate had worked within the prison system—treating inmates, testifying in court, and participating in multidisciplinary teams with a fervent desire to shed more light on the psychological aspects of criminal behavior with a focus on prevention and rehabilitation.

To say she loved her job was an understatement. She lived and breathed her job.

Even when her colleagues doggedly refused to see things her way, she felt that she was making a difference. Right up until the day she'd been assaulted, robbing her of her most basic sense of safety. Looking back, she could see that safety had been an illusion.

She'd been recovering physically from the assault when her mother was killed, and she returned to New Mexico to grieve. But instead of readying her to resume her life, going home had made her feel small, like she'd ventured out into the big world only to be returned battered and broken. She'd climbed back into her childhood bed that first night and gone to sleep, knowing deep down that she would never go back to her former life.

Taking the counseling job at the school had been practical once she decided on staying. For the most part, she dealt with students who were full of the kind of teenage angst that only time and experience would rid them of. On the bright side she rarely took her work home with her, and when difficult situations presented themselves there was a chain of authority that allowed her to shuffle off the stressful cases into a wider system built to address them. She recognized that this behavior was textbook avoidance, but the one thing that she'd gained by moving back home was that sense of safety.

Until now.

Now the world was spinning out of control again.

She was on the verge of losing her father. Her sister still wasn't around. And something sinister was happening to her students—something that, in her former life, she would have tackled head on like one of the detectives in the books she'd read. In an academic sense, Kate saw criminal behavior as a puzzle. Unfortunately, the resulting complacency had cost her more than her career.

Her quick escape from Roman's house was a direct result of the pull she'd felt in her stomach at the mention of getting involved. It was a sharp tug in that place where she'd buried her passion and her curiosity. She told herself she wasn't that person anymore. But it was a lie. And Roman knew it. Knew he could appeal to that part of her she'd buried. She'd fled because, somewhere deep down, she wanted to be part of his investigation. Oh God, she wanted to.

The spark that drove her in her career had ignited into a full-fledged flame. Seeking out Roman, offering her expertise, had been an impulse she simply couldn't control. But hearing her father's prognosis had sobered her. Up to that point, she'd been deluding herself. Thinking that she'd misunderstood, that things couldn't really be as bad as her father had made them out to be. After the trip to the doctor, she couldn't deny the truth anymore.

Kate loved her father, and she knew taking care of him had to be her priority. The part of her that longed to jump into the fray needed to be smothered before it got her into trouble again.

The rational part of her knew she needed to stick to the boundaries she'd constructed for herself. The irrational side told her to hide, to avoid Roman's calls, and to hope that by Monday he'd have put aside that notion and she could return to just being a school psychologist. She would pass any new information on to school administration or law enforcement, but she would not try to interpret it herself. She would not engage.

Things at school would settle down. And Kate could go back to pretending that this life was the one she wanted.

She should have known it wouldn't be that easy.

At noon on Sunday her father knocked at her door and then

walked in, taking a seat at the foot of her bed. "Feeling any better?"

"I'm doing okay," Kate replied, feeling ridiculous for lying to her sick, frail father about being ill. She hated to do it but she knew it would keep him away, letting her wallow in peace.

"Do you want to talk about it?" he asked.

"About what? It's just a cold."

"I'm your father. I live with you. I know you're not actually sick. I figured you needed some time to yourself, so I let you have it." He smiled kindly. "I also know that you were with Roman on Friday night and you've been laid up ever since. So, you can either tell me what's going on or I'll go out in the living room and ask him."

Kate shot up in bed. "He's here?" She groaned when her father nodded. In high school Roman had been a regular figure in her house, often dragging her out of bed on the weekend so they could go off and do something fun. She should have known he wouldn't give up so easily. But, given the rocky state of their barely-existing relationship, she'd never expected him to appear at her house. She couldn't decide if she was more amused or annoyed.

"He wants me to help with his investigation into Gabby Greene's murder," she said, hoping that mentioning the girl's name would shut her father up the way it had every single time she'd brought it up before. No such luck.

"And you don't want to?" By the look he was giving her, she knew there was no point in lying.

"I'm a school psychologist now. I'm not in law enforcement. What I did before, that's not me anymore. I don't have anything to offer him." Kate got out of bed and threw on her bathrobe.

"Listen, Kate." Her father's tone was so serious she sat back down again. "You've been hiding out for five years now. You know it and I know it." She started to protest, but he raised his hand. "Let me finish. I know something happened to you at the prison. I saw you walking around like an injured animal. And the bruises. It was like seeing a shell of the person you used to be. We were all wrapped up in what happened to Mom, but I kept hoping you'd eventually tell me about it. When you decided to stay in town, I was suspicious. But when you took the job at the high school, then I knew I was right."

"It was nothing..."

"It was something, Kate. And I'm not saying you have to tell me about it. Now or ever. But staying in bed all weekend just to avoid talking to Roman isn't going to help you. If you don't want to help him, don't. But I know the way your mind works, and I understand why he's asking for your help. You're brilliant and tenacious. You always have been. Roman knows you."

Kate felt the color creep to her cheeks. Her father was right. Nothing about Kate had fundamentally changed over the years, and Roman knew her better than almost anyone. And though she might not know all the details of Roman's life over the years, she knew him, too. He wouldn't let this go.

"I don't want to get involved," Kate said. Her voice shook.

Her father scrutinized her for a moment, then got up and walked to the door. "I'm going to make Roman a cup of coffee. If you're not dressed and out there in twenty minutes, I'm sending him in to get you." He winked, and then shut the door behind him.

CHAPTER EIGHT

Roman hadn't stayed for coffee. When Kate came out of her room, showered and dressed, it was to a quiet house. Her father was watching television, his feet propped up in his recliner. Kate couldn't help feeling a twinge of disappointment, followed immediately by irritation.

"Where's Roman?" she asked.

"He left." Her father chuckled. "It's nice to see you two talking again. I always did like Roman." He sounded tired, but cheerful, which didn't improve Kate's reaction.

"What do you mean, he left?" Kate was full-on annoyed. "You dragged me out of bed and he doesn't even have the courtesy to stay long enough to tell me why he came by? Where did he go?"

"I assume to the police station. He got a call a few minutes after you got in the shower. But he did ask me to have you call him."

Kate was fuming, but angry was better than scared. She could feel a little bit of the fight coming back to her. She went back to her room, ready to have a telephone showdown with Roman but when he finally answered his phone, she'd calmed down. Her dad was right—about a lot of things. For the past five years, she'd been letting circumstance guide her actions. She needed to take control of her life again.

"Hi, Kate," Roman said when she answered.

"What can I do for you, Roman?" she asked, hoping she sounded annoyed.

"Can you come in to the station today?"

"Roman, I..."

"I understand that you're hesitant to get involved," Roman interrupted. "I want to go over something with you. Whatever you decide from there, I'll respect." His words were measured and formal, leaving Kate feeling very uneasy.

"All right," she replied. "I'll be there in half an hour."

The call disconnected.

Kate sat back on her bed, frustrated. Every interaction with Roman sent her reeling. When things were easy, it brought back all those good feelings from when they were friends. Inseparable. But the weight of their history, and the lack of closure—which Kate knew was her own fault, having cut Roman out of her life without warning—laced those easy moments with strained and uncomfortable pressure to keep some professional distance. It made Kate's chest tight. And it was clear that Roman was feeling it, too; his moods shifting from friendly to formal, like he couldn't decide which was the correct tactic.

After stalling for as long as she could Kate gave her dad a kiss goodbye, grabbed her purse, and headed out to her car.

The drive to the police station took about five minutes. Finding parking took considerably longer. The police department was in a brand new building near the renovated city complex and recreation center. The lack of adequate parking seemed a serious oversight in the new design. Kate circled the parking lot twice before giving up and looking for a space on the street.

The hairs on her neck began to prickle, like someone was watching her. A quick scan of the area revealed nothing. She had parked on a quiet side street. Traffic rolled by on the main artery she'd soon be crossing. Neatly manicured lawns graced the small but charming houses on this block.

As she stood at the corner, waiting for a break in traffic, Kate looked back toward her car. Everything seemed quiet, but she still couldn't shake the feeling of eyes on her. She crossed the street and began walking the two blocks to the police department, but the persistent feeling of being watched made her glance back one last time.

She saw a figure in a dark hoodie standing near her car, staring in her direction. She had no idea where he'd come from or if it was even a he.

"Hey!" she shouted, turning back. She expected the figure to move, to turn and walk away, but he didn't. He stood still as a statue, his head fixed in her direction. For a moment Kate thought about walking across the street to confront the lurker, but something stopped her. She'd been squinting, trying to make out any features, when she noticed one thing—the person was smiling, or maybe sneering.

A cold chill ran down her spine.

Kate turned and closed the distance between herself and the safety of the PD lobby. When she looked back, the figure was gone. In a panic she scanned the streets, but the person had disappeared.

Roman was waiting for her at the police station door. She wondered if he'd seen the man across the street but Roman's expression was hostile, making her forget her previous panic.

"Thanks for taking the time to come by, Kate," he said a bit too loudly, causing the few people milling around to look up. Kate gritted her teeth, feeling her cheeks color. A dozen responses were forming in her mind, but Roman had already started walking briskly toward the stairs and all she could do was try to keep up.

When they reached his office and the door closed, Kate exploded. "What the hell was that about!" She threw her bag onto the floor with a thump and turned to face him, arms crossed tightly over her chest.

"What?" Roman asked, the picture of innocence, though his expression was cold. "Have a seat, please." He started tapping the keys on his keyboard, ignoring her completely. She finally sat down in the chair across from him, feeling awkward and embarrassed. She regretted coming.

"I need you to look at this." Roman turned his screen to face her, revealing a Facebook feed. At first Kate didn't understand what she was looking at, but as she began to read the posts the color drained from her face. She reached across to take control of the mouse and continued reading through the posts.

"Oh my God," she whispered as she scrolled.

"I have to ask you," he said, his voice grave. "Are you sure there isn't anything you can tell me about Gabby Greene? Any bullying incidents that were reported? Anything the school didn't think was relevant?"

It took Kate a few moments to gather her thoughts. The Facebook feed supposedly belonged to Gabby, but it was full of pictures of horrific sexual acts—images of Gabby Greene subjected to every vulgar act imaginable. The posts were all dated from Friday. They all came from the same account, and just looking at the profile picture Kate knew the account was a fake. She was horrified that the posts hadn't been taken down yet.

"Who did this?" she whispered, finally looking away from the screen. A sour taste filled her mouth as she fought back nausea.

"We're not sure yet. Look, I know you think I'm incompetent, but..."

"What are you talking about?" Kate interrupted, suddenly furious. "Why are you treating me like I'm your enemy, Roman?"

"Right. Like you don't know." His expression was hard.

"Actually I don't," Kate spat, standing up and heading toward the door. "I don't know what your problem is, but *you* asked *me* to come here, remember? I'm leaving. Feel free to call me when you grow up." She reached for the door handle but Roman grabbed her arm making her gasp. She hadn't even heard him get up.

"If you had a problem with me, you could have told me. I deserve at least that much from you. And this bullshit walking away thing that you do is getting old."

Kate turned. "I'm going to give you about three seconds to tell me what's going on or I really am leaving. And get your hand off me." He relaxed his grip, letting his hand fall to his side. He walked back to his desk, grabbed a piece of paper, and handed it to Kate.

Kate skimmed the letter, her eyes growing wide as she reached the signature at the end—hers. Well, not hers. But someone had done a fairly decent job of forging her name. The letter accused Detective Roman Aguilar of every manner of inappropriate contact, including stalking. Kate shook her head. "I didn't write this."

He was staring at her so fiercely she backed up a step. But she softened her tone before she spoke again, knowing how he must have felt seeing this letter. Seeing her name on it.

"I would never write something like this, Roman. You know me better than that."

"Do I? It's been twenty years since we had any kind of real conversation. I don't know anything about you, not anymore," he said, echoing Kate's own internal dialogue. Then his face relaxed a little bit. "But okay, fine. I'm sorry for overreacting. The chief made a point of calling me in to discuss this *complaint*. Told me to stay away from you."

Kate frowned. "Why would someone write this?"

"I don't know. I guess someone wanted me off the case."

Kate thought about it for a moment. "Not you, Roman. Me."

"What do you mean?"

"One of the reasons I was reluctant to get involved in this investigation is my position at the school. My duty is to my students, and I can't do anything that would cause them not to trust me. When I got those notes on Friday, I wasn't sure I should give them to you. No, that's not true. I knew I had to give them to you, but I worried that it would cause a problem." Kate paused. "Someone saw us talking."

Kate's mind flashed to the man who'd been watching her.

"No one knew what we were discussing," Roman argued.

"It doesn't matter," Kate said. "You've been to the school several times now to question the staff and students. I'm sure I didn't look all that calm after seeing the notes. It wouldn't take that much to put two and two together, even if they didn't know what I was reacting to."

Roman didn't look convinced.

"This is a small town, Roman. You know that as well as I do." She took a deep breath, thinking things through carefully before she spoke. "I think we have to at least consider that someone at the school is involved in Gabby's murder. At the very least, they know something."

"We?" Roman asked, his brows raised high in surprise.

"I don't know how I'm going to navigate this, but it looks

like someone doesn't want me getting involved. I flatter myself to think that means I'm in a position to help, and someone knows it. So it looks like I have no choice." Kate sighed, putting her bag down again. The gravity of the situation weighed heavily on her, but she also felt a rush of adrenaline as her old life and her new life crashed into each other there in Roman's office.

CHAPTER NINE

"Tilly?" Kate asked when she returned home and found her father and sister talking at the kitchen table.. She couldn't quite believe her eyes. As far as she knew, Tilly hadn't stepped foot in their childhood home since graduating from high school. And since she hadn't gotten back to Kate about visiting, Kate assumed it wasn't going to happen.

"Hi, Kate," Tilly said, her tone casual. The kettle started to whistle and Tilly hopped up to attend to it. "Making Dad some tea. Do you want some?" she asked over her shoulder.

"Sure," Kate said. She put her bag down by the door and walked over the table, giving her dad a quick kiss on the cheek before sitting down next to him. "When did Tilly get here?" she asked him.

"About an hour ago," Tilly answered. "You know, you can talk to me directly, Kate. I promise I won't bite."

Kate felt her face flush, but a look at her father made her swallow her snarky comeback. "It's nice to see you, Tilly. I'm glad you're here." Her words were sincere even if her tone didn't quite match.

Tilly set three steaming mugs of tea down on the kitchen

table, dealing them out to her father and sister like delicate playing cards. "So, what were you up to this afternoon? Dad said you were out with Roman. I didn't realize the two of you were friends again."

"I wasn't out with Roman," Kate said, shooting her father a death glare. "He asked me to meet with him about an investigation."

Tilly tilted her head. "Oh? In trouble with the law?" Kate was about to retort, but she could see the corners of Tilly's lips turn up slightly. She took a deep breath.

"You know me," she replied, but she hadn't even come close to a jovial tone.

"I'm teasing, Kate. So what's the investigation?"

"Let's not talk about that tonight, girls," Frank said wearily. He pushed his untouched tea a few inches away and then stood up. "I think I'm going to turn in for the night."

"It's not even 7 o'clock," Tilly complained.

"It's okay, Dad. Get some rest," Kate said. As soon as she heard her father's bedroom door close, she turned back to Tilly. "So, how long do we get you?" Tilly's eyes glistened, and she stared after their father.

"Just a few days," Tilly said quietly. "I'm on call starting Thursday, so I'll have to leave late Wednesday night."

Kate let the news sit a minute. "I have to work all week, but it'll be good for Dad to have someone around during the day."

"How's he doing?" Tilly asked, a hint of shakiness in her voice.

Kate sighed. "Not well. It seems like ever since he told us about his prognosis, he's been going downhill fast. He goes to sleep earlier. Takes a lot of naps. And I think he's in more pain than he's letting on, but he's stubborn."

"And how are you?"

"Exhausted. I'm working full-time, taking Dad to all his appointments, and then this investigation thing sprang up. I don't know how I'm going to handle it all. I keep thinking about taking a leave of absence, but every time I bring it up Dad argues." Kate let the words rush out, enjoying the release.

"What does the investigation have to do with you?" Tilly asked.

"A high school girl was murdered a few weeks ago," Kate said, noticing the color draining from her sister's face. "He's hoping the students will come to me and I'll learn something new. A glorified snitch, I guess." Kate didn't want to get into the details, and she certainly didn't want her sister to know how involved she truly was. It was best for everyone if Kate kept Tilly focused on their father. "I doubt I'll have much to contribute, but it's nice to have a challenge."

"A challenge? Leave it to you to perk up when some girl dies." Tilly's face had turned a strange shade of purple.

"I'm not happy she's dead," Kate fumed. "Don't judge me, Tilly. You're like a ghost in our lives. You have no idea what I've been through these last five years."

"God, I hate this place," Tilly said, her voice thick with emotion. "I should've known things would start to fall apart the minute I got here."

"None of this has anything to do with you," Kate spat. "The whole world doesn't revolve around you, Tilly. In case you hadn't noticed, Dad and I have been carrying on quite well without you." Kate had aimed her words like weapons, but as Tilly's face fell, Kate regretted them. "I'm sorry, Til," she offered weakly.

"I get it, Kate. I know I haven't been here, and I'm actually very sorry for that. But you have no idea what coming back here does to me. I wish I never had to set foot in this place again." Tilly stood and walked back toward her old bedroom, now the guest room and office. She closed the door quietly, but the click of the lock turning still felt like a punch to Kate's stomach.

The next evening, Kate eased open the front door, anxious to see how Tilly and Frank had done on their first day together. It didn't take long to see that something was wrong.

"Hi, sweetie. How was your day?" her father asked, straining to inject some normalcy into his words. Tilly remained expressionless.

"Uneventful. Mondays are usually pretty quiet for me. All my regular appointments start tomorrow." She looked between her father and Tilly. "Is everything okay here?"

Tilly finally turned to Kate. "It's fine. I made dinner, but it won't be ready for about twenty minutes."

"That's great, thank you. What did you guys do today?" Kate asked Tilly, studying her sister. "Did you get out of the house at all?" Tilly stiffened.

"We went out to lunch," Frank said. "At the steakhouse."

"Was the whole gang there?" Kate asked, smiling at her father. The local steakhouse was a popular hangout for all the older residents in town. When Kate and her father ate there, it often took half an hour to make their way from the hostess station to their table. Kate only took him there when she knew she had a good long time to spend on a meal and she wasn't starving.

"Yes," Frank replied, but he didn't elaborate. Kate had no idea what was going on, but the tension in the air had grown so overwhelming that she wasn't sure she wanted to poke at it any further. She grabbed the remote control, flipping to an episode of Wheel of Fortune, hoping to fill the silence with some mindless noise.

Tilly only moved from her position on the couch to pull a casserole out the oven. Kate turned off the television, plunging the house into gloomy silence again as they all made their way to the table.

It was maybe the hundredth clink of fork hitting plate that finally pushed Kate over the edge. "Enough already," she said roughly, pounding her fists on the table for effect. "Whatever happened between you two you either need to get over it or let's have it out right now, because I can't stand another second of this."

Tilly looked down and Frank shifted in his chair, but he finally broke the silence. "Your sister and I had an argument after lunch. It was nothing."

"Nothing?" Tilly asked, staring icily at her father. "I'd say it was more than nothing, wouldn't you?"

"What happened?" Kate asked.

"I got up to use the restroom, and when I got back to the table Allen Parks had taken a seat next to Tilly. You remember Allen?" Frank said. When Kate nodded, he added, "There was a scene."

"I simply told him to get his disgusting hands off of me. Not my fault that the people at the next table heard me," Tilly said, gritting her teeth.

"He didn't mean any harm," her father argued. "He just patted your shoulder..."

Tilly stood, throwing her napkin onto the table. "He had no right to talk to me, much less touch me." Tilly's face was red and her hands were shaking. "And you..." She glared at her father. "How dare you scold me. You're my father. You're supposed to protect *me*. To defend *me*. Not him. But we all know that's not your strong point."

Kate gasped. Tilly stomped down the hall, slamming her bedroom door. Frank sagged in his seat, his skin ashen. Kate stood. "I'll go talk to her."

"No," Frank said wearily. "She's right, Kate. I shouldn't have been so hard on her."

"She's only been here one night and she's already causing

drama." Kate could feel the anger burning in her stomach. "She shouldn't speak to you that way, Dad."

Frank sighed. "I haven't been the best father to your sister. She deserved better."

Kate walked over and knelt beside her father. "You've been a wonderful father."

Frank gave a small smile and put her hand on Kate's cheek. "Thank you, mija. But I've made some big mistakes, and your sister has every right to be angry with me." He shifted, readying himself to stand, and Kate moved aside to help him up. "I'm tired. I need to sleep. I love you, Princesa." Frank kissed Kate lightly on the cheek and shuffled down to his bedroom. When he'd closed his door she sat back down in her chair, feeling confused.

The next morning Kate found Tilly sitting at the kitchen table, sipping a cup of coffee. Tilly was dressed in jeans and a t-shirt, but she'd pulled her hair back in a colorful scarf. If it weren't for the dark circles under her eyes, Kate might not have suspected her sister's distress. She poured herself a cup and sat down across from Tilly.

"Morning," Kate said, trying to keep her tone casual.

"Good morning," Tilly said with a sigh. "I'm sorry about last night, Kate. I didn't mean stir things up. That's part of the reason I don't come back to visit. Being here in this town and in this house puts me in a bad place."

Kate chose her words carefully. "I would like to understand, Tilly. Maybe if you tell me what happened from your perspective, I could help."

Tilly stiffened. "It's not your job to make me feel better, Kate." She took a deep breath. "I don't mean to snap at you. I'm just very on edge."

"We could talk..."

"I don't want to talk about it," Tilly said, shutting down any chance Kate may have had to open the lines of communication.

They sat in silence for a few minutes. The house was quiet—no noise coming from their father's bedroom. It wasn't unusual these days. Kate rarely saw her dad before she left for work, and it was still very early.

"Maybe after you get home from work, we can talk about what I can do to help you and Dad out. I can't spend a lot of time here physically, but I can help arrange care or even talk with his doctors." Tilly's eyes were pleading now as she fumbled with her words.

Kate's heart deflated a bit. She'd known Tilly wouldn't stay. Hell, it was amazing she'd come at all. But sitting there are the table, just the two of them, she wished they were closer. "Sure. I should be home around six."

A few minutes later, having dressed for work and downed a protein shake, Kate picked up her bag and was getting ready to walk out the door. Tilly was still sitting at the table quietly.

"Tilly?" Kate said, putting her bag back down and walking over to stand beside her sister. Tilly looked up and Kate could see tears forming in her eyes. "If you need someone to talk to, I'm here."

Tilly nodded, but she seemed to be struggling to keep the tears at bay. Kate didn't want to push her so she walked back to the front door, picked up her bag, and headed to school.

CHAPTER TEN

The house was quiet again when Kate got home from work, but her presence seemed to alleviate the tension. By dinnertime, conversation was steady and everyone seemed relaxed. When Tilly announced that she'd be leaving early the next morning, it almost didn't feel like the end of the world for once.

Tilly had refused to leave the house for anything other than groceries and prescriptions, but she'd been busy at home getting updates from Frank's doctor, finalizing plans for hospice, and putting Frank's papers in order. Kate was amazed by the amount of progress that Tilly had made in just two days.

" …And for the most part, the day went smoothly. I have one student who keeps missing meetings," Kate said as they ate dinner. She'd been telling them about a funny incident at school, but Tilly had kept her talking by asking questions.

"What happens if the student doesn't show up?" Tilly asked.

"We usually call the parent. Unfortunately, this girl's mother has yet to return my phone calls. She hasn't even filled out the intake forms, and I've been seeing her daughter for over a month now. Though I'm not sure it counts as *seeing* her, since we've only managed to meet three times, and the last time she only stayed for about five minutes." Mandy had been absent from school today, so it wasn't a surprise that she missed their appointment. Still, Kate was concerned by the continuing lack of communication or concern from Mandy's mother.

"I wish we'd had a psychologist on staff when I was in high school," Tilly lamented. She looked at Kate and smiled. "It's good that they have you."

A rush of warmth filled Kate's body, but was interrupted by the doorbell ringing. "Who could that be?" Roman stood at the door when Kate answered. He was wearing his usual jacket and tie, but he looked tired and disheveled.

"Can I come in?"

"Oh, um, sure. Come in. We were just having dinner."

"Sorry to interrupt," he said. "Hello, Mr. Medina. And Tilly? Wow, I didn't expect to see you again." Kate noticed her sister blush at the attention.

"It's so good to see you. I thought you had too much sense to hang around with this riff-raff." Tilly meant her words to be playful, but Kate noticed the twitch in Roman's jaw. She felt the same flutter of shame that seemed to be a near constant companion in Roman's presence.

"Come in and have something to eat," Frank said, gesturing to an empty chair at the table.

"Thanks, but I can't stay. I'm on duty. I need to speak with Kate for a moment and then I'll let you get back to your dinner." Roman gestured for Kate to follow him to the living room. He moved as far from the kitchen as he could get before turning to Kate.

"There's been a development," Roman whispered.

"With Gabby?"

Roman shook his head.

"David Garcia came in to the station today. He said you've been seeing his daughter Mandy for sessions at school."

"Wait, what? Roman, you know I can't..." Kate started, but Roman stopped her mid-sentence.

"I know. David came in to file a missing persons report. It looks like his daughter has missed her last three visits. We know his ex-wife has sole custody, so normally we wouldn't be able to do much, but David says his ex-wife hasn't been answering his calls. We did a welfare check, and the house they were renting is cleaned out. The landlord didn't even know they'd gone."

"She can't have left town with the girls without at least notifying someone. The custody arrangements aren't final yet," Kate said, a feeling of dread in her core.

"I'm hoping there will be a simple explanation, but when David mentioned that you'd been seeing her I decided to stop by. Because a police report has been filed, I was hoping you might be able to tell me something that will help us find her. Has she been at school?"

"I'm not sure—she wasn't today. But she missed her last two appointments with me as well, so maybe not. There's been so much going on, I hadn't thought to check." She tried to remember if she'd even seen Mandy in the halls these last few weeks.

Kate wrestled with her emotions. She wanted to help Mandy, but she didn't know the girl that well. In the end, it was her father's coughing fit coming from the kitchen that jogged Kate's memory.

"Actually, there might be something," Kate said. Roman's eyes widened. She guessed he hadn't actually been expecting to make headway. "When I was at the doctor with my father last week, I noticed a picture of Mandy in his office. She's friends with his daughter. They'd been waitressing at a hospital function." She paused. "Anyway, I remember asking about it and the doctor said Mandy's stepfather had encouraged her to take the job. But Mandy doesn't have a stepfather."

Roman was quiet for a moment. "Do you know who he was talking about?"

"No. I don't know the family well, and Mandy's mother hasn't been in contact with me either, so I don't know the particulars of their situation. But I did hear that Mandy's mother was dating someone. I remember thinking it was odd, given that the divorce is a long way from final—and also very contentious from what I hear. Anyway, the picture was only taken a little over a month ago, so maybe Mandy's mom moved in with her boyfriend? Either way, seems like Dr. Nivens's daughter might know a little more than I do."

When Kate went to the kitchen the next morning to get breakfast, she was surprised to find Tilly sitting at the table. They'd said goodbye the night before, so that Frank wouldn't have to get up early.

"Tilly? I'm surprised you're still here."

"I was getting ready to hit the road but I wanted to talk to you first."

"What's going on?"

Tilly looked nervous. "First, I have to fess up. I heard your conversation with Roman last night. By accident. Sort of."

Kate probably should have been irritated by her sister's eavesdropping, but she would have been doing the same thing if their positions were switched. She grinned. "And?" But the look on Tilly's face cooled her amusement. "What is it, Tilly?"

"You're one of the smartest people I know, Kate. This is going to sound extra corny but I've always admired your drive, your determination. And I'm scared for you."

"Scared? Why?" Kate waited as Tilly struggled for words.

"The people here in town are ruthless. Trust me."

"What are you talking about?" Kate asked, frustration

growing. "You haven't lived here in twenty years. I'd be surprised if you even remembered anyone. Not many people stuck around."

Tilly's expression turned cold. "Nothing ever changes here, Kate. Don't get me wrong. There are things I love about this place. It's my hometown. But I've seen what the people here are capable of."

"I don't understand." All Kate could picture was the reckless teenager that Tilly had been, so out of control. Not at all concerned about who she hurt. It had been a relief when Kate left for college. And though she knew Tilly didn't like being home, Kate didn't like the tone the conversation had taken.

"I've spent nearly twenty years trying put this place behind me. I've missed out on so many things, but I knew if I came back here it would put me in a bad place." Tilly shook her head and held up her hand to stave off Kate's questions. "No, I'm not going to go into any detail. I've got enough demons to deal with without inviting them in. But I want you to be careful."

The ominous tone of Tilly's voice, the all-too familiar shadow that crept across her face as she spoke, made Kate shiver as she began to put the pieces together.

"What happened to you?" she whispered, but Tilly was already gathering her things and heading toward the door.

"Take care of yourself, Kate," Tilly said, and then she was gone.

Kate left for work before her father got up. The quiet of the house as she walked out the door amplified the gloom left in Tilly's wake, and Kate had finally run out of patience, opting for an early start to her workday over worrying about her sister. Of course, by the time she arrived at work, she regretted not making sure her father was okay. A call home went unanswered, and Kate decided to drop by the house at lunch to assuage her worries.

She'd barely gotten settled when there was a knock at the door. She looked up in time to see Pete walk in, closing the door behind him.

"Morning, Pete," Kate said with a smile.

Pete frowned. "Morning, Kate. Sorry to drop in so early, but I have to discuss an urgent matter with you."

"What it is?" Kate said, her anxiety ramping up.

"Are you working with the police?"

Kate sighed. "I'm doing some consulting for Detective Aguilar. I was hoping he'd keep it quiet so it wouldn't interfere with my work. Is he here?"

"No. I received a letter this morning, slipped under my office door, from a parent who is very concerned about you working with the police. Seems to think it creates a conflict of interest. They were very upset."

"They? Who sent it?"

Pete shifted. "I'm not exactly sure. It's anonymous."

"I'd like to see the letter. How do you know it was from a parent? It could have been written by anyone."

"True." Pete sighed. "But you know I have to take this seriously, Kate. I can't just ignore it because the sender didn't provide contact information. You know how it goes."

"Well, I can't say that I'm surprised," Kate said. "The police department received a similar complaint—anonymous, of course—trying to get Detective Aguilar thrown off the case. Or at least trying to make sure he wasn't working with me. Though they accused him of some awful stuff."

"I'm assuming this has to do with Gabby Greene?" Pete asked, looking more and more pained as they talked.

"Of course." Kate paused. She'd been ready to tell Pete about the notes she received at the health fair, but decided maybe pointing out that she'd shared student information with police wouldn't be the best way to alleviate his fears. Even if the surveys were anonymous. "That reminds me. Do you happen to know if Mandy Garcia was at school the last few days?"

"I'll check with Steph when she gets in. Why do you ask?"

"Her father filed a missing persons report with the police."

Pete looked queasy. "What is going on around here?" he asked of no one in particular.

"I've been asking myself the same question," Kate replied. "Is me working with the police going to be a problem?"

Pete shook his head. "There's nothing in your contract expressly forbidding it, but I'd be remiss as your principal—and as your friend, Kate—if I didn't tell you that the fact that we're already getting complaints about it might come back to kick us in the buttocks."

Pete was the most proper, well-mannered person she knew. His choice of words cracked Kate up, though she knew he must be stressed out to have gone to such lengths.

"Noted," she said. "Thanks for your concern, Pete. Hopefully they'll find whoever killed Gabby and we'll be able to get back to some semblance of normalcy around here." She smiled, hoping to convince him that he had nothing to worry about despite her own growing fear that they did.

CHAPTER ELEVEN

Roman walked into Kate's office as she was packing up for the day.

"Hi, Roman," she said with a sigh.

"Nice to see you, too," Roman replied with a grin that didn't reach his eyes. "Do you have a few minutes to talk?"

Kate put her bag down and sank back into her computer chair. "Sure. But I have to get home soon. Tilly left and I don't want to leave my dad alone any longer than I have to."

"Understood," Roman said, taking a seat across from her. "We found Mandy Garcia's mother and sister last night."

"Found them?" Kate asked, dreading the answer.

"They're fine," Roman said, this time with a real smile. "It looks like Mrs. Garcia has moved in with her boyfriend. She wasn't happy to see me, and she didn't want to answer my questions, but that part of the mystery is solved."

"That's a relief," Kate said, allowing herself to relax.

"Unfortunately," Roman continued, "she wasn't any help in locating Mandy. She claims that Mandy left home a few days before the move, refusing to live under the same roof as mom's new boyfriend. Didn't seem too shaken up by it. She says she thought Mandy would go to her dad's."

"She thought? Nice parenting. So she hasn't had contact with her daughter for, what, weeks?"

"A week or two," Roman said.

"And?" Kate asked, unnerved by the look on Roman's face.

"When I told her that Mr. Garcia filed a missing persons report, she didn't seem concerned. In fact, I'd say she showed no emotion at all. Until she started on about how her ex has a tendency to overreact. When I asked her why she hadn't returned his calls, she claimed she never got them."

"That should be easy enough to check, right?"

"Right. Thanks for the advice." Roman's tone was mildly sarcastic, but he looked tired.

"You came to talk to me, remember? You don't have to be such an ass." Kate had meant the words to be more playful than they sounded, and she flinched when she saw Roman stiffen. She wondered if they'd ever reach a point where they weren't offending each other at every turn.

"You're right, Ms. Medina. I'll go get back to work." He stood abruptly, turning to the door. He was halfway out when Kate stopped him.

"I'm sorry, Roman," she said softly, hoping to repair the damage. "I'm just stressed. It's been a rough day."

Roman turned toward her, but didn't step back into her office. He stood in the hall, waiting.

"We got an anonymous letter today—a complaint about my involvement with the police department. I thought Pete was going to have a coronary, and I get the feeling I'm on pretty rocky ground here. And with Tilly gone, I have to be careful about how much energy I'm putting into all this. My dad needs me. I don't have a lot of extra bandwidth right now."

"I know I'm asking a lot from you right now, Kate. I'll try to keep you out of it as much as I can, but that doesn't change the fact that you're more in tune with what's going on here at the school than I am. I can't afford to lose…" He paused, "I need your help. These girls need your help."

Kate sighed. "I checked today, and it looks like Mandy hasn't been at school all week."

"Do you know who she hangs out with? Who she might be dating? Anyone I can talk to who might know where she is?"

"She's a cheerleader. She hung out with the popular kids until recently. I've never known her to date anyone but, again, I don't know much about her. Honestly, I'd only met with her a few times before she stopped coming to sessions. And I didn't know Gabby Greene at all, except by name. I don't know how much help I can be, but I'll do my best."

Kate hated the winter months, even in the New Mexico desert. It never got very cold, but since she had to be at school early in the morning she was always walking in and out of a dark building. Her office, an extension of the main office, had no windows, and was pitch black even in the summer. But in the winter the darkness permeated, making everything feel colder.

She'd headed into work especially early, hoping to get several files updated before things got busy. She flipped on the light in her office and screamed.

"Mandy?" she asked once she'd regained her composure. The girl was huddled in the corner of the office in the dark, barely moving as Kate dropped her bag and knelt beside her. Mandy's face was battered and bruised, blood crusting her lips and one of her eyes nearly swollen shut. Her hair was filthy and matted, several strands stuck to the carnage of her bloody cheek. When she didn't speak, Kate put her hands on Mandy's arms. The girl flinched.

"Mandy, honey, what happened?" Kate tried to keep her voice calm but adrenaline surged, causing her heart to race.

Mandy looked up at Kate, her eyes vacant. "Please help me." Her voice was barely a whisper, raspy and broken.

"Of course." Kate held Mandy's elbow, lifting the girl to her feet and leading her to the visitor chair. Mandy's movements were slow and clumsy. Kate saw her wince as she sat down, raising the hairs on Kate's neck. Kate moved to her chair and scooted the phone closer. "I think we should call your mother."

"No!" Mandy yelped. Her voice was gravelly, as if she hadn't had any water for days. It sounded painful. Mandy's eyes were wide and her hands had begun to shake. "Please. You can't tell anyone I'm here."

"You need to see a doctor," Kate said, mulling over her options. She reached into her bottom desk drawer and handed Mandy a bottle of water from her stash. The girl struggled to remove the lid and then gulped thirstily.

"I need to tell you something first." Mandy's breathy words were like ice on Kate's heart. Mandy closed her eyes, and for a moment Kate wondered if she had dozed off, but her eyelids slid open slowly, revealing freshly formed tears. "I ran away from home. From my mom's house." Mandy sighed. "I wasn't planning on coming back, ever."

"Where were you going to go?"

"Anywhere. I stayed with a friend in Las Cruces for a few days, and it didn't matter where as long as it wasn't here. But…" Mandy's breathing became labored and a tear slid down her cheek, streaking the dried blood and dirt it touched. "But I can't leave my sister. She won't be safe. They'll get to her, too." As if a floodgate had been opened Mandy's face crumpled and she sobbed, long and hard with heaving breaths in between. Kate slid the box of tissues across her desk and then moved to Mandy's side, holding the girl as she cried. This was the closest she'd ever been to Mandy Garcia.

When her tears finally subsided, Mandy wiped her eyes and looked at Kate. "Do you know how I get one of those rape exams?"

"You were raped?"

Mandy smiled an eerie, jaded smile. "They call it service." Her smile faded.

"They who?" Kate asked quietly.

Mandy ignored her. "Can I stay with you? After?"

Kate sighed. She looked at her watch. It would be another hour before the rest of the office staff arrived. "Let's get you out of here before anyone sees you," Kate said. She knew she was crossing a line, felt the weight of it in her abdomen. Just as she knew that if she didn't act now—if she called the police, which she knew she should do—that Mandy would disappear. And they might not get another chance to help her.

Kate and Mandy sat in the car until they saw the nurse walk into the small office building. Mandy slumped down in the passenger seat.

"Are you ready?" Kate asked. She'd called the sexual assault hotline and arranged for Mandy to receive an exam. Kate had worked with forensic nurses at the prison and was familiar with the process, but she knew it would be hard on Mandy. It would also take hours, so she'd called in sick to work.

"Okay." Mandy's voice was shaky.

"They're going to take good care of you, I promise," Kate assured her.

"Can you stay with me?"

"If you want me to."

"Okay," Mandy said again, this time opening the car door and stepping out. She and Kate entered the building. The space was small, but warm and cozy. It didn't feel sterile, which was a good thing. Kate saw lots of literature in magazine racks, but the central focus of the room was a seating area with soft, cushy sofas draped in fuzzy blankets in soothing colors. They were greeted as they entered by a middle-aged woman in teal scrubs.

"Hello. Mandy? My name is Jennifer. I'm a registered nurse, and I've been specially trained to do sexual assault exams." Mandy seemed to grow smaller, but Jennifer smiled. "Don't worry. We'll move slowly. And you are completely in control here. If you want to take a break or stop altogether, tell me. I will explain everything to you step by step before we do anything, and if you have any questions at all, ask."

"Do we have to call the police?" Mandy asked.

"No," Jennifer answered with confidence. "We'll talk a lot about your options, but your time here is about making sure you're physically okay and that you get the help you need." Jennifer had been focused intently on Mandy, but she turned her attention to Kate. "Are you her mother?"

"No," Kate said. "I'm the high school psychologist—Kate Medina."

Jennifer returned her attention to Mandy. "Would you prefer to have Ms. Medina step outside during the exam?"

"No," Mandy said with urgency. "No, I want her to stay with me." She grabbed Kate's arm.

"No problem," Jennifer said soothingly. "You're the boss in here. Whoever you want with you is fine with me." She turned her attention again to Kate. "That being said, you're here as a friend, not in an official capacity. Everything said in this room is confidential."

"I understand," Kate said.

Jennifer ushered them into a small waiting room. Kate sat next to Mandy on a plush loveseat, feeling a little bit unnerved by the way Mandy leaned into her. The intimacy made her uncomfortable, especially since she hardly knew the girl. But she didn't flinch, knowing that she needed to model calm even if she didn't feel it.

On a small table Jennifer had laid out a clipboard with a small stack of papers, a pen, and a large white envelope that looked lumpy.

"We're going to start by taking your history. This process can take a while, so it's fine if you need to take a break. I have snacks and drinks in the fridge, but I'll need to take a few swabs before you eat or drink anything." She reached into the white envelope and pulled out a series of smaller packages. "These are the swabs and vials in which we'll store any evidence we collect. We seal and sign off on each sample to maintain the chain of custody, in case you decide to go to the police. But that decision is up to you, and you don't have to make it right now."

Jennifer made small talk as she swabbed the insides of Mandy's cheeks, her hands working deftly. Mandy didn't say much in return, but Kate noticed that the nurse didn't push her, didn't demand any sort of reaction. Her chatter was more a rehearsed distraction. When she was finished, she packaged up the samples. "I'm going to get you cleaned up, but I'll need to take pictures and more samples first so let's get started on the history, okay?"

Mandy nodded.

Jennifer worked as quickly as possible through a page or two of basic personal information, which Mandy answered like a robot, her tone flat. But then the questions became very personal.

"Are you sexually active?" Jennifer asked, then added, "with someone other than the person who raped you."

"No," Mandy said.

"I want you to tell me, in your words, exactly what happened. Try to be as detailed as possible, especially about your attacker."

"What if there was more than one?"

Jennifer didn't miss a step. "That's fine. I'll take down everything you tell me and no one will see these notes unless you want them to."

Mandy clutched at Kate's arm, squeezing harder as she began to recount the events that had led her to this place. As Mandy spoke, Kate was grateful for the pressure on her arm, because the details of Mandy's story made her stomach roil.

The interview took two hours. Jennifer's calm, soothing demeanor never wavered. Kate admired the woman's self-control, because with every word that Mandy spoke, with every indignity she described, Kate felt her blood boil. She watched as Jennifer took photos of each of the cuts and abrasions and bruises on Mandy's face, arms, and abdomen. But she had to move close to Mandy's face and focus her gaze there as she examined more intimate areas.

Kate understood why Mandy had come to her—why she had come back. Girls in Alamogordo were being preyed upon right this very second. Kate's hands shook as she wondered how to stop it from happening again.

CHAPTER TWELVE

By the time Mandy's exam was done, Kate was exhausted and conflicted. She'd listened in horror as Mandy told her story. It started when her friend's father offered the girls alcohol. The drink had made her feel woozy, and she'd woken up to him pushing his way inside her, her skirt and underwear pulled down around her ankles. She tried to cry out, but the man had held his hand down on her mouth as he finished. A glance to her side revealed Mandy's friend, passed out a few feet away. When he let her go, Mandy got dressed and fled.

She'd told her mom immediately, who'd insisted on telling her boyfriend, Benny, who'd insisted that Mandy was making things up. He'd known the man in question for years, he said. To Mandy's horror her mother believed him.

Mandy scrubbed her body until her skin was raw. She dropped out of cheerleading—something Kate hadn't been aware of—and started wearing baggy clothing, hoping to not draw attention to herself.

She thought she could forget about it. Until they came for her. Then she knew it would never end.

The second time, Mandy had been approached after school by a man she knew from the hospital banquet she'd waitressed. The man offered Mandy a ride home, which she refused, sensing danger. Unfortunately, the parking lot had been empty. Mandy walked away but the man followed her, pulling up and insisting that she get in. His voice left no room for argument— she either got in the car on her own or he'd make her. Resigned to her fate, she tried to prepare herself for what was about to happen.

But nothing could have prepared her. She was taken to a house she didn't recognize in one of the newer developments, where she was passed around. They gave her alcohol again, though it made her feel dizzy almost instantly, and told her that she would be rewarded for service to her community. She remembered being with at least five different men, but she had lost consciousness several times and couldn't be sure. She was dropped off at her house, where her mother found her vomiting in the front yard.

Mandy's mother demanded to know where she'd been, but the man who'd taken her had made two things clear. First, if she told anyone he would kill her and hurt her family. Second, he'd be back for her.

She kept her mouth shut.

———

Mandy's abductor had come for her three more times before she stopped going to school altogether, hiding out in her room, feigning illness. That had been a week ago.

On the day that she ran away, her mom's boyfriend had come to find her.

"Come on, Mandy. You're going to school today." He wasn't kind. Mandy was pretty sure he hated her, and the feeling was mutual. Despite her mother's story, Mandy had moved with her family into Benny Parks's house, taking her away from her neighbors and all the things she knew.

"I don't feel well," she croaked, pulling the covers back over her head.

He stepped up to her bed, yanking the blanket off, leaving her curled in a ball in the middle of the mattress.

"Get up," he demanded, grabbing her arm and pulling her up. "You're not going to be hiding out today. People have been asking about you." When she saw the look on his face, she'd nearly vomited.

Mandy fought back. The next thing she knew he was punching her, grabbing her head and slamming it against the bed frame. The attack didn't last long but he left her lying on her bedroom floor, locking the door behind him. As if that would somehow stop her from leaving. He must've known what she would do.

When Mandy came to, she packed a backpack and climbed out her window. She took the bus to Las Cruces. For nearly two days she stayed, practically comatose, on the couch of a friend's sister. She didn't shower. She didn't eat. Finally, her host threatened to call an ambulance if Mandy didn't drink some water. Mandy obeyed and then left, heading back to Alamogordo. By then it had dawned on her what might happen to her mother and sister if she stayed away

Kate had gleaned these details while listening to Mandy's story at the SANE office. She wondered how she would be able to honor the privacy of this girl when her job required that she report physical abuse to the police. Apart from the sexual assault, Mandy's mother had moved both her girls into the home of a man who was physically violent. Mandy's sister was also at risk. And from what Mandy described, so were many more girls.

The nurse had asked a lot of questions about Mandy's attackers, but she hadn't focused on the bigger picture. That wasn't her job. As a newly minted consultant for the police department, Kate knew that she should take her theories to Roman, that she should talk Mandy into pressing charges. And she would. But when she looked over at Mandy, all she could think about was getting her somewhere safe.

Frank's reaction to Kate showing up with Mandy was another blow.

"What are you thinking?" Frank fumed, pacing the living room while Kate ate her fast food from the coffee table. As soon as they'd arrived, Kate had settled Mandy into Tilly's room, and within moments of lying down Mandy was sound asleep.

"Shh, Dad. You're going to wake her," Kate chided. She'd introduced Mandy, but it was only after the girl was safe and sound that Kate gave her father a highly edited version of what had happened. She'd expected his support. Maybe some disgust at what had happened to the teen. But nothing had prepared her for the explosion that followed.

Frank gritted his teeth. "Does anyone know she's here?"

"No. She asked me not to tell her parents. And she's not ready to talk to the police. She needs to rest. The nurse gave her a ton of antibiotics. She's got cuts and bruises all over her body. I think she deserves to feel safe for a day or two before she has to make any big decisions, don't you?" Kate laid her head back on the couch, ready for sleep despite the fact that it was only five o'clock in the evening.

Frank sat beside her. "Kate, you need to be careful here."

Kate opened her eyes and was surprised to see fear in her father's eyes. "Careful of what? Her mom's boyfriend doesn't know she's here. So as long as she stays inside, there's no reason to think he'd come after her. He was never violent before the attack. She'll be eighteen in a few months. I can help her come up with a plan for what to do next." Kate's voice had trailed off.

"You're not listening to me, Princesa." Her father's voice was thick with tension. "Having her here... it puts us all at risk."

"I can have Roman have someone patrol our street tonight..." Despite the urgency in her father's voice, exhaustion was making it hard to concentrate.

Frank grabbed her arm, interrupting her mid-sentence. "Listen to me!" His voice was a near shout, causing Kate to wince. She also looked toward the hall, wondering if this outburst would disturb Mandy. "Look at me, Kate. What happened to that girl, it's none of our business. We shouldn't get involved."

Suddenly Kate was on high alert. "Why does it sound like you know something about this?" Kate's heart pounded as she waited for his answer.

Frank sighed, letting go of her arm, his body sagging. He was breathing very heavily, and Kate could see sweat forming on his brow. "Some things we can't do anything about, Kate. Some things just happen. And it's unfortunate. And it makes us angry. But we have to move on and try to look forward."

"What are you talking about?" Kate hissed, feeling her anger rise. "What things? Because I don't believe that we need to let a teenage girl get raped; repeatedly, I might add. Not for a minute should we allow that to happen." Kate had expected to shock him, but Frank's expression didn't so much as twitch. She felt bile rising in her throat. "Oh, God. You do know something about this, don't you? How?"

Kate was on her feet before she realized she'd moved. She looked down at her father, small and hunched on the couch. His head had fallen forward, and she could see a slight tremor in his shoulders. Her insides were at war. She wanted to comfort him. She wanted to tell him everything would be fine. That they would all move forward the way they always did—the way she always did—never looking back. But she couldn't, not after seeing and hearing about the things that had been done to Mandy Garcia. "What do you know?"

"What I know," Frank whispered, "is that in this town a few hold all the power. And to cross them, even to question them, leads to devastation."

Kate looked at her father as if seeing him for the first time. The way his eyes now stared blankly, as if he'd retreated to a safer place in his mind, made Kate wonder if she was ready to know whatever secrets he was keeping.

That night, Kate couldn't sleep. After the requisite tossing and turning, she flipped on her bedside lamp and pulled her laptop on top of the covers. She logged in to Facebook and was casually sifting through friends' posts, but her mind kept replaying the conversation with her father.

Gabby Greene's Facebook profile had been disabled, but Kate scanned the pages of every high school girl she could think of, searching desperately for clues. But of course there were none to find.

Switching over to Google, Kate searched for articles about the girl who was killed when she was in high school. Laura Fuentes had been a quiet girl. Kate could barely muster a picture of Laura in her memory, and seeing the few photos that circulated online didn't help. Laura had died before the days of social media. It was sad, like the girl had just disappeared one day.

Except that she hadn't.

Laura's car, with her body inside, had been dumped in the

creek. According to the few newspaper clippings Kate found, authorities believed Laura had been dead for a few days before she was located. Her body was found lying across the front seat, her shirt pulled up over her breasts to reveal carvings made with some kind of rough-edged blade. She'd been stabbed, strangled, and there was evidence of sexual contact, though the journalist didn't mention rape.

Kate broadened her search, looking for any teenage girls who'd been killed in the area. As she sifted through listings for cold cases and disappearances, her body began to sag under the weight of all these lost lives. She read about men and women who'd been killed in drug and gang-related territorial disputes. Children who'd succumbed to abuse and neglect. Significant others who'd chosen the wrong partner.

When the sky revealed the first signs of morning, Kate had had enough. She flipped through another page of search results and was about to put her computer away, when she saw a peculiar headline. Another teenage girl found dead, not in the creek but out in the desert on the south side of town. She'd been stabbed and strangled, though the newspaper coverage lacked detail. What caught Kate's eye were the references to "liberties taken"—code for sexual assault. And the date. This girl had been killed in 1968.

Kate sat back against her headboard and let her laptop slide onto the covers beside her as she processed everything she'd read. But as soon as she settled back, her eyelids felt leaden. Fatigue took over and Kate woke a few hours later to the sound of her alarm, groggy but grateful that she'd managed to get a little bit of sleep.

A soft tapping on her door signaled an end to her lounging.

"Come in," Kate said.

The door creaked open slowly. Mandy peered around the corner. "Is it okay if I take a shower?"

"Of course," Kate said then smiled, yawning. "There are clean towels in the bathroom cabinet."

Mandy nodded and retreated, closing the door softly behind her.

Kate got up and slipped on her bathrobe. She padded out into the kitchen to start the coffee brewing, wondering what the day would bring.

CHAPTER THIRTEEN

Kate made breakfast, setting out the medications Mandy would need to take. The teen emerged from the bathroom a while later, her hair wet and stringy. After a full twelve hours of sleep, the girl looked almost alive again. The cuts and bruises spoke of pain but her eyes were brighter. Kate dished out eggs and toast, refilling Mandy's water before sitting down to eat.

"How did you sleep?" Kate asked, keeping her tone casual.

"Pretty good," Mandy mumbled. "I didn't dream."

Kate nodded. She knew that Mandy would be dealing with post-traumatic stress from the abuse she'd suffered, and nightmares were part and parcel of PTSD. "I don't want to put any pressure on you, Mandy, but we need to talk about what happens next."

"I know," Mandy said.

"I think we should talk with the police. I can take you to the station this morning if you want."

Mandy cringed.

"I can call a detective I know and have him come here if you're more comfortable." Kate hesitated. "Or we could call your father." When Mandy started shaking her head, Kate added. "He's really worried about you, Mandy. He reported you missing."

Mandy's hands were shaking. "He can't know I'm back. Not right now."

"Why?" Kate couldn't hide the exasperation in her voice.

"It's too dangerous."

"Mandy, the police will keep you safe…"

Mandy laughed. "Like they kept Gabby Greene safe?"

"Wait. Are you saying Gabby was part of this?" When Mandy nodded, Kate asked, "Were there other girls?"

"Yeah, a few," Mandy whispered. "I saw Gabby once. The first time they took me to one of their parties. It was like… we were the party favors, you know? The men laughed and drank, like it was just another day. I saw Gabby being led into one of the rooms. She looked at me and her eyes were so empty. I wondered if that's what I would look like." Mandy's voice had become almost inaudible as she spoke.

"When was that, Mandy?" Kate asked, knowing the answer would turn her stomach. She pushed her plate away.

"A few nights before they found Gabby in the creek," Mandy answered, confirming Kate's suspicions. Silence hung heavily between them while Kate considered their options.

"I know you're scared," Kate said. "But Mandy, we need to put a stop to this. We need to stop more girls from being hurt."

"I know," Mandy muttered. After a few minutes, Mandy said, "Okay, who's the detective you know?" Her tone hinted at suspicion.

"Roman Aguilar," Kate replied, studying Mandy's reaction. When she didn't seem to recognize the name, Kate continued, "I've known Detective Aguilar for a long time. I trust him. You can trust him, too."

Mandy sighed. "You can call him, but please don't tell him I'm here until he gets here."

Mandy went back to her room to lie down while they waited for Roman to arrive, so when Kate answered the door the girl was nowhere in sight.

"Playing hooky?" Roman might have meant to be playful, but his expression was dead serious.

"No," Kate said. "Though I did call in today."

"Can I come in?" Roman asked and Kate realized she was still standing in the doorway, blocking his path.

"Yes, of course," she said, moving aside. Roman was dressed for work, his suit jacket neatly pressed, his holster visible inside. He made his way to the sofa, sitting with his back to the hallway. Kate sat across from him.

"Why am I here?" Roman asked. He was sitting at the edge of the sofa with his back rigid, ready to stand at any moment. Kate felt flustered. His posture was anything but friendly, and she wondered how his state of mind was going to affect his interaction with Mandy.

"There's been a development," Kate said.

"A development?" Roman asked with a hint of irritation.

"Why do you always have to be so difficult," Kate muttered.

Kate could see Roman's anger brimming under the surface, but she wasn't going to back down. She wasn't about to hand Mandy over to a hostile police officer, no matter how badly she wanted to extricate herself from the situation. No matter how her father felt. Things were hard enough for sexual assault survivors. Luckily, Roman took a few deep breaths and his color began to return to normal. His teeth were gritted when he said, "Fine." Kate decided to give him the benefit of the doubt.

"Okay," Kate said, keeping her voice calm. She'd heard the click of a door in the hallway, and knew that Mandy was coming down the hall. "Yesterday, Mandy Garcia showed up at my office."

"Where is she?" Roman's whole demeanor changed.

"She's here. I'll get her in a few minutes," Kate said, hoping that Mandy heard her and would stay in the hall until she was ready. "She did run away from home. But she came back, Roman. And she was not in good shape."

"How do you mean?"

"She'd been raped and beaten. I don't know how long it had been since she'd eaten or slept. She asked me to take her to SANE."

"And did you?" Roman said, fully calm now that he was in work mode and over whatever had been bothering him before.

"Yes. She had a full exam yesterday and I brought her here to sleep."

"We'll need to call her parents..." Roman started, but Kate interrupted him.

"She doesn't want her parents to know where she is, and I think you'll agree when you hear her story."

Roman looked skeptical. "Why?"

"Well, first, because the person who beat her up is her mother's boyfriend." Kate saw Roman's brow rise. "And also because she knows something about what happened to Gabby Greene."

"Come join us, Mandy," Kate said. Mandy walked around the corner, eyeing Roman suspiciously as she made her way over to Kate and sitting down beside her. Kate watched as Roman's eyes moved over the girl's injuries. Mandy had dressed in one of Kate's baggy sweatshirts and leggings. She pulled her knees up inside the sweatshirt, making herself small and self-contained.

"This is Detective Aguilar."

Mandy stayed silent but kept her eyes locked on Roman.

"Hello, Mandy," Roman said. His voice still held an

authoritative edge, but he'd infused it with calm. It was clearly his *talking-to-victims* voice. Kate was glad to see how he changed his strategy to fit the situation—not all police officers did. "Kate told me a little bit about what happened to you. Can you tell me about it?"

Mandy hesitated. This was the part of the process that Kate hated. Victims of violence were made to recount their story so many times as they moved through the legal system, ripping open barely closed wounds at every turn. Kate put her hand on Mandy's shoulder. "It's okay, Mandy. You can take your time. Just like yesterday. This is your story and you're the one in control here."

Kate met Roman's eyes, but couldn't read his expression.

"If I talk to you, will you tell my parents I'm here?" Mandy asked.

Roman hesitated. "How old are you?"

"Seventeen."

"Technically, I can't even talk to you on the record without a parent present," Roman said, causing Mandy to wilt. "But in cases where the parent might be abusive, I have a little latitude. At least at first. So why don't you tell me what happened, one piece at a time, and I'll let you know if that changes. Right now, I'm here as Kate's friend."

"Okay," Mandy replied cautiously. She was silent for a few moments. The whole room seemed to hold its breath until she finally began to talk. She told Roman about the beating she'd taken from her mom's boyfriend first.

"Does your mother know he hurt you?" Roman asked Mandy, interrupting her flow. Kate nearly reprimanded him, but Mandy looked relieved by the break.

"I don't know," Mandy replied. "I didn't ask her. But ever since she started dating him, she's been different."

"How?"

"She doesn't care what happens to us anymore. She believes

him, no matter what he says. She won't let me see my dad when I want to." Mandy's tone became angrier. "It was never like this before."

"Before your parents separated?" Roman asked kindly.

"Yeah," Mandy replied.

"Did he ever hit you before? Your mom's boyfriend?"

"No."

"What about your sister?"

Mandy stiffened. "Not that I know of." She paused. "But I'm scared. I'm worried about her."

"I can understand that," Roman said. "Was he inappropriate with you, Mandy?"

Kate hated Roman's choice of words. As if beating Mandy to within an inch of her life was appropriate, but sexual contact was not.

"No," Mandy whispered. "Not him."

"Okay. I'm sorry I have to ask you all this, Mandy, but I want to help. Who else hurt you?" Roman looked very serious, but his tone remained calm, soothing.

"The first time," Mandy said, so quietly that even Kate had to strain to hear her, "it was Mr. Craig. From the hospital."

The name didn't sound familiar to Kate. She wondered if Craig was the first or last name.

"Then it was other men." Tears began to stream down Mandy's cheeks.

"We can take a break," Roman said, handing Mandy the tissue box from the coffee table.

"No," Mandy said, dabbing at her eyes. "I want to say it all right now." Kate could hear a vibration of fear and anguish in Mandy's voice. She knew Mandy was hoping that this would be the last time she had to tell her story. Kate knew that it wouldn't be.

"Okay, when you're ready then," Roman said.

"After the hospital banquet, the one where I waitressed, I

went home with my friend Gina after school. Her dad gave us some drinks. When I woke up, he was on top of me." Mandy went through as many details as she could, though her voice got quieter and quieter. Finally she got up to get a drink of water. Roman and Kate sat in silence. It took a few minutes after she returned to her seat before she could continue.

"After that, another man would wait for me after school. I don't know his name. Sometimes there were other girls. He gave us beer, but I think it had something in it because I always started feeling fuzzy right away. Then he drove us to a house. I'm not sure exactly where. South of Panorama. He walked us to the door and handed us off to another man. I didn't know him. He took us into a room with couches and a TV. I could always hear men's voices, talking. Laughing. One by one, we'd get picked."

"What do you mean 'picked'?" Roman asked.

"Someone would come and take my hand. Sometimes I recognized them. Sometimes not. We'd walk to one of the bedrooms." She'd begun to shake again. "I would try to focus on the ceiling. Sometimes I fell asleep. They didn't seem to care if I was awake or not."

Mandy swallowed hard, choking over her words. "The last time, the guy asked me if I liked it. Like, 'I bet you like this, huh?' I threw up. He was mad, but after I puked I fell asleep. I woke up when they pulled me out of the car and left me on my front lawn."

Kate put her arm around Mandy's shoulder.

"I remember thinking that I couldn't go back. I would die if I did. I felt so sick all the time. Every time I looked in the mirror, I felt so gross." Finally Mandy's voice faded away, replaced by silent sobs.

Mandy buried her face in Kate's shoulder, and for the next ten minutes they all sat in silence, letting Mandy regain her composure. Kate and Roman exchanged glances throughout, but Kate didn't want to push Mandy too far. She suspected Roman felt the same way, though she knew he must be bursting at the seams to ask the question that was lingering between them. *Who were these men?*

"I don't want them to do this to my sister," Mandy said, wiping away the tears that were still flowing. "I don't want them to do this to anyone. But I'm afraid they're going to kill me if they find out I told you." She looked at Roman, her eyes pleading for a promise that Kate knew he couldn't give her. Not after what she'd said.

"I understand," Roman said. "And I'm sorry this happened to you. I promise I will do my best to make sure it doesn't happen to anyone else." He paused. "But I can't do much unless you file a police report and press charges. And you're going to have to have one of your parents with you."

Mandy started to protest but Roman stopped her. "I know that's not what you wanted to hear, but right now you're the only person who can verify what happened."

"I want to help," Mandy said. "Here's the thing, though. I didn't recognize many of the people at those parties, but a few I did. And one of them was a police officer."

Roman was quiet, but his expression couldn't entirely hide his shock. "Can you tell me who?"

"Yes. But you have to promise to keep me safe. And to keep my sister safe." Mandy voice was small but determined.

"I will do everything I can to protect you," Roman promised.

Mandy scrutinized him. Finally she said, "It was the chief." She hesitated, and then added, "And he picked Gabby. The last time I saw her, he was leading Gabby up the stairs."

Roman asked a few more questions, but Mandy was visibly drooping. Kate sent her back to bed, promising that she'd wake her up in a few hours. When Kate was sure Mandy was settled, she returned to the living room and sat across from Roman.

Kate sat back and closed her eyes. It gave her mind a moment of much-needed peace. Between the emotional turmoil and her lack of sleep the night before, Kate was beginning to wish she could crawl back into bed as well. She looked over at Roman, whose mind seemed to be a million miles away.

"Thank you," she finally said, getting his attention.

Roman cleared his throat nervously. "I'm sorry I was such an ass when I got here this morning," he said. "I had no idea what you'd been going through."

"I know," Kate said, letting him off the hook.

"Is your dad home?"

"He's sleeping. He doesn't get up before noon most days, and we had a pretty big argument last night over Mandy being here."

Roman seemed surprised. "Why?"

Kate remembered how Frank's reaction had thrown her, and how his words had kept her up at night. "Can we talk about it another time?"

Roman nodded, and they sat silently for another moment before Roman started asking questions. Questions Kate knew were coming and was prepared for.

"You were present during the SANE exam?" he asked.

"Yes. She asked me to stay."

"Anything I need to know?"

"Not until she files a report. Maybe not even then," Kate said, bracing herself for his reaction.

"For God's sake, Kate! I don't want to invade that girl's privacy, but if we have some kind of sex trafficking operation going on... I mean, she talked about parties. How many men are involved? And how many victims are there?" Roman sounded a little frantic. Kate was thankful he'd kept it to himself until Mandy was out of the room.

"I'm not being arbitrary here, Roman. I know what's at stake.

But after hearing the story again, I'm convinced that this is going to be a nightmare for Mandy—and the least we can do for her is respect her privacy as much as we can. If she says it's OK, I'll tell you everything I saw. Everything I heard. But I'm going to ask her first. It's not fair to Mandy."

"Look, I'm not disputing that Mandy has been violated here, and I do intend to get every bastard who hurt her locked up, but she just implicated someone in Gabby Greene's death. I have a duty to keep the community safe, too." Roman was whisper-shouting, his face beet-red.

"Whatever I am, Roman," Kate hissed, "I am not naive. I know the terrible things that can happen to people, even in the most secure environments." Kate's voice cracked. She could feel heat flooding her face. She hated that she couldn't keep her own trauma from rearing its ugly head when she got emotional, when she felt cornered. And she hated that it was coming out now with Roman. "I wasn't with Mandy in an official capacity. Otherwise, the nurse wouldn't have let me stay. And it's important that we respect that."

Roman studied Kate closely, but he didn't say more. He stayed still while she breathed. While she cleared her head. Until she could look him in the eye again.

"Here's what I can say," Kate said slowly, keeping her emotions in check. "Based on what I saw yesterday, something terrible happened to Mandy and there is plenty of physical evidence that it happened. I know that it's your job to tie that evidence to whoever committed the crime. Mandy came to me yesterday because she didn't have anywhere else to go. And she still doesn't. So until she consents to file a police report, or you can show me how you intend to protect her from further harm, I'm not going to tell you anything else. What happened to Mandy never should have happened. What happened to Gabby Greene never should have happened. And while I want to make sure it doesn't happen again, I cannot, in good conscience, betray this girl's trust just to make your job easier." Kate had kept her voice level throughout her speech, but anxiety churned through her core. She waited for Roman to argue, but he surprised her.

"I get it," Roman said, standing. "As far as I'm concerned, I have no new information about Mandy Garcia's whereabouts until I hear from her." He sighed. "I know you think I'm a brute. I know you think I don't care about Mandy's well-being. You're wrong. I do care. But I am duty-bound to protect this community and I need Mandy to work with us. That being said, you're absolutely right. I've got to find a good way to keep her safe, and until I know more this is probably as safe a place as any for her to be."

"She can stay with us for now," Kate said. "But my dad wasn't happy when I brought her home yesterday. I'm not sure he can handle too much drama right now."

"Really?" Roman asked, confused.

Kate hesitated. She still didn't know what to make of her father's reaction, but she knew she needed to tell Roman in case there was something there. "He says this is a small town and the people in power are dangerous."

"Sounds like he knows something." Roman's expression darkened.

"It does," Kate agreed. "I'd love to tell you that his health is making him say crazy things." She paused. "But I've never heard him say anything with such conviction." *And such fear*, she thought.

CHAPTER FOURTEEN

Kate returned to work the following day. She'd been wary of leaving her father in charge of Mandy, but Frank seemed resigned to the situation. By dinnertime, he and Mandy were joking the way that Frank and Kate used to when she was in high school. Kate caught glimpses of Mandy's real personality, and it made her feel both happy and sad. Those fleeting unguarded moments gave way to moody, withdrawn behavior, alternating back and forth through the evening. But Mandy had slept well again. Kate hoped she could get back to work without incident.

When Kate walked into the office, though, she wondered if she'd made a huge mistake. She could see police uniforms through the frosted window of Pete's office. She slipped into her office, turning on her computer and getting settled. She hoped that whatever was going on next door didn't have anything to do with Mandy, but she wasn't surprised when there was a knock at the door. Pete peeked his head in.

"Hi, Kate. Feeling better?"

"Much better, thanks."

"Um. Can you join us in my office?"

"Us?" Kate asked, stalling for time as she considered what might be waiting for her.

"Chief Gunnison is here to ask a few questions."

"Sure," Kate said, hoping she sounded casual. "I hope everything is all right."

She followed Pete into his office. Mandy's mother, Sarah Garcia, and another man who Kate assumed must be the boyfriend were standing next to the police chief. She counted to ten in her head, trying not to look directly at the man until she could do so without obvious fury. In the meantime, she noticed scratches on his knuckles and made a note to mention it to Roman.

"Ed, this is our school psychologist, Kate Medina."

The chief walked over to Kate with a smile, offering her his hand. "You're Frank's daughter, right?"

Kate smiled back. "That's me." His grip was strong, and he held her hand for a fraction of a second too long.

"And this is Mandy Garcia's mother, Sarah, and her friend, Benny Parks."

Kate nodded at them. "Nice to meet you." She stood next to Pete, angling her body away from Benny. "I hope Mandy's doing okay. She's missed our last few sessions. I hope you got my voicemails."

"That's why we're here," Chief Gunnison said. "Mrs. Garcia came to us this morning. Her daughter ran away from home."

"Oh no!" Kate exclaimed, hoping she hadn't overdone it. "That's awful. When did she go missing?" She wanted to kick herself for using that word, but once it was out she couldn't take it back.

The chief seemed umimpressed by the tragic story of this teenage runaway. "Interestingly enough, her father, David, filed a missing person report a few days ago. Mr. Garcia has visitation, and Mrs. Garcia hasn't seen Mandy since her last visit with her father."

Kate kept her expression neutral, but she didn't like the implications. She had seen her share of custody drama, with parents competing and putting their sons and daughters in the middle. Kate had known Mandy was one of those students, but after meeting David Garcia she felt a little bit defensive of him.

"Have you tried calling her cell phone?"

"She left it at home," Sarah said, turning away.

"Why would she..." Kate began to ask, but the police chief cut her off.

"Pete mentioned that Mr. Garcia was in to see you last week." The chief's expression had grown dark, almost menacing, as if he could read her thoughts. "We wondered if you could tell us about his state of mind—how he seemed to you."

"Well," Kate said, pausing for effect, "he seemed agitated and worried. But I'm aware that he and Mrs. Garcia are going through a divorce, so I did my best to calm him. He wanted information about Mandy, but I explained that student files are confidential."

"That can't be true," Sarah exclaimed. "Mandy is a minor. Surely her parents can access her files, not that I'd want David invading her privacy like that." Sarah's tone was full of indignation. Kate really didn't like this woman.

"I am a mandated reporter, Mrs. Garcia. If a student appears to be in physical or emotional danger, or presents a danger to other students, I'm required to report it. Otherwise, students are granted some privacy. Most of the ones I see talk about issues in friendships or relationships, the usual teenage topics. They need a safe place to talk, and my office provides that."

"That's great. My daughter's missing and you're telling me you don't have to tell me anything about your work with her?" Sarah's voice was rising in anger. Benny Parks put a hand on her forearm. Kate wondered if he'd given it a squeeze to keep her calm, because she took a pronounced deep breath and turned to Pete. "Is that true?"

Pete's cheeks were red. "I'm sure that if Ms. Medina had learned something that would help you find Mandy, she would tell you. Right, Kate?" Pete looked at her pleadingly.

"Of course," Kate acquiesced, though she was pretty sure she'd be reluctant to tell this woman anything about her daughter. By comparison, David Garcia had seemed much more concerned about Mandy's welfare. Kate held out her hands, hoping to de-escalate the conversation. "I assure you, Mrs. Garcia, I didn't learn anything in my sessions with Mandy that would indicate she was thinking about running away. In fact, she barely talked to me during our sessions. I was hoping to get that intake form back from you in case there was something in there that would help me get through to her. I know your initial concern was her anger and problems with authority. Unfortunately, I haven't spent enough time with her to get a clear picture."

Kate was thankful that her voice stayed steady. She kept her eyes locked with Mandy's mother, but she could feel Benny Parks looking at her. She didn't want to meet his gaze. Something about him made her uncomfortable and it wasn't only the fact that she knew he'd beaten up his girlfriend's daughter. There was something inherently menacing about him.

Here he was, listening to a discussion about his girlfriend's missing child, and he seemed calm. His hand still held Sarah's arm as if he were a puppeteer.

Pete escorted Sarah Garcia and Benny Parks out of the school. Kate exhaled deeply as she shut the door of her office behind her but her relief didn't last long. A quick rap at her door jolted her back to attention. Chief Gunnison slipped into her office, closing the door behind him.

"Oh, Chief Gunnison," Kate said, shrinking despite herself. Gunnison was standing tall, his back to the door, a grin on his face. "What can I do for you?"

"I just wanted to get to know you a little bit better." He took a seat across from her without invitation. "I saw Detective Aguilar's request to add you as a paid consultant and I started to wonder, who is this woman? I mean, other than Frank Medina's daughter. Good man, your dad. Anyway, I did some checking..."

Kate forced herself to sit down, unwilling to give this man even the tiniest hint that she was uncomfortable. "You did? Well, I suppose that makes sense. You've got to know who you're working with." she said with a smile. "Boring task, I bet. Not much to tell."

"I don't know about that," he said, leaning toward her. "You have an impressive educational background. More than I would have expected from a school counselor."

"I'm a trained psychologist, not a guidance counselor," Kate clarified, meeting his gaze. "Doesn't matter where I work. That's still my job. Detective Aguilar knows I have a background in forensics. I'm sure you know that I worked in the prison system for almost a decade."

Gunnison gave her an amused look, letting his eyes linger a little too long on her body. It made her shiver. "Don't sell yourself short, Ms. Medina. I'm sure the good detective is interested in more than your mind."

"I don't appreciate what you're implying..." She felt her face flush, panic flaring as the police chief continued to study her. She wanted to escape, but he was blocking her exit and she didn't want to get even a bit closer to his looming figure.

"I'm going to deny Detective Aguilar's request, Ms. Medina. You've got your hands full with the kids here at school, and I don't believe that your expertise is going to be beneficial to our investigation." He stood, walking toward the door. But before he walked out, he turned to her and smiled, saying, "Well, it's been a pleasure, but I've got work to do. I don't guess I'll see you around, will I?" Kate was sure that last question was an order, meant to intimidate her. It worked.

On her lunch break, Kate called Roman.

"Hi, Kate," he said, sounding like he'd just woken up.

"Chief Gunnison was here this morning," Kate said. She'd locked the door of her office and was whispering, feeling paranoid about who might be listening. "So were Mandy's parents. Well, Mandy's mom and her boyfriend."

"Why?" he asked. "I haven't been into the station yet, but I'm surprised the chief would get involved on that level. He's been pretty hands-off of our investigations lately."

"I didn't realize you'd put in an official request."

Now she had his attention. "It's protocol for all our consultants, and with your background I figured it wouldn't be a hard sell to get you paid. Not that the PD has a huge budget or anything. Gunnison told you?"

"He did. Right before he told me he was going to deny it. And then pretty much told me to stay away." Kate's blood rushed thinking about the way the man had cornered her in her own office.

Roman groaned. "Great. He's not my biggest fan, so I imagine that's going to create some problems."

"It was odd that they showed up today. Do you think he knows I have Mandy?"

"No," Roman said with confidence. "Though he might be fishing. One thing I do know is that he doesn't like outsiders involving themselves in police business."

"You don't sound very angry," Kate accused.

"And you sound distraught," Roman volleyed back.

"You're damn right I'm distraught." Kate was surprised to hear the hysteria making its way into her voice. She'd tried all morning to push down all the bad feelings, but talking to Roman made it impossible to keep herself in check. "Gunnison barged into my office uninvited. Insulted me. Ogled me. Threatened me. The least you could do is get a little angry in my defense."

The line was silent for a moment.

"I'm sorry that happened. I didn't realize this was going to get ugly for you." Roman's voice was hard as stone.

Kate steadied her breathing. Roman had no way of knowing that the chief's behavior had triggered panic in Kate. She hadn't even seen it coming herself, though she supposed she should have. The minute the chief had closed that door, pressing his back against it, she'd felt the familiar prickle of fear creep up her neck. Looking back, she was amazed that she'd managed to keep herself collected up to this point. She'd come a long way since moving home.

"You still with me?" Roman asked, and Kate realized she'd missed something he'd said.

"Sorry for the outburst. I guess I didn't realize how badly the situation had affected me. What did you say?"

"I asked if we could meet up this afternoon. When do you get off?"

"At four. But I have to be honest, Roman. As much as I hate to bow to that kind of bullying, I also don't want to lose my job right now. Not with Dad being so sick."

"You don't think Pete would back you up?"

Kate thought about the way Pete had skittered into her office, already overwhelmed by the situation.

"I don't think Pete has much of a backbone. He already gave me a warning about that letter he received. I doubt he's going to put himself or the school is a position of being scrutinized just on principle. And I'm not sure that I would blame him."

"So what do you want to do?" Roman asked. He was leaving the decision up to her, which she both appreciated and resented. She already knew what her answer would be.

"I'll meet you at my house at 5:30."

Kate stayed at her office until 4:15, long enough to see both Pete and Steph leave for the day. When they'd gone she walked over to the file room and propped the door open, turning on the lights. The school kept current files in the main office, under lock and key of course. Old student records had been archived in hundreds of file boxes and stored in this room. In her five years working at the school, Kate never had a need to access these files.

It looked like the room didn't see many visitors. Thick layers of dust coated the file boxes, getting darker as Kate worked her way back. It took about twenty minutes for her to locate the boxes containing records from her high school years and another ten to find the file on Laura Fuentes. She pulled the file and put it on the floor next to her, closing up the box and replacing it on the shelf. Then, on a whim, she pulled out a nearby box and flipped to the Ps.

She located the file she wanted and added it to her pile, returning the file box to its shelf. Grabbing the two files, she exited the file room and locked the door.

A few minutes later, she'd packed up and was on her way to her car. The parking lot was nearly empty but Kate glanced around, happy to see no one around but wondering why she felt like she was being watched.

Sliding behind the wheel, Kate put her bag on the seat beside her and started up the engine, when she caught a movement in her peripheral vision.

Someone *was* watching her.

The figure was standing in the field across the parking lot, near a copse of trees, his dark hoodie pulled over his head to hide his face, but there was no mistaking that the figure was a man. Kate jumped back out of her car.

"Hey!" she yelled, and started walking across the parking lot.

The man backed behind the trees, losing himself in the shadows. Kate stopped in her tracks. She'd been close to running after him, but the lights in the parking lot had come on and she realized how little daylight was left.

She took another tentative step toward the place where the man had been standing, but he was gone.

Kate walked back to her car, locking the door the minute it closed. She looked around her again, but the lot was still. She knew there were security cameras at the school entrance, and she wondered if the mystery man might be on film. But she couldn't think of a reason to demand to see the footage without opening up a new can of worms.

CHAPTER FIFTEEN

Kate picked up food on the way home and was setting the table when the doorbell rang. She shooed Mandy, who'd been sitting at the kitchen table, down the hallway before she went to answer the door. She peered through the peephole. When she was confident it was Roman and that he was alone she unlocked the door.

"Sorry," she said, locking the door behind him. "Feeling a little paranoid today."

"Understood," Roman said, taking off his jacket and hanging it over a kitchen chair. "Smells good in here. What's for dinner?"

Kate allowed herself to relax. "Enchiladas. Not Grandma's, but beggars can't be choosers, right? Do you want some wine? Or are you on duty?"

"I'm off, so yeah I'll take a glass. How's Mandy doing?"

"Better," she said, handing him a glass. "The bruises get uglier before they go away, so she's not happy looking in the mirror. But I think she's caught up on sleep. Still not talking much, but I can't say that I blame her."

As if on cue, Mandy walked into the room and took a seat at the table.

"Hello, Mandy. How are you today?"

"Alive," Mandy answered without enthusiasm. "Kate told me that my mom came by the school today."

"Yeah she told me that, too." Roman looked up at Kate. "Where's your dad?"

"He's lying down. He doesn't have much of an appetite these days, and he wasn't interested in being anywhere near whatever we'll be talking about tonight."

"What are we talking about tonight?" Mandy asked.

Kate smiled. "We," she said, gesturing between Roman and herself, "will be discussing next steps. When that has to do with you, you're welcome to join us. When it doesn't, I'll ask you to go hang out in your room."

"You sound like my dad," Mandy grumbled, but her tone was light, almost playful. It was hard to reconcile the typical teenage petulance with the damage on her face, and the memories Kate knew would be affecting her life for years to come.

"But first we eat." Kate served up enchiladas, rice, and beans from her favorite local dive. She poured Mandy a glass of water and refilled her own wine glass, noticing that Roman hadn't drunk much from his. After a few minutes of eating in silence, Mandy started asking questions.

"So, you really worked in a prison?" she asked Kate.

"You've been talking to my father," Kate replied with a sigh. "Yes, I worked in a prison for almost ten years."

"Did you work with killers and stuff?" Mandy asked, trying not to sound too interested, though her eyes gave her away.

"I worked with inmates who were in prison for a variety of reasons," Kate said. She thought about her last prison client with a shudder. "What else did you and my dad talk about today?" she asked, hoping to shift the conversation away from herself.

Mandy cocked her head to one side. "He told me you got hurt... when you worked at the prison."

Kate winced. "Well, it was inappropriate for him to share

that." She wondered just how much her father knew about *the incident*.

"He told me so I would know I could trust you. That you knew what I had been through," Mandy said, returning her focus to her food.

Kate felt her cheeks color. She didn't dare look up at Roman until she'd taken a few steadying breaths. Kate had never spoken to her father about what happened at the prison —never shared a single detail about the assault, her hospital stay, the PTSD, quitting her job, and all the things that followed. With her mother's death, she thought she could put those days behind her without having to tell her father anything. She knew he suspected, but she had no idea he knew so much.

"You *can* trust me," Kate said in all seriousness. "Not only because I know how it feels, but because I would never betray your trust." Only then did she look at Roman. He was studying her, but there was no shock in his expression. Kate wondered whether she had any secrets at all, or if she'd been living in denial for half a decade.

"Thanks." Mandy cleaned up her plate and excused herself from the room, asking them to come get her when they needed her.

While she cleaned up the dishes, Kate thought about how much of her personal life was on display. She didn't know what Roman knew—or what he suspected—but she was positive he wasn't going to let it drop. He didn't disappoint.

"I'm not trying to push, Kate. But if you want to talk to me about what happened to you, I'm here," Roman said when they settled into the living room.

"I can't believe my father brought it up with Mandy. I've

never even talked to him about it," Kate muttered. "Is that how you knew?"

Roman smiled. "I actually don't know anything but I didn't want to freak you out by having some big reaction. I assumed there was a reason that you left your job, but I've never wanted to pry into your life." He hesitated, but didn't end up saying more.

"Well, the long and short of it is that an inmate attacked me. I had a broken rib, some cuts and bruises. It took a while to recover, and then my mom died. It seemed like a good time to move on." Kate looked past Roman as she spoke. She knew she'd crack if she made eye contact, and she was hoping a no-frills story would suffice.

When Roman didn't speak right away, forcing Kate to look in his direction. His eyes were alight with rage. Kate could see he was fighting for control over his emotions. She wondered if he would ask her for more detail, make her tell him the whole story. She hoped not, and she was grateful when he didn't. Intellectually she knew the attack wasn't her fault, but a part of her felt like damaged goods. She didn't want anyone, especially Roman, thinking she was weak.

"I spoke with my team this afternoon," Roman said after a long, awkward silence. "To see if we'd gotten back the labs from the crime scene."

"And?" Kate asked when he didn't finish.

"And it looks like the samples we collected were misplaced before they made it to the crime lab."

"You've got to be kidding," Kate said. "In a murder investigation? I mean, I know this is New Mexico but..."

"I know what you're going to say," Roman interrupted, holding up a hand to stop her tirade. "I'm pissed off, too, but I also know that the detectives I work with are good people. Please don't put us all in that 'small-town cop' lump."

Kate calmed herself down. "I don't understand how that could happen," she said without a hint of conviction.

"There's only one way, as far as I can tell. Someone took the evidence out of lockup before we shipped it. And before you ask, we do keep tabs on who goes in and out of the evidence locker. I'm sure you know that. The evidence would have only been in the room for an hour, maybe two. I've requested the video footage but I have to go through IA. And the minute I put in that request the chief was in my office, threatening to kick me off the case."

"He's not subtle, is he?"

"No," Roman said with a sigh. "It's never popular when someone brings in Internal Affairs. Gunnison's been looking for reasons to get on me for years, but usually I just do my job and he can't find any. This case is a nightmare."

"Can he take you off the case?"

"Sure," Roman said. "But he won't. I'm a senior detective and, despite whatever might be going on around the town, I've got a few friends in high places. It would be pretty suspicious in the wake of my IA request. But it does mean that I'm going to have to be working under immense scrutiny. And that means following the rules to the letter. He can't forbid me from working with you on an informal basis, but he's not going to officially condone it." Roman's expression turned dark. "And I can't guarantee he won't try and intimidate you. He's obviously already decided to go that route."

"I'm not worried about me," Kate said. She could stand up to some bullying, especially now that she knew what she was dealing with. "I don't want my involvement to be a problem for you, though."

"So we're agreed. Let's not cause each other problems, and get to work," Roman smiled. Kate marveled at how cheerful he could be under the circumstances. He'd gone from enraged to smiling in a matter of minutes. That kind of compartmentalization took a lot of cultivating. She wondered if it was the job alone that had forced him to become such a master.

Roman stood up and began to pace. "Okay, first, I changed my mind about how to deal with Mandy—at least for now."

"Deal with Mandy?" Kate said, a sour taste in her mouth.

"Meaning I'm not going to take her to the police station, and filing an official report is going to require making her whereabouts known. Right now I'm not sure who to trust outside my team, so I'm going to assume we can trust no one."

"You sound like a cop on television," Kate teased.

"I'm serious," Roman chided, making Kate feel ridiculous. "Until I figure out if there's something going on in the department, it's not a safe place for her. The problem is, where is safe?" Roman looked hard at Kate.

Kate shook her head. "She can't stay here much longer. I don't think Dad can handle it."

"I understand that, Kate. But no one knows that she's here right now, and moving her only makes it that much more likely that she'll be seen. It seems easiest to keep her here until we have a solid plan for a more permanent safe house."

"There are no safe houses?"

"None with the kind of security we need to keep her safe. We'd have to take her out of town, and I'd rather not do that."

"Okay, let's pretend like there's even a tiny chance that I would keep her here. Don't you think someone's going to notice if you're at my house every day? And what if my dad has an emergency during the day?"

"Wouldn't it be better if you had someone here with him anyway?" Roman asked.

"That's not fair to Mandy," Kate said. "She's just a kid, and she's been through a horrible trauma. I can't ask her to take responsibility for a sick old man she hardly knows. It's not fair to either of them."

"I'm pretty good at taking care of people." Mandy's voice cut through their argument like a knife. She was standing in the hallway. "Anyway, I thought you were going to come get me when you started talking about me. Don't I get a vote?" Kate couldn't help being comforted by Mandy's petulant tone. It was a sign that, though Mandy might be broken, she was also strong.

"You get a vote," Kate assured her. "But being in charge of my dad isn't your job. What we need to decide is if there's somewhere you can stay where you'll be safe and where no one will find you."

"Impossible," Mandy said, plunking herself down in an armchair. "The guys who hurt me...I know they'll find me." Her voice had grown breathy, labored—her face ashen.

"You're safe right now, Mandy. Take some slow breaths," Kate said, kneeling beside the teen. "Remember what we talked about last night. Victims have flashbacks and memories. We have triggers. When you start feeling overwhelmed, get grounded. Rub your feet on the floor. Rub your hands on the arm of the chair. Bring yourself back to your body." She kept her voice low and soothing, her words infused with as much calm as she could muster. Kate loved to see her clients learn to breathe through their anxiety It reminded her to take stock of her own emotional state and practice good self-care.

"You're good at that," Roman said, standing much closer to Kate than he'd been. Her breathing hitched. She patted Mandy's hand and stood again, stepping away from Roman to the other side of the coffee table, needing room to breathe.

"Who were you staying with in Las Cruces?" Roman asked Mandy.

"My friend's older sister. Ruth," Mandy said. "But I can't stay with her. She lives near campus, and there are, like, a million people walking around all the time. It's not safe. Besides, I think I freaked her out so bad she'd probably call the cops if I showed up at her place again."

"What if Mandy files her report with Las Cruces PD?" Kate asked.

"The crime took place here, so they don't have jurisdiction. The most we'd accomplish is having another agency in the loop, but in the end the case would go back to APD."

"Will they process the SANE kit without a police report?"

"I'm not completely sure. The lab is usually pretty backed up," Roman said. "I'll find out. But in the meantime Mandy needs a place to stay, and I think the safest plan is to keep her where she is for at least a few more days."

"I can do chores while you're at work," Mandy said. "I can get your dad to eat. Do the dishes."

Kate chuckled. "Thank you, Mandy. But that's not the issue."

They all turned at the sound of a throat clearing from the hallway. "It's okay, Katie," her father said as he ambled into the room. "Mandy can stay with us. It's time I started to atone for my mistakes. I don't want to be the reason we send her away."

"What mistakes?" Kate asked, frowning.

Her father gazed at her with clouded eyes as he whispered, "I wish I could go back and make the right choices. I'll be meeting my maker soon, and I'd like him to see I've been a good man at the end." He turned and walked back to his room.

Kate swallowed the lump of fear building in her throat. "Well, I guess that settles it." The expressions on Mandy and Roman's faces told her she wasn't the only one feeling far from settled.

CHAPTER SIXTEEN

Kate loved being proven right. But when she walked into her office to find Pete stationed behind her desk the next morning, she realized being right wasn't all it was cracked up to be.

"What's up, Pete?" she asked, not bothering to take her jacket off or put her bag down. She could only think of one reason Pete would be in her office, and it didn't bode well for a productive workday.

"Hi, Kate," Pete said. His whole body screamed defeat.

"Let me guess," Kate said, taking a seat in the visitor chair. "The chief of police?"

Pete nodded. "I got a call from the school board this morning. Seems the President got a call yesterday from Chief Gunnison. He raised concerns about your ability to do your job. Said you weren't cooperating with an investigation."

"Don't they have to at least hear my side of the story before they fire me?" Kate asked. She'd only been working in the school system a few years, but she'd never heard of an employee being fired without a huge hullabaloo.

"Oh, they're not firing you," Pete said. "They're suspending you without pay, pending investigation. That way they can string you along."

Kate groaned. "Wonderful. And what exactly are the stated grounds for suspension?"

"Misconduct having to do with blatant disregard for student welfare, or some such nonsense. Unfortunately, somehow the whole school board has signed off on it. Even Carol Stanhope. And you know how she feels about her fellow school board members. They've asked me to inform the staff that you are taking leave."

"Right," Kate snorted. "So they don't have to explain themselves."

"I tried to tell them that you had no information to offer Chief Gunnison, and that you'd been very cooperative, but they weren't in the mood to listen."

"It's okay, Pete," Kate said, choosing to let him off the hook. She'd never expected Pete to put up much of a fight for her, and he hadn't. No harm, no foul. "I'm assuming they'll send someone down to fill in?"

"Probably, especially with everything going on right now. You won't have access to school email or anything in your office until this is resolved. Starting now. I have to ask for your badge and your keys." Pete paused. His features were strained, as if he had something more to say and the effort was causing him physical pain. "Listen, Kate. I know this job isn't exactly the most thrilling—certainly not compared to your previous position. But I think if you'd just agree to whatever the chief is asking for, we could get you back to work ASAP." Pete was practically begging. It didn't improve her opinion of him.

"Sorry, Pete," Kate said. "For five years I've done my job, taken care of my dad, and tried to be unobtrusive. Hiding out after a series of personal disasters. And I do love my students, but I'm not going to stand by and let them be victimized. Chief

Gunnison reminded me that there are always going to be bullies. I'm done trying to avoid confrontation because it's easier. I've done absolutely nothing wrong here, and I'm being punished anyway. Might as well try to do some good."

Kate turned her back and walked out of the office before Pete could respond.

When Kate got home Mandy was in the kitchen, fixing breakfast for Frank.

"What are you doing home?" he asked when Kate walked in.

"They suspended me," Kate said, her tone flat. She put her down her bag and walked toward the table. "Is there any coffee?"

"Coming up," Mandy said. She set a mug down in front of Kate.

"Thanks, Mandy." She took a sip and looked at her father, who was frowning. "What's wrong, Dad?"

"What's wrong?' he asked, eyeing her suspiciously. "You've been suspended from your job and you're wondering what's wrong? What happened?" His voice was shaky, a combination of weariness and anger.

Kate was about to tell him not to worry, when he started to cough. When he didn't stop coughing, she hopped up to pat his back. "Mandy, get some water." The girl put a glass down in front of him but it took several minutes before he was able to drink, and several more before he spoke again.

"I can't get enough air," he whispered, fighting back another coughing fit. "It. Hurts." Her father was pale, his lips turning a touch blue.

"He's been coughing a lot this morning," Mandy said, looking concerned.

Kate put her hand against his cheek and then his forehead. "You're a little warm. I'm going to call the doctor."

"I'll be fine," he muttered, but every word caused more coughing. Kate grabbed her cell phone from her purse, stepping into the living room to have a muffled conversation with the receptionist. Mandy sat with Frank, rubbing his back.

"Nivens wants to see you in half an hour," Kate said, pulling his jacket off the coat rack near the front door. "Mandy, can you grab his shoes from his room?" While Mandy was gone, Kate leaned down next to her dad and said, "I know you worry, Dad. But right now let's work on getting you feeling better. Maybe this work break will be a blessing in disguise."

Frank didn't look satisfied with that explanation, and she knew he wouldn't let it go, not for long. But for the moment he kept quiet, trying to keep his coughing under control.

Mandy delivered Frank's shoes, and busied herself cleaning up the breakfast dishes.

"Hopefully we won't be gone long," Kate said to Mandy as she ushered her dad to the front door. "Don't answer the door, okay?"

"Got it," Mandy replied. The girl's face was ashen, her eyes glistening with unshed tears.

Kate wished there was someone she could call to come be with Mandy, but another round of coughing returned her focus to Frank and getting him to the doctor as quickly as she could.

Kate and Frank were at the doctor's office for less than ten minutes before he sent them over to the hospital. A chest x-ray confirmed pneumonia, and with Frank's weakened immune system they admitted him right away. At the hospital the doctor was optimistic, insisting that they'd take care of him and get him on his way home soon. Still, there was something very ominous—almost prophetic—about the turn of events. And Kate was pretty sure she wasn't the only one feeling it.

When Frank was finally settled in a room, Kate pulled a chair up beside his bed and took his hand. They'd put him on oxygen, and the color was returning to his cheeks.

"I can't believe," he started, pausing for breathes between words, "I'm stuck here."

Kate chuckled. "Think of it this way, room service and a whole staff of people to wait on you hand and foot." She teased him, but her heart wasn't in it. She knew that these days were going to become more common, and then one day he'd be gone. She wondered how much time they had left. "I'm going to run back to the house and get a change of clothes. I'll be back in an hour or two." She started to move, but Frank gripped her hand.

"Kate," he rasped, "listen to me." Every word was a struggle, but she knew telling him to save his breath would only agitate him. "I'm not blind. I can see what's going on right in front of me. First Roman starts coming around. Then Mandy turns up. Now your job is gone."

"Not gone, Dad. It's just a break. I didn't do anything wrong, so eventually they'll have to take me back," Mandy argued but Frank squeezed her hand hard, silencing her.

"Don't. Argue." His voice was urgent. "I've lived in this town my whole life. I know these people. They're not going to let this go. If you keep working with Roman, if you keep Mandy in our house, they're going to find out and they'll make you sorry. They can be very cruel." Tears glistened in his eyes.

"Come on, Dad. What's the worst they can do?" Kate asked with a bravado she didn't feel. "I won't let them push me around."

Kate kept her tone upbeat, but Tilly's warning buzzed in Kate's mind.

Kate looked into Frank's eyes, firming her resolve. He didn't argue, and after a few minutes Frank let his hand go slack. He closed his eyes, and though Kate knew he was still awake she hoped sleep would help to settle his nerves. She checked in with the nurse and then headed home.

CHAPTER SEVENTEEN

As Kate drove to her house, she tried to figure out what to do about Mandy. With her father in the hospital, Kate wouldn't be home much. She pulled out her cell phone, dialing Roman's number—hoping he'd have a solution for her.

"Everything okay?" he asked.

"No," Kate sighed. "My father is in the hospital with pneumonia. I'm heading home now to pack an overnight bag. Not sure what to do with Mandy while I'm out of the house."

"I'm sorry, Kate" Roman said

"Thanks," Kate said. "Unfortunately—or maybe fortunately, depending on how you look at it—I got suspended from my job this morning, without pay, adding insult to injury. But that's one less thing I have to worry about, I guess."

"What happened?"

"Looks like your chief upped the ante. He had unanimous school board support in less than 24 hours, which is nothing short of miraculous. Anyway, it doesn't matter. I hadn't been home ten minutes before I had to take Dad to the hospital, so it's probably good timing. But I don't know what to do about

Mandy. I'm not sure when I'll be home, and I hate to leave her alone right now."

Roman was silent so long Kate wondered if they'd lost their connection, but a quick glance at her phone showed he was still on the line. "Roman?"

"I'm going to call a friend with the state police." Anger made his voice shake. It was a relief to hear someone feeling what she knew she should be feeling, but was too weary to care.

"I bet that's not going to make you popular," Kate said. Law enforcement departments could be very territorial. Roman was already on shaky ground. Getting the state police involved was crossing a line.

"I'm not so popular now, and this is getting out of hand," Roman said. "If I can get them involved, they can take Mandy's case and get her out of town. Keep her somewhere safe while we get this figured out."

"I'm just around the corner from my house. What should I tell Mandy?"

"Nothing yet. I'll call you as soon as I have more information..."

"Oh, shit!" Kate yelped, interrupting Roman mid-sentence. She'd turned in to her driveway and could see that her front door was ajar.

"Kate?"

"Front door's open. I told Mandy not to go outside." Kate parked and had her hand on the door when Roman stopped her.

"Don't go in," he said. "Wait for me. I'll be ten minutes."

"I'm sure it's fine," Kate said, but something in Roman's tone made her pause. What if it wasn't? A vision of her hooded stalker flickered across her mind. She still hadn't told Roman about that.

Kate felt her heart rate surge and her breathing become labored as panic took hold. *Not now,* she pleaded with herself, taking slow breaths and rubbing her palms against her thighs, trying to reorient to her body. She felt her cheeks flush and the skin on her arms and chest burned red-hot, causing her to sweat.

The world began to spin and all Kate could do was curl forward and wait until the panic attack subsided.

Kate heard Roman's car pull up behind hers, but she kept her head pressed against the steering wheel until she heard him knocking on her window. Only then did she lift her head and meet his eyes. He looked concerned. She hated that his concern made her feel so fragile. She opened the door, putting both feet on the ground. But she didn't stand right away, afraid that any sudden movement might set off another round of anxiety.

Roman squatted in front of her, resting his hands on her knees. "Are you okay?"

"No," she answered. "I had a panic attack. I'll be fine, I just need another minute to let my head settle."

Roman didn't move. The warmth in his hands provided an excellent focal point for Kate, so she used it. Allowing her breathing to slow back to normal before she put her hand on the door handle and stood. Roman hopped back to give her space.

Kate stepped past Roman without looking at his face. She heard him follow her.

"I'm going in first," he said, pushing past her as they reached the front stoop. He drew his weapon and pushed the door, swinging it open. "Police!" he yelled, pausing to listen for any sound. Then he advanced, gesturing for Kate to wait as he walked inside. When the waiting threatened to swallow her, she followed him in.

Roman was walking down the hallway. Kate stopped in the doorway and looked around. As far as she could see, nothing had been disturbed. The dishes Mandy had been washing were drying by the sink. The chair Kate had been sitting in was still angled the way she'd left it.

"Mandy?" she yelled. All she heard were Roman's footfalls as he made his way through each of the house's bedrooms.

Finally he reappeared, his weapon back in its holster. "She's not here." Kate nodded, not trusting herself to speak yet. Roman walked up beside her. "How long have you been having panic attacks?" he asked, his full attention back on her.

"For a few years." She was tempted to tell him the whole story, but the words wouldn't come so she changed the subject. "It's fine. So, where's Mandy?"

"Do you think she left on her own?" Roman asked. "I didn't see any of her things."

"She didn't have much. And why would she leave the door open?" Kate walked toward Mandy's room, scanning all the surfaces as she entered. Not a thing out of place. Not until her eyes fell on the mirror in Tilly's old vanity. There were smudges along the top right corner. Kate moved closer, reaching out to touch the mirror. Roman grabbed her hand, stopping her.

"What is it?" he asked.

"The smudges on the mirror," she said, pointing. "Probably nothing."

Roman pulled a handkerchief from his pocket and used it to grab the edge of the mirror, careful not to touch the prints. The mirror turned, the bottom edge hitting the wall. Roman reached down and pulled the vanity away from the wall a few inches. Then he turned the mirror over so that the back was facing out, revealing a brown paper backing attached around every edge but the top right where something white had partially slipped out as he moved it.

When Roman pulled on the white corner, a lined piece of notebook paper came out. It was folded in half, and then again, and looked dingy with age. He unfolded the paper, his frown deepening as he stared at its contents.

"What is it?" Kate asked, curiosity overcoming the humiliation she'd felt from her driveway confession.

"I don't know," Roman said, handing it to her.

The paper contained a list of men's names in pencil, a few of whom Kate recognized.

"Allen Parks... wait, are he and Benny Parks related?"

"His uncle," Roman replied. "He and your father were on the bank board."

"And Darren Parnell," Kate said, going down the list. "Didn't he die a few years back?"

"Rings a bell, but I'm not sure I ever met him."

"Mark Nivens. That's my dad's doctor. Donald Copeland. Jacob..." Kate put her hand over her mouth.

"I wonder what this list means," Roman mused. "What was Mandy up to?"

"Mandy didn't write that list," Kate said, moving her hand down to her throat. "That's Tilly's handwriting."

"Tilly?" Roman asked, looking very confused.

"Yeah," Kate murmured. Her mind was racing, trying to understand the list. "When Tilly was home a few weeks ago, she took Dad out for lunch and they ran into Allen Parks. Tilly was furious because he put his hand on her shoulder."

"But what..."

"*Shh.*" Kate was pacing now. "Let me think for a second. Okay, Tilly dated Jacob Copeland in high school. That relationship ended badly but I can't remember why." She looked at Roman. "Wasn't Donald Copeland involved in some sort of scandal a few years back?"

Roman thought for a minute. "His wife caught him in bed with a younger woman, but I don't remember there being much to it. In fact, it seemed like the rumor went away pretty fast."

"When Tilly was here, she told me to be careful. Like she

thought this town was dangerous." Kate was hesitant to say more since she was operating on assumptions.

"Careful of what?" Roman asked.

"I don't know," Kate muttered, more to herself than to Roman. She hadn't told him about the person following her or the strange things her father had been saying. She'd been thinking about each thing, including Tilly's warning, as separate. But if they were all connected... The implications were terrifying.

"I don't know what to think, Roman. I don't see why Mandy would have left. I thought we were going to come in here and find the place torn apart. This whole situation has me completely paranoid."

"Can you take a look around and make sure there's nothing out of place?" Roman said, his face a network of worry lines. They spent another twenty minutes going through the rooms, finding nothing worth noting. When they returned to the living room, Roman let out a frustrated sigh.

"Without Mandy, I can't go to the state police. They won't pull rank without a good reason," he said.

Kate sympathized with his frustration. If there was something going on in town, Mandy might have been the key to solving it. Without her, Roman was back where he started in his investigation and Kate was out of a job. Kate hoped Mandy had left on her own, that nothing bad had happened to her. But Mandy wasn't the only person who needed Kate's attention.

"I've got to get back to the hospital," she said reluctantly.

"I'll wait while you pack," Roman offered. Kate was glad. She didn't want to be in the house alone. Not even for a few minutes. When she finished he walked her to her car, making sure the house was locked up good and tight.

"I hope she has somewhere safe to sleep tonight," Kate said, knowing there would be no way for Mandy to get back inside short of breaking and entering. She couldn't see the teen doing something that might get her picked up by the police. She made herself believe that Mandy had left of her own volition. The alternative was too frightening.

"Do you have Tilly's list?" she asked Roman.

He took the lined paper from his jacket pocket and handed it to Kate.

"Do you mind if I take a picture?" He pulled out his phone when she nodded and snapped a quick image. "What are you going to do with it?"

"I'm going to ask my dad about it," Kate said, causing Roman to give her a look. She knew that look. "I don't know how much time I have left with him, but I think he knows a lot more than he's saying. Maybe he'll know something about the list."

"Let me know if he does," Roman said, walking toward his car. "Take care of yourself, Kate." She watched him drive away, a knot of emotion building under her ribs.

CHAPTER EIGHTEEN

Frank was still in the hospital two days later and Kate was starting to suspect that he wouldn't be coming home. He'd been transferred to ICU. His resistance was low, and he wasn't responding to the antibiotics he'd been given. Kate had left Tilly at least a dozen messages, but hadn't heard a word back. Normally she would have been outraged, but she didn't have the energy for that kind of anger.

One positive side effect of the situation was that Kate had no choice but to completely disconnect from the world outside. She wasn't working. There was no one at home for her to worry about. She could focus her energy on her dad. She hadn't asked him about the list she and Roman found. Something about the list gnawed at her insides, and she worried about what Frank might say on the subject. In the face of great emotional turmoil, she clung to the comfort and familiarity of avoidance.

"Dad?"

Frank had begun to stir. He'd been sleeping most of the day, and while the doctors assured her that he needed rest they'd also hinted that if he couldn't wake up enough to eat they might have to put him on a feeding tube. She knew he wouldn't want that and Kate wouldn't go against his wishes.

"Daddy?"

His eyes fluttered open. "Katie." His voice was a rattling whisper, but he smiled at her.

"Hi there," she said. She was glad to see his eyes bright and alert, even if the rest of his body was unable to match.

"What time is it?" he asked, each word punctuated by a short breath. She could tell that it took everything he had just to form words, but she was happy to have him do it. The silence from Tilly had made the last few days lonelier than she could have imagined.

"It's dinner time," she said. "Are you hungry?"

"Not really. Thirsty mostly."

"Good enough," she replied, hitting the call button. Soon she was helping him sip water through a straw. The nurse had bought in a cup of chicken broth, and though it took him almost an hour to get it all down he didn't complain. By the time he finished, his eyelids were drooping again.

"Katie?" he murmured. "You should go home and get some rest."

She smiled at him, tears forming in her eyes. "I will, Dad. Don't worry. Just get better." She brushed her hand against his cheek. His skin was no longer on fire, his fever finally having broken after 48 hours and who knew how many bags of fluid. He was on a morphine drip that managed his pain, and he looked peaceful. Kate leaned back in her chair and had nearly dozed off, when the door opened. Kate waited to see which nurse was on duty, and nearly fell out of her chair when her sister walked through the door.

"Hi, Kate," Tilly said, putting her bag on the floor and walking over to their father's bedside. "Hi, Daddy," she whispered.

Frank stirred. "Tilly?" His voice was almost inaudible and he fell asleep again, but this time with a smile on his lips.

Kate was sipping a cup of tea in the cafeteria when Tilly sat down across from her. Neither sister seemed to know what to say, so they sat in silence. After emptying her cup she finally looked up at Tilly. Her sister's eyes were red-rimmed and puffy. Her hair was pulled into a messy bun and she was wearing scrubs.

"I came straight from work," Tilly said, following Kate's gaze. "They were short in the ER and I had to cover."

"You couldn't call me?" Kate asked, her voice thick with accusation. All the anger and disappointment she'd been shoving aside for days was forcing its way out.

Tilly was so quiet, Kate couldn't even hear her breathe. Finally she said, "I'm sorry, Kate. I wish there was something I could say, but you deserve better than any excuse I could come up with."

Kate felt a lump forming in her throat, making it impossible to speak. She could feel tears begin to roll down her cheeks and she wiped at them furiously.

Tilly began to cry, too.

"I haven't been a good sister to you, Kate. I haven't been here for you, and it's not your fault. It's not his, either," she said, gesturing in the general direction of her father's hospital room. "I've wanted to blame him for a lot of things, but the truth is, I've made my own choices. And one of those choices was to cut you all out of my life. I've been telling myself it's easier this way, but it's not." Her voice was shaky, and she made no attempt to dry the tears beginning to pool on her scrub top.

"He always defends you."

"I know. He's tried to make things right with me over the

years, and I wish I'd let him. It's frustrating how much perspective you gain by getting older. I wish I could do things differently."

"What happened to you, Tilly?"

"Something terrible. And before you ask, I'll tell you. You need to know. But can we wait until after?" Tilly asked.

"I don't think he's going to make it much longer," Kate said, finally finding her voice.

"No," Tilly agreed, looking miserable.

Tilly got up and sat in the chair next to Kate, leaning over and wrapping her arms around her sister. Kate folded herself into the embrace and let out all the anguish she'd been suffering. She cried for her father, for her mother, for the relationship she'd never had with her sister. And she cried for herself. For the life she'd had and lost. For the life she'd never had that she suspected she might have wanted. She felt her energy and resistance leave her body with each tear.

A whole life of sorrow came out in those tears, adding to the puddle on Tilly's scrub top. When Kate finally sat up, she saw the spot and started laughing. Soon Tilly was laughing, too, and it was a long time before the torrent of emotions finally ceased. They must've looked crazy, laughing and crying in the hospital cafeteria. It was such a relief to let those emotions out. When they returned to Frank's room, Kate felt like she might be able to handle what was coming.

———

Another day passed. Then two. Tilly and Kate took turns sitting with their father. His decline was slow but steady and he slept most of the day. The sisters drifted through the hours. Sometimes together. Sometimes alone. But always in silence. Any conversation was with their father when he came to. Or they chatted about the weather. Never anything more substantial. Frank's well-being—the uncertainty of his situation, or the certainty that his time was running out—held them in a state of limbo.

Roman kept his distance. Kate suspected that he was making an effort to respect her time with her father, and she appreciated it. She missed her friendship with Roman now more than ever, but she didn't have the energy to give it much thought. She felt depleted, but she was grateful for the chance to let the rest of the world go for a time.

Kate was sitting with her father one evening, curled up in the armchair, her legs tucked up under a blanket, listening to his ragged breathing. The room was warm. The lights were low. And Kate's mind was wandering from the book lying open in her lap. She'd been on the same page for hours, but she didn't try to force her concentration into check. Her eyelids drooped but when the door opened, the breeze it created jostled her awake. She expected to see Tilly, so she only cracked her eyes a sliver. When she saw the visitor was a man, and when she recognized that man as Benny Parks she bolted upright.

Parks had stepped into the room, closing the door behind him. She felt cornered.

"What are you doing here?" Kate hissed, not wanting to wake her sleeping father.

Benny Parks smiled, an expression that sent a chill down Kate's spine. He stepped closer to her, his smile becoming a sneer. The dim lighting cast his face in and out of shadow as he moved. "Such manners, Ms. Medina. My uncle asked me to stop by and see how your old man is doing." He looked over at Frank. "Not looking very good, I see." His tone was somber, but she still saw a slight upward tilt to his mouth.

Kate stood and stepped toward him, planting her feet firmly on the floor, forcing Benny to step back. The power shift was slight, but it made Kate feel less afraid. "No, Mr. Parks. He's not doing very well. Mission accomplished. Feel free to let your uncle know. Now, please leave."

Benny held up his hands in a mock conciliatory gesture, but his eyes were cold. "I'll be on my way. Sorry to disturb you." He turned and walked to the door, but when he touched the handle he paused and turned back to Kate. "One thing, Kate."

Kate cringed, hearing her name from this man she didn't know. It was too familiar. Too intimate. And it made her feel small again.

"It's good that you're here with your dad. It'd be best if you kept your focus here. It's not smart to get involved in things that don't concern you. Not when you have more important things to worry about, like family to protect." He smiled again, and then left.

For the first time in days, Kate thought about Mandy and prayed that she was all right.

CHAPTER NINETEEN

When Tilly arrived at the hospital, Kate decided it was time to take a break. She hadn't set foot in her house for days and Benny Parks's visit had been a wake-up call. All the fury and resolve she'd felt before Frank ended up in the hospital surged back. She was done being bullied. Done hiding.

"Are you all right?" Tilly asked as Kate gathered her things.

"I don't know. No," Kate admitted. "I'm tired. Emotionally drained. You know, all the good stuff." She smiled weakly at her sister. "I'll be fine. I just need some sleep and maybe a meal that doesn't come out of the hospital cafeteria."

Tilly laughed softly. "Good plan. I stopped by the house yesterday and turned on the porch lights, so don't freak out if it looks like someone has been there. It was just me."

"Thanks," Kate said, feeling grateful at her sister's thoughtfulness. "I'll be back in the morning."

"No rush," Tilly said, taking up Kate's spot in the armchair and pulling out a book. "I got a good nap this afternoon. I'm going to binge read. I don't usually have the time."

Kate nodded and made her way out of the room and down

to the nurse's station. Her favorite nurse was sitting behind the desk typing.

"Hey, Barbara," Kate said as she approached. "I'm heading home. Give me a call if something comes up, okay?"

Barbara smiled. "Get some sleep. Oh, I forgot to tell you…" She reached across the desk to pull out an envelope. "Someone left this for you. You were in with the doctor, so I didn't want to interrupt."

"Thank you." Kate put the envelope in her purse and walked out to her car. It was after nine o'clock, but Kate was starving so she drove out to one of the chains near the highway, knowing they'd be open. Either that or a truck stop, and she wasn't sure she could stand the ambiance of the latter.

She sat in a booth near the back, the only quiet corner in the restaurant. She could hear boisterous laughter near the bar. It made her tired. She ordered a burger and was sipping some iced tea, when she remembered the letter in her purse.

Her name was written in blocky letters on the outside and, given the unsettling visit from Benny Parks, she wondered for a moment if it was safe to open. But she slid her finger through the paper at the top leaving jagged tears.

Kate smiled. There was something satisfying about the sound of the paper ripping.

Inside the envelope she found one sheet of folded printer paper with a note written in the same blocky handwriting. Before reading, she skipped down to the end where an "M" was written in caps. The letter was from Mandy. Kate vacillated between relief—Mandy was okay—and anger. She'd tried not to worry while tending to her father, but it was a losing battle.

The letter was brief, but it created a whole new set of worries for Kate.

Ms. M.

I'm safe. Sorry for worrying you. After you left, I saw a truck I recognized drive by about five times and I figured I'd better leave before they found me. Then, when I came back, you weren't there. I had a friend deliver this. I'll be in touch.

- M

Kate folded the letter, tucking it back in her purse as her food arrived. She'd intended to go home and get some sleep before calling Roman, but as she ate the thought of going to her house by herself sounded less and less appealing. Was it possible that someone knew Mandy had been at Kate's place? Even if that wasn't the case, someone was keeping an eye on her house. Neither possibility was appealing.

She dialed Roman's number, getting his voicemail. She left a message saying where she was and where she was headed, then disconnected and nibbled at the rest of her dinner. When she couldn't stall any longer, she paid the bill. She was heading toward the door when she saw Roman walking in.

"Glad I caught you before you left," Roman said. "Let me follow you home."

Kate stared in disbelief at the mess.

Roman had been at her house when she called, along with a couple of patrol officers, investigating a break-in. Frank's neighbor had called the police to report some suspicious activity next door. By the time the cops arrived, someone had trashed the house. Every drawer and cabinet had been rifled through. Worse, whoever had done it seemed bent on destroying everything they could get their hands on.

Kate leaned over and retrieved a picture frame lying face-down near a fallen bookshelf. The floor was covered in broken glass and the damaged bric-a-brac that Kate's mother had collected and her father never touched. Kate turned the frame over in her hands and saw her parents' wedding picture. The glass had broken and several violent scratches ran across her mother's face, as if a wild animal had mauled it. The photo wasn't salvageable. Kate felt her insides twist into a knot as she wiped away glass shards and pulled the ruined paper out of the frame.

She walked into her bedroom, which was in a state of shambles. She pulled a suitcase out of her closet and began retrieving clothes from the floor, folding them carefully into the case.

"Try not to touch anything you don't have to," Roman said from the doorway behind her. "And let me know if you see anything missing." She nodded, keeping her focus on the task at hand. She didn't ask him who had done this. It really didn't matter. Her childhood home had been ravaged. For just a moment, she was thankful that her father might never come home to see it. She made a mental note to pack up some of his belongings and take them to the hospital.

"Kate." Roman had moved much closer. His nearness was her undoing. Her hands began to shake. She dropped the piece of clothing she'd been holding and leaned over, grasping at the side of her bed for support as tears spilled down her cheeks. Her body shook as sadness and anger and hopelessness coursed through her, flowing onto her face in big, hot drops that formed a dark puddle on her bedspread.

Roman pulled her into his arms, but she barely noticed, having given herself over to despair. He held her while she sobbed. He didn't say a word—just held her until she'd cried herself out. Then he helped her sit down on the edge of her bed and handed her a handkerchief. Even as a teenager, Roman had carried handkerchiefs. He'd endured a lot of good-natured ribbing, but Kate knew the cloths Roman carried had been hand-embroidered by his grandmother. She'd thought it was sweet then. Now she understood that they were a symbol of Roman's character—of the things he valued and the way he kept those things close. Something inside her stirred.

"Thanks," she said, drying her eyes with the soft, worn fabric. "I haven't gotten much sleep since Dad's been in the hospital. This is too much to deal with." Her voice was weak. Part of her wanted to leave the wreckage of her father's house and never look back. The hatefulness and disregard made her feel ill. She knew this was just the beginning, but if she let herself go down that path now she wouldn't be able to function. "I'm not exactly sure what to do."

Roman sat beside her, near enough that their legs touched. "We'll be collecting evidence and witness statements. In the meantime, we'll have patrol keep an eye on the house until you can get the door repaired and the lock fixed."

Kate nodded then closed her eyes, shutting out the world for a moment.

"You can stay at my house," he offered. "I have a spare room."

"I need to get back to the hospital," Kate protested, though her heart wasn't in it. She needed sleep, and a lot of it.

"If you're not comfortable staying with me, you should at least get a hotel room. You need to rest, Kate. Frank's in good hands." Roman sounded resigned. Kate wondered if he was as tired of all this as she was. It couldn't be easy to be a cop in this town. Not if you wanted to keep your integrity intact.

"I appreciate the offer, Roman. But I don't want to impose." She stood up again and started folding clothes to keep her mind busy. She almost jumped when she felt his hand on her arm again. She turned.

"I want to help. Please let me help you." His eyes were bright, intense. The back of her neck tingled and she was aware of the warmth of his hand through her sleeve, the firmness of his grasp. Firm but gentle.

He was opening his home to her, and it wasn't a request she could take lightly. It felt like all their history, good and bad, was heaped into this one moment. Like that day in the canyon. Back then she felt the thrill and exhilaration of realizing he loved her, followed closely by the utter terror of the implications. How her life might change if she heard what he had to say.

In her youth, and in her haste to get out of town, she'd let fear guide her. Turning away from her best friend, the one person she could always depend on. She'd built a wall between them, convincing herself that time and distance would make him forget her. He'd move on like she planned to do. She'd been a fool, thinking that time could heal all wounds. Every moment with Roman seemed to teeter between comfort and agony, and she could see the same struggle in him.

Now, amidst the chaos, Kate realized something. Life had brought her back to this town for a reason. It had been a convoluted path, full of ambition and accomplishment as well as pain and sorrow. She'd been in denial, thinking that this was just a hiccup in her journey, a place to hide out while she licked her wounds and tried to find her courage again. When she looked at the disaster all around her and at Roman, standing beside her like he always had, she made a choice.

"If you really don't mind," Kate said, giving Roman the best smile she could muster. Roman seemed surprised by her response, but he smiled back. Then he left her alone to pack.

Her brain screamed at her to be cautious. She'd already been warned to stay away from the investigation, and especially from Roman. The disaster that was her father's house should have been enough of a warning to keep her away. But Kate felt the world shift a little—things falling into place for the first time in a very long time.

CHAPTER TWENTY

Kate followed Roman to his house where he got her settled into his guest room. He was on duty so he headed out soon thereafter and she had no idea when he finally got in. She'd called the hospital, letting Tilly know where she was and what had happened. Then she laid down. She was asleep almost before her head hit the pillow.

Kate slept hard. Dreamless. She didn't stir until she heard a soft knock at her door.

"Come in," she called. She'd changed into sweats and a t-shirt before collapsing. Her neck was stiff and her hair was flying all over her head, but she was much too tired to care how she looked.

The door opened a crack. "I'm heading back into the station, but I left you some breakfast in the microwave and some coffee in the pot."

"You didn't have to…"

Roman held up a hand. "I know, but I did so don't worry about it. You needed to sleep. And you need to eat."

"What time is it?" she asked, yawning.

"Eight o'clock," he said. "I wasn't supposed to go in today, but after last night I wanted to follow up on a few things. I'll be home around noon."

"Oh, okay,'" she said. "I'll get showered and head up to the hospital. I'm sure Tilly needs a break."

"I'll leave a key next to your purse. Feel free to come and go as needed." Roman began to back out of the room.

"Roman?" Kate said, causing him to peek his head back in. "Thanks."

Roman smiled the first genuine, unreserved smile Kate had seen from him since she moved back to town. Her heart swelled.

After he left, Kate got out of bed and stretched. Sitting up all day and night in Frank's room had taken its toll on her body. Sleeping so hard made her achy in places she wouldn't have expected. She was sweating by the time she'd loosened up her muscles enough to consider getting out of bed.

Roman had left her a pile of clean towels and his bathroom was immaculate. It didn't quite fit with the messy teenager she remembered but, then again, nothing about adult Roman was what she'd expected. She'd spent so much time avoiding him, she still hadn't wrapped her brain around the fact that they'd both grown up. In her mind, he was still that same goofy teenage boy.

Kate got showered and dressed, taking a few moments to wolf down the breakfast Roman left for her before heading up to the hospital. She'd packed up a few of her dad's most treasured positions—the ones that had survived—and was hoping she'd find him awake so she could surprise him.

Instead Tilly met her in the hallway looking like she'd been crying.

"What's going on?" Kate asked, panicked.

Tilly shook her head. "Dad's blood pressure and oxygen saturation dropped. It was sudden."

"Is his pneumonia worse?"

"I don't think so. It might be his heart," Tilly said. "The treatments aren't helping. That combined with the cancer... his organs might be shutting down."

Kate tried to process what her sister was saying. She'd always been more interested in the mind, not the body. She wondered if that ignorance was better or worse. She was scared, yes, but Tilly looked undone—like she knew what was coming. And that made Kate feel so much worse.

They waited what felt like hours before a doctor emerged from Frank's room. Several nurses filed out behind him, but the monitor was still beeping in her father's room and Kate took that as a good sign.

"We did an EKG. His heart is having trouble keeping up. We upped his oxygen, but if he doesn't improve we're going to have to intubate."

Kate shook her head. "He has a DNR."

The doctor nodded and walked away, leaving Kate and Tilly to wander back into Frank's room. A nurse was monitoring the machine his IV ran through. Kate noticed several new bags and wondered what medications they'd given him. Frank was awake, but his eyelids drooped.

"Girls," he whispered. Kate put her bags down next to the armchair and both girls leaned in closer so he wouldn't have to try so hard to be heard. "Listen to me," he said. Sweat glistened on his forehead from the effort. Kate would have protested, but the look in his eye told her he needed to say his peace.

"Tilly, my love. I should have believed you. I'm so, so sorry."

"I know. I love you, Daddy," Tilly said, tears forming in her eyes. It took Frank a few minutes to gather the strength to continue.

"Katie. You're so strong." He began to cough, and his monitors started beeping loudly. Kate waited for the fit to calm. "Don't let what happened to you keep you from living a good life. Don't be afraid."

Kate couldn't speak. Her words were stuck in her throat, painful and heavy. She leaned over and kissed him gently on his cheek.

"I love you both." Frank whispered. His eyelids slid closed and Kate began to cry. The nurse passed her a tissue.

"He needs his sleep," she said, patting Frank's hand as she walked out of the room. She closed the door behind her, leaving the girls to sit vigil.

Another day passed before Frank took his last breath, and in that time Kate made the most of their moments alone. Telling him how much she loved him, thanking him for all the wonderful years together. She'd sometimes thought of those years as a burden, but she knew how precious they'd been. Kate wondered if Tilly had similar conversations with their father when Kate left them alone.

Tilly had spent each night in the armchair giving Kate an opportunity to return to Roman's house and get real sleep. Kate had a new door installed at her father's house and had all the locks rekeyed, but she couldn't bring herself to stay there. She knew she'd have to clean up the mess at some point, but the shadow of her father—the reminder that she would soon be grieving the loss of another parent—kept her away more effectively than any threat could.

Roman's house was warm and safe. Over the last few days, whenever they were home at the same time, they watched TV or simply occupied the same space. Roman didn't push Kate to talk. He offered her comfort and consolation, but in the sweetest, most unobtrusive way Kate could imagine. Allowing her room to think and to grieve.

Kate was sitting in Roman's living room, reading a book, when the call came telling her that Frank had passed. She nodded as the nurse gave her the news, knowing that no one could see her but unable to conjure words. Then she cried. When Roman came home he found her sitting in the dark room, her eyes red and swollen. He sat down beside her, taking her in his arms, opening up the floodgate again. Kate realized this was the second time in a week she'd cried herself dry on Roman's shoulder.

"Your father?" he asked when the sobbing slowed. Kate nodded, wiping her eyes on her sleeve.

"Can you drive me to the hospital? Tilly's still there. She's waiting for me to come. I couldn't drive."

"Of course," he said, helping her to her feet. He grabbed her jacket and led her to car. The tenderness he showed her was the only thing holding her together.

She barely remembered the ride to the hospital nor the hours that followed, making arrangements, speaking to doctors, nurses, administrators. After, Roman drove both sisters to his house, where Kate and Tilly huddled together on the couch until they both fell asleep.

When Kate woke, she saw that Roman had covered them each with a blanket. The house was dark and quiet. Kate glanced at her watch and saw that it wasn't quite four in the morning. She listened to the sound of Tilly breathing, praying she'd fall back asleep.

"You awake?" Tilly asked.

"Yeah," Kate replied. "Is everything OK?"

"No," Tilly said. Kate had expected that answer, and she knew there was nothing she could do. She felt the same. Instead she cuddled closer to Tilly, thankful for the physical contact.

"Roman's awfully sweet," Tilly whispered. "I don't remember that about him. He always annoyed me when we were kids. He teased me a lot."

Kate smiled. "Well, he was my best friend. It was his job to drive my little sister crazy." Kate felt Tilly laughing.

"I don't know why this feels so surreal," Tilly mused. "We knew he wasn't going to make it. Why does it feel like we're..." She couldn't seem to find the word.

"Orphans?" Kate suggested.

"Yeah," Tilly said with a sigh. "Orphans."

The word hung between them, threatening to bring on another round of sobs. Kate wasn't ready. She thought Tilly felt the same because they both took deep breaths, one after the other.

"Tilly?"

"Yeah?"

"What was Dad talking about? About believing you?" It wasn't the right time, but in the stillness of the dark house Kate felt compelled to ask. She wondered if Tilly would answer. It was a very personal question, one that Kate felt she had no right to ask. They didn't have that kind of relationship. It was quiet for so long that Kate wondered if she should get up and give Tilly space. "I'm sorry, Til. It's really none of my business."

Tilly put her hand on Kate's. "It's okay." She sighed. "I spend hours talking to sexual assault survivors about the power in telling their stories. But I've never told mine—not in full. I started to tell Dad once..."

"You can tell me," Kate said.

"It happened when I was in high school. I was hanging out with a shitty group of girls. Hard to imagine what I ever saw in them."

Kate remembered those girls. Not exactly the cheerleader types but popular, and awful. Even though she was older, being around them made Kate feel insignificant.

"One of them, Diana Zamora, introduced me to her cousin, Jacob."

"Jacob Copeland," Kate said.

"Yeah. He was cute and he had a great car. I felt about a thousand times cooler than I actually was when I was with him."

She hesitated. "One night he invited me to a party. He said his dad was having some people over, so we'd hang out with some friends downstairs. But when we got there, it was almost all older men. I felt uncomfortable and out of place. I asked Jacob if we could go, but he told me to relax and got me a drink. It wasn't my first red Solo cup, believe me, but the room started spinning."

"He put something in your drink," Kate said, the familiarity of the story making her weary.

"I'm sure he did. He took me into his bedroom, told me to lie down, that I looked tired. I woke up with him on top of me. But I was so out of it, it almost felt like a dream. So I closed my eyes and went back to sleep."

"Oh, Tilly," Kate said, taking Tilly's hand in hers.

"It didn't end there," Tilly said. "I woke up several times that night, and each time I woke up to a different guy. A different man, because Jacob was the only one even near my age. First, Jacob's father. Then other men I didn't recognize. I have no idea how long I was there. I finally woke up and found Allen Parks staring down at me. He was thrusting into me, and it hurt. Everything hurt. I wanted to scream, but somehow I couldn't make my voice work."

Kate felt bile rising in her throat.

"When he was done with me, Jacob came in and told me to get dressed. I was crying. He told me that I'd done a good job. With a smile, like I had just waited his table or something. He smiled, but he looked at me like I was garbage. I felt so dirty. I had to look away. I couldn't stand him looking at me like that. I got dressed and he brought me home."

"When we got home I got out of the car, but before I could close the door he told me that if I told anyone what happened he'd kill me." Tilly's whisper had turned heavy. Weary. Kate's heart felt like it was trying to fly right out of her chest, but she fought off the mountain of panic. "Then he said—" She choked back a sob. "He said, 'I'll let you know when we need you again.'"

It was an unbelievable story, but Kate knew it was true. She thought back on those years. Tilly had become impossible to be around. She was moody. Angry. She screamed at their parents. She stayed out all night. And all Kate had thought at the time was how selfish Tilly was behaving. How much energy and grief her parents experienced. How much of their attention was on Tilly, and not on her.

Even now, with all her training and with everything she'd gone through, it hadn't occurred to her that Tilly might have been assaulted. Now it all made sense, and the truth was more brutal than anything she could have imagined. Kate felt guilt sink its claws into her heart.

"You told Mom and Dad?" Kate asked.

"I told Dad," Tilly said. "I told him Jacob raped me. He looked like he wanted to kill someone. Then I told him about the others. And I could see that he didn't believe me, even before he said it. He told me that he had known those people for years, that it couldn't have happened. Then he asked me if I was on drugs. It was the last time I had a real conversation with either Mom or Dad."

The weight of Tilly's story threatened to crush Kate. The room was suddenly too hot, the blanket too confining. Kate shoved the covers away and hopped up.

"What's wrong?" Tilly asked, looking concerned.

"I'm having a panic attack," Kate mumbled, walking into the kitchen for a glass of water as her heart thumped wildly and the world started to spin. She was surprised to feel Tilly's hand on her back.

"Take some slow breaths," Tilly cooed, her voice soft and soothing. "Here, let me get that." She took the cup from Kate's hand, filling it with water. Then she took Kate's hand and led her back to the couch. "Take a few sips," she said as she rubbed small circles on Kate's back.

Usually Kate fought hard to keep control during an attack, but with her sister there she surrendered—giving herself over to wave after wave of suffocating anxiety. She could feel sweat trickling down the back of her neck as terrifying visions of her attacker—the feel of his hot breath on her face as he cut off her ability to breathe—appeared in her mind, distorted and misshapen with smells and sounds repeating until she felt like throwing up.

After being attacked Kate had withdrawn, both emotionally and physically. When her medical leave ran out, she took personal leave. A few days before her personal leave ran out, her mother died. Kate knew she would never go back but it was easier to live in denial, to focus on her family tragedy and to make herself a martyr in its wake.

Kate's thoughts spiraled out of control, but Tilly's hand on her back kept her grounded, giving her the freedom to succumb to her out-of-control emotions without the worry that she would die. Without the fear that her body would be found too late, that this time it wasn't just panic.

"Don't forget to breathe," Tilly said. Kate calmed, her breaths coming without strain. Her heart slowed. The room started to brighten as the sun climbed in the sky outside. Finally Tilly asked, "How long have you been having panic attacks?"

Kate sighed. "Five years, seven months, three days, Give or take."

"Right before Mom died?" Tilly asked, confused. "What happened?"

Kate turned to face Tilly. She looked into her sister's wide eyes. "I was raped."

Tilly's face paled, and she nodded.

Kate wasn't strong enough to tell her story, not at that moment, but Tilly knew enough.

CHAPTER TWENTY-ONE

In the days that followed, Kate and Tilly began to make sense of their father's house, throwing out bags of broken belongings that were a perfect reflection of their own shattered lives. Frank had insisted that he and Kate make all the funeral arrangements ahead of time, so there was not much to do on that front. Frank had transferred ownership of the house to Kate, but she knew she'd never be able to live there. Not on her own. Tilly agreed that selling the house was the thing to do.

Kate and Tilly spent the week leading up to Frank's funeral going through every inch of the house, taking boxes of donations to the thrift shop, and setting aside any personal effects they wanted to keep until all that was left was an empty shell, with only a few pieces of furniture left to keep it inhabitable until it sold.

"It's funny." Kate sat down on the sofa, one of the few remaining items in the living room. Despite her words, there wasn't a trace of humor in her voice. "A few weeks ago, I thought going through all this would be impossible. I guess the assholes who broke in did us a favor."

Tilly walked into the kitchen, grabbing two sodas from the

refrigerator. She popped the top and took a long swig as she walked back into the living room and handed the other can to Kate. Tilly sat down on the floor against the wall, scanning the room. "It just looks like a house now. I'm kind of glad we did this. I don't think I can come back to this house again, not without Dad here. I'm glad you're not planning on keeping it."

Kate felt a little pang of sadness, but she understood where Tilly was coming from. "When do you head back?" Kate asked, not wanting Tilly to leave but knowing it was going to happen sooner or later. She needed to prepare herself.

"Saturday," Tilly said. "I wanted to help you with anything that still needed to be done after the funeral." She paused. "Why don't you come back with me?"

Kate couldn't hide her surprise. "What?"

Tilly smiled. "Why not come back with me? You'd love Colorado. You could find a job doing whatever you want to do. I've got a lot of connections in the system. And it's so much better than staying here. I worry about you."

Kate hesitated. There was a certain appeal to leaving. The idea of going back to work at the school, assuming she ever got her job back, didn't leave a good taste in her mouth. And being closer to Tilly, working on their relationship, was a serious consideration. But something held her back, tugging at her heart.

"I can't." Kate sighed. "Not yet."

"Why?" Tilly asked, a hint of irritation in her voice. "This town is poison, Kate. Sometimes I don't know how either of us survived it."

"I know, Tilly. And I'm so sorry for what happened to you..."

"It's not just what happened to me," Tilly said, her voice rising. "It's what it's done to our whole family. To all of those girls who've had their lives ruined. There's nothing good here. And I don't ever plan on coming back." She nearly spat the last words. "Please don't stay here."

Kate walked over to Tilly and slid down to the floor, sitting next to her. She was right. The house looked very ordinary. She'd never thought about it before. The floor plans of the houses in this neighborhood were all similar, at least from the outside. Without the things that tied the house to their family, it looked inconsequential and unfamiliar.

"I know what you're saying, Til. And I appreciate your concern. I feel like my whole life, and definitely our whole relationship, has been based on a series of lies and omissions. It's a lot to sort through. And I don't intend to do it in this house. Too much baggage. Too many memories." Kate sighed. "But I think I have a chance to make something good happen here."

"You're going to jump back into the investigation." It wasn't a question.

"I'm already waist-deep, Tilly. For some reason, someone sees me as a threat. That has to mean that I am, right? I don't want to give up this opportunity to do something important." She paused, taking her sister's hand. "And I can't leave without knowing I tried to stop this. Not now that I know what they did to you."

"Don't make this about me," Tilly muttered.

"I'm doing this for me," Kate replied, glad to know that she meant it.

Tilly didn't respond, but she gripped Kate's hand tighter. Her face was a mixture of fear and anguish. Kate hated to think she was causing Tilly more pain, not after what she'd already been through. But ever since that morning at Roman's house, Kate had been thinking about her sister. About how, despite what she'd gone through, Tilly had chosen to work with victims of sexual assault. She'd chosen to be triggered again and again, because she wanted to help. Kate had spent years running away, still a victim of her circumstances.

Kate had never thought of her sister as strong. She'd been

selfish, believing that she was the strong one. Now she realized they were both strong, and that she had a choice. She wouldn't let the monster in her past keep her from doing what she felt, in her heart, was the right thing to do. And she wouldn't let the monsters lurking in this town send her into hiding again. A veil had lifted for Kate. And her new direction led straight into the path of danger.

Kate sat in the same front pew, in the exact same place in the church where she'd said goodbye to her mother five years ago. Now she was saying goodbye to her father. The thought was bittersweet. In many ways, she felt lost. Untethered. It was strange to think that she'd never talk with her father again. But Tilly sat beside her this time, holding her hand, and for that Kate was grateful.

The service was short. The church full. Frank had been a very active member in the community before his wife died, and people had come out in droves giving Kate the feeling that there was something worth fighting for in this town.

When it was over Kate and Tilly stood and walked to the back of the church, forming a two-person receiving line. Tilly was dreading this part, and Kate wasn't much more enthusiastic. Things were moving smoothly, when Tilly suddenly excused herself. "I have to go," she whispered, walking quickly toward the bathroom. Kate looked to her left and saw Allen and Benny Parks approaching.

When Allen stepped up to shake Kate's hand, she gave him a formal nod. "Mr. Parks." She didn't acknowledge Benny.

"Hello, Kate. I was sure sorry to hear about your father. He was a fine man."

"He was," Kate agreed, but she kept her expression hard. It was impossible to look at these men without seeing a monster.

She turned her attention to the next person in line, but as he moved past her Benny grabbed her arm.

"I imagine you'll be heading out of town now that your father's gone," he said coldly. Kate looked to see if anyone was watching this exchange, but a bubble seemed to have formed around them—encapsulating her with this vulgar, horrible man.

"Get your hands off of me," Kate hissed through gritted teeth. She pulled away, but Benny held on tight.

"There's nothing left for you here, don't you think? No mother. No father," he said quietly, leaning in so close that his breath was hot on her ear. Kate shivered. It was unimaginable that this man was threatening her in public, and at her father's funeral no less. And yet here he was, with his fingers digging into Kate's arm. She was ready to scream when Allen Parks reappeared next to his nephew.

"Come on, Benny." The elder Parks smiled, but his eyes weren't kind as he stared at Kate. "There's no need to cause a scene."

Benny let go of Kate's arm and stalked off, several sets of eyes following him as he left the church. The elder Parks turned back to Kate. "My nephew loves drama. He never seems to learn." His words twisted Kate's stomach.

As soon as Parks walked away the receiving line seemed to come back to life, moving back into Kate's sphere again as if a barrier had lifted. She felt rattled but she shoved those feelings aside and greeted the mourners, one by one, as quickly as she could.

Tilly never came back.

By the time Kate got home, her sadness and fear had turned to a solid ball of anger. A crushing weight that made it hard to breathe. Hard to think. She walked into the house to find Tilly packing her bags.

"You left me!" Kate shouted at her sister. Tilly was bent over her bed, folding clothes. She froze at the sound of Kate's voice. "I thought you were here to help me, Tilly. What the hell was that?"

Tilly was completely still, as if she'd been turned to stone. Kate's fury swelled.

"Look at me!" she screeched, surprising herself with the wild, feral quality of her voice.

Tilly tuned. Her face was blotchy, her eyes red and so puffy she struggled to open her eyes all the way. Kate almost felt sorry for her sister.

Almost.

"You left me to the lions back there, Tilly. Benny Parks pretty much told me to get out of town. And his uncle was even worse. It would have been nice not to have to face that alone." Kate's voice had quieted but anger hummed just beneath the surface of her skin, coloring her cheeks and making it uncomfortably hot in the chilly house.

"What did you expect me to do, Kate?" Tilly muttered, her voice hoarse.

"I don't know. Be there for a change," Kate said. "But you did what you always do. You ran away."

Tilly's back straightened. "That man ruined my life," she said, her voice tight and hard. "I can't be in the same room with him again. It makes me want to kill him. If I had stayed, I might not have been able to control myself." The hatred in Tilly's voice sent chills down Kate's spine. She didn't doubt that her sister meant it, and she couldn't blame her, but she was still too angry to have sympathy.

"Today wasn't about you, Tilly. It was about Dad. You had no right to leave. Dad deserved better."

Tilly's face lost all trace of color. Kate knew she'd gone too far, been too dramatic, but it was too late to take it back.

"How dare you," Tilly whispered, her expression murderous. She walked up to Kate, put her hand on Kate's chest, pushed her out the door, and slammed it in her face. Kate stood in the hall, stunned, as the lock on the door clicked. To Kate, it felt like another death.

CHAPTER TWENTY-TWO

For a few days after Tilly left, Kate did nothing. She barely ate. She slept most of the day. All she felt was overwhelming despair and emptiness. Tilly was the only family she had left, and now she was gone.

After their fight, Kate had retreated to her room to lie down. When she'd gotten up, Tilly had already vacated the premises. After the third or fourth voicemail Kate knew that Tilly wasn't going to answer. The burden of moving forward was too much for Kate, so she invited the grief and depression in, shutting herself away from the rest of the world.

Then the phone calls started. Kate answered the first one. A man's voice growled on the other end, telling Kate to move on. A subtle threat, but nothing explicit. After that, Kate let the calls go to the answering machine. The calls came at all hours, and after the second day Kate turned off the ringer.

She was sitting on the couch with a movie playing on her laptop, though she hadn't been paying attention, when there was a fierce rapping at her front door. Kate tensed. The knocking felt angry and forceful. She huddled under the blanket, hoping whoever it was would go away.

"Kate, are you home?" Roman's shout was severe. "Open up!"

For a moment Kate sat there, wondering if she ignored him if he would go away and leave her to her misery. But the knocking started again and she finally got to her feet.

The concerned look on Roman's face gave her a pretty good idea of how bad she must look. She couldn't remember the last time she'd showered. He walked past her, shutting the door behind him. Kate shambled back to the couch and took up her previous position.

"I'm not going to ask you if you're okay," Roman said, taking a seat beside her. "Obviously you're not."

"No, I'm not," Kate parroted. "What are you doing here, Roman?" His frown deepened, but Kate couldn't muster enough energy to feel bad for being so blunt. They sat silently, the movie creating tinny background noise. Kate could almost imagine that she was alone again, so it made her jump when Roman put his hand on her arm and pulled her gently to him. She didn't resist, though the gesture caused her eyes to tear. She took a deep breath, trying to keep herself from crying. Once she got started, it was hard to stop.

Once again, Roman held Kate. Without talking. Without offering advice or platitudes. It made Kate feel whole.

It was too much.

Kate's heart began to pound and she gulped for air, feeling her chest turn to stone as panic gripped her body, refusing to let go. Her vision dimmed and she began to shiver.

Roman looked at her, alarmed. "What's wrong?"

"Anxiety. Attack." The words came out in short bursts that took so much effort she began to feel faint.

"What can I do?" Roman asked.

"Nothing. Just wait," Kate said, curling herself into a ball on the couch and closing her eyes. The skin on her arms and face felt like it would burst into flames, but her shivering turned violent. She felt Roman pull the blanket over her, tucking it around her shaking body. He sat on the floor with his face close to hers and rubbed her arm gently.

"Is this okay?" he asked. Kate nodded, focusing on her breathing. Jagged at first. More even as her heartbeat slowed. Her chest felt sore from fighting so hard to breathe. Her limbs ached. She began to uncurl herself, little by little, still focusing on her breathing, keeping her breaths regular. In and out. In and out. It wouldn't be the first time she'd gone straight into a second attack, and she was feeling embarrassed to have Roman see her this way. Again.

Finally she sat up on the couch, pulling the blanket around her. Roman took up his position beside her. She leaned her head on his shoulder and wondered how she was going to make it through another day.

Kate awoke with a start to the sound of pots clanking in the kitchen.

"Who's there?" she said, her voice shaky. Her mind felt dull and disoriented.

The living room light came on. Roman was standing by the front door, a saucepan in his hand. "Sorry, didn't mean to scare you. I was going to make some dinner, but it looks like slim pickings around here. Hope you like no-frills spaghetti."

Kate looked around her. It was dark outside. "How long was I asleep?"

Roman smiled. "A long time. You needed it."

Kate stretched. Her throat was scratchy and irritated. She thought she might be getting sick until she realized it had been at least half a day since she had anything to drink. As if reading her mind, Roman brought her a big glass of water and returned to the kitchen. He was not a quiet cook, and Kate thought there was a pretty good chance he wasn't a neat one either.

"You don't have to cook," she said, getting up and walking into the kitchen. She made it to the table before the dizziness kicked in.

"Sit down," Roman said, a look of concern on his face. "You're dehydrated."

She wanted to protest, but he was right. She sat down at the table and began sipping the water he'd retrieved from the living room. When she finished the first glass, he filled it up again. Soon the smell of spaghetti sauce filled the air. Kate's stomach rumbled loudly.

"When was the last time you ate?" Roman asked, sounding stern.

"I don't know," Kate answered. "What day is it?"

"Wednesday."

"Damn," Kate muttered. It had been almost five days since the funeral. It was a little bit scary to think how far gone she'd been when Roman showed up. And even more disconcerting when she realized how long she must have been passed out. "When did you get here?"

"Yesterday," he said over his shoulder.

Roman served up two plates of spaghetti. "No frills," he said, taking a seat across from her. "Looks like you haven't been grocery shopping in a while either."

Kate bristled. "While I appreciate your concern, if you're going to criticize, you can leave. I haven't shopped because I wasn't planning on staying here. It's been a hard week."

"I know it has," he said, though his tone was still scolding. "But you're falling apart, Kate. I came over because I've been calling for three days. You're not answering your phone. I was getting worried."

"I'm not a child," Kate snapped. "You don't have to check up on me."

"Someone needs to," Roman replied, shoving a mouthful of spaghetti into his mouth. "You're not eating. You look wrecked."

Kate wanted to throw him out but her stomach demanded that she follow his lead, cramming as much spaghetti as she could chew into her mouth. No frills was right, and yet it was the best meal she'd eaten in her entire life. It was possible that her perspective was skewed from the total neglect she'd suffered at her own hand, but she didn't care. She wolfed down the food until her plate was clean. After she took her last bite, her stomach objected.

"Oh shit," she said, putting her hand over her mouth.

Roman laughed. "Yeah, you might need to slow down a bit, Tiger. You're going to make yourself sick."

Kate wanted to smack the smile right off his face. "Why are you being such an asshole!"

"So you'll wake up." Roman's volume was just shy of a yell. "You seem to think you're the only person who's ever lost someone. I know the last few weeks have been shitty. Worse than I can imagine. But I've known you a long time and I've never seen you fall apart like this."

"You don't know me at all, Roman. You know the teenage me. The girl who had something to prove, who couldn't wait to get out of this horrible town. And you know what, I shouldn't have come back. It's been one bad thing after another since I got here." Kate's anger chased away the nausea she'd been feeling. She was right back where she was after the funeral—ready for a fight.

"Yeah, so why *did* you come back?" Roman's glare was cold. "You got out of here so fast the first time. Didn't care who you left behind. I get that you had to come back when your mom died, but why did you stay? Why did you take that shitty job at the high school?"

Kate was on her feet. "Who the hell do you think you are? What I do with my life is none of your business, Roman." She was seething.

"You've always made that abundantly clear." Roman stood

now, too, and she could see that his hands were shaking despite the neutral expression on his face. "Regardless, there are people here who care about you. Who love you." His voice sounded strangled. "If you're going to self-destruct, you can do it alone. I won't check on you again."

Roman stormed out the front door, slamming it behind him. Kate sat down again and put her head down on the table.

CHAPTER TWENTY-THREE

Roman had accomplished his mission. After he left Kate went back to bed, waiting for the depression to take hold again. But she couldn't sleep. She was fired up—fully awake for the first time in days.

The next morning Kate got up, took a long-overdue shower, and began cleaning the house from top to bottom. She scrubbed until her arms ached and her skin was red and irritated. She channeled every bit of anger and frustration and sadness she'd been feeling into her work.

It felt so good.

Kate started looking into realtors. Every time she came across a familiar name, she crossed it off the list. She finally narrowed her search down to two young female realtors who seemed to be new to the area. It made her feel less vulnerable, working with someone who couldn't be part of the issues going on in town. She made an appointment to have each woman see the house, and then she started on her second task.

Kate pulled into the animal shelter parking lot, full of trepidation. An hour later, she pulled out again with a big Labrador mix named Rusty in the backseat. She'd picked up enough supplies from the shelter store to get her through the next few days.

By dinnertime she'd cleaned up about a half-dozen doggie messes, but Rusty had finally calmed down. She realized how much she liked having him around. It made her feel less lonely. She'd almost started to doze on the couch, Rusty at her feet, when a knock at the door had him barking again.

"Just a second," Kate called, grabbing Rusty's collar as she made her way to the door. When she opened it Roman stood on the other side, holding a paper grocery bag.

"Roman?" Rusty had stopped barking and was sniffing at Roman's pant-leg.

"Who's this?" Roman asked, leaning down to let Rusty sniff his hand. Rusty struggled to get free, his tongue lapping in the air as he tried to get close to his new best friend.

Kate suppressed a grin. She wasn't ready to forgive Roman yet.

"I figured I needed some protection, as long as I'm staying here."

"Can I come in?" Roman asked, holding out the bag. "I brought a peace offering."

Kate stepped aside, letting go of Rusty the minute she shut the door. The dog jumped up on Roman, sniffing him enthusiastically. If Rusty was going to be a guard dog, she had to assume that Roman was a good guy. Otherwise, she'd chosen very poorly.

She took the bag from Roman and put it on the table. Inside, she found a half-gallon of rocky road ice cream—her favorite— and a plastic folder containing a huge stack of papers. "Let me guess. Sugar in exchange for slave labor?"

"I'm sorry for the other night, Kate. I was being a real jackass."

"Yeah, you were," Kate replied, but her tone had softened.

"You scared the hell out of me," Roman continued. "You

looked half dead when I got here. And, with everything that's been going on, I started thinking something might have happened to you." His voice broke.

Kate flushed, emotion surging through her. She distracted herself by putting the ice cream in the freezer and then laying the papers on the table. "What's this?"

"My notes on Gabby Greene's murder."

"Official?"

"My personal notes. The chief is watching me like a hawk, but I keep a lot of my own notes on a thumb drive I carry with me. Most of the other detectives write all their notes into their reports, but I like to be able to think about what I'm writing before I submit it to the official record, you know?"

Kate smiled. In a lot of ways, she and Roman were so alike. It's probably why they'd gotten along so well once upon a time.

"So what do you need my help with?" Kate asked, trying to keep her tone casual. She was glad that Roman had come back but she wasn't ready to unpack all her feelings yet.

"I was hoping you would read it over and let me know if anything stands out to you." Roman walked to the living room and took a seat on the couch. Rusty lay down by his feet.

"Traitor," Kate said in mock fury. "Don't forget who feeds you." She grabbed the stack of papers and headed over the armchair. "I'm not sure what good it'll do to have me look through this, Roman. I'm not an investigator."

"Fresh set of eyes," Roman replied. He leaned back on the couch and closed his eyes. "Besides, you're a trained psychologist. You *are* an investigator, even if you're not a cop."

Kate set the papers on her lap and began reading.

———

Kate looked up when Roman and Rusty started snoring in unison. A quick glance at her watch told her she'd been reading for almost three hours. It was nearing eleven o'clock. Roman's notes were thorough. Kate was impressed by his insights on the possible motivations and intentions of the people he'd interviewed.

"Roman," she said, hating to wake him. He didn't even stir. She put the papers on the coffee table and sat down beside him on the couch. "Roman," she said again, this time jiggling his shoulder.

"Hmm," he mumbled. His face was relaxed with sleep. Kate looked at him, noticing the fine lines around his eyes. Roman had changed. He'd aged—they both had—but as she studied him she noticed the sturdiness of his jaw, the touch of gray at his temples. She wondered what he worried about. Was it his job? Roman took his job seriously. Kate marveled at how he'd managed to keep his integrity intact in this town, though Roman had always been strong.

"Admiring me, eh?" he asked, making Kate jump. His eyes remained closed, but he was smiling.

Kate moved away an inch or two to ease the fluttering in her stomach. "Sorry. I didn't want to wake you," she stammered. "I finished reading the notes. And it's getting super late."

"Oh," Roman said with a hint of sadness. "Did you find anything useful?"

"Not sure yet," Kate said, gathering up the pages and returning them to the plastic protector. "There are a few things I don't understand."

"Such as?" Roman was awake now and back in cop mode.

"Well," Kate said, sitting back down in the armchair. She took a deep breath to clear her head. "If Mandy and Gabby were both being preyed on by the same group, why kill Gabby? Mandy made it sound like they went to great lengths to keep her alive and well. That behavior fits the way sexual predators groom their victims."

"I can understand your frustration." Roman sighed. "The

chances of getting caught grow exponentially if the girl being trafficked is murdered. Whoever killed Gabby made no effort to hide her body. To destroy evidence, yes. But there are a thousand better places to hide a body. Millions. Why leave her in a place we'd be sure to find her?"

Kate thought for a moment. "Maybe..." she said, an idea forming in her mind. "The killer was sending a message to the other girls. Maybe Gabby threatened to go to the police and they made an example of her."

Roman considered that. "It could be. But if that's the case, we're talking about a very organized effort. That's a lot of calculation."

"Mandy talked about so many different men. All older. Maybe there *are* a lot of people involved. People who protect one another. I mean, it makes sense right? This is happening right under our noses."

"I hope not." Roman shuddered. "I'm not sure we have the capacity to deal with an issue that big. Especially if there's a problem in the department. And it sounds like so many people are involved. How are we supposed to narrow it down?" Roman locked eyes with Kate, who'd stiffened in her chair, her eyes wide.

"Oh crap. I forgot." Kate jumped up out of her chair. She raced over to her purse and dug around until she felt the folded paper they'd found in Tilly's room. She unfolded it and held it out for Roman, who was now standing beside her.

Kate read the names on the list, a pang of guilt and shame filling her heart. "We do know a few of the people involved. Remember? Tilly made a list," she whispered.

"Tilly?" Roman asked. He looked pained. Kate nodded.

"She told me after Dad died. While we were staying at your house, actually." Kate paused. "Thank you for that, by the way."

Roman seemed frozen in place, his face ashen. "Are you telling me that this happened to Tilly? In high school?"

"I didn't know," Kate said, nodding. She felt her cheeks flush with shame.

"And this." Roman pointed to the paper in Kate's hand. "These are the men who did it?"

"I assume so," Kate replied. "I meant to ask her about the list, but Dad's health got so bad it slipped my mind. And then Til and I got into a huge fight. I haven't heard from her since." Kate took a breath. "But she told me some of the people who raped her, and they're all here on this list."

Roman started pacing. "Why did she make the list?" He was talking more to himself than to Kate, but it made her think.

"Revenge," Kate said with certainty. "She was always making lists. Do you remember when we were in high school, and Tilly was always looking for a fight?"

"Yeah. She was so angry."

"Exactly," Kate said. "It makes sense to me now. She kept track of the people who abused her. But when she realized she couldn't get back at them, she left town instead and never came home." Kate remembered something that Tilly had said, about the town being bad. "She didn't come home for Mom's funeral, and she didn't want to come home when Dad got sick. I made her feel guilty—that's the only reason she did."

"You needed help," Roman said, but the words didn't make her feel better.

"Can you imagine what it must have been like—being back here?" Kate muttered, thinking about the last words she'd said to Tilly. How vile she'd been.

"Maybe," Roman said, causing Kate to study him.

"Roman..."

"No. No, I just meant that I know how it feels to have to face someone who's hurt you badly."

"It's not the same." She felt the blood rush to her cheeks and she turned her eyes to the floor, doing a silent count to ten to calm herself.

Now it was Roman's turn to study Kate. She could feel his eyes on her, but she didn't look up until she felt that she'd regained her composure. When she met his gaze, the look in his eyes made her groan.

"Kate." He whispered her name, like his voice might break her. Roman always looked a little bit weathered, especially around her. But the sorrow that had etched its way deep into his eyes and expression made Kate want to cry. Instead, she stood and started to pace.

"You wanted to know why I stayed here in town, right?" Kate had to force the words out, and she felt more weary as she let each one go. "That's why. I was attacked by an inmate I worked with."

"Attacked?" Roman asked.

Kate looked away so she wouldn't have to see the look of pity she knew would be on Roman's face.

"One of my new patients... we hadn't been working together long, but I was confident. Over-confident. I thought I had him all figured out." She started to sweat but drew in a long, deep breath to steady her nerves. "He was fast. Grabbed my neck with one hand while he slid up my skirt with the other hand. He was inside me so fast. I kicked and clawed. I couldn't scream but I tried. I was starting to see spots. It only lasted a minute before the guard realized something was wrong. The inmate let go of my neck and slammed me onto the floor, climbing on top of me. They dragged him off of me. He fought them hard, like a wild animal. I was gasping so hard, trying to get some air back into my lungs. I didn't realize how hurt I was until the ambulance arrived."

Kate looked at the floor, wishing she could dig a hole and crawl right in. She could still feel her attacker's breath in her face. The pain as her entered her, like he was stabbing her with a knife. The pure terror of knowing that she was going to die. And then the shame and humiliation that followed.

"He'd planned it. Had been planning it from the minute he first saw me. That's what he said. He was laughing when they pulled him off of me." Kate cringed. "He broke one of my ribs, and it took about a week for my voice to come back."

She finally looked up at Roman. His face had lost all color and his jaw and fists were clenched.

"Mom died shortly after. I put in my resignation via email. Couldn't even bring myself to call and talk to my boss. The thought of going back was... unfathomable." Kate shivered. "When you asked for my help. It was, well, hard." She hated how difficult it was to articulate what she was thinking. She started pacing again.

"I thought taking the job at the high school was a safe choice. I thought being back here was safe. But it's not." Kate's voice rose, becoming more shrill. "Now I'm here, alone, and I have people threatening me, breaking into my house. I can barely handle being here. I can't imagine how Tilly could even bear it. Now she's not speaking to me. I don't even know how to get a hold of her."

Roman walked over to Kate and stood in front of her. He grabbed her arms, and looked at her with such fierceness that she felt a pang of fear surge through her. But she also knew with complete certainty that Roman would never hurt her.

"You are not alone," he said, his face so close to hers that their noses nearly touched. "I'm so sorry that happened to you, Kate. I truly am. But I promise you I will not let anything happen to you here."

"How can you say that, Roman?" It frustrated her, how simple he made it all sound. She slipped out of his grasp, sinking back into the armchair. "There is a group of men in town preying on teenage girls. Raping them. Killing them. They've been doing it for God knows how long. And they've made it clear that they don't want me here."

Roman frowned. "What do you mean? Did something happen? Apart from the break-in?"

Kate sighed. "I've been getting phone calls. I finally turned off the ringer. That's why you couldn't reach me."

"What kind of phone calls? What do you they say?"

"For me to leave town," Kate said. "Which is pretty much what Benny Parks said at the funeral."

Roman's eyes glowed with anger. "He approached you at the funeral?"

"Yes. It seemed like everyone there was giving him a pretty wide berth. His uncle pulled him away, but not before mentioning that Benny loves drama. You should have seen how he looked at me, Roman."

As if on cue, Rusty walked over and rested his head on Kate's leg. She scratched his head.

"I'm going to sell this house. I can't stay here. I feel suffocated and exposed. I don't know what I'm going to do."

Roman had taken a seat on the couch and was tapping his fingers against his knees, his face rigid. Kate knew he must be processing all this new information, and she wondered how he was going to react. But before he could say anything his cell phone rang. He excused himself to the kitchen, and Kate listened to his hushed voice while she ran her fingers along Rusty's ears. When Roman returned, he looked bleak.

"I have to go." He grabbed his coat from the arm of the couch. Before walking through the door, he turned to Kate. "Lock the door behind me."

CHAPTER TWENTY-FOUR

Kate thought about turning on another movie hoping she'd fall asleep, but something niggled at the back of her mind. She replayed the conversation with Roman, trying to track down whatever it was that was bothering her.

She assumed Roman had suspicions about her return to town, especially after Mandy mentioned her getting hurt in her job at the prison. She'd never imagined herself telling Roman all the details. She hated the idea of anyone pitying her, especially him. She hadn't been prepared for how much it upset him.

Then again, given the new and unimaginable horrors that they'd uncovered—the violence and predation taking place in their hometown—Kate couldn't blame him. She vacillated between a deep, abiding fury for the horrible things these girls had experienced and a sense of helplessness over how to break a cycle that had been in play for decades.

Kate tried calling Tilly, sighing when she got voicemail. She left a brief message and set her phone aside. Before she started dwelling on her sister, Kate returned her thoughts to the events unfolding in town.

Could Benny Parks have killed Gabby?

Benny was definitely a violent man but that didn't make him a murderer. Then again, given that Allen Parks's name was on Tilly's list, it seemed clear that both Parks men were trouble.

Kate had never noticed before how avoidance seemed to be a family characteristic. Her father had forever been dodging topics that were uncomfortable. Kate had been openly critical of her sister for avoiding things, but that was Kate's go-to strategy for dealing with most of her problems in life, too. In fact, the decision to stay in town and continue working the case was very out of character. She'd had the chance to cut and run, and she'd chosen to stay.

Finally, the thing that had been poking at the recesses of Kate's memory made its way into the light. Kate hopped up off the chair and grabbed her workbag, which she hadn't touched in weeks. The file folders she'd taken from the school were still inside. Kate pulled out the file on Laura Fuentes and began reading.

As Kate read through Laura's file, she looked for similarities between all the known victims. On the face of it, the girls couldn't have been more different. Gabby and Laura had been quiet girls. Good students, hard workers, ambitious. Laura had been a tall, thin girl with light brown hair that brushed her shoulders. Gabby was a curvy Latina, dark-complected, with curly black hair that reached her waist.

Tilly and Kate looked a lot alike, having inherited a mix of their father's darker features and their mother's fair ones. Tilly had filled out sooner than Kate had, and even in high school she was often mistaken as the older sibling. She had their mother's deep green eyes and a smattering of freckles across her nose and cheeks. Kate's hair was a lighter shade of brown, and she'd gotten her mother's fairer complexion, but her eyes were a rich chocolate brown like her father's.

Mandy seemed to be an anomaly. Blond and petite. A cheerleader. Involved in after-school clubs and volunteer organizations. She was an average student, but her outgoing nature made up for any academic failings. Her teachers loved her. Right up until the last month, when everything had gone south.

It took a long time for Kate to glom on to the only thing the girls had in common. Accessibility.

Gabby Greene had spent very few hours at home, filling her spare time with work and volunteer projects that would help her get into the college of her dreams. She'd disappeared one night after work.

Laura Fuentes had been a latch-key kid, with both parents working long and often opposing shifts in their contract jobs for the military. Before moving to Alamogordo, a nanny had helped care for her. But she'd been left to fend for herself after the move. She, too, had spent hours away from home each day at school and then the library. It had taken her parents nearly twelve hours to notice she was missing.

The turmoil in Mandy's home life had given her plenty of reason not to spend much time at home. Mandy's mother seemed more concerned with her own personal life than with the well-being of her girls. And if Benny Parks had been involved in trafficking Mandy, it was only a matter of time before Mandy's little sister was victimized.

Kate turned her attention to her own family. Kate's mother had stayed home when the kids were little but returned to work in their teenage years, leaving the hours after school free for Kate and Tilly to do as they pleased. Kate had worked a part-time job. Tilly had been restless. She wasn't a terrible student, but academic life wasn't her forte. She spent more time with her friends and boyfriends than she did studying. Kate was always the one receiving praise for her accomplishments.

Kate had always felt loved by her parents, but Frank had often taken a critical view of what he viewed as Tilly's laziness and lack of ambition. Kate wondered what it must have felt like for Tilly. Once again, she felt stabbing remorse at not having made more of an effort to be a better sister.

Kate poured herself a glass of wine, setting it down next her to silent cell phone and pulled out the other file she'd snagged before leaving the school. The student file on Benjamin Parks.

Benny's file was much thicker than Laura's. Kate flipped through pages of minor transgressions which would have landed other kids in detention. Benny seemed to have a special knack for avoiding punishment. The juvenile delinquency described in those pages should have been a red flag for any school psychologist, but the only reference to counseling in Benny's file appeared to have been redacted. Like she was reading an FBI report rather than a high school student file.

Benny was younger than Kate. He'd squeaked thought high school and went to work for his uncle's real estate company. Allen Parks had since retired, but he still sat on the board of directors for several civic organizations.

Thinking about the Parks men made Kate furious, and she had to check her anxiety.

She pushed the student files to the center of the coffee table and pulled her computer into her lap. Kate typed each of the girls' names in the search bar and then combined those with Benny and Allen Parks, as well as the other men on Tilly's list. Finding nothing useful, she changed tactics. She'd been looking for something to link the girls to the men, but maybe she didn't need to make that connection. Not yet. First, she needed to find out what connected the men to one another.

Two minutes later Kate was scrolling through photo after photo taken at countless events around the city featuring Benny and Allen Parks, Donald Copeland, and a number of the other men on Tilly's list. Chamber of Commerce events. Civic clubs. Grand openings. City Council meetings. These were the business elite, the men who ran the big organizations in town.

Burned out, Kate was about to put her computer away when one final photo caught her eye. It was some sort of business gathering. She saw the usual faces, including the Parks. But standing beside Allen with a big smile on his face was Dr. Nivens, her father's oncologist. He had an arm flung around the shoulder of a man Kate hadn't expected to see—her father, Frank Medina.

CHAPTER TWENTY-FIVE

Kate curled up on her couch, Rusty beside her, and spent the rest of the night in a trance. Not quite asleep. Not quite awake. Her mind darted from one image to another, each more terrifying than the last. She managed to keep her anxiety at bay, but when the sun began pouring in through the living room window she felt like a zombie.

It took most of the morning before she finally hauled herself into the shower and began puttering around the house, trying to convince herself that she was accomplishing something. In reality, she was waiting for Roman to call. She needed to tell him about her research and how disturbed she was seeing her father among all these horrible, vile men.

And she needed to know Roman was okay.

His extended visit and the conversation they'd had left her feeling vulnerable. She told Roman more than she'd told anyone about the attack and the mess her life had been ever since. More than she ever intended to tell anyone. The weight lifted and what was left was emptiness, exhaustion, and loneliness.

Kate found it ironic that she bottled up all her feelings when she was constantly telling others to journal, to talk, to let it out.

What was that saying about doctors being the worst patients? She supposed the same might be true for psychologists. It was much easier to give advice than to take it. But now that she'd started talking, there was no going back.

Digging into her purse, Kate found her therapist's card right where she'd shoved it more than five years ago. The embossed type was sticking to the card in front of it, but when Kate pried it off she found the information intact. Kate hadn't added the information to her phone—another attempt to bury her past when she'd come home to take care of her dad—but she was glad that some part of her had known not to get rid of it.

She placed a call and scheduled a phone appointment a few weeks out.

Kate was finishing lunch when a knock at her door made her jump. Rusty stood by the door, wagging his tail, completely silent. A quick look through the peephole revealed the reason for Rusty's sudden happiness. Kate opened the door and let Roman inside.

"I swear, this dog likes you better than he likes me," she said with a groan.

"Did you sleep?" Roman asked, looking concerned. She'd seen the circles under her eyes after taking a shower and wasn't at all surprised by the question.

"Not really," Kate said, walking toward the kitchen. She poured Roman a cup of coffee without asking and they both took up stations at the kitchen table. The caffeine did nothing to ease her fatigue, but she was relieved to have company.

"Thanks for the coffee," Roman said after a few more moments of silent sipping. He seemed on edge, reminding Kate that she hadn't heard the reason for his visit yet. Or for his hasty departure the night before.

"So are you going to tell me or do I have to ask?" she said, assuming the best playful tone she could muster. Roman's rigid posture and tired eyes was starting to stress her out again.

"Dispatch got a call last night about a break-in. They picked up Mandy Garcia."

"What?" Kate said, her body tensed, ready for a fight. "Oh my God. Is she okay?"

"The report says that she broke into the real estate office on Florida Avenue."

"The one owned by Allen and Benny Parks?" Kate felt her whole body begin to pulse with adrenaline.

"Yes." Roman's face was etched with worry lines. "And before you say it, yes, I find it very convenient. Anyway, I wasn't there. I got a call from a friend on patrol. By the time I got there, the case had been closed. Benny agreed not to press charges as long as Mandy was remanded to her mother's care and put on house arrest."

"That's insane!" Kate yelled, standing up abruptly. "You're telling me Mandy was sent back to live in the same house as the man who assaulted her?"

"It appears so." Roman sighed. "I asked for regular welfare checks. But the chief has made it clear that I'm not part of this case, and therefore what I say has no weight. I put in the request with the officer in charge, but I don't know if he'll follow up."

Kate was furious. "How in the hell are we supposed to protect these girls when the whole system is in cahoots! I should have taken Mandy somewhere safe when she showed up at my house."

Kate hadn't realized she was hugging herself until Roman appeared in front of her and held her arms. The warmth of his touch brought Kate back into her body, cutting short the downward spiral she was about to take.

"I know, Kate," Roman said. "I feel like I'm beating my head against a brick wall. I've never felt this way in my entire career and, I'm not going to lie, I hate it. But this isn't your fault. Mandy showed up on her own and she left on her own."

Kate looked deep into Roman's eyes. "We're the adults here,

Roman. We're the responsible ones. It's our job to protect these girls. These children."

Roman nodded. "And we will find a way to shut these bastards down." He let go of Kate and went back to the table. "I put in a call to my friend at the state police. It'll probably get me fired. Stepping outside the chain of command doesn't usually make anyone very happy. I asked her to meet us here. I hope that's okay."

Kate returned to her seat as well. "Yeah, why not. When?"

"Around four. I'm going to go home and try to get a few hours of sleep. You should do the same." Roman got up, rinsed out his cup and headed for the door, Rusty on his heels, tail wagging.

"I'll see you in a while," Roman said, and before Kate could say a word he was gone.

Kate was still groggy when Roman arrived just before four o'clock, and he was not alone.

"Hi, Kate. This is Detective Lopez."

"Angela." The woman was striking. She wore her hair in a severe bun, and her suit was fitted, showing her curves. Kate could see the edge of a shoulder holster inside the suit jacket. But it was her eyes that caught Kate's attention. They were dark and piercing, made even more so by eye makeup applied to make them pop.

"Can we come in?" Roman asked, and Kate felt flushed with self-consciousness.

"Of course, yes. Sorry. I'm still a little bit tired." She held the door open to her guests and they sat down in the living room. Roman settled next to Detective Lopez on the couch. They joked around like old friends and the way they moved around one another made Kate uncomfortable.

"Kate, Roman tells me your background is in forensic psychology." Angela's voice was husky and soft. She studied Kate, but her expression was warm and inviting.

"Yes. I worked in the prison system for over a decade."

"We've been looking to hire someone like you for almost a year now. There aren't a lot of people with that background who want to work out here in the sticks. But Roman tells me you grew up here?"

Every time Angela used Roman's name, Kate felt her heart squeeze. There was nothing offensive about this woman. She was polite, well-spoken, and seemed interested in what Kate had to say—a far cry from the way Roman sometimes treated her.

"Yes, this is my parents' house. I'm getting ready to put it on the market."

"I'm sorry about your losses, Kate. My mother died a few years ago, and I've felt at loose ends ever since."

"I invited Angie here so we could fill her in on what's been going on," Roman interrupted, earning himself a glare from the detective. Kate cringed at his use of her nickname. They definitely knew each other. Well. "I'm just saying that I think we should get to business." Roman looked agitated, taking Kate's anxiety up a notch.

Angela pulled out her laptop. "I'm going to take notes if that's all right with you both." Kate nodded, still fixated on the tension in the air.

"Leave my name out of things until we make this more official," Roman said.

"Roman filled me in on his investigation," Angela started. Kate wondered how long they'd been together before coming to her house. Roman had only been gone a few hours. Where had Angela driven in from? "Sounds like you've been dragged into things. Can you start by giving me a rundown on what's been going on?"

Kate paused for a moment. "On the contrary," she said, hearing the irritation in her voice. "I agreed to help, but now my family is being targeted. I'm being bullied by people in this town who seem to be above the law. Though I guess I should thank those people, because being a target seems to be the only way to have my voice heard."

"Kate," Roman said, his voice soothing, but Kate wasn't in the mood to be calmed. Maybe it was the sleep deprivation, or the grief, or the growing frustration she had with the whole situation. Maybe it was the way Angela was angling her body toward Roman. Whatever the reason, Kate could feel anger surging.

Kate held up her hand, silencing Roman. She put her full focus on Detective Lopez. "I've had the chief of police intimidate me in my own office. My house has been broken in to. I was suspended from my job. And it looks like this horrifying sex trafficking business has been going on since I was a kid. My sister was a victim. Roman wants me to be calm, but I'm *not* calm, and there's no way around it. It's been the worst few weeks of my life, and that's saying something."

As Kate's rant died down, the room sank into silence. Angela looked at Kate with concern. Roman looked out the window, refusing to make eye contact with anyone.

Finally Kate said, "I guess what I'd like to know, Detective Lopez, is how we can stop this insanity. I am not a member of law enforcement, but I'm right in the middle of this mess. I need to help these girls."

Angela nodded. "I understand, Ms. Medina," she said, parroting Kate's switch back to formal titles.

Kate was relieved. The intimacy between Roman and Angela had been palpable. Besides feeling like the odd man out, Kate had felt a surge of jealousy. It was not a pleasant feeling. And she'd be damned if she wasn't treated as an equal part of this team from this point forward.

Two hours later, Detective Lopez left. Kate was glad to see that she'd arrived in her own car, though it made the jealousy she'd felt all the more unseemly. She knew she had no claim over Roman, but the last few days he'd been such a comfort. It felt like they'd been growing closer, and it was unnerving to think of him in the context of other relationships.

Kate watched as Roman walked Angela to her car. She wondered if they'd slept together. Finally she closed the door and began tidying up the living room to distract herself. She was starting to look through her cabinets for something to eat for dinner when Roman knocked at her door.

Kate opened the door, allowing Roman to come inside though she didn't say a word. The look on his face told her she was in for a confrontation, and she wanted a few minutes to prepare herself. She busied herself in the kitchen.

"Do you want something to eat?" she asked.

"No," Roman answered. Kate didn't have to see his face to know he was frowning. "I thought we were doing okay, Kate. I thought we were starting to let go of the past."

Kate's head drooped. Roman didn't sound angry. He sounded sad, and it broke Kate's heart. She put her palms down on the counter and focused on her breathing. She didn't know what to say, and she couldn't look at him.

For weeks, Kate had been fighting a flood of feelings about Roman. Having him around her had brought back all the warm, friendly feelings she'd had for him in her teens. And more. No matter how hard she tried to fight those feelings or how conflicted she felt, the rush of jealousy when seeing Roman's easy manner with Angela made it hard to deny. She'd pushed aside her feelings for Roman in their youth, but she wasn't sure she could do so now. Or that she wanted to.

"I know this is hard." He was standing by the table, just a few feet behind her, when he spoke. She pressed her palms harder into the counter, praying that she could get her emotions under control before she had to interact.

"I know you're scared, and angry, and sad." He was moving closer. Kate's palms began to sweat and her breathing was labored. Why couldn't he just sit down? Give her a minute to get herself together.

"How long have you known Angela?" she whispered, stopping Roman in his tracks.

"Years," Roman replied. He was standing a foot away, but he'd stopped moving. "Since right after high school. We went to the police academy together."

"She seems nice," Kate said.

Time stood still in Kate's kitchen. Roman was quiet for a long time. Of all the things she could have said, why did she bring up Angela? If they had a history, she wasn't sure she wanted to know the details.

Finally, when she couldn't stand the silence anymore, Kate turned around. She was startled to see Roman crying.

He was standing a foot away, but tears were slipping down his cheeks, leaving dark spots on his shirt. He was looking at her, so their eyes met as soon as she turned.

Having never seen Roman cry, Kate panicked. "What's wrong?"

Roman wiped his eyes with his sleeve. "I'm tired, Kate. My whole life has been turned upside down. When I'm out there, I have to be hard. I can't afford to slip. And then when I'm here with you, my emotions are all over the place. I figure if you're allowed to go all ape shit on me, I can get away with a few tears." His tone remained somber.

Kate wanted to say a lot of things. That he was being harsh. That he was overreacting. But her behavior during their meeting had been over the top. She wanted to be treated like a professional but she'd led with her emotions. Letting her jealousy and confusion guide her words.

"I'm sorry, Roman. I'd like to tell you that all the sadness and frustration of the last few days were to blame, but I'd be lying." Kate wrapped her arms around her middle, holding tight. She was a master of holding back, and even in this tender moment she couldn't let her walls down.

"I know I haven't exactly been easy to be around," Roman said. "But I do appreciate your insights. I'm sorry you have to be involved in this case at all."

"That's the thing, Roman," Kate said, feeling a twinge of confidence. "I'm not. I mean, I wish this wasn't happening. But working with you on this case has been the only thing getting me through the day. I didn't realize how much I missed this." Whether she meant the job or being with him was anyone's guess—even she didn't quite know. She turned away again, hiding the color in her cheeks, and jumped when Roman put his hand on her hip.

Her face burned. She could feel his breath on her neck. It wasn't the first time Kate's heart had gone on point for Roman, but it was the first time she been willing to admit how much she liked having him near her.

They stood like that, his hand at her waist, her back turned to him, for what felt like hours. Then Roman's cell phone rang and he broke away to answer it, shattering the spell. Kate felt her body deflate like a balloon as he walked into the living room. She could hear his side of the conversation, but her brain was spinning too fast to pay attention.

What was happening between them? It was hard to believe that Roman still had feelings for her after all these years; after all that she'd done. She'd pushed her own feelings so deep down that she'd almost convinced herself they didn't exist. What a fool she'd been.

"I have to go," Roman said, causing Kate to jump.

"Oh," she replied. Once again, there were so many things she wanted to say to him, but the words caught on her tongue.

"Goodnight, Kate," he said. He leaned down and kissed her cheek. Then he turned and walked out the door. Kate locked it behind him.

CHAPTER TWENTY-SIX

The next morning, Kate left the house early to run errands. Rusty gave her a doleful look as she closed the door, and she wondered what kind of disaster she'd be coming home to. Kate dropped her last two boxes of donations at the thrift store. She was ready to put her dad's house on the market.

Kate pulled into the Sonic parking lot and ordered a cherry-limeade. She sipped the drink and enjoyed a few moments of quiet, when her phone rang. The name on the caller ID flooded Kate with relief.

"Tilly?" Kate answered. "Oh my God! I'm so glad to hear from you. I am so sorry for being such a jerk. I didn't mean to be so awful!" The words poured out of Kate's mouth in one long stream.

"Slow down," Tilly said. Her voice sounded strained. "It's okay. I understand. I'm sorry I've been so absent. I needed some time to process."

"I know," Kate said, her body flush with relief at hearing her sister's voice.

"I'm all right. Well actually I'm not. Have you thought about coming up to stay with me for a while?"

"Things have been a little chaotic here." Kate gave her sister a rundown on her work to get their parents' house ready to sell, avoiding mention of the investigation.

"Listen, Kate. I know I've been pretty cryptic about things lately, and I want to be clear. You need to come and stay with me. Let the realtors take care of things."

"I can't leave my job," Kate stated.

"The school knows how to get a hold of you if they need you. In the meantime, you can be looking up here."

Kate tried not to take it personally, but the cavalier way that Tilly was attempting to rearrange her life was starting to rub. "I'm not sure I'm going to stay at the school anyway. I might take a job with the state police." A slight exaggeration, but one that made her feel more in control of her own life.

"In Las Cruces?" Tilly's tone was wary.

"No. Well, I don't know actually. I'm not sure."

"You won't be working on Roman's case, right?" It didn't sound like a question.

"I might. I don't know."

"No."

Kate paused. "No? No, what?"

Tilly sighed so loudly Kate could practically feel her breath through the phone. "You need to stay away from that case, Kate. Move to Las Cruces. Come up here. Whatever you want. Just please get the hell out of there."

The urgency in Tilly's voice made Kate shiver. "What happened, Tilly? Tell me."

"I got a call last night. On my unlisted number. Not sure who. A man. Young. He didn't sound familiar, but that's not surprising. He told me to get you out of town. That they were going to hurt you."

"I've gotten some threats here, too," Kate admitted.

"That's the thing, Kate. It wasn't a threat. It was a warning."

"What do you mean?"

"He sounded worried. I don't know how to describe it, but it gave me the creeps. I don't scare easily, Kate. And I'm terrified. I want you to be safe. You're all I have left."

"But why would he call you, Tilly? It doesn't make any sense."

"I don't know," Tilly answered, then the sisters fell silent.

"Listen, Til. I'm not at home right now. I'll call you this afternoon and we can talk some more."

"Okay," Tilly said, but she sounded defeated. "Be careful."

"I will."

Kate found Roman waiting on her doorstep when she arrived home.

"Hi," she said with a smile as she approached him. He didn't return her smile. That was all it took for her to know that something was wrong. "What happened?"

"Can we talk inside?" Roman asked, letting her by so she could open the door.

Rusty had greeted them at the door and was now lying at Roman's feet. There were no obvious signs of destruction from the dog's first stint at home alone.

Roman took the cup of water Kate offered with a quiet thank-you. His shoulders slumped. The dark circles under his eyes told his level of stress and worry. In response Kate's posture became straight and rigid, like her own anxiety was pulling her to attention.

"Mandy Garcia is in the hospital," Roman said.

"What happened?"

"She tried to hang herself in her bedroom. Her mother found her."

Kate's hands shook. "When was this?"

"Last night." Roman sighed, finally looking up at Kate. His

eyes were bloodshot. "I found out this morning when I went on shift. Seems no one thought I needed to know."

"Will she be OK?" Kate's voice trembled.

"I don't know. She'd currently in ICU. They're not sure how much damage the lack of oxygen might have caused. They're supposed to call when she wakes up, but no one knows how much time that will take. Or if it will even happen."

Roman got up and started pacing.

Kate watched him for a few minutes. This was her Roman. The one she'd been friends with so long ago. Whenever something troubled him, he paced. And she'd learned, even back then, to let him walk it off. He finally stopped moving and stood staring at a picture hanging on Kate's wall. She got up and walked over to him, putting her hand on his shoulder, trying hard to ignore the jolt that she got from the physical contact.

"Hey. What're you thinking?"

Roman turned to face her. She dropped her hand to her side. As it was, they were nearly touching they stood so close.

"It's always frustrating when I hit a wall in an investigation, but usually it's a lack of evidence or stonewalling suspects or victims. I've never had my own department cut me out of a case."

"Did they take you off the investigation?" Kate asked.

"Not officially," Roman admitted. "I wish we'd had Mandy file a police report that first night she was with you."

"She wouldn't have done it."

"I could have made her. I could have taken her into custody. Kept her safe. Called in social services. She might have hated me, but at least there would have been a record of what happened to her. I shouldn't have waited."

"You blame me." It was a statement, not a question. Hadn't Kate had those exact thoughts when she learned Mandy had returned to her mother's custody? Hadn't she felt that way as soon as Mandy entered her office?

"I don't blame you, Kate. Mandy sought you out. She needed someone on her side. I'm glad you were there for her. I hope she'll fight her way through this. She didn't seem like the type of kid who would attempt suicide."

"I don't think she is," Kate said.

Roman crossed his arms across his chest. "What do you mean?"

"She doesn't fit the profile for a suicidal teen. And she gave no indications of being suicidal, not even with what had happened to her." Kate's mind was cranking faster. "Who took the report?"

"One of the patrol officers. Guy named Davis."

"Did he note anything out of the ordinary about Mandy's physical appearance when she was brought in?"

"I'm not sure. I didn't read the report very closely." Roman's eyes were wide. "I can't believe I just assumed. God, I used to be so thorough. I'm not even doing my job well anymore." He lifted his gaze to the ceiling.

"Considering the monster she's living with, I'm not saying Mandy hadn't finally had enough. But I'd very curious to see her injuries and to talk to her mother about her demeanor prior to the incident." Kate stopped short. "If it were me. I know it's not that simple."

Despite the circumstances, Roman smiled. "You're exactly right." He started moving to the door. "I'll let you know what I find out."

———

For two days, Kate cleaned to keep her wild thoughts at bay. Occasionally she thought about what Detective Lopez had said, about the state police looking for someone in her line of work. She wondered what it would be like working for law enforcement. Maybe nothing but document review and expert testimony, but you never knew. Maybe she'd be in a position to work with law enforcement on cases like these, helping victims of violence. The thought wasn't unappealing.

Kate was taking a break, admiring her handiwork from the comfort of the living room couch, when there was a knock at the door. She stiffened. It had been ages since a knock at the door had resulted in anything but bad news.

Kate's eyes grew wide when she opened the door to find Tilly, suitcase in hand.

"What are you doing here?" Kate asked, unable to mask her surprise.

Tilly smiled. "Nice to see you, too, big sister." She pushed past Kate and dropped her bag by the front door. "I took some time off to help you get the house on the market. Looks like you don't need my help. Good grief, did you hire a cleaning company? It looks like you've been scrubbing with a toothbrush in here."

"I always need your help, Til. Though I've had a lot of time on my hands lately, so the house is pretty much ready to go. I've been re-cleaning the same spots for days. The realtor is dropping by this afternoon. Have you eaten?" Kate started walking toward the kitchen.

"I grabbed a wrap on the way down."

Kate studied the shadows under Tilly's eyes. "How long will you be here?"

"What's that?" Tilly asked, drawing Kate's attention to the barking coming out of the backyard. She'd put Rusty out while the floor dried and hadn't let him back in. Her dog was clearly unhappy at not being present to inspect their guest.

"That's Rusty. He's mad at me for shutting him up outside while I cleaned." Kate let the dog in and Rusty rushed to Tilly, giving her an enthusiastic sniff before taking up a spot at Kate's side. "Yes, I know," Kate said, retrieving a treat from a canister on the counter. The dog inhaled his snack and then retreated to the living room to lie down.

"How long have you had him?"

"A week. I needed the company."

"That's a good idea. Having a dog around."

"Not sure how good a guard dog he's going to be. He seems to love everyone at first sight."

"He's pretty sweet," Tilly said, patting Rusty's head.

Tilly's demeanor was friendly and conversational, but Kate could sense the tension lying just below the surface. She changed the subject.

"Well, the next thing I was going to work on today was packing up my bedroom. I'm going to put a lot of my things in storage until I figure out where I'm going to end up."

"How's the investigation going?"

Kate frowned. "It's not great. Roman called in the state police, though I don't know how much they can do right now. It seems like he's being pushed off the case."

"Not surprising," Tilly replied. "It's not easy to stand up to the powers that be."

"Detective Lopez—she's Roman's contact at state police—mentioned they might have an opening for a forensic psychologist."

Tilly quirked an eyebrow. "Angela Lopez? I think I remember her. Didn't Roman used to date her?"

Kate felt ice running through her veins. "I don't know. I didn't ask her, and it's none of my business."

"Sorry. Didn't mean to stir something up." The smile on Tilly's face was so smug, it felt like they were teenagers again. Tilly always knew how to push Kate's buttons.

"You didn't. Roman did mention that they'd been at the academy together. It's not surprising that they dated." Kate tried to keep her tone casual, but the news still burned.

"She's local, you know. She grew up here in town. She was a

year behind me. I remember her being super snotty and superior."

"Really? She seemed nice enough to me."

"I guess we've all changed a lot," Tilly said. "I'm pretty sure they dated after high school. You were already gone, but Roman still popped up around here every once in a while. I remember thinking that Roman was way out of her league."

Kate didn't respond. She was too busy wondering why Roman hadn't mentioned that Angela was local, or why Tilly seemed to know more about Roman's personal life than Kate did.

Before the day was through, Kate and Tilly had met with the realtor and rented a small storage unit for some of Kate's belongings. When they returned home, Kate felt a little pang of sadness to see the "For Sale" sign in the front yard.

Tilly made dinner while Kate paid some bills online. Over dinner, they talked about the past, trying to stick to the good times.

"Like that night you got caught sneaking back in. And Mom threw your CD collection out on the lawn," Kate said, chuckling.

Tilly smiled. "God, I was so mad at her. I remember being out in the yard in the middle of the night, scooping up jewel cases with mascara streaking down my face. I was so horrible! I put Mom through so much."

"I'm sure you'll get it back times ten when you have kids," Kate teased.

"Probably," Tilly replied, but her voice was distant.

"Tilly?" Kate asked, reaching out to take her sister's hand.

"I'm okay," Tilly said, wiping away a tear that hadn't quite materialized. "You have Netflix, right? Let's watch a movie."

Tilly got up and started clearing dishes. Kate recognized the nervous energy for what it was and left Tilly to work off whatever she was feeling.

Kate was flipping through movie options when someone knocked at the door. Once again, she felt a surge of anxiety.

"I'll get it," Tilly said, making her way to the door with Rusty hot on her trail.

"Hi, Roman," Tilly said, moving aside to let Roman into the house.

"Hey, Tilly," Roman said. "Didn't realize you were back in town." Roman reached down and ruffled the fur on Rusty's head.

"I got here today. Kate and I were going to put on a movie. Do you want to join us?"

Roman looked over at where Kate was sitting, a question in his eyes. Kate smiled.

"Hi," she said. "I can't vouch for our choice of movies, but you're welcome to join us if you'd like."

Tilly had gone back to the kitchen, making herself scarce.

Roman took off his jacket and slung it over a chair. He came over and sat down next to Kate on the couch, stretching his legs out in front of him and leaning his head back against the pillow.

"Rough day?" Kate asked. She was desperate for news on Mandy and the case, but with Tilly in the next room she wasn't sure she wanted to bring it up.

"Yeah," Roman groaned. He laid his arm over his eyes. "You could say that."

"Want to talk about it?"

"No. No change on Mandy, by the way. She's still out. But I did read the patrol officer's report. He didn't include much detail, and I haven't been able to track him down to ask him in person."

"That seems strange."

"It's not. He's not on shift until Saturday, and a lot of us try to disconnect when we're not on duty." Roman raised his arm and looked over at Kate. "How was your day?"

"Good, actually. Tilly came down to help get the house ready. Or to keep me safe. Either way, it's nice to have her here."

"I saw the sign in the yard," Roman said, sitting up. "Not sure how to feel."

"Me either. But I'm not going to miss being here alone." Kate put the remote back on the coffee table. Tilly still hadn't materialized. "Not sure how long it will take to sell the house, but I put stuff in storage today so it's not so cluttered."

"How long is Tilly staying?"

"I asked, but I don't think she ever said. Tilly?" Kate called.

Tilly came padding down the hall from her room, her phone to her ear. She gestured to her phone and then to her room.

"Probably a sign that movie night is off," Kate said, but she didn't mind. She was tired from the day and looking forward to going to bed. Having Tilly in the house had calmed her anxiety. She was praying that she'd get some sleep for a change. "Did you hear anything from Angela?" Kate asked, hoping that the state police were ready to jump all over the case.

"I touched based with her today," Roman said. "Nothing much to report. Though she did say she enjoyed meeting you."

Kate sat up straighter. "Why would she say that?"

Roman eyed Kate warily. "I guess because she enjoyed meeting you."

"You were talking about me?"

"We were discussing the case and your name came up, yes. Why are you getting so defensive?"

"I don't love the idea of you talking about me when I'm not there." *Especially with her,* Kate thought.

Roman looked like he wanted to say something, but instead he sighed and put his arm back over his eyes. "I don't know if I can do this, Kate. Not when you're so angry with me all the time."

"I'm not angry," she whispered, but that wasn't entirely true. She wasn't angry with Roman. Why was she always lashing out at him? She leaned back into the couch. She'd begun to edge away from Roman but now she shifted closer and closed her eyes, trying to salvage the situation. "I'm all over the place right now, you know? I've never felt quite so...directionless."

It was easier to talk when she didn't have to look into his eyes. She felt him sit up beside her, but she stayed put.

"The thing is," he said, "when you left town, I changed. At least I thought I did. I figured out how to be me without you. And then when you came back, everything was the same as it had always been for me. Every time I saw you, it tore me up. It still does."

Kate felt tears forming. "I never meant to hurt you."

"I know," Roman said. "But you did, and it doesn't matter because I still feel the same way about you."

They sat for a few more minutes before Roman got up to leave. "I'll call you tomorrow, Kate. Get some sleep."

As the door clicked shut, she let the tears fall.

CHAPTER TWENTY-SEVEN

Kate was resistant to the idea of leaving New Mexico despite Tilly's urgings. True, the opportunities in Colorado were probably better—more choices and better pay—but she wasn't ready to leave again. Not when she finally felt she had a purpose. She didn't want to run away. And she wouldn't leave Roman again, not without trying to make things right between them.

As she sat in the quiet house, waiting for Tilly to wake up, Kate thought about Mandy lying in the hospital. Mandy, who had come back to keep her sister safe and now was battling for her life. She called Roman, but his phone went straight to voicemail. She didn't know what to say, so she hung up without leaving a message. By ten o'clock, she was going stir crazy. She gave Rusty a treat, left Tilly a note on the kitchen table, grabbed her purse and phone, and headed out.

At first, Kate drove aimlessly. She'd almost made it into the hospital parking lot before she knew where she was going. Her palms began to sweat.

Kate parked and made her way into the hospital, stopping by the gift shop to buy flowers and a box of chocolates. She headed up to the Intensive Care Unit, wondering if they would let her in. Luckily, one of her father's nurses met her at the door and escorted Kate to the nurses' station.

"It's good to see you," Kate said, placing the flowers and chocolate on the counter. "I thought I'd stop by with a thank-you gift. I really appreciate all the care you gave him."

The charge nurse smiled at Kate. "That's what we're here for. Though we will never turn down chocolate."

Kate chuckled while trying to figure out how to approach the next topic. "Listen, I know this is irregular, but one of my students is in here after a suicide attempt. Mandy Garcia? I wanted to see how she's doing. I've been worried."

A shadow crossed nurse's face. "She's still unconscious, though her physical injuries are healing."

"Could I see her?"

"For a few minutes. Her mother hasn't been in today, and I think it would do her some good to hear a friendly voice."

The nurse led her down the hall. "Do they know what happened?" she whispered.

"The mother says she found her daughter hanging from a rope in her closet." Something about the way she spoke gave Kate the confidence to ask her next question.

"You don't believe her?"

The nurse paused outside a patient door. Kate could see Mandy lying in the hospital bed, a ventilator tube down her throat. "No, I don't. But her mother refuses to allow anyone in to see her. And the police didn't seem particularly concerned."

"Is it going to cause problems? Me being here?"

"Maybe. But her mother hasn't been here for two days. The girl needs someone. Just keep it short."

She shuffled back toward the nurses' station, leaving Kate to slide the door open and enter Mandy's room.

Stepping inside, Kate was overwhelmed for a moment with memories of her father. The whir of the ventilator. The beeping of the monitor. The smells of antiseptic and latex. Kate focused hard on Mandy to steady her breathing and ground her in the present. She approached the bed and took Mandy's hand.

"Hi, Mandy," Kate said. "I'm so sorry that this happened to you." She reached over and pushed a strand of Mandy's hair away from her eyes. As her eyes traveled down, Kate took in the marks on Mandy's neck—red and angry.

Leaning in close Kate said, "I'm going to make sure this doesn't happen to anyone else."

Knowing she was running out of time, Kate pulled out her phone and began taking pictures. She photographed the bruises and abrasions on Mandy's neck, face, and hands. Then she put her phone back in her purse, gave Mandy's hand a gentle squeeze and left the room, sliding the door closed behind her.

As Kate was exiting the hospital, Benny Parks was walking in. Kate caught him glaring at her as she passed. She shuddered and walked a little faster.

Kate returned home to find Tilly still in bed. She made herself some lunch and puttered around the house, but by early afternoon her agitation had grown. She walked down the hall and knocked on Tilly's door.

"Tilly?" she called, trying to make her voice sound pleasant despite her irritation. When she didn't get an answer, she pushed the door open. Peeking around the door, she repeated in a whisper, "Tilly?"

"Hmm?" The sound came from somewhere in the direction of Tilly's bed. The mound of pillows and blankets shifted.

"Do you want to take a walk?" Kate asked.

Tilly lifted her head. "Um, not today. I didn't sleep well. I need to just take it easy today."

"Are you feeling okay?"

"Yeah," Tilly mumbled. "I just need sleep."

"OK," Kate said. She backed out of the room and headed back down the hallway, grabbing Rusty's leash from the peg near the front door.

Kate did a few laps around the block and then headed back home. She called Roman again, but to no avail.

Frustrated, Kate sat down at her computer and uploaded the photos she'd taken. She opened each image and studied them. The rope marks on Mandy's neck gave Kate pause. The skin was a raw, purplish-red, the patterns from the rope still visible on Mandy's skin. From a distance, it almost looked like a garish choker-style necklace. There were other bruises around Mandy's neck, but the low lighting in the hospital room had created shadows. Making it difficult to tell between discolored skin and a trick of the light.

Moving on, Kate examined the pictures of Mandy's hands. The girl's fingernails were clipped short but bits of dark red nail polish remained, chipped and irregular. Kate zoomed in closer and realized something she'd missed in the hospital room. The tips of several of Mandy's fingers bore abrasions, and a few of her fingernails showed signs of damage the clippers weren't able to remove. Defensive wounds? Kate didn't know. She hoped Roman would call her back.

Feeling paranoid, Kate made copies of the images and saved them to the Cloud. Then she pulled out a notebook and started to do searches for rental houses, listing the ones she wanted to drive past over the weekend.

The room was growing dim when Tilly finally came out of her room. Kate could hear Rusty barking in the backyard.

"Hey," Tilly said, throwing herself onto the couch. Kate put down her pen and turned to face her sister. Tilly looked completely disheveled. She was wearing sweatpants and a shirt that Kate recognized from their high school days. "What're you doing?"

"Looking at houses," Kate replied with a sigh. "Hungry?"

"Not really," Tilly said.

"Are you sure you're okay?"

"I'm not sick, if that's what you're asking," Tilly replied. Her sarcastic tone riled Kate.

"I'm glad you're not sick. And for the record, I'm not an idiot. What's going on, Til?" Tilly sat up. Her eyes were puffy and red. Kate's level of concern outweighed her annoyance.

"Bad breakup," Tilly said with a sniffle.

"I didn't know you were dating someone." Kate realized how little she knew about her sister.

"Almost two years. We were living together."

Kate walked over and sat beside her sister. "I'm sorry, Tilly. I didn't know."

"Of course you didn't," Tilly replied with a sardonic laugh. "I've been such a stubborn ass about being part of this family."

"So, you taking some time off wasn't about selling the house?" Kate asked.

"Not really," Tilly said miserably. "But I didn't want you to think I didn't want to be here. I just wanted to be with you."

Kate laughed, putting her arm around Tilly's shoulder and pulling her close. "God, we're pathetic," she said. "How the hell did we get here, Til? We're both smart, capable women."

Tilly laughed, too. "Guess it's never too late to be a walking disaster."

Rusty's barking was beginning to get on Kate's nerves. She got up to let him back inside the house. As soon as she did, he raced to the front door and continued barking ferociously. Kate heard yelling in the street. She raced to the door, grabbed Rusty's collar, and pulled it in time to see two figures running around the corner. Something wet dripped down the screen in streaks.

Kate and Tilly stepped out onto the porch. Kate was not the

least surprised to see the words "DIE BITCH" slashed across her doorway in bright red paint.

Kate figured things couldn't get any worse.

Then Roman and Angela arrived at her house, together.

Tilly had wanted to try to wash the paint off the house before it dried, but Kate had insisted they call Roman first.

Roman took notes to file a report, but Kate had no faith that anything would be done to keep it from happening again. The sooner she sold her father's house, the sooner all this madness would end. Or would it? If this trafficking ring had been operating for decades, was it realistic to think she'd ever be safe in her hometown again?

"I don't know how we're going to sell this house if this keeps happening," Kate said when they got inside.

"Can you have patrol keep an eye out until the house sells?" Angela asked Roman.

Roman looked tense. "I can try. Not sure how effective my orders are these days."

"I'm going to start looking at rentals this weekend. I'll just have to get out of the house sooner rather than later. They want me out of town. I'll give them what they want."

Kate didn't look at Roman while she spoke. She couldn't. Instead, she turned to Angela.

"I stopped by the hospital today. I was able to see Mandy Garcia. She's the student I told you about. The one who'd been returned to her mother's care. I don't know if Roman told you, but she's in the ICU. Attempted suicide."

"Yes, Roman told me about that this morning."

Kate cringed, trying not to read too much into Angela's response.

"How did you get in to see her?" Roman asked.

"I sweet talked the nurses. I think they share my suspicion."

"How did she look?"

"Bad." Kate pulled up the images on her phone. She passed the phone to Angela, still unable to look at Roman even when he sputtered, "You took pictures?"

"I figured since they aren't letting anyone see her it was the only chance we'd have to see her injuries."

"Smart," Angela said, flipping through the images. Despite herself, Kate was beginning to like Angela. She passed Kate's phone to Roman. "Didn't you tell me the mother found her hanging?"

"I did," Roman said. Deep lines furrowed his brow as he and Angela exchanged a look.

"What?" Dread seeped into Kate's question.

Roman took another moment to study the images, zooming in and peering at the details. Finally he handed Kate back her phone and said, "The marks on her neck. They're not consistent with hanging."

Tilly took the phone from Kate and studied the image. "See how the mark circles her neck like a necklace, in a straight line?"

"Yeah."

"If the mark was made by hanging, even if she wasn't up there for long, the line would be at an angle. Like a V. From the pressure of her weight against the rope."

"So what does this mean?" Kate asked, though she was pretty sure she knew.

"She was strangled," Tilly answered.

Roman added, "And her mother lied."

CHAPTER TWENTY-EIGHT

"What about mandatory reporting?" Tilly asked. Kate had almost forgotten her sister was participating in the conversation.

Angela answered. "Yes, I was wondering about that myself. The patient is still a minor. If the nurse had suspicions of child abuse, she should have reported it."

"It's not that simple," Kate said, though she wished it was. "Doing the right thing can be a heavy task. Especially when the patient's mother is involved with one of the hospital trustees."

Angela sighed. "I'd forgotten what a small town Alamogordo can be."

"It's also probable that the nurses didn't recognize the injuries for what they were. Especially the neck injury. As forensic nurses, we're trained to recognize signs of strangulation since it's often seen in abuse cases. Not all nurses get that training," Tilly said.

"So what can we do?" Kate asked, desperate for something positive to cling to.

"Now that you've reported it, Kate," Tilly said with more enthusiasm. "And now that you've given the police the information," Tilly gestured Roman and Angela, as if to underscore her point. "That's enough to warrant a CYFD investigation and forensic exam."

"She already had a rape exam," Roman interjected.

"Did she file a police report?" Tilly asked.

"No."

"Given that she's currently unconscious due to child abuse, I think you could justify a new forensic exam without parental consent. Then we could document her injuries for the official record. You'd at least be able to justify further scrutiny and protection while she recovers."

Tilly's optimistic tone gave Kate some hope.

"Would you be willing to do the exam?"

"Wait a second..." Roman started to protest, but Angela held up a hand.

"I know what you're going to say, Roman. But I think the best chance of keeping this girl safe and keeping you out of trouble with your department is to have the state police order the exam. We can contract with Ms. Medina to perform the exam so that local jurisdiction is not involved until it's done. That keeps all the local rape responders out of it as well, in case there's more trouble than we know."

Roman didn't argue, but he looked defeated.

"I don't like the idea of you getting involved," Kate said to her sister. "You of all people know what this town is capable of."

"It doesn't matter. I can't perform the exam. I'm not affiliated with the hospital here," Tilly said.

"That's unfortunate." Angela frowned. "But I'll call the SANE office here in town and see if we can arrange to have you consult. I'd still like for you to be there."

"Are you sure, Tilly?" Kate's insides felt twisted in knots.

"It's okay, Kate," Tilly reassured her. "This is what I do. No one even needs to know I was involved."

Kate didn't argue. The energized look on Tilly's face was

contagious. Almost. Kate knew better than to think anything that happened in this town would stay quiet for long.

Roman and Angela left Kate's house. Tilly changed to scrubs and left for the hospital, leaving Kate at loose ends and alone. She and Rusty curled up on the couch to watch some mindless television while she waited.

When her phone rang Kate knew it was too soon to expect news, but she still hoped. It was the realtor.

"Hi, Janet," Kate said without much enthusiasm.

"Hello, Ms. Medina." Janet tended toward formality, but Kate didn't mind. She'd had enough of the people of Alamogordo. "I have good news. We have a cash offer on your house and the buyer is offering your asking price."

"You're kidding. Sight unseen?" Kate asked. "What's the catch?"

"It's not much of a catch. The buyer wants to move in by the first of the month."

"Wow, that's fast but I think I can do it. I need to get moving on finding a rental. Let's go for it."

"Wonderful!" The realtor had become much more animated. "I'll start working on the contracts. Would you like me to send you some rental listings?"

"No," Kate said, but another glance at the date changed her mind. "Actually, yes. I'm looking for a small rental house with a yard for my dog."

"Here in town?"

Kate hesitated. "Mostly in Las Cruces, but I'll take a look at what you have here if you want to send it over. Not sure what my next plan is."

After hanging up, Kate opened up her laptop and continued her search for properties. She made a few calls and set up two viewings for that afternoon. She didn't expect Tilly to be back in time, so she left a note on the kitchen table and headed over the mountains.

Kate grabbed lunch in Las Cruces and then set out for her appointments. Two hours later, she wasn't convinced that Las Cruces was where she wanted to end up. To complicate matters, the current limbo of Kate's employment didn't make her feel entirely secure making a decision. Both properties she viewed were looking for one-year leases. Kate wasn't sure she was ready to commit. She returned home feeling down.

When she got to her house, it was getting dark. Tilly's car was gone. Kate wondered if the exam had happened or if they'd run into interference. She unlocked the door and walked inside. As soon as she stepped across the threshold, she knew something was wrong. Rusty didn't run to the door to greet her, and she didn't hear him barking in the backyard. She put her bag on the floor and flipped on the living room light.

Benny Parks was sitting in her living room.

Kate screamed in fright, but her fear turned to fury.

"Get out of my house!" she shouted.

Benny smiled, but made no effort to move. He crossed his legs, all the while glaring at Kate.

"I heard you dropped in on Mandy this morning." When Kate didn't respond, he continued. "Doesn't seem very smart, Ms. Medina. Not very smart at all."

"I wanted to check on my student," Kate said, holding her ground.

"She's not your student anymore," Benny said, sneering. "I also heard your employment would be terminated. Seems that the school district has no need for you anymore. Guess you should have taken my advice, eh, Katie?"

"Why are you here?' she asked, placing her hand on the door. She hadn't closed it yet, and she was grateful for the easy escape route.

"I figured it was time you and I had a little chat. In private." Benny uncrossed his legs and stood, letting the rocker he'd been sitting in bob behind him. The *thump thump thump* reverberated in Kate's head.

"I don't think so," Kate said. Her ears were ringing and her heart was racing. Benny took a few slow steps toward her. "You need to leave."

From the kitchen behind her, Kate heard movement. She turned to find a strange man approaching her. Benny used Kate's moment of distraction to walk over and slam the door shut right out from Kate's hand.

"Well, maybe not entirely private," Benny hissed.

Benny loomed over Kate, whose back was now pressed against the front door. She was starved for oxygen. No one was touching her, but she felt like she was going to pass out anyway. Panic had gripped her more effectively than human hands could.

"Hey, Rick. I have an idea," Benny said to the other man. "I think Kate's having a hard time understanding how things work around here." Benny breath was hot on Kate's cheek, but she kept her eyes on Rick. The man swaggered closer. His eyes were dark, and the way he was looking at her made her blood run cold.

"Sounds like she needs a lesson on what we expect from our women," Rick croaked, his voice ravaged from years of smoking or drug use. The effect was frog-like. In any other situation, Kate might have laughed. As he moved closer, Kate could see old tattoos peeking out from his shirt sleeves. The difference between Rick and Benny was clear. Rick was the muscle, and that made the situation much more dangerous.

"Detective Aguilar was here earlier. He'll be coming by again," Kate stammered.

"Oh, yes. The ever-present Detective Aguilar. I could have sworn I saw him leave with another woman. Trouble in paradise? Well, whatever. He can't help you now, Kate. Pretty soon he'll be lucky to get a fast food job in this town."

"Roman is a good cop," Kate said despite her fear. She hated that this man felt like he could take Roman's career away from him.

Benny ran his hand along Kate's cheek. She slapped it away with a shaky hand.

"Hold her," Benny ordered. Rick closed the gap between them and grabbed Kate's hands, pinning them above her head. She struggled, but her anxiety made her muscles weak and uncoordinated. Rick leaned in and licked Kate's cheek. His breath was putrid. Kate's stomach began to roil. She hoped she puked right on him.

"Now," Benny said, putting his face inches from Kate's, "I want to make sure we're clear, Kate, because I feel like you've misunderstood me. You are no longer welcome in this town. We don't need you here. We don't want you here. And if you continue sticking your nose in things that don't concern you, you'll be sorry."

Benny ran his hands down Kate's sides as tears slid down her face. He pulled at her tucked shirt roughly, sending a button flying across the room as it rubbed against the waist of her pants. Her body began to shake. She twisted against Rick's hold. He shoved a knee hard against her pelvis, keeping her from moving as Benny continued exploring her body with his hands.

Rick laughed, pressing harder against her to keep her still.

Benny reached down and unzipped Kate's jeans, running his fingers along the inside of her waistband.

"Please don't," Kate whispered as the edges of her vision began to blur.

With his hand sliding further inside her pants, Benny leaned in close again. "Don't worry, darling. You're not my type. Too old." He chortled. "But here's the thing. You're exactly Rick's type, and the only thing keeping him from having a go at you is me. Because I know you know how to follow directions. Right, Kate?"

Benny ran a hand through Kate's hair, pulled her head forward, and bashed it into the door. Both men released her, letting her slump to the floor and into peaceful darkness.

CHAPTER TWENTY-NINE

"Kate? Oh my God!"

Kate's head pounded and she felt cold. She opened her eyes slowly, and as they came into focus she saw Tilly peering at her. She closed her eyes again as the pain in her head intensified.

"Tilly?" she rasped. She struggled to sit up, but Tilly pushed her back down.

"Stay still a minute," Tilly cooed. "Can you tell me what happened?"

Kate's memories were foggy, but only for a moment. Then Benny Parks and his thug came back to her in full color. She heaved a huge breath and started to cry. Tilly stroked Kate's forehead while she wept.

Opening her eyes again, Kate saw that she was on the floor in her living room. She wasn't near the door anymore. Someone had moved her a few feet away so that she lay splayed across the entrance. It was dark outside. Kate wondered how long she'd been out.

"What time is it?" she whispered when her sobs quieted.

"A little after eight," Tilly said. "When I finished at the hospital, I called to see if you wanted me to pick up dinner.

When you didn't answer, I came straight home and found you here. Do you remember what happened?"

"I went to Las Cruces to look at some houses."

"Today? I thought we were going this weekend."

Kate sighed. "We got a cash offer on the house." She shook her head in frustration. "Let me get this out, okay?"

Tilly nodded and sat back on her heels.

"When I got home, the house was dark. Rusty didn't come to the door." Kate's heart sped up. "Where's Rusty?"

"I don't know," Tilly said. "I'll go look for him in a few minutes. Tell me what happened."

"Benny Parks was here. And another man. Rick. I didn't recognize him." Tears began forming in Kate's eyes again. She tried to keep them away. "I don't know how he got in."

"Did they hurt you?" Tilly asked, her tone serious.

Kate's hands wandered to her shirt and the waistband of her pants. The zipper was still undone. Kate heard Tilly suck in a breath.

"It's not what you're thinking," Kate said, though she felt thoroughly violated. "He threatened me. Then he slammed my head against the door."

"I'm calling Roman," Tilly said, her fingers flying over her phone screen. "Lie still a bit longer."

Kate could hear Tilly speaking on her phone in urgent tones, but she didn't have the energy to listen. She closed her eyes.

"Stay awake, Kate," Tilly said, patting her face. But it was so hard to obey.

———

Kate awoke a while later in an unfamiliar room. Her pulse spiked and she shot up in bed, only to have pain surge through her skull and the room spin.

"Lie back down," a soothing voice said. It took Kate a

moment, but she finally identified the voice as belonging to her sister. Another moment and she realized she was in a hospital room.

"I need some water," Kate rasped. Now that she was awake, she remembered everything leading up to her current situation. The attack. Tilly calling Roman. Being put on a stretcher and taken to the hospital. She'd been in and out of consciousness the whole time, but she had enough details to piece the story together.

Tilly put a straw to Kate's lips and she sucked in small sips of water until her throat felt less like a bed of hot coals. "Slow down. You've got an IV so just take it a sip at a time, okay?"

"Where's Roman?" Kate asked when she'd finished drinking.

Tilly put the cup down and took a seat on the bed beside Kate. "He's here somewhere. He called an ambulance on his way to the house, so it's been a little hectic. I'm sure he's called in the cavalry, so don't be surprised when you get bombarded with questions."

"Ugh," Kate groaned.

"Listen, Kate. One thing they may or may not ask you is whether you want to do a forensic exam."

"I wasn't raped," Kate protested.

"I know," Tilly said. "But we might be able to get fingerprints or DNA. You could put this asshole away before he can hurt anyone else."

"Oh."

As Kate was thinking it over the door opened, and a plainclothes detective strolled through with Roman on his heels. The look on Roman's face was murderous.

"Hello, Ms. Medina. I'm Detective Wellman from APD. I'm here to take your report."

Kate used her bed controls to raise herself into a sitting position, then waited a moment for her head to settle before responding. "Okay. Though I'm sure Detective Aguilar could have done that."

"Detective Aguilar has been reassigned," Detective Wellman said. He didn't look at Roman, and Roman didn't make eye contact with Kate. He stood by the door, seething.

"Reassigned? From what?" Kate asked.

"That's not what I'm here to discuss, Ms. Medina." The detective's tone had gone cold. "I'm here to take your statement. I understand you were attacked in your home."

"Yes," Kate said. "I arrived home and found two men inside my house."

"Was the door unlocked?"

"No."

"Any sign of a break-in?"

"No."

"How did they get in?"

Detective Wellman made no attempt to take notes or record Kate's statement.

"That sounds like a question for the police," Kate responded, trying to keep her voice calm despite her rising agitation at the interrogation.

"Look, Ms. Medina. I can't help you if you don't cooperate."

"It doesn't sound like you want to help me," Kate replied, beginning to lose her cool.

"Who attacked you, Ms. Medina?"

"Benny Parks and a person named Rick."

"A person named Rick?" The detective was mocking her now.

"Yes, Detective. I didn't catch his name as he pinned me down. Though I was told he'd be back if I didn't leave town."

After a pause, Detective Wellman said, "I'll look into it," and left without another word. Only then did Roman speak.

"Benny Parks called the police station about an hour ago. He said that you two had a private meeting and that you attacked him." Roman was gritting his teeth so hard Kate could see his jaws muscles popping out on either side. "Then the chief called me and reassigned me to desk duty indefinitely. He says I'm not objective and should take some time to get perspective."

All Kate could do was nod. "Can I go home?"

"The doctor says you have a concussion, but they'll release you to my care," Tilly said. "We were waiting for you to wake up so we can get the paperwork going."

"Okay," Kate said. She looked up at Roman. He was staring at her with such emotion in his expression, it made Kate want to cry. "It's going to all right."

"I'm sorry, Kate," he said.

"Me, too," Tilly said, holding Kate's hand. "I should have been home with you."

"You couldn't have known," Kate said.

"True, but there is something I can do now." Tilly pulled a big white envelope out of her bag. Kate could see the chain of custody form on the front. "Now tell me every single place on your body that those bastards touched."

"Wait, should you be doing this?"

"You're an adult, you're awake, and you can consent to the exam. We'll worry about liability issues later. For now, let's collect evidence."

As Tilly began laying out swabs, Kate recounted the whole story in painstaking detail.

"Rusty!" Kate wailed as she and Tilly walked through the front door to a quiet house.

"Let me get you settled on the couch and I'll go investigate," Tilly said. Kate could hear her trepidation. Kate was still off-kilter, her head pounding, so Tilly led her to her armchair to rest while she did her search. After only a few moments Tilly returned, shaking her head.

"Well, I guess our home invaders didn't want to add animal abuse to their list of misdemeanors. They must have thrown something over the fence. Rusty is sound asleep on the porch. He's probably been there all afternoon. He didn't wake up when I shook him, but he's breathing and he seems okay. If he's not up soon, I'll call the vet."

"Thank goodness," Kate sighed, though she wasn't reassured. "A lot of good it does having a guard dog."

Tilly sat down on the couch. "Don't blame Rusty. It's not his fault these assholes are good at being assholes." Tilly rested her head against the back of the couch.

"Did you have any trouble getting in to see Mandy?" Kate asked, hoping to get her mind on something else.

"No," Tilly said. "She hasn't had many visitors in the last few days. Angela gave the floor nurses the spiel about an anonymous report regarding Mandy's safety. They led us straight to her. We were able to take pictures and swabs. Angela has the kit. She thinks she'll be able to fast-track it. Then they put a guard on Mandy's room with instructions not to allow any visitors to be alone with her, including the parents. Hopefully she'll wake up soon."

"What do you think?"

"You called it. The wounds on her hands look defensive, and the rope burn on her neck definitely doesn't look like a hanging. We'll see what the lab comes up with."

"You didn't see Mandy's parents at all?

"No. Why?"

Kate thought for a moment. "I don't know. Benny saw me when I was at the hospital this morning, but I don't think he'd have let me off the hook if he knew a forensic exam was in progress."

"You call that being let off the hook? That knot on the back of your head looks pretty painful."

"It is," Kate said, gingerly running her fingers over the lump. "Benny was trying to scare me, but I don't think he meant to hurt me that badly. When he finds out about the cops being brought in, I don't know what's going to happen. I believed him when he said he'd send Rick back for me. He seems like the kind of coward who'd have someone else do his dirty work."

"Then I guess we'd better get out of this house sooner rather than later," Tilly said.

"We? Does this mean I get to keep you for a little longer?"

"I'm not going anywhere," Tilly replied, and when Kate moved she added, "So there's no reason not to get some rest. Roman's outside sitting in his car. I think we're safe enough tonight."

CHAPTER THIRTY

Kate slept fitfully, especially with Tilly waking her up every two hours, but other than a dull, thrumming pain in the back of her skull she felt better the next day. She could hear dog paws in the hall, and was relieved to have Rusty jump on her when she opened her bedroom door. She took her time getting showered and dressed. Tilly made them both breakfast. And then the sisters headed out of the house in search of safe lodging.

"The two houses I looked at the other day are definite no's," Kate said, crossing the addresses off her list. "Let's start on the north end of town. It'll make it easier to get back to Alamogordo anyway."

Tilly was driving. "You still want to go back?"

"I want to keep my options open," Kate answered, though she knew she was dodging. Now that moving was a reality, the pull of her hometown was stronger. It was ironic. Kate had been counting the days till she could move on with her life. Why was she hesitating now?

"What are you thinking?" Tilly asked, interrupting Kate's internal dialogue.

Kate hesitated. "You're going to think this is crazy." Kate

hated sharing her ideas when they were only half-baked, but she wasn't feeling grounded and needed someone to drag her back to Earth. "Moving away feels like giving up, and despite everything that's happened I'm not ready to give up."

"Explain," Tilly said, agitation clear in her voice.

"It's our hometown, Til. Our parents and grandparents are buried there. Mom and Dad lived their whole lives there."

"This is the same place you couldn't wait to get out of." Tilly's voice was tense.

"I know," Kate said. "But every time I come to Las Cruces to look at rentals, I'm calculating how long it would take to drive back. It means something."

"What? That you've gone completely nuts?"

Kate laughed. "Maybe." She ran her fingers through her hair, wincing when the motion tugged against her injured skin.

They drove in silence. As the car crested the Organ Mountains and the city of Las Cruces came into view in the distance, Kate's phone began to vibrate. When she picked it up, she realized she'd missed several calls in the mountain pass.

More than one had come from Detective Lopez.

"Hi, Angela. I'm heading into Las Cruces. No reception in the pass. Sorry I missed your calls."

"Since you're heading this way, can you come by the department?"

The hairs on Kate's neck prickled. "Tilly is with me."

"Bring her, too. We've got a situation."

"We'll be there in 20 minutes."

Kate recapped her conversation for Tilly's benefit and the two headed to the state police headquarters.

"She's awake?" Kate couldn't mask her frustration. "Why didn't you tell me on the phone?" Tilly had taken a seat in the detective's office, but Kate had been much too agitated. She paced in front of Angela's desk.

The detective looked grave. "I didn't want you to try to see her, especially in your current state."

Kate paused, realizing that if she didn't calm herself down she was in danger of looking crazy in front of the one person who'd shown her nothing but professional courtesy and respect.

"Don't worry," Angela said, as if reading Kate's mind. "You're entitled to feel like hell right now. But the situation with Ms. Garcia is complicated."

"Because child welfare is involved? I've worked with many children in the system…"

Angela held up a hand. "I'm aware of your qualifications, Kate. Would you please sit down? You're starting to make me nervous."

Kate took a seat next to Tilly, who had remained quiet.

Angela leaned back in her chair. "The local police are aware that the state has stepped in. Judge Vega from the 12th District has issued an injunction, pending a full investigation."

"An injunction against what?" Kate asked.

"Against you." Seeing Kate's confusion, Angela continued. "And Tilly. Seems someone mentioned that Tilly was present during the exam. And given your connection with the victim, the judge ruled that neither you nor Tilly can have contact with Mandy until an investigation concludes that you will not cause further harm."

"Are you kidding me?" Kate was back on her feet. "Whatever happened to patient confidentiality? What about the child abuse report?"

Angela sighed. "We've still got a guard watching Mandy. The complaint seems to hinge on her being a minor, but since the exam was ordered by the state police, local law enforcement has to tread carefully. Looks like they've decided to go after you two in order to delay our child abuse investigation as much as possible. Or it could be a way of discrediting you both."

"Wouldn't be the first time," Tilly said. When Kate glared at her, Tilly shrugged her shoulders and said, "Come on, Kate. You testify in court. It's no different than having a defense attorney go at you."

"We're not in court, Tilly. These people are manipulating the system to try to keep Mandy Garcia from getting the help she needs. And they'll make it impossible for me to get a job in this area if they keep it up. Who's going to want to hire a forensic psychologist who's unable to testify in court?"

"It's only one judge," Angela said. "And if you're right about the amount of corruption in town, making a go of things in Alamogordo was always going to be a long shot. But like I said, you've got other options."

Kate tried to muster up a smile, but she couldn't quite get there. "I hear what you're saying, Angela. I'm so tired of this bullshit. I know it wasn't possible, but I wish I'd kept Mandy with me."

She slumped back into the chair next to Tilly.

The drive home was silent. After the meeting with Detective Lopez, Kate had insisted they go straight home, putting off house hunting. When they neared town, Kate sat up straighter.

"Let's take the bypass," Kate said.

"What are we doing?" Tilly asked, though she passed the exit and headed north without pause.

"Do you remember that big house off the highway? Almost in Tularosa? The one Mom used to call a compound"

"I think so," Tilly said. "Why?"

"I ran across the listing when I was looking for realtors. It's for sale."

Tilly laughed. "And what, you're thinking of buying it? That house is huge. Do you remember when it was built? Mom took us to see it. There's even a chapel."

Kate smiled. "I do. I remember thinking how old-fashioned it looked. But it was also lovely. Very New Mexico. Anyway, I'm curious."

The highway north ran parallel to the mountains in the distance. It had been a rainy summer and the creosote bushes were still very green, despite it being almost winter. As they drove, Kate thought about the things she loved about living in southern New Mexico—the smell of rain in the desert, the sunsets, the thunderstorms that created spectacular light shows during the spring and summer, the monsoons. She wondered if she'd ever stopped to consider all the beauty of her native state. And she wondered why now, with all the terrible things happening around her, she chose this moment to appreciate it.

"I think you turn here," Kate said, pointing to a dirt road a few miles outside the city limits. Tilly turned right and the car bumped along, creating a cloud of dust behind them.

"That one," Kate said, indicating a property about a mile off the highway. A tall wooden fence wrapped around the property. The owner had landscaped using rock and desert cactus, some having grown so large their thorny pads stuck up over the wall. The creosotes and mesquite trees that surrounded the property had run wild, giving the compound a foreboding quality.

Tilly pulled over near the front gate and Kate hopped out to grab the one-sheet from the attached container. She got back in the car, and for a few minutes both women studied the information and pictures contained on the sales flyer. The house looked like it belonged in a Santa Fe luxury real estate guide. She admired the Spanish-style red tile roof. The house wasn't something you'd likely see outside the trendier northern part of the state, and yet the desert camouflaged it.

"So are you going to tell me what we're doing here?" Tilly

finally asked, though she seemed as much in awe of the place as Kate.

Kate sighed. "I've been thinking about Mandy—how much I wish I could have kept her safe. Tucked her away somewhere secret. So I started thinking about places in the area that were big enough to house several residents, but out of the way enough to make security doable. Roman said there aren't any local safe houses that would be suitable for girls like Mandy."

Tilly laughed. "And you thought of this house?"

"I remember seeing it in the listings when I was looking at rentals. Obviously I wasn't thinking about it for myself. But the girls..."

"Hold on," Tilly said, her face draining of color. "I see where you're going with this, but those men—they could have killed you. You don't think they're going to let you set up a safe house not ten miles from their home base, do you?"

Kate understood her sister's fear, but she couldn't shake the feeling that what she was thinking was right.

CHAPTER THIRTY-ONE

Two days later, Kate left her father's house for the last time. She and Tilly spent the weekend packing the rest of her things and stuffing a small storage room to nearly overflowing. Tilly griped about Kate's optimistic rental of the smallest storage unit she could get her hands on. Kate vacillated between feeling untethered and anticipation about what would come next in her life.

"I hope I got everything," Kate worried out loud for the thousandth time as she and Tilly walked toward their cars. Kate had rented an Airbnb for the week, needing a place to stay where Rusty would be able to run around. She'd found an interesting property out on the south side of town. The house sat on five acres and was completely fenced in. She'd dropped Rusty off on her last trip and was anxious to get back to him. She wasn't convinced he couldn't jump the fence.

Kate led their two-car caravan out past the golf course and into the rambling desert, where the houses became sparse. It felt good to be out of the middle of town. The home she'd rented was owned by a couple in Texas, and for the first time in a long time Kate felt anonymous and safe. When they arrived Rusty met Kate at the gate, barking happily and jumping around like a maniac. Kate laughed as she got out of the car, opened up the gate and then followed Tilly through, stopping on the other side to close and lock it again.

Parking under the carport, Kate grabbed two suitcases out of the back of her car and made her way inside. Tilly followed a few minutes later with an armload of boxes they'd unearthed in the back of their father's closet. Neither Tilly nor Kate had been up to another trip down memory lane.

"This place is nice," Tilly said taking a look around.

The floor was tile, except in the bedrooms, which were carpeted in commercial- grade neutral tones. Though stucco on the outside, the inside of the house had exposed adobe bricks and wood beams, giving it a rustic, Southwestern feel. It made Kate's thoughts drift to the red-tiled hacienda they'd looked at a few days ago.

"I was going to go for groceries, but I'm too tired," Kate said, plopping onto a sofa in the living area.

"I don't think we can get delivery out here," Tilly said, picking up her phone presumably to scroll through Grubhub or one of those other food delivery apps.

"Why don't we run down to Taco Bell and call it a night."

"Perfect," Tilly said.

Twenty minutes later they were camped out on the sofa again—this time with the television on, munching on tacos. Kate had staked out the master bedroom at the end of the hall. It had its own bathroom with a soaking tub. Kate figured she could use a good soak right about now. As if on cue, her phone rang.

"Hi, Roman," Kate said as she answered.

"Hey, where are you? I stopped by your house tonight and it looks empty. Are you all moved out?"

"Yeah. We have a cleaning company going over tomorrow to deep clean, but we got the last few boxes out this afternoon," she replied. She hadn't actually answered his question about her whereabouts. She felt more secure with no one knowing where she was, at least for one night.

"Listen, Roman. I'm exhausted. I'll call you tomorrow, okay?" She disconnected before he had time to respond, hoping he wouldn't call back.

He didn't.

For two peaceful days, Kate and Tilly hung around the rental house. During the day Kate lounged on the porch, reading while Rusty ran around the yard barking at birds and chasing jackrabbits that wandered in through the fence. At night Kate and Tilly took turns cooking dinner and then settled in for sappy, feel-good movies that reminded them of happier times. Kate started to feel almost normal.

But she knew it wouldn't last.

On Tuesday, Kate went into town to sign the final paperwork in the sale of her father's house. Afterward, she stopped by the post office and then the grocery store. She was about halfway home when she realized someone was following her.

About three car-lengths back, she noticed a dark sedan with tinted windows that had been behind her for some time. Not wanting to overreact Kate decided to take a spin through the nearest neighborhood, hoping her suspicion was wrong. She took three very random turns, but the car stayed with her.

Kate used her phone's voice command feature to dial Roman's cell phone.

"Hey," Roman said when he answered. He sounded grumpy.

"Sorry to bother you," Kate said, feeling awkward. "I think someone's following me."

"What?"

"I stopped by the grocery store and was heading home. There's a dark car following me. The windows are tinted. I can't see who's driving. And they're not following close enough for me to get their plates."

"Where are you?"

"I'm turning back onto First Street."

"Okay. Take White Sands to 10th and then head to the library parking lot. I'm going to try to spot whoever it is. I'll meet you there. Don't get out of your car until you see me."

Kate hung up and turned onto White Sands Boulevard, hoping her movements seemed casual, as if she'd forgotten something and was swinging back into town to correct the error. By the time she reached the library parking lot the car was gone. A few minutes later, Roman pulled in beside her.

"Did you see it?" Kate asked, as she stepped out of her car.

"I was hanging out in the Albertson's parking lot. No one went by after you turned. They must have dropped out a few blocks back."

Kate's heart was thumping hard. "They must have realized I saw them. I was already on my way out of town when I doubled back. I wondered if they'd notice."

"You gonna let me in on where you're staying?" Roman asked.

"South of town. I found a short-term rental on some acreage. Figured it would be a good out-of-the-way place to stay while I'm figuring out what to do next."

"Is Tilly with you?"

"Yeah. She hasn't mentioned going home yet. Not sure how long she's planning on staying."

Roman looked concerned. "I thought you were looking at places in Las Cruces."

"Trying to get rid of me?" Kate hadn't meant her words to sound bitter, but they did, and she wasn't the least bit surprised to see Roman's face twist in anger.

"I'm not the one who leaves town."

Kate threw her hands up in the air. "God, Roman! Are you ever going to stop punishing me for wanting to make something of my life?" As soon as the words escaped Kate wished she could yank them back, take a deep breath, and keep her mouth shut instead. The look of pain on Roman's face was unbearable. "Roman, I..." But he'd already gotten in his car, slamming the door to shut her out.

———

Angela had reserved a small conference room at headquarters, and when Kate arrived Roman was pacing. Angela was sitting at the table, drumming her fingers across the veneer surface in quick bursts. Her face was grim.

When Kate closed the door behind her, Angela said, "Another girl has gone missing."

Kate shivered. "Who?"

"Rachel Telles. She's a sophomore," Roman replied. The lines on his forehead looked like they'd taken up permanent residence.

"I don't think I know her," Kate said.

"No reason that you would. According to her mother, Rachel is a very shy girl. Not a lot of friends. Keeps to herself."

"Sounds like the profile of a perfect victim," Kate said. "When did her mother report her missing?"

"This morning. Last seen yesterday before school. She never came home. Mom filed the report at 24 hours on the nose."

"No chance she ran away?" Angela asked.

"According to her mother, not a chance." Roman finally stopped pacing and slumped down into a nearby chair.

"Who's in charge?" Angela asked.

"Not me," Roman sighed. "The chief pulled me off the case, and there seems to be a gag order going around the department. I was told to stay away if I wanted to keep my job."

"So what can we do?" Kate directed her question to Angela. An idea was formulating in her mind, but she was sure it would be shot down immediately. When Angela hesitated, Kate decided to go for it. "Did Roman tell you about the person following me?"

"No," Angela said, glaring at Roman. "When was this?"

"A few days ago, " Kate said. "I managed to shake them by driving back into town, but Roman wasn't able to see who it was. Anyway, I've moved out of my father's house and into a rental out in the boonies. They'll eventually figure out where I am, but it's been nice to have a couple of minutes of peace."

Kate felt herself rambling. She was still working up the courage to say what she wanted to say.

"Anyway," she continued, "it occurs to me that the best way to catch these guys might be to a set a trap."

Roman looked alarmed. "What? And you're going to the bait? Jesus, Kate. This isn't an episode of *Scooby-Doo*. Those guys could have killed you."

"Yes, they could have. And they still could, Roman. If I stay in town, they're going to find me. If I leave town they'll leave me alone, but I can't give up on these girls. And I don't want to let them drive me away." Kate tried to keep her voice level, but the edges were tinged with hysteria. She couldn't believe what she was saying, but she also knew it was the right thing to do.

"What do you propose?" Angela asked.

"I can't believe you're entertaining this." Roman had risen again, and his face had gone from red to an ugly purplish color.

Ignoring his outburst, Kate said, "The house we're renting is on five acres. Plenty of room to set up surveillance at the very least. Maybe we can catch Benny Parks or one of his goons trespassing."

"Trespassing won't be good enough. We have to aim for a felony. Breaking and entering, maybe," Angela brainstormed.

"Why don't you just let murder her?" Roman shouted. He was glaring at Angela. She walked over to him and placed a hand on his arm. The gesture stopped his tirade, but it also sent a jolt of molten jealousy through Kate. She had to turn away. She fished through her purse, pretending to look for something.

"I don't want Kate to get hurt either, Roman," she said, with a tenderness that made Kate's stomach roil. While she was glad to be valued by this woman, she also wanted to scratch her eyes out. The turmoil was overwhelming.

"I'm not suggesting that we let the bastards get inside my house, Roman," Kate said, trying to regain her composure. She shifted her attention to Angela. "The house has an active security alarm and a locking front gate. I have Rusty with me. He barks like a maniac when someone approaches the house, including me."

"Can we go out to your house today and look around?" Angela asked.

"Absolutely."

"I'll ditch my car at Roman's and then we can follow you over," Angela said, looking at Roman for agreement to this new plan.

"Ride with Kate," Roman said. "I'll drive you home later."

Trying to push aside the jealousy gnawing at her gut, Kate led Angela out to her car and they headed back to Alamogordo with Roman trailing close behind.

CHAPTER THIRTY-TWO

When they arrived at Kate's rental house, Rusty came rushing to the gate to meet them. Tilly waved from the back patio. She got up and walked around to the carport, where Roman pulled in behind Tilly's car.

"Hello, Angela," Tilly said, extending a hand. She was wearing a flowing peasant skirt with a University of New Mexico sweatshirt. Somehow, she made the look passable. Kate smiled at her sister. Tilly gave a quizzical look in return.

Over iced tea, they debated the pros and cons of Kate's half-cocked plan.

"I guess the big question I have is how to keep us safe. How can you guarantee that these people won't get past whatever surveillance you're setting up? And what should we do if that happens?" Tilly asked without a hint of emotion. She was strategizing, and enjoying it by all accounts.

"I'll have to take a look around the property, but I assure you I won't move forward on any plan unless I can guarantee your safety."

Roman huffed. "How can you make promises like that, Angela? You and I both know how many things can go wrong.

This property is pretty big, and the fence has gaps. If you station enough patrol officers to ensure there's no breach, you'll give yourselves away. And then what? If they know Kate's gotten the state police involved we lose any advantage we might have."

"Your confidence is overwhelming," Angela said, but she was teasing, trying to ease Roman's mind. He wasn't taking the bait.

"I'm serious. What good is this supposed to do? You make an arrest. Great. But you can't watch Kate's house forever. If we're on the right track this network goes way beyond Benny Parks, and we don't have enough information to make a move yet."

"And how are we supposed to get that information, Roman?" Kate asked. She tried to keep her voice even, but she was getting agitated with all the arguing. "You've been shut out of the case, likely because someone in your department is involved. I was attacked in my own home, and I have no doubt they'll come at me again if I stay here. So, then what? Either I let these assholes run me out of town or I stand up and fight."

"This isn't a game, Kate." Roman turned to Tilly, pleading. "Come on, Tilly. Help me out here."

Tilly took a moment before answering. "Sorry, Roman. Kate's right. I lost my family because of these people. No one is more concerned about Kate's safety than I am, but she can't live her life in fear. And since she can't seem to pry herself away from this damned town—" She gave Roman a meaningful look that made both him and Kate turn red. "Someone has to stop this."

Roman's expression was unreadable. He looked from Tilly to Kate, holding her gaze long enough to make her stomach turn. Then he said, "Fine. I'll check in later," turning and walking out the door.

The women stood in silence listening as Roman's tires crunched in the gravel. The clank of the gate closing made Kate's heart jump, and she could feel tears welling in her eyes.

When the world became still again, Angela was the first to break the silence. "Don't worry, Kate. He'll come around."

Kate nodded. "I can give you a ride home."

"II'll check in to a hotel tonight. I'd still like to spend some time walking the property, and it's getting too dark out there. I'm not on duty tomorrow. Can you give me a lift to whatever's closest?"

"Why don't you stay here?" Tilly offered. Kate wasn't sure how she felt about it, but when Angela turned Kate nodded and smiled.

"We've got plenty of room. This house is huge."

Kate showed Angela to one of the guest rooms. Tilly made dinner, which they shared over small talk. No one mentioned Roman or Benny Parks, or anything to do with the case. It felt like the whole house was holding its breath.

The next morning, Kate was up bright and early. She took Rusty out and did a little stretching as the sun came up over the mountains, bathing the landscape in warm orange light. Tilly was a late sleeper, and Kate was used to spending the early morning hours in solitude, so she wasn't prepared to find someone at her kitchen table.

"Coffee?" Angela said, scooting the pot and an empty mug toward Kate.

"Please," Kate said, sitting across the table. Rusty curled up by the window, basking in the morning sunlight pouring in through the window.

"Tilly remembers you from high school," Kate said when the silence became unbearable. "I didn't realize you were a local girl."

Angela smiled. "Born and raised right here in lovely

Alamogordo. I was a sophomore the year you and Roman graduated. I couldn't wait to get out of here."

"I know the feeling," Kate said, studying Angela's expression. "You and Roman were at the police academy together?"

And there it was, a flicker of something in Angela's eyes. A momentary upturn of her lips. She'd been looking out the window but she turned her attention back to Kate, her expression neutral.

"Yeah," Angela replied. "We were in the same class at the academy. I'd been dreaming about becoming a cop since I was a little girl. Lots of police officers in my family. Roman was a harder sell."

"I don't remember him ever talking about law enforcement as a career," Kate said.

"Do you remember the girl who was killed in high school? Roman told me that he was walking in the creek and saw her car there, before the police found it. He says it was the thing that made him consider becoming a cop."

"I remember," Kate said. Her mind drifted back to that day. What would have happened if she'd let Roman tell her what he wanted to tell her that day? How would their lives be different now?

"That girl, Laura Fuentes? I pulled her student file before I was suspended. I wanted to look for any similarities between the girls we know have been victimized," Kate said.

"You think the cases are connected?"

"It could be a coincidence. But I've read enough crime novels to know better."

"You're right. The fact that Laura Fuentes and Gabby Greene were both dumped in the creek does link them, though you know we get a lot of weird things happening in the creek. They're not the only people we've ever found there."

"I know," Kate said. "And as I thought about the girls there didn't seem to be much in common, at least not on the face of it.

That may be why whoever is victimizing these girls has been able to go undetected for so long. The only real similarity I could see had to do with access."

"Go on." Kate had the detective's full attention now.

"I don't remember much about Laura, but she's described as quiet. A good student, hard-working. With the exception of Mandy, the girls all had jobs or after-school activities that kept them out of the house a lot. Not saying that Mandy didn't have those, too, but her life was more insulated. Her main contacts were through school. The other girls had a lot of contact with the businesses in town."

"How did Mandy end up in the mix?"

"Her mother is dating Benny Parks," Kate replied.

"He's the guy who attacked you?"

"And Mandy. When she showed up at my office after running away, she'd been beaten so badly she could hardly open her eyes. The SANE nurse documented all her injuries." Kate thought about Mandy. Would she ever be the same girl she was before?

"So Parks had instant access to a teenage girl..." Angela started, but Kate interrupted her.

"Two. That's the reason Mandy came back. She has a sister. About two years younger. Mandy was convinced that her sister is in danger and I don't doubt it."

Angela sighed. "CYFD has an open case now for Mandy's family, but so far they've seen nothing to indicate any problems. That's usually the way it goes. Everyone is on their best behavior when they're being watched."

"I know," Kate said. "And I don't expect Mandy's mother to be much help. I don't know what's wrong with her, but she seems pretty detached from the welfare of her children. I couldn't even get her to return my calls or fill out the intake paperwork for Mandy at school."

"She had some choice words about you," Angela said with a small chuckle.

Kate smiled. "I bet she did."

"Well that's good information, but we need to get to the task at hand. I have an idea or two about how we catch the person who's been following you. With any luck, it'll be Benny Parks."

CHAPTER THIRTY-THREE

Angela's plan turned out to be pretty conservative which Kate appreciated, given that it was her neck on the line. Kate drove the detective back to Las Cruces, and later that evening Angela was back with an overnight bag. Kate would be making a trip into town the following day, hoping to pick up her tail. The detective would be staking out the road leading to Kate's house to get a positive ID on the lurker.

The plan involved giving away her location, which made Kate a little bit queasy, but she knew it was necessary. Besides, she'd only be there for a little while longer.

The more time Kate spent with Angela, the more she liked her.

After breakfast the following morning, they went over the plan one last time.

"I'm going to stop by the grocery store, the bank, and then head over to the realtor's office. I have an appointment at ten, so I should be out of there around 10:30. I'll text you when I start heading home, but I'll drop by the post office first. That should make me plenty visible around town. If someone's trying to find me, it shouldn't be hard," Kate said.

"I'm going to park up at the intersection of Yucca Drive. When you drive by, I'll head back toward town. I'm looking for a dark sedan, but I'm going to take down plates on anyone I see on your road. There are only two houses out here, so there shouldn't be much traffic." Angela turned to Tilly. "I'd like you to have Rusty outside once Kate heads home. He'll notice if someone tries to approach the house from somewhere other than the front gate."

"I thought I'd set up lunch on the patio. When Kate gets home we'll hang out there, keeping our eyes open."

"We may have to try this a few times. There's no guarantee that whoever was following you the other day is going to try the same thing again today. Especially if they think you saw them. And they may not be looking for you if they think they scared you off. So don't get discouraged if it doesn't happen today."

Kate smiled. "I'm not worried."

And she wasn't. Her mind was buzzing with a new plan. With the sale of her father's house and the considerable amount she'd put in savings, Kate could afford to buy a house instead of renting one. Her trip to the realtor was pure reconnaissance. She felt excited and full of purpose despite the circumstances.

Kate polished off her second cup of coffee, gathered her things, and headed out. Her first few errands required little thought, so she used the time to consider whether her safe house idea was as crazy as it sounded. And whether that would deter her from doing it anyway.

She arrived at the realtor's office ahead of schedule.

"Oh hi, Ms. Medina. I'll be right with you," the realtor said from her desk in the corner.

"Take your time, Janet. I'm early." Kate walked over to the far wall where all the agency's current listings were represented with glossy sales sheets. The properties were sorted, though it was hard to tell the scheme at first glance. Kate spotted the hacienda flyer and grabbed a copy.

"That's one of my favorites," Janet said, approaching.

"I remember when it was built," Kate said, following Janet back to her desk. "I was surprised to see the price so reasonable."

"It's been on the market a long time. The price is pretty high for most folks in this area, and it's very out of the way. With so much new construction, it's hard to talk buyers into spending the money on such an old house when they could get a new one for the same price."

"Makes sense," Kate said.

"I admit, when you called to say you were thinking of buying, this wasn't the type of house I was envisioning." Janet paused. "I'm assuming you're interested in taking a look?"

"I am," Kate replied.

"It's a lot of upkeep for one person. The inside will need to be sealed. The previous owner left the adobe exposed, which causes a lot of dust."

"When can I see it?"

After leaving the realtor's office, Kate headed to the post office. When she parked, she sent a quick text to Angela. The same dark sedan pulled into the parking lot behind her, settling into a spot a few cars down from her. She was amazed at how relentless these people were, and how brazen. She'd expected her tail to at least be in a different vehicle.

She drove home as casually as she could, trying to keep her adrenaline from finding its way to the gas pedal. She turned onto the road leading to her house and made it almost all the way to the driveway, when she saw a dark car turning down the road in the distance. Rusty met her at the gate, and Kate made sure the lock was engaged before parking.

She unloaded the groceries and headed out to the patio,

where Tilly was lounging with a full picnic spread out on the table.

"Expecting company?" Kate teased.

"I figured Angela would want to eat once she got here. I don't think she had much at breakfast. And I suspect we'll have another visitor shortly."

"Oh?" Kate said, grabbing a few carrot sticks to munch on.

"Roman called."

Kate frowned. "He called you?"

"He did," Tilly replied, giving Kate a funny look. "He was feeling a bit guilty for abandoning ship the other night, especially given that he was Angela's ride home. I got the feeling she gave him a good talking to."

Kate laughed, but her lungs felt tight.

"He's going to drop by in about an hour. Angela should be back by then." Tilly had laid out sandwich fixings, and was piling ingredients high on a slice of multi-grain bread.

"That looks like the Leaning Tower of Pisa," Kate said, chuckling as Tilly put another piece of bread on top and then leaned on the tower with her whole weight, compressing it into a still-too-big-for-her-mouth but at least more manageable size.

The sun was shining bright and the yard was heating up. Rusty had found a shady spot under a window ledge to nap in. The day was so pleasant, it was easy to forget why they were eating on the patio in the first place.

"What happened after I locked the gate? I assume you were watching," Kate asked.

"I was trying to look disinterested, but a few minutes after you pulled in, a dark car drove by and headed up the road."

"Doesn't that road dead-end?" They hadn't explored the area much since arriving. The web of dirt roads often led to dead-ends where development had stalled. When Kate and Tilly were little, the area was undeveloped desert. Now, little by little, houses were popping up, camouflaged by the desert flora.

"It must not," Tilly replied. "The car hasn't been back by."

Kate's phone started buzzing on the table nearby.

"Steph?" Kate hadn't heard a word from the school since she was sent home. In all the drama that followed, she'd hardly noticed. "How are you?"

Steph's voice was strange, like she was holding her hand to her mouth to block the sound. "I don't have much time to talk, but I wanted to give you a heads up."

Kate flinched. "Let me guess, they're firing me."

"Unfortunately, yes. Pete will be calling you with the official news in a few hours. But that's not all. The school board is pushing for a formal inquiry into a complaint they received. They're accusing you of improper contact with a minor."

Kate felt like she'd been punched in the stomach. "*What?*"

"Pete asked me to call you. He said if you get a letter of resignation in before he makes the official call, it'll stop the process."

"So, I'm not fired. I quit," Kate said blandly.

"I'm sorry," Steph whispered. "I have to go."

Kate put her phone back down on the table. Tilly didn't ask. Kate supposed she didn't need to. It has been pretty clear that Kate's job at the school was over. She grabbed her laptop and typed the most brief, wooden resignation letter in the history of such letters. She attached it to an email to Pete, cc'ing Steph, pressed send, and just like that her prospects for employment were wide open.

She wished it didn't feel like another blow.

Kate was feeling pretty low when Angela arrived. Roman was right behind her, causing an involuntary twitch.

"How'd it go?" Kate asked Angela without greeting Roman.

Tilly offered them both drinks, and the detectives dug into the food Tilly had laid out.

Between bites, Angela said, "I called in the license plate number." She picked up her phone and typed in the passcode while shoving another chip into her mouth. "2017 Buick Regal. Graphite Gray. Registered to David Jennings of Cottonwood Drive, here in Alamogordo."

"Hmm. Never heard of him," Roman said. He was speaking to Angela, but his attention was on Kate. When their eyes met she looked away, feeling her cheeks flush.

"I drove by his house. It's a nice one. Not too far from here actually. Golf course property."

"Wait," Kate said. "He lives near here? Does that mean he already knew where I was staying?"

"It's possible, but why go to all the lengths of following you if he already knew where you were? That being said, his proximity makes me nervous."

"Me, too," Roman said. "Were you able to get a background on him?"

"Not yet," Angela said. "Working on it. In the meantime, "We'll want to install the cameras and security features we discussed yesterday, Kate. We'll get a patrol set up, but I want to make sure we've got eyes everywhere."

"We'll keep the alarm armed at night," Tilly said.

"Keep it armed all the time," Roman said. "If you're home and you're hanging out inside the house, arm it. And definitely when you leave the house. Even if Rusty's home."

Kate shivered. "Considering what happened to Rusty last time I'm all for leaving him inside when we go out, Til. Don't you think?"

"I do," Tilly said.

The group finished eating and Angela volunteered to help Tilly clean up, leaving Roman and Kate alone to talk.

"I'm sorry for overreacting the other night," Roman said. He sounded weary.

"I'm not mad," Kate said. "I mean, I was for a few seconds. I don't know. Every time you go all bossy and protective, it puts me on the defensive. Then again, one concussion later, I'm very aware that these creeps mean business. I understand why you're worried."

Roman looked like he wanted to say something, but he kept his lips shut. Kate decided to change the subject and let him off the hook.

"I got a call from the school today. I was expecting to be let go. Turns out, someone was pushing for an investigation into my professional conduct. So I resigned. As of this afternoon, I'm unemployed." Kate sighed. "The good news is that every single thing these people do to try to drive me out of town firms my resolve to stay."

"I put in an application this morning with the state police," Roman said, sounding deflated. "The chief has managed to completely undermine my authority in the department. Even if I'm not working on this particular case anymore, it's getting harder to do any part of my job."

"I'm sorry, Roman. I wish knowing me wasn't messing with your career."

"You don't have to apologize, Kate. If you hadn't been working at the school when Gabby Greene disappeared, who knows if we ever would have learned about the other shit going on in town. It might have continued unnoticed for God knows how long. Now, at least, we have a chance to help these girls."

Kate turned her head to hide her blush. "I've got to run out to Home Depot to pick up the home security stuff Angela mentioned. We worked on a plan last night and I called the store to check stock. It should be a quick trip, and then I'll be in for the night."

Kate stood up and Roman followed her into the house. Angela and Tilly were standing in the kitchen, talking.

"I'm going back to my office," Angela said, picking up her bag as she headed for the door. "Remember to lock up, and I'll have my tech guy out here tomorrow morning to get everything set up."

Before she walked out the door, she turned. "Keep your cell phone charged and with you at all times. If you see or hear anything suspicious, call me immediately."

CHAPTER THIRTY-FOUR

Rusty barked at everything that moved all night long. When Kate stumbled out of bed much easier than usual, she found a red-eyed Tilly working on her cup of coffee.

"How long have you been up?" Kate asked, pouring herself a cup.

"I don't think I slept at all," Tilly rasped.

"Go back to bed," Kate said, her voice thick with sleep. She wished she could take her own advice. "The tech guy's going to be here in about twenty minutes and then I have an appointment." Kate sighed and rested her head on the table.

"Do you want me to come with you?"

"You can if you'd like to. I'm going to look at a house."

Tilly's eyes perked up. "Where?"

"The red-tiled fortress we looked at the other day."

Tilly laughed. "You're going to buy a seven-bedroom house in the middle of nowhere?" Then she frowned. "Wait, you're still thinking about a safe house, aren't you?"

"I am," Kate said, holding her head high to fortify her new confidence. "I'm at loose ends now. A crossroads. Yes, I can come to Colorado and find a job. And I'm not ruling it out. But when I think of creating a safe place for these girls to go, one where I can use my skills to help them make their way through the trauma they've experienced... It feels right. Like a calling, you know?"

Tilly nodded. "I do. But I can also tell you from personal experience that healing others when you're not fully recovered yourself is a hard path. My first two years working with victims were a nightmare. It was like reliving my own rapes over and over again."

"I get what you're saying," Kate argued. "But I'm here now while these horrendous crimes are taking place, and I can't let that go. I would feel like I'm abandoning these girls. I don't know if I could live with myself."

"I'll come with you," Tilly said, sighing. "I'm curious to see what the fortress looks like on the inside."

Rusty started barking at the door. Other than the fact that the tech guy turned out to be a girl named Jamie, the whole process was seamless. Kate and Tilly had unpacked all the parts, so installation went quickly. A little over an hour later, Jamie was explaining how to pull up the cameras on the computer and how to make sure everything was set to record.

"I've pointed the cameras toward the doors and the back wall of the house, so we shouldn't get a whole lot of animal interference."

"Animal?" Kate asked.

"Sometimes birds or bugs trigger the camera, so don't be alarmed if the screen comes on at odd times. But do check when it does. Anything that triggers the camera should also trigger the motion-sensor lights, so if someone tries to approach the house they'll get lit up for the camera."

Jamie packed up her gear and handed Kate the tablet she'd programmed.

"You can also control the system from the tablet. Keep this with you while you're in the house, especially at night. That way if something happens, you'll be able to react quickly. There's a panic button here that will alert local law enforcement. In this case, I've set it up to call our dispatch. We'll have people in the area who can respond."

"Thank you," Kate said, though she was beginning to feel uneasy. The situation was becoming more real. Someone might come for her, and she hoped all the preparations they'd made would keep her safe.

That afternoon, Kate and Tilly met the realtor at the hacienda. The drive over had been tense, with each woman quizzing the other about locking doors and arming alarms. They'd spent the last few minutes in silence.

When Kate parked and stepped out of the car her worries were pushed aside temporarily. She was determined to scrutinize the house objectively to determine if it would work for her proposed safe house, but being on the grounds gave her an immense feeling of joy. The house looked like a fortress situated in the middle of a five-acre plot. As skeptical as Tilly had been about Kate's half-baked safe house plan, she seemed just as impressed by the property. Both sisters stood at the gate, staring in wonder.

Janet jingled her keys. "Let's go take a look, shall we?" She unlocked the padlock on the gate, unwinding a length of thick chain. Kate could see that the hinges were rusted, and the gate creaked loudly when Janet pushed it open.

Stepping into the courtyard felt like visiting an ancient city. The thick adobe walls that surrounded the house gave an immediate sense of separateness from the desert outside. Unlike other adobe walls that featured decorative cutouts with wrought iron bars, this wall had no openings, like the builder wanted to keep the people inside safe from barbarian invaders.

It was perfect.

"How long has it been on the market?" Kate asked, noting the overgrown weeds and general disrepair of the courtyard.

"Almost five years," Janet replied. "Notice the padlock instead of a lockbox? We've only shown the house a few times. Every once in a while we get a couple—usually new transfers from out of state—looking for something 'southwestern'. But between the obvious repairs needed and the distance from the Air Force base, they always end up going with a new build on the south side of town."

Janet led them through the front doors of the residence, two enormous slabs of knotted pine that looked hand-carved. The house itself was two stories and shaped like a C. The front door led to a comfortable living area, with skylights brightening what would have otherwise been a dark room. The downstairs held the kitchen, two bathrooms, and the chapel. The master bedroom took up one whole wing of the bottom floor.

The six remaining bedrooms and three shared bathrooms were upstairs. The rooms were modest in size, but cozy and airy, each opening to a covered balcony the stretched along the inside of the property and the courtyard below. The interior hallway was lined with small windows that overlooked the desert outside. These windows were screened to keep insects outside, but they were also barred with wrought iron— presumably to keep them from being used for entry or exit. Kate wondered which.

Janet stayed downstairs in the living area while Kate and Tilly explored the property.

"What do you think?" Kate asked. They were standing on the balcony. A breeze rustled the leaves of the creosote bushes outside, but otherwise the desert was quiet.

"It needs a lot of work," Tilly said with a sigh. "But it's gorgeous. It's so peaceful here. I would never have imagined feeling this relaxed anywhere near here." She turned and looked at Kate, her expression serious. "I can almost see your vision, Kate, but I'm scared. You won't be anonymous here. They'll know where you are. How can you stay safe and keep anyone else safe?"

Kate inhaled the scent of rain in the air. "I promised myself I would be realistic, but it's hard to think of the cons when we're standing here. Let's go back to the house and talk about it." As they turned to leave, Kate imagined herself stretched out on a lounge chair, watching lightning fly across the sky from the safety of the courtyard. What would she do to make this dream a reality?

"We've been all through that," Kate said, feeling the weariness of a long afternoon spent arguing with Tilly over the merits of the safe house plan. She'd kept her temper in check, knowing she'd be rehashing this entire argument with Roman if she decided to go forward.

"I know," Tilly replied, sounding tired. "Okay, let's put aside all the obvious dangers. The house needs a lot of work. You're going to eat up a lot of your savings trying to make it inhabitable. And you'll need a good security system. That's a lot of ground to monitor."

"I could look into hiring a night guard."

"Hire? With what money? You make it sound like you're starting a business here."

"Maybe that's what I have to do," Kate replied, earning an exasperated gasp from Tilly. "No, hear me out. Most victim service programs rely on grants and government funding, right?"

"Right," Tilly said. "But those funds aren't easy to get and they don't amount to much in the long run."

Rusty, who'd been sleeping near Kate's feet on the couch,

suddenly leapt off the couch and ran down the hall, barking like a maniac. Kate, who thought he'd been sleeping, jumped, knocking her head against the back of the couch. "Ow," she said, gingerly rubbing the sore spot on her skull.

Before she could call for Rusty, the screen on the security tablet came on.

Tilly reached for the tablet. The camera on the back of the house had been activated, and the motion-sensor light illuminated a dark figure standing behind the back gate. It wore a hoodie and a ski mask, both of which were plainly visible as the figure stared up into the light, as if mugging for the camera.

"That's eerie," Tilly said. "The way he's standing there like he wants us to see him."

"He does," Kate said, her voice shaking. Both sisters sat paralyzed, staring at the screen, until the figure reached into his pocket. A bright flare flashed on the screen, like a light being shined into the camera. It wasn't until Kate heard the glass break that she knew.

"Oh no. Push the panic button!" Kate screamed as she sprinted down the hallway. Rusty was running around frantically barking at a flaming object lying on the floor. The fire crept toward the bedspread. Kate raced back to the kitchen and grabbed the fire extinguisher. Back in the bedroom, she held tight, spraying flame retardant until the lump was a smoldering pile of unrecognizable black and foam.

"Kate! What is it?" Tilly yelled, her voice coming down the hall. Kate could hear sirens in the distance.

Kate coughed from the pungent smell emanating from the recently burning mass. Rusty had stopped barking but he crouched near the lump, growling low in this throat, ready to attack if need be.

"What is that?" Tilly asked, approaching Kate's position near the fireplace in the master bedroom.

"I don't know," Kate said, inching closer. Tilly put a hand on her arm, pulling her back.

"The police will be here in a minute." Kate was surprised to hear Tilly so rattled when her own anxiety levels were in check for a change. She was scared, but she wasn't spiraling out of control.

It was a start.

CHAPTER THIRTY-FIVE

The person who'd thrown the flaming mass through her window was the same person Kate had seen outside the police station and the school, Kate was sure of it. An officer from the state police was sitting in the living room, studying the security camera footage, having already sent copies to their specialist.

The mask, the hoodie, and the quality of the video footage made it impossible to tell who the figure might be. Visions of Benny Parks's lackey Rick flashed through her mind as she told the story once again.

Roman stood in the corner listening, his expression fierce. Kate hadn't told him about her stalker, and he was furious with her, as usual. Unfortunately there were a lot of things she'd hadn't told him, so she imagined he'd stay mad at her for a while. She hoped he'd come around.

Tilly had gotten a phone call and retired to her room. Kate could hear the ebb and flow of conversation through her bedroom door. She wondered who Tilly talked to. There'd been quite a few nights when Tilly excused herself to take a call and then stayed in her room for the rest of the night.

"Ms. Medina?" Kate realized she'd been lost in her own thoughts and had stopped paying attention to the officer taking her report. She was exhausted and wanted to go to bed.

"Sorry," Kate muttered.

"That's okay. I've got everything I need. We patched up the window and picked up the debris. It looks like a rock with some fabric wrapped around it. Must've soaked it in gasoline, which was actually a good thing because it kept the damage continued to a small area. That, and your quick work with the fire extinguisher."

"Did you find anything outside?"

"No, ma'am," the officer said, making Kate feel old. "Two of our duty officers will walk the perimeter of the property tonight to keep an eye on things. Detective Lopez mentioned that you're renting this house. I'll get a copy of the report to you for the homeowners insurance."

"Thank you. We'll be checking into a hotel tomorrow. I hate to think of the damage these guys might do if we stay here and I don't want to cause the owner any more trouble."

The officer left. Kate watched him lock the gate on his way out, and she could see the flashlight beams of the officers patrolling her house. She turned to Roman.

"I'm staying," he said. For a split second, Kate was tempted to argue, but she was glad Roman would be there.

"I'm going to go clean up the mess in the master bedroom," she said. Roman nodded, then went back to brooding in the corner.

Kate went into the bedroom to assess the damage. The floor was singed and dirty where the rock had landed, and a path of scorched carpet had made it almost to the bed. The floor was wet from the fire extinguisher. Kate went to the kitchen and found some carpet cleaner. She sprayed around the damaged areas and then went searching for a vacuum cleaner. She found a small steam cleaner and decided she might as well get things as clean as she could. She was too shaken to sleep, and wasn't about to spend the night in this room anyway.

She filled the tank and plugged the machine in, getting on her hands and knees to start scrubbing the carpet. Before long, her arms and back were aching. The physical exertion pushed her over the edge. She turned off the cleaner and curled up into a tight ball, her body wracked with sobs.

Her mind was swimming with so many conflicted thoughts and feelings. The usual panic was there, threatening to take control, but somehow she managed to keep it at bay. That didn't stop the self-doubt and fear from taking her breath away. It seemed crazy now to think that she could stay here. To buy the red-tiled house and build a safe haven for the battered girls in this town. She couldn't even make it through a night without someone trying to beat her down, and as much as she hated to admit it their methods were effective.

"Kate?"

Tilly was standing in the doorway, her eyes red and swollen from crying. She padded across the room and knelt next to Kate, taking her in her arms. Together they cried.

When Tilly and Kate finally emerged, Roman had made tea and was setting steaming mugs down on the coffee table.

"Thank you," Kate said, sitting down. She'd gathered the thickest blanket she could find around her and huddled inside, pulling her legs up to her chest. Roman remained quiet. Tilly snuggled in next to her, leaving an armchair open for Roman.

"I'm going to camp out on the couch in the other room," he said. When no one protested, he excused himself to the den and turned out the lights.

"I wonder what's going on in his head," Tilly said.

"I don't know. He hasn't said a word to me since he got here," Kate replied, not wanting to get into the reason Roman wasn't speaking.

Tilly looked miserable. She took a deep breath, held it for a few seconds then exhaled loudly, like she was working up the nerve to continue. "There's so much drama right now. It's exhausting."

When she didn't continue Kate asked, "Are you going to tell me who was on the phone?"

Tilly smiled. "I wasn't going to, but I guess I will. I keep thinking the whole thing will go away if I ignore it. But we both know how well that works." She gave Kate a sidelong glance. "Jim, he's my boyfriend. Well, my ex-boyfriend now, I suppose."

"Sounds complicated," Kate said.

"It's not. I met Jim a few years ago. He works for the district attorney's office. I knew he liked me but I don't do relationships, so I started making the case for us not dating by being the biggest bitch possible."

Kate laughed, and got a smile in return.

"He's persistent, I'll give you that. When I finally figured out he wasn't going to give up, I decided I'd go one better and date him. That'd teach him." Tilly's self-deprecation made Kate a little bit sad. She and her sister were more alike than she'd ever imagined. "So we dated, and I started letting my guard down. He's a genuine and kind person. Next thing I know, I'm in love."

Tilly started fidgeting with the edge of the couch cushion. "I thought if I was 100% clear with him about what I wanted and what I didn't want, things would be okay. Like I didn't want to get married. Neither did he. Great, right? We were both so involved in our careers, and the time we spent together was wonderful. He asked me to move in, and like an idiot I did."

"That's not a terrible thing."

Tilly laughed miserably. "Not for normal people, no. But

when we moved in together, we started talking more about our lives. He started asking me about my family. And when I didn't want to go there he was hurt. He felt like I didn't want him to know me. Which was true, I guess."

"So you broke up with him?"

"No. I left him and came here. It was an act of desperation."

"Because he wanted to know about your family?"

"No," Tilly said, her eyes filling with tears. "Because, as it turns out, he wants to have a family of his own. We agreed that marriage wasn't a priority, but we'd never talked about children. He wants them."

"And you don't?"

A tear slipped down Tilly's cheek. "I can't. One of the side effects of an untreated STD—one that I picked up from one of those disgusting men. By the time I'd made it out of Alamogordo, the damage was done."

Kate felt the tears sliding down her cheeks before she realized she was crying. "Oh, Tilly."

"Don't," Tilly said, though her words weren't angry. "Please don't pity me, Kate. That's one of the reasons I never wanted to talk about it. And why the topic never seemed to come up with Jim."

"I know exactly what you mean," Kate said between sobs. When she'd calmed down, she asked, "Why does he keep calling you then?"

Tilly sighed. "I still haven't told him. I just left. He wants me to come home."

Tilly eventually went to bed, but Kate couldn't convince herself to leave the couch so she lay down and slept where she was. When the first light started streaming through the kitchen windows, Kate was awake. She knew she wouldn't get another good night's sleep until they were somewhere else.

Kate stared at the ceiling, replaying her conversation with Tilly. After Tilly had finished her story, Kate decided it was time to tell hers. She went through all the horrifying details of her attack, without a trace of anxiety this time. Each time she told her story, it got easier. She was able to see the incident for what it was and separate herself from the guilt and shame.

In the morning, Kate was resolved on at least one thing—the victimizing of girls in Alamogordo was going to stop and she was going to be involved in stopping it, even if it meant putting herself in danger.

Kate startled when Roman came walking out of the kitchen behind her, brandishing two cups of coffee and a plate of toast.

"Thought you might need some sustenance. I heard you tossing and turning in here last night. Did you sleep at all?"

Kate sat up, keeping the blanket twisted around her body. "A little," she said, her stomach rumbling traitorously at the smell of the buttered toast. She picked up the coffee and took a sip. "Thank you for staying."

Roman furrowed his brow. "I know you told the cop last night that you were checking into a hotel today, but I thought it might be better if you guys come back to my place."

"So you can keep an eye on us?" Kate said, thankful that he was talking to her again. His frown softened, but he didn't look at Kate.

"Yes. And Rusty will have a yard. There aren't a lot of pet-friendly hotels in town."

"You won't mind having us there?" she asked. "I was going to ask if Rusty could stay with you for a few days, but I don't want to be in the way."

Roman finally turned to her. His eyes looked tired. Had he slept?

"I don't know how many times I have to say this to you,

Kate. but let me be clear. You matter to me." His gaze was fierce, intense. Kate held it as long as she could. When she looked away, she realized she'd been holding her breath.

"I'm off today," Roman said. "I'm going to go check in with the officers patrolling the house. If you and Tilly want to stay with me, come by when you're ready. You still have a key." He didn't wait for her response.

CHAPTER THIRTY-SIX

By the time Tilly got out of bed, Kate had called and made an offer on the hacienda.

"I guess that's that," Tilly said, though Kate could see a slight upward tilt at the corner of her mouth.

"Roman offered to have us stay with him. It's probably a good idea. Rusty will be much happier there." Kate had already begun packing her things. The owner of the rental had been understanding when she explained what happened, but he also sounded relieved to know they'd be out of the house sooner rather than later.

"Roman's not mad at you?" Tilly asked.

"No...I don't know. He was acting strange when we talked this morning. Very intense. And he seemed out of sorts."

Tilly laughed. "I'm not surprised. You can tell he's not thrilled the state police are so involved."

"He's the one who brought them in," Kate snapped.

"Come on, Kate. Did you see the look on his face when you were talking about the guy who's been stalking you?" Tilly's expression turned dark. "I was worried *before* that you were working on this case with Roman, but to be honest now I'm more worried that you've gone rogue."

"That seems a little dramatic."

"You think so?" Tilly said, her words dripping with sarcasm. "There's a lot you haven't told Roman, and it's his case. Or it was. How much investigating have you been doing on your own?"

"Not much," she muttered, annoyed at having to defend her actions. "Besides, Angela seemed impressed with what I dug up on Laura Fuentes."

"Laura Fuentes?" Tilly's shoulders slumped. "Wow, I haven't thought about her in years."

"Did you know her?"

"Not well. But I remember when she was killed. Things got a little better."

"What do you mean?" Kate asked.

Tilly looked up at Kate, though her mind seemed miles away. "I stopped getting calls. Things were quiet for a while. It didn't last, but it seemed like they were being more careful."

"Were you and Laura friends?"

"No," Tilly replied, frowning. "I never saw her outside of school. But when she was killed and the abuse stopped, I was terrified. I'd been dreaming of ways to get revenge on those fuckers for a whole year, and when Laura died I realized they could kill me, too. And no one would care."

Kate sat in stunned silence.

"Do you remember how it was after she died?" Tilly asked. "How the police were around asking questions, and then they just weren't? It was like she'd never even existed. No one talked about her. Her family moved. I'd been so reckless and out of control up to that point, but something about her death was sobering. I realized I wanted to live. I wanted to survive long enough to make it out of this hellhole. So I stopped fighting."

The resignation in Tilly's voice opened a chasm in Kate's heart, a black hole that seemed to swallow all the joy and hope in the room. The vision of her beautiful, wild teenage sister making the decision to be abused in order to survive. Deep in the pit of Kate's stomach, a white-hot ball of rage began to fester.

It didn't take long for Kate and Tilly to pack up their belongings, load Rusty into Kate's car, and head over to Roman's house. Kate hadn't been expecting Roman to be home, but he was. He corralled Rusty into the backyard and then helped Kate bring her things into the house. Tilly, who'd driven her own car, stopped for fast food on the way. After unpacking, they sat down at Roman's dining table to eat.

"Thanks for lunch," Roman said. He was in much better spirits than he'd been that morning. He let Rusty back inside and the dog was beaming at him.

"Thanks for letting us crash here."

Rusty chimed in with a happy yip, and then stretched out on the carpet in front of Roman's couch for a nap. Kate noticed a pile of bedding on the couch.

"I'll take the couch," she offered. "Tilly can take the guest room."

"Not necessary," Roman replied. "I straightened up my bedroom. I'll take the couch. You two need your rest."

"We couldn't..." Tilly started to protest. Roman held up a hand to silence her.

"My house, my rules," he said with a grin.

"Wow, you sure are bossy in your old age," Tilly teased. "If you insist, I'm going to go take a nap." She gathered up her purse and suitcase and headed down the hall to the guest room. A thick silence sat between Kate and Roman. She started picking up their wrappers and cups, tidying up to keep herself from speaking. She didn't know what to say to Roman, or even how to start. When she turned to wipe down the table, he'd gone. She could hear the water running in the bathroom.

Finishing her task, Kate pulled her laptop out of her bag and sat down on the couch. She was logging in to check her email when Roman emerged from his bedroom, freshly showered. His hair was damp, and he was wearing jeans and a faded t-shirt with the Atari symbol. The shirt was snug, clinging to the muscles in his stomach and arms. Kate shifted her gaze back to her computer, trying not to notice.

Roman shoved the stack of bedding aside so he could sit next to Kate, their legs touching. He smelled like soap and some kind of cologne. Kate's heart beat a little bit faster.

"Roman, I'm sorry," she said without looking at him. Being this close was intoxicating and Kate wanted to say what she had to say before dealing with the emotions causing her heart to race. "I'm sorry I didn't tell you about the hoodie guy. There was so much going on that it slipped my mind. I didn't mean to keep that from you."

"I'm sorry for being such a jerk the last few days." He inhaled deeply, steadying himself.

The space between them seemed to grow smaller, consuming the air that Kate needed to keep breathing normally. Whatever he was building up to was going to change everything. Like that day in the creek. And Kate's first instinct was to change the subject, to move them in a different direction. One that she could control.

For once, she resisted.

After a few agonizing moments, he began again. "You're right. There's too much going on. Like the shit hit the fan from all directions, and I couldn't figure out how to deal with it. The truth is, I've spent the last twenty years trying to put my feelings for you aside. When you moved back to town, it was hard. I was angry for so long. It was easier when you weren't here. Then it was easier when I tried to hate you."

Kate knew he didn't mean to hurt her, but the words still stung. Intellectually, she knew that leaving Roman the way she did all those years ago had caused irreparable damage. Admitting to herself now that she had feelings for him didn't erase how much she'd hurt him. She knew the road ahead of them would be a long one. But it still felt like a knife to her heart to hear him talk about her this way.

"Now," he said, surprising her by sliding his fingers between hers. "Now, I'm just terrified that something's going to happen to you."

Kate couldn't breathe. The feel of his skin on hers was so sweet it was almost painful. She felt tears welling in her eyes, and she couldn't think of a thing to say that would be significant enough for the moment. She hoped her silence wouldn't scare him away. She squeezed his hand then let his fingers go so that she could run one along his palm. She heard his sharp intake of breath. Felt him tremble at her touch.

Kate closed her eyes, with her hand lying in Roman's open palm. She rested her head on his shoulder and focused on her breathing.

Sometime later she woke up, alone.

———

"Hey there," Tilly said, walking into the living room. While Kate slept, Tilly had showered and changed. "How're you feeling?" she asked, taking a seat beside Kate.

"Groggy," Kate said, trying to mask the conflicted feelings coursing through her.

"Roman had to run out for a bit, but he said he'd be back soon. And that he'd make dinner." Tilly smiled. "Much better than a hotel, wouldn't you say?" Kate could feel the tears threatening to fall. Tilly wrapped her arm around her shoulder. "Do you want to talk about it?"

"Not really," Kate said. "I'm just feeling overwhelmed right now."

"I heard you and Roman talking."

Kate closed her eyes again, forcing several large tears to spill down her cheeks. "You heard *Roman* talking. *I* couldn't figure out what to say."

Tilly pulled away from Kate, facing her. Her smile was bright. "I think I can safely say that whatever you did or didn't say, it was the right thing. Roman was fine when he left. Did you tell him you love him?"

Kate jerked away. "Why would you say that?"

"Calm down, Kate. You're not nearly as mysterious as you think you are. You get that same stupid look on your face when he's around now that you did when we were kids."

"I did?" Kate felt a smile creeping up on her, despite herself.

"I always assumed you guys quit hanging out because he rejected you."

Kate laughed a bitter laugh. "Not even close. The opposite actually. Or at least I think he might have been trying to tell me his feelings. I wouldn't let him."

Tilly winced. "Ouch."

"Yeah. I mean, I wanted to go to school and get out of town. I made that choice. But I wish I hadn't hurt him so much."

"Well you can't be good at everything, right?" Tilly teased.

The sisters turned when Rusty sprinted to the door, tail wagging furiously. Kate wiped away her tears The key clicked in the lock and then Roman walked in, using his leg to move Rusty away from the doorway as he balanced a bag of groceries in one arm.

"Whoa, let me help with that," Tilly said, hopping up to grab the grocery bag before Rusty dislodged it.

"Thanks," Roman said, closing the door and locking it. He

looked over at Kate and his cheerful expression turned to one of concern. "Is everything all right?"

"Yeah," Kate told him. "I just woke up. Sorry for falling asleep."

"You needed it. I tried not to wake you."

"You succeeded in your mission," Kate said. "Let me wake up a bit before I talk so I don't sound like an idiot the whole night." She smiled and was rewarded with one of Roman's dazzling smiles in return.

Kate grabbed her bag and headed to the bathroom for a quick shower. When she finished, the delicious smell of dinner and the sound of Roman and Tilly talking wafted down the hallway. Tilly had taken the spare room so Kate took her things to Roman's bedroom. Kate found her cell phone charger and searched for an outlet to plug in. She found one next to Roman's dresser, the same dresser he'd owned since she'd known him. Back in their teen years, the dresser was covered in odds and ends from school. Medals and trophies. Discarded notes. Candy wrappers.

Now the dresser was clean and organized, with only a few framed pictures. Kate picked up one of Roman and his parents. She'd always liked being at Roman's house. His mom and dad were so warm and welcoming. Her father mentioned that they'd moved out of state some years ago, but she couldn't remember where.

"Dinner's ready."

Roman was leaning against the doorframe, looking intently at Kate. She put the framed photo back where she'd found it and followed him into the kitchen.

Dinner tasted as good as it smelled. Roman had thrown together tacos with hand-fried corn tortillas. The mix of oil and corn meal took her back to her childhood. "This looks amazing," she said, digging in.

When they'd all eaten their fill Kate reached for their plates, but Roman stopped her. "I've got it," he said, clearing the table and filling the sink. He sat back down at the table. "I quit my job today."

Kate sputtered on some water she was drinking. "You quit?"

"I turned in my notice, and the chief made it clear that I wouldn't be receiving a favorable recommendation from him, so I rescinded my two weeks and got the hell out of there."

"Are you okay?" Kate asked, a little shaken by the abruptness of his announcement.

"I didn't join law enforcement to sit on my ass and do nothing. And I didn't want to spend another day working for such a corrupt department. I applied for a job with the state police in their Special Investigations unit. Until I hear from them, I've got enough savings to get by."

Tilly and Roman fell into an easy back-and-forth about the hijinks of multi-disciplinary teams, but Kate's mind wandered. With Roman out of the police department, what would happen in the Gabby Greene investigation?

CHAPTER THIRTY-SEVEN

Kate woke up in the middle of the night, disoriented. She sat up in bed fast, her body drenched with sweat, her face wet with tears. She was shivering despite the heat she felt in her cheeks and forehead.

"Damn," she mumbled as she rubbed her hands along her bare legs and focused on her breathing. Waking up in the middle of a panic attack was always bad, but being in an unfamiliar setting meant she didn't have quick access to the tools she needed to calm herself. She swung her legs over the side of the bed, frantic, wishing she'd remembered to bring a glass of water with her into the bedroom.

She stumbled toward the door, tripping over her suitcase. Trying to be quiet while in the throes of anxiety just wasn't possible.

In the kitchen, she sensed movement. She nearly screamed when Roman appeared beside her. Her vision began to blur at the edges. She reached for the counter and let herself down onto the kitchen floor before she passed out.

She wrapped her arms around herself and started rocking, trying to steady her breathing so her heart would follow suit.

Roman wrapped his arms around her. He was sitting beside her on the floor.

"Breathe," he said, his voice soft and soothing. He rested his cheek against hers, his mouth near her ear, and took slow, deep breaths. She mimicked his breathing until they were in sync.

"I need to lie down for a minute," she whispered. He released her as she curled onto her side. The cool tile against her cheek felt like heaven. Roman ran his fingers through her hair and she closed her eyes, counting every inhale and exhale until breathing didn't seem like such a harrowing task. Even after her body calmed she laid still, keeping her focus on Roman's movements.

"Better?" he asked. She sat up slowly and nodded, but she could feel tears running down her cheeks.

"I'm sorry."

Roman pulled her against him.

"You have nothing to be sorry for," he said. "Let me get you some water."

He stood, pulled a glass from the cabinet, and filled it with cold water from the fridge. Then he returned to his spot on the floor, handing her the glass. The cool liquid slid down her throat, washing away the rest of her anxiety. She shivered.

"Where's Tilly?"

"She fell asleep on the couch, so I left her there and took the spare room. Let's get you back to bed," Roman said, holding her hand as he helped her to her feet. Part of her felt ridiculous for accepting his help, when she knew she was capable. But part of her relished the feeling of someone taking care of her. She'd spent many nights alone on the bathroom floor or in her bed, fighting back waves of panic. She knew they'd ease, but it felt nice to have someone comfort her.

Roman led her back to bed. While she got settled, he refilled her water and set it on the bedside table. She'd propped herself up against the headboard, knowing that she needed to do some calming exercises before she tried to go back to sleep. Roman sat down on the edge of the bed, his features tense. He'd been so steady and calm while Kate was spinning out of control. Now that she was feeling better, his distress was showing.

Kate smiled. "Thank you for sitting with me." She wanted to reach out and touch him, but her hands still felt a bit shaky and she didn't quite trust herself to move yet.

Roman fidgeted. It reminded Kate of herself, the way she couldn't stop moving when something was making her nervous or she didn't know which course of action to take. Her panic attack had woken them both up. Poor guy.

"I hope I didn't scare you," she said, finally reaching out a hand and touching his.

Whatever mental battle he'd been fighting seemed to reach a resolution. He leaned in, taking Kate's face in his hands, and kissed her. It was a tentative kiss, gentle and hesitant, testing to see if she would push him away. She didn't. Wrapping her arms around his neck she pulled him to her and kissed him back, making up for every missed opportunity.

Life was so chaotic and frightening. It had been a long time —too long—since Kate felt safe, but having Roman in her arms, feeling the heat of his body pressed against hers, she was secure. The fears that had been keeping her up at night were gone, at least temporarily.

It was a strange sensation, being in the moment. Kate slid her hands under the soft shirt Roman was sleeping in and explored his body. He groaned, barely audible, but the sound made Kate's head spin with desire. Roman turned off the lamp, plunging the room into darkness as he slid under the covers beside her.

Kate awoke with a start the next morning, flinging her arm out to ward off the attacker from her dreams.

"Ow," Roman yelped. "You're safe, Kate. No need to beat me senseless."

The goofy grin on his face made her laugh out loud despite her embarrassment. Soon, they were both laughing. Kate put her hand over her mouth to curb the flow. "We're going to wake Tilly."

"Too late. I heard her out in the kitchen a while ago." Roman rolled toward Kate, his chest bare, making her aware of the thin sheet between them. The whole night came back to her in a series of vivid images. Her breath caught and she closed her eyes to savor the feeling.

Roman leaned in and kissed her shoulder, then her neck. "Good morning."

Kate opened her eyes, turning on her side to face him. "Hi," she said, feeling bashful. She ran her fingers over his cheek, feeling the soft skin and the stubble around his jaw. He closed his eyes, his breathing coming in ragged bursts. Why had she waited so long to do this?

The buzzing of Kate's cell phone brought an abrupt end to the moment. Roman rolled over and reached for her phone, handing it to her. She lay back, staring at the ceiling so she wouldn't have to think about the fact that she was still in bed, naked.

"Hello?"

"Good morning, Kate. Sorry to call so early." It was the realtor, Janet. "I thought you'd like to know the owner accepted your offer!"

"Really?" Kate's tone must have sounded completely incredulous, because Janet laughed.

"Yes. I told you the house has been on the market forever. The owner was thrilled that someone finally made a serious offer. I think we could have gone lower and he would have been happy."

Kate had been feeling guilty about the low-ball offer she'd made, knowing the house would have cost ten times as much in another town. "I'm glad we didn't. He shouldn't have to give the house away. It's beautiful."

Kate felt Roman shift in bed and her stomach flopped. She hadn't told him about the house or her plan for it.

After disconnecting she laid on her back for a moment, her eyes closed, wondering how to break the news.

"You got the house?" Roman asked. His tone revealed nothing about how he was feeling. Kate finally got brave and opened her eyes. Roman was propped up on one elbow, looking at her.

"Yeah, I got the house," she replied. "I'm sorry, Roman. I completely spaced about it."

Roman smiled, though there was wariness in his eyes. "It's okay. Tilly mentioned that you'd been looking at houses and that you found one you liked. Is it in Las Cruces?"

Tilly hadn't told him everything.

"Tularosa. Well, not quite in town. It's off the highway. Do you remember that big house with the red-tiled roof they built when we were kids?"

"That house is huge." Roman's gaze turned suspicious. She figured she'd better go for the whole truth and nothing but.

"I want to turn it into a safe house. For abuse victims. It's like a compound. Thick walls. Barred windows. I swear the guy who built it must have been paranoid. It's like a fortress really. Totally defensible."

Roman chuckled, but his expression was serious. "Defensibility. That's what I usually look for in the place I call home."

Kate sighed. The situation was getting away from her fast. She pulled at the sheet so that there was nothing but air between them, and then scooted toward him. His arms went around her almost reflexively. A good sign, she hoped.

"After what happened to Mandy, I thought these girls could use a safe place to be while law enforcement is straightening this mess out."

Roman's face was a mask, expressionless, though he stared at her with an intensity that made her nervous. She thought about their night together, and hoped it wouldn't be the last one.

Finally, he sighed. "When do I get to see it? I've always wondered what that house looked like on the inside."

After revealing her plans about the hacienda, the atmosphere in the room turned cooler. Roman excused himself to take a shower. Kate watched his pull his shirt and jeans on with a pang of regret.

She put on some sweatpants and a t-shirt then padded out into the kitchen, her feet bare. Tilly was sitting at the table with a cup of coffee. She looked up at Kate with amusement. Between Tilly's expression and the sound of the shower running in the background, Kate felt her cheeks heat up. She held up a hand and said, "Not a word."

"I wasn't going to say anything," Tilly said, but she was grinning behind her coffee mug. Kate poured herself a cup and sat down across the table.

"The realtor called. My offer was accepted."

Tilly raised an eyebrow. "So you were celebrating, eh?" Her eyes moved to the door of Roman's bedroom.

"You're not going to let it go, are you?" Kate asked, exasperated. "Fine. I had a huge panic attack in the middle of the night. It woke Roman up. He helped me get back to sleep." If Kate's face could have combusted, it would have.

"Mmm." Tilly folded over the newspaper she'd been reading

and handed it to Kate. "Sorry to ruin the moment, but I thought you'd want to see this."

Gabby Greene's school photo appeared above the fold with the headline: "Gang violence turns deadly." Kate skimmed the article, dumbfounded. Local police had deemed Gabby Greene's murder an act of gang retaliation, fabricating a vague account of jealousy turned deadly. The plot sounded like it had been taken right out of a cheesy paperback, and there wasn't a shred of evidence to support it.

"The case remains open, though no suspects have been identified," Kate read.

"What's that?" Roman said, appearing in the kitchen. He reached for the paper and read the article, his forehead creased in consternation. "Sounds about right," he said, tossing the paper back onto the table. His voice was calm, but he rifled through the cabinets with more force than was necessary. Coffee in hand he sank down into a chair at the table, looking dejected.

Kate took Roman's hand, eliciting another eyebrow raise from Tilly. "I've been meaning to ask you. Did you look up the report about Laura Fuentes' death?"

"I tried," Roman said with a sigh. He tangled his fingers with Kate's and she took comfort in his touch despite the topic of conversation. "The file was never entered into the digital system, and I wasn't able to locate it. Apparently, it was *misplaced.*"

"Sounds familiar," Kate said.

"How long has Gunnison been police chief?" Tilly asked.

"About eleven years. He was a detective when I started on the force. He was an asshole back then as well. Why?"

"I thought of something," Tilly said. "Well, two things actually. First, was Gunnison involved in the Fuentes investigation? And second, who was the chief back then? Could he have been complicit?"

Roman sat back in his chair, thinking. "When I started, the chief was Charlie Munroe. He died not too long after. A heart attack I think. Then we had musical chairs for the position for a while. Seemed like no one wanted it."

"Law enforcement hot potato," Tilly said, joking, though her brow still furrowed as she thought through the situation.

"Another thing I forgot to tell you," Kate said. Roman cringed, but she'd been expecting it. "I grabbed the student files on Laura Fuentes and Benny Parks before I was suspended. I only looked at them a few days ago."

"And?" Roman asked, looking a little less than thrilled at the latest revelation.

"Not much. Benny's file actually had things blacked out. Like some CIA cover-up. About a million reasons he should have been suspended or expelled, but he wriggled free. And Laura's was small. But when I started thinking about her and the other girls I knew about…" A quick glance at Tilly revealed her rapt attention. "A lot of latch-key kids and girls volunteering in the community. Mandy said that the hospital banquet was where she was singled out. If we look at the girls' after-school activities, maybe we can find some connections to the men whose names we know."

"I'll have to see if Angie can take a look," Roman said, letting go of Kate's hand and taking a sip of his coffee. "Since I'm sans access right now."

Tilly scooted her chair back. "Since you're staying here right now, I'm going to head back up to Colorado."

Kate felt deflated. "Probably a good idea. You've got a life to get back to." She wanted to argue, but now that Kate knew Tilly's story, what she really wanted was for her sister to be happy. And safe.

Kate walked Tilly out to her car, tears already forming.

"I'll be back," Tilly said, hugging Kate fiercely. "After everything that's happened, I'm feeling guilty about leaving Jim hanging. He's been a wonderful partner. He didn't deserve me walking out on him like that."

"Relationships can be difficult, but it seems like such a shame to walk away without at least trying to talk things out," Kate offered.

Tilly sighed. "I've kept my relationships short and manageable for this exact reason. I really never wanted to be in a position to hurt someone like this." Tilly tossed her bag into the backseat, and then turned to Kate again. "Listen, I've had a crazy idea of my own. But I'm not quite ready to divulge. I'll call you when I get there." She gave Kate another long hug and then slid behind the wheel.

Kate watched her drive away. She was still standing in the driveway, staring down an empty street, when Roman came out to find her.

"You okay?" he asked, wrapping his arms around her. The gesture was both exhilarating and comforting.

"No, but I'll figure out how to cope," Kate answered. When she turned to face him, she realized he had on his jacket and sunglasses. She gave him a quizzical look.

"I'm going to run down to Las Cruces," he said in answer to her unasked question. "Do you want to come? I wanted to give Detective Lopez an update."

"Detective Lopez?" Kate had that sinking feeling in her stomach, the one that preceded disappointment.

"Angie," Roman said, his cheeks turning pink. He put his hands on Kate's waist and rested his forehead against hers. "Not gonna lie. Things are a little complicated right now."

Kate pulled away. "What do you mean complicated?"

Roman shifted, giving Kate some space. He ran his fingers

through his hair. "I've known Angie for a long time. We've dated on and off over the years."

"And right now you're on," Kate finished. She wasn't surprised. It was clear from her body language that Angela Lopez was attracted to Roman. And Tilly had hinted at a history that dated back to high school. Roman's head hung low, his eyes trained on the ground.

"I've been in love with you since I was 17 years old, Kate." Roman's words pulled at Kate's heart, causing both pain and a flutter of hope. He didn't look at her while he spoke. "When I brought Angie in on my case, it seemed like a sign that I needed to move on. Every time you and I were in the same room it ended in a fight or in hard feelings. It was agonizing, and I started to wonder if I was just a stupid masochist. If I was going to keep punishing myself, and you, for the way things ended twenty years ago."

Roman finally raised his eyes to Kate's. They were filled with tears. "I thought I wouldn't still feel this way after a while. That every single time I look at you, I wouldn't want to touch you."

Kate's breathing came in gasps as she processed what Roman was saying. *He would have said this to you that day in the creek.* His sad eyes made her wonder if he was regretting their night together, but she pushed the worry aside. *No. Otherwise, why stand here and go through this torture?*

This had always been Kate's problem. She could think herself in circles, overanalyzing any situation until she felt frozen with fear. Roman would have told her he loved her when they were kids. She'd known it was coming, and she'd broken his heart without even letting his express his feelings. She'd been cruel. Unintentionally, but intentions didn't change the facts.

"Kate?"

Roman's sadness had turned to concern. She studied those

hazel eyes, trying to the find the right words. Finally she settled on the only thing that mattered.

"I love you, too."

Saying the words out loud didn't make the situation any less complicated. Roman looked startled for a moment, like Kate had spoken in tongues. Then he smiled, nodded, and walked to his car.

He didn't kiss her.

He didn't reach out to her.

Kate was left standing in the driveway for the second time that morning. She'd said *I love you* to a man for the first time in her life. She didn't know what would happen next. What Roman would say to Angela. What it would feel like when he came home. She was surprised to realize that the uncertainty was palatable. Saying the words out loud had freed her. Whatever happened next, at least he knew, for once, how she felt.

CHAPTER THIRTY-EIGHT

The rest of the day flew by. After lunch, Kate left a message for Tilly, receiving only a quick text in response to say she'd arrived home. Tilly had her own personal disaster to attend to and Kate knew she'd call when she was ready.

Kate turned on her computer to do some research. Rusty nestled at her feet. She needed to find out how to open a safe house that could serve minors without being raided by the police. Being arrested for harboring runaways wasn't high on Kate's list of fun things to try, especially when she knew local law enforcement didn't like her much.

Luckily the new property was outside city limits, and subject to the county sheriff's jurisdiction. Kate hoped the sheriff's department had a few more friendly faces.

She'd been at it for an hour, taking copious amounts of notes. Her list of questions was a lot longer than her list of answers, but she felt like she was making progress. Her phone buzzed on the table beside her, an unfamiliar number appearing on the caller ID.

"Kate? It's Angela." The detective's tone was flat. Kate's began to sweat.

"Hi, Angela. How are you?" she asked, crossing her fingers this wasn't going to be a confrontation.

"I've been meaning to call you, not that we've made much progress on your rock-throwing stalker. I spoke to Mandy Garcia's doctor today."

Adrenaline pulsed through Kate's body. "How is she?"

"The doctors are saying it's too early to tell if she'll have any lasting brain damage, but she's able to talk a little bit. They took her off the ventilator early this morning."

"Have you guys picked up Benny Parks?"

Angela was silent. "No, not yet. Miss Garcia is heavily medicated, so she hasn't been able to give us enough information for an arrest. We still have a guard on her room. Her mother asked to be with her—well, demanded actually—but Mandy refused to see her."

"I can imagine," Kate said. Her heart ached for Mandy. "And I'm still barred from seeing her?"

"Yes. There's not much we can do until she's recovered some. It may be a few more days. But at least she's safe."

"Yeah," Kate said without enthusiasm. She didn't believe that anyone could keep Mandy safe, not with the connections Benny had in town. But she held on to hope. "Thanks for letting me know. Will you keep me updated?"

"Of course. But Kate—" Angela paused again, putting Kate on edge. "I had one more thing I wanted to ask you."

Here it comes.

"Have you talked to Roman?"

Kate was confused. "You mean today?"

"Yeah. He stopped by my office this morning and we had a bit of a misunderstanding. He was very angry when he left, and he's not answering his phone."

"Sorry, I haven't. Do you want me to give him a call?" Kate hated the way this conversation was making her feel. The way

Angela was talking, it didn't sound like Roman had broached the topic of their new...situation.

"If you hear from him, would you have him call me?"

"Sure," Kate said. After another few words, the call disconnected. Kate dialed Roman's number but got his voicemail.

"Just checking in. Want me to make dinner? Give me a call back." She hung up, feeling a little queasy.

Mandy was awake. She wished there was something more she could do for the girl, but she knew that going against the injunction would cause problems for everyone. She'd have to have faith that the state police would do their part to keep Mandy safe.

And Roman was incommunicado. What had gone down between him and Angela? Kate and Roman had only one night together, and everything was a little tense after. Was she setting herself up to be hurt?

Faith was another of Kate's weak points.

———————

When Roman wasn't home by dinnertime, Kate started to worry. What they'd shared, that was real. But she wondered if he was having second thoughts. If his talk with Angela had made him rethink things. It felt like too much to ask, that Roman wanted her after all these years, after everything they'd been through. As the sun began to set, Kate felt less confident.

Kate tried his phone again, but it went to voicemail. Restlessness turned to agitation, and when her phone rang she pounced on it.

"May I speak with Kate Medina?" The unfamiliar voice startled Kate.

"Speaking."

"I'm calling from Mesilla Valley Hospital." Kate's stomach tied in a knot. "Roman Aguilar was brought in this evening."

"Oh my God, is he all right?" Kate's voice was shaking.

"He was assaulted. Stabbed. They're taking him to surgery now, but he asked that we call you. Are you a relative?"

"Stabbed?" Kate couldn't follow what the woman was saying.

"The police are here. If you'd like to come in, you can talk with them." The woman's curt tone brought Kate back to her senses.

"I'll be there in an hour," she said, hanging up the phone. She called Angela's cell phone, but started crying when the detective answered.

"What's wrong?"

Kate explained between sobs. By the time she finished, she'd managed to calm down

"Are you okay to drive?" Angela asked.

"Yeah, I think so," she said, but as soon as she hung up the phone panic began to creep in and she wondered if it was true. Wishing Tilly was around didn't help. She gave Rusty his dinner plus some, knowing she might not be back right away.

As she headed out of town, the night swallowed the landscape. She passed the entrance to White Sands National Monument, and for a few miles the white gypsum deposits made the landscape seem less bleak. But the effect was gone too soon. The road was quiet, which only added to Kate's growing feeling of isolation.

When she finally pulled in to the hospital parking lot and opened her car door, the air felt different. Like the darkness had sucked all the oxygen out of the atmosphere and the lights of the city were finally allowing her to breathe.

Kate entered the building at a sprint. Angela was waiting in the lobby near registration. When Kate approached, Angela said, "He's in surgery."

"What the hell happened? Where are the police? The woman

who called me wouldn't give me any information," Kate panted, trying to calm her breathing.

"Let's go sit," Angela said, leading Kate over to a quiet corner. When they were seated, Angela said, "The police *were* here, but they left when he was taken in for surgery." Kate couldn't tell if the detective's tone was defensive or irritated, but there was something behind her words. She shook her head like she was clearing away some unwanted thought. "I guess Roman went to the bookstore downtown after he left my office. Or he ended up there. Someone came at him from behind. Stabbed him twice with some kind of hunting knife then ran. He never saw it coming. He was able to walk back to the building and get help but serrated blades do a lot of tissue damage."

A million things raced through Kate's mind but she couldn't make her brain slow down long enough to make sense of her thoughts.

"Was he robbed?"

"No. There weren't a lot of cars in the parking lot, so Roman thinks the attacker was hiding behind his car. It was over quickly. Too fast for a robbery attempt."

"You talked to Roman?"

Angela looked thoughtfully at Kate. "I came straight over after you called. He was still in prep, so they let me in to see him for a few minutes. The cops had already gone over everything with him. Not that there's much to go on."

The pressure building inside Kate was reaching critical mass. She wanted to scream and punch someone. She was scared, but she was mostly angry. Angry that she hadn't gone with Roman when he asked, as awkward as it might have been, and that Angela had been able to see him.

Roman was right. This was complicated.

"How is he?" Kate asked.

"The knife didn't hit any major organs, but there was some damage to his abdominal muscles. He lost a lot of blood and there's the risk of infection, but he should be okay." As Kate digested that information, a doctor in scrubs walked across the lobby.

"Detective Lopez?"

"Yes," Angela answered, standing.

"He's out of surgery. Everything went well. He'll be in recovery for about half an hour and then you can see him." The doctor had been speaking to Angela. He finally looked at Kate. "Are you here for Detective Aguilar?"

Kate nodded.

"Are you a relative?"

Before Kate could answer, Angela spoke up. "She is. Let us know when we can see him." When he was out of earshot, she said, "I told him Roman was my partner so he'd let me in." Angela sat again, picking up a magazine and started flipping through it. Kate stood a moment longer, fighting off prickles of jealousy.

CHAPTER THIRTY-NINE

It took an hour but Roman was finally settled into a room, and someone came to take Kate and Angela back. They'd spent the hour waiting in silence. Occasionally, Kate looked at Angela and wondered what the woman was thinking. Her face was like stone, except when she was looking back at Kate.

Meanwhile, Kate had dissected every moment of the day—starting when she woke up in Roman's bed. She wondered what Roman had been doing when he was attacked, and what he and Angela had argued about. Had Roman told Angela he couldn't see her anymore? If so, why hadn't he come straight home?

Kate tried to figure Angela out. The detective hadn't been unfriendly to Kate, but the easiness they'd experienced before was gone. Kate tried not to imagine Roman and Angela together. She wondered if Angela's feelings for Roman were strong. If he felt something for her. How could he not?

That question was answered when they walked into Roman's room. Angela's eyes filled with tears and she went to Roman's bedside, taking his hand in hers and stroking his cheek. Jealousy, red-hot and pulsating, filled Kate's body, making her sweat. She stood frozen by the door of Roman's room, unable to move closer. Angela seemed oblivious to Kate's presence, which riled Kate even further.

After a few moments, Roman opened his eyes. His face was ashen. Kate watched as he looked up at Angela and smiled. "Angie." His voice was gravelly.

"Do you need something for the pain?" Angela asked.

"It's not too bad," Roman replied, but he couldn't hide a grimace.

Kate wished she could slip out of the room without anyone noticing. Seeing Roman smile at Angela, and the way she looked back at him with such affection, was more than Kate could take. She wanted to disappear, to find somewhere quiet to be before her anxiety got the better of her. Instead, she closed her eyes and tried not to be present.

"Where's Kate?" Roman asked, his voice a whisper. Kate's eyes popped open in time to see Angela look in her direction, her expression cold.

"I'm here, Roman," Kate said, approaching the opposite side of Roman's bed. She didn't look at Angela, but she could feel the woman's eyes boring a hole through her. "I'm here," she repeated, her words failing her. Roman's eyes brightened when she approached, erasing her worries. She told herself that his happiness at seeing her was enough, no matter where things went from here.

Kate looked up at Angela, and the two women locked eyes in what felt like an unspoken standoff with Angela still holding Roman's hand. Kate's hands remained at her side. For twenty years she'd left Roman behind, and Angela was one of the people he'd turned to for comfort. Kate wouldn't stake a claim on Roman, not if his heart wasn't in it. Even if it hurt.

But if Roman wanted to be with Kate, she was ready. If he chose Angela she wouldn't turn his friendship away. She owed him that much. As they stared at each other, Angela's features began to soften.

"I'm going to go get some coffee," she said. She gave a sad smile as she walked away.

When the door closed, Kate took Roman's hand and held it tight. All the jumbled up emotions she'd been shoving aside made their way to the surface and she started to cry.

"Come here," Roman whispered. She leaned closer to his face, resting her cheek against his. "I'm going to be okay."

"I know," she whispered back. His cheek was cool, but the feel of his breath on her skin felt real and solid. She pulled back so she could look at him. "Who was it?"

Roman sighed. "I don't know. I suppose it could have been a random act of violence, but..."

He didn't have to finish.

They both knew it wasn't.

"When can you come home?" she asked. His eyelids were beginning to flutter, but he smiled.

"Maybe tomorrow. I guess the damage wasn't as bad as expected but they're worried about infection." He gestured to the IV pole beside him. "They're going to pump me full of antibiotics, just in case."

"You should get some rest," she said, straightening up. He squeezed her hand a little tighter.

"Stay," he said, shutting his eyes. Soon he was snoring softly. Kate pulled her hand from his and settled into the armchair in his room. Another night sitting vigil in a hospital room, but this time the outcome would be different.

Angela did not come back that night, and Kate fell asleep in the chair. When she woke, her neck was stiff and sore. Pins and needles attacked the arm she'd used to prop up her head. She shook her hand, trying to speed up the recovery process, and then stretched. It was early and Roman was sleeping.

Kate went in search of coffee.

When she reached the cafeteria, she saw Angela sitting alone at a table near the window. Kate filled her cup, doctored her coffee with sugar and creamer, and walked over to the table.

"Mind if I join you?" she asked. Angela nodded in the direction of the empty chair, but didn't speak. They sat in silence until Kate felt like she was going to explode. "Angela..."

"Stop," Angela said, clasping her hands. "You don't have to explain, Kate. I see the way he looks at you." She sounded like she was trying to convince herself, and Kate knew there wasn't a thing she could say to make it hurt less. "I'm not going to say it's okay. It's not. I've always known that Roman wasn't entirely available, at least not emotionally."

Kate cringed.

"Anyway," Angela continued, tapping her fingernails on the tabletop. "I'm going to have to process this—to make peace with it—and I don't want to talk about it. Especially not with you."

It was a slap in the face but Kate nodded, thankful that Angela was so direct no matter how uncomfortable she felt. "Do you want to go see him?" she asked. "I'll hang out here for a while."

"I do, but I wanted to talk to you first."

Kate felt her nerves go on point. "Oh."

"I got a call last night. Benny Parks was arrested."

"For what?" Kate's hands shook a little. She picked up her own coffee and wrapped her hands around the cup for warmth.

"Sexual contact with a minor. Remember the missing girl, Rachel Telles? Apparently she wasn't missing. Looks like she and Benny are an item. She was furious when they took him away. Screamed at the officers about being in love. Then they took her into custody. She wasn't too happy about that either."

"Is it weird that I'm relieved?"

Angela made a face. "Relieved?"

"She'd not dead somewhere in a ditch. Not saying this isn't

horrible." Then Kate frowned. "I guess that means Benny isn't the person who attacked Roman."

"No, he wasn't. But I didn't think he was, did you? From what you've said, Benny doesn't do his own dirty work."

"True," Kate said, thinking. "Could it have been Rick?"

"We still don't know who Rick is. But back to Mr. Parks. It also looks like they may pin the Gabby Greene murder on him."

Kate bolted upright in her chair. "What the hell? I thought they were calling that gang violence."

"And they're implicating him in another death, an older one. A girl named Laura Fuentes."

"No," Kate said, feeling the fury grow. "That's bullshit. He would have been, like, fourteen when Laura died."

"I know how you feel. Seems like APD is able to solve several cases all at once. Very convenient." Angela rose. "I'm going to go check in with Roman."

CHAPTER FORTY

Roman was discharged with a laundry list of restrictions and instructions. A nurse wheeled him to Kate's car, but getting him into the front passenger seat was an ordeal. He'd been stabbed in the side so every twist, turn, and maneuver caused him to groan. The nurse gave Kate his pain medication with orders to give him one every four hours whether he wanted it or not, at least for the first few days.

Roman fell asleep on the drive back to Alamogordo, giving Kate time to think about everything she'd learned in the past few hours. To the public, it looked like the Alamogordo Police Department was taking a stand against a sexual predator, but Kate had major reservations. Could Benny have been responsible for so many crimes? Even if he was, Kate knew he wasn't acting alone. As Angela said, Benny didn't do his own dirty work.

"Hey," Kate said as she pulled into Roman's driveway. She reached over and rubbed his shoulder. "Home sweet home."

Roman opened his eyes and moaned.

"Tell you what, let me go in and get Rusty squared away so we can get you to your bed without incident."

"Probably a good idea."

Kate put Rusty in the backyard and found Roman asleep again in the car. It was an arduous struggle to get him to bed, but when he was finally settled she felt an immense sense of relief. She didn't like seeing Roman this way, but it felt less unbearable when he was in his own clothes in his own bed. He looked exhausted, but he was awake and alert.

"Can I get you anything?" she asked from the doorway.

"Water, please. And a pain pill if it's time. The ride home about killed me."

Kate looked alarmed. "I thought you were sleeping."

"I tried," Roman said, smiling. "I felt every bump, but there wasn't anything you could do and I didn't want you to worry."

She got him a glass of water and his pain medicine, both of which he accepted without argument.

"Now catch me up on what's been going on around here. At least until the meds kick in and I pass out."

Kate chuckled. "What an offer. I talk and you fall asleep on me." She leaned back against the headboard and took his hand. "Things were pretty uneventful until you went and got yourself all busted up."

"I can be a real pain sometimes," he said with a grunt.

"Did Angela tell you about Benny Parks?"

Roman nodded. "A little bit. What a farce. I mean, he needs to be put in jail, but..."

"I know, I felt the same way," Kate said. She went to the living room and grabbed Benny's student file out of her bag. She returned to the bedroom and started flipping through the file. "While I was waiting for you to get sprung, something occurred to me. I want to see if I'm right."

"About what?"

"Hold on a sec." She scanned each page until she found the one she wanted. "There." She turned the file around so Roman could see. "In April of 1996, when Laura was killed, Benny was at juvie. It was one of the very few times he actually got caught for one of his misdeeds." She closed the file.

"He couldn't have killed Laura. So why are the cops digging this up now?"

"I don't know," Roman said, frowning. "But it doesn't feel like a good thing."

Despite Kate's best efforts to make Roman rest, after twenty-four hours in bed he was having none of it. Kate helped him onto the couch, creating a barrier of pillows around him to deter Rusty from getting too friendly. After his initial excitement, Rusty seemed content to lie at Roman's feet. Roman read the newspaper while Kate sat on the opposite end of the couch with her laptop.

"Did you see today's front page story?" Roman asked. Kate looked up to see a picture of Benny Parks staring back at her. She took the paper from Roman's hands and read the article.

ALAMOGORDO, NM - Benjamin Parks, 32, was taken into custody on Tuesday for having an inappropriate relationship with a minor.

The student contacted police earlier this month to say she had been in an eight-month-long relationship with Parks, beginning in January of this year.

According to the police report, the victim told investigators she was 15 years old when the two began having sex. She claims Parks would "have her cut classes and he would drive her to a nearby motel room and they would have sexual intercourse."

The victim also told officers Parks "would take photographs and videos of their sexual acts on his cell phone."

A source from the police department states that Parks has

been under investigation for a variety of crimes, dating back nearly twenty years.

Kate put the paper on her lap. "Something's very wrong here. Why did this girl come forward now? Angela made it sound like Benny was caught in the act, but that's not how this reads."

"I agree," Roman said, frowning. Kate watched as the creases in his forehead grew deeper. "I wonder..."

A knock at the door brought them both to attention. Rusty leapt up, but didn't bark. Kate got up to answer the door, giving Roman a wary look.

"Who is it?" she called.

"Tilly. Open up."

Kate unlocked the door and threw herself into Tilly's arms. Tilly wrapped Kate in a hug, laughing. "Wow. That's quite the greeting. I've only been gone a few days."

"It was a long few days," Kate said.

When Tilly spotted Roman on the couch, her expression changed.

"What happened?"

Kate sank back into her position on the couch and Tilly took a seat on a nearby chair.

"Let's see. Roman got stabbed. Benny Parks was arrested. Oh, and Mandy is awake but, of course, no one is allowed to see her." Each word was packed with bitterness. As she tried to calm herself she realized that Tilly had shown up with nothing on her person, not even a purse. "Did you bring a bag? How long can you stay?"

Tilly smiled. "My bag is at the hotel with Jim."

Kate raised an eyebrow. "Jim is here?"

"Who's Jim?" Roman piped in.

Kate could hear the strain in his voice. She looked at her

watch. "Med time," she said, retrieving Roman's pills and a glass of water. Tilly was smiling at her. "What?"

"It's fun to watch you play nurse."

"I always wanted a hot nurse," Roman said with a self-satisfied grin. Kate blushed, which made Tilly laugh out loud. Roman managed to chuckle, but then groaned. Tilly stopped laughing and gave Kate a sympathetic look.

"So, Jim?" Kate asked as Roman settled back into the cushions and closed his eyes.

"I laid it all out and told him I was thinking of moving back to New Mexico," Tilly said.

"You are?"

Tilly smiled but her tone was serious. "I know the SANE clinic here can use trained nurses, and I was thinking about opening up a practice."

"What? Did he follow you?"

"Sort of," Tilly said with a grin. "He was pretty pissed that I'd kept so much from him, but then he took a week off of work and came with me. Said he wants to see where I grew up so he can understand me better. Ha!" Tilly's tone was sarcastic, but Kate wasn't buying it. Tilly looked more content than Kate had ever seen her.

A soft snore from Roman made both sisters smile.

"So, what really happened?" Tilly said, gesturing to Roman.

"Someone attacked him in a parking lot in Las Cruces. He's okay, though. They had to do a quick fix on a torn ligament, but he'll heal. He's in more pain than he's letting on though. And stubborn. After the first day, I've had to pretty much shove the pain meds down his throat."

"Sounds romantic," Tilly teased. "And you two are good?"

"Yeah," Kate said. "I think we are."

Every day Roman grew a little stronger. And every day Kate grew more apprehensive. The police had no leads on Roman's attacker. Things had been quiet around town, like the whole community was holding its breath.

Tilly brought Jim to meet Kate. Kate hadn't known what to expect, but she immediately liked him. Jim had been an investigator with the district attorney's office for a decade after a stint in law enforcement. He was tall, burly, and handsome. But his best feature, at least in Kate's opinion, was his infectious laugh. He was one of those people who laughed deep in his belly, and the joy reached all the way to his eyes.

As Roman recovered the four of them sat around his kitchen table, poring over documents and news articles. As the outsider Jim was the perfect sounding board for Kate's wild theories, and there were many.

"I'm not saying it's impossible," he said one evening after dinner. "I'm saying that, from what you've told me, Mandy's mother may have been oblivious."

"How can that be?" Kate's voice had gotten loud as they'd gone around in circles. Angela called to say that Mandy was talking, but that her memories of the attack and even some of the weeks leading up to it were fuzzy. She couldn't debunk the attempted suicide theory, and so it was slow-going trying to build a case. They all suspected that Benny Parks, or one of his minions, had strangled Mandy to within an inch of her life. But there was no way to prove it. Not unless Mandy's mother changed her story, and the woman wasn't budging. They were all waiting impatiently for the results of the forensic exam.

"We know he beat the living daylights out of Mandy the first time. We know that she was 'found' in Benny's place of business —a place I would think she would avoid like the plague—and that he magnanimously chose not to press charges if she was returned to her mother's care, under *his roof* of course. Tilly did the forensic exam. We know her wounds are not consistent with a suicide attempt. How can the DA even consider sending Mandy home with her mother?!"

Kate knew she was preaching to the choir, but she didn't have a better outlet for her frustration. She'd reached a dead end in her research. Roman had been reaching out to his friends at the department, trying to figure out who he could trust. Tilly and Jim would be returning to Colorado for a few months— long enough for Tilly to give notice, and for the two of them to decide the direction of the relationship.

"We also know," Kate said, standing up to pace, "that Benny couldn't have been responsible for the death of Laura Fuentes." Benny's arraignment was coming up fast, and as far as anyone knew he wouldn't be charged with Laura Fuentes' murder despite speculation in the local newspaper. Kate still wondered how Laura's name had come up in the first place.

"True," Roman chimed in. "Unless they charge him that piece of information is irrelevant. At least right now."

Kate slumped back into her chair. "I know, but I don't like it."

"What's to like?" Jim replied. "On the face of it, this is a huge win for local law enforcement. The situation is resolved. They can take all the credit, and whoever is running the trafficking ring can lay low for a while."

"And we wait until another girl is killed?" Kate asked. She already knew the answer, but that didn't make it any less abhorrent.

Kate tried to focus on the positive. The arrest of Benny Parks took one very bad man off the streets, and his conviction would ensure it. The injunction involving visitation of Mandy Garcia was removed. Within minutes of hearing the news, Kate was in her car heading to the hospital.

Mandy had been moved out of ICU. When Kate stepped off the elevator she saw Mandy's mother, Sarah, sitting in the waiting room. She braced herself as she approached the nurses' station.

"I'd like to see Mandy Garcia. My name is Kate Medina."

"You don't have permission to see my daughter," Sarah said, rising from her seat. Her eyes were red and swollen. The fury in her eyes kept Kate from feeling sympathy.

"Where was that anger when Benny Parks beat your daughter up, or when he tried to kill her," Kate hissed, unable to hold back.

"She lied to you," Sarah said, but her voice was shaking. "Mandy's a liar like her father. She…"

"Don't," Kate said. She turned to the nurse, who was watching the exchange warily. "What room is Mandy in?"

"3345," the nurse responded. "Her father's in with her. She's been asking for you." Kate started walking down the hallway, but after a few steps she turned and faced Sarah once more.

"You have another daughter. I hope you take better care of her than you did Mandy." Sarah gasped, but Kate walked away.

When she reached Mandy's room, she knocked on the door.

"Come in." David Garcia greeted Kate with a weary smile. "Hello, Ms. Medina. Thank you for coming."

"Hey, Ms. M," Mandy said, her voice a raspy whisper. The petechiae that Kate had seen on Mandy's face last time she saw had faded, but the angry wounds around her neck were bruised and the skin was still puffy. "Not very pretty, I know," Mandy said, touching her neck.

"Injuries usually aren't," Kate said, taking a seat next to Mandy's bed.

"I'm going to go get some coffee, if that's okay," David said, standing to leave. He waited by the door until Mandy nodded.

When he was gone, Mandy smiled. "He's been here pretty much 24/7 since I woke up. Poor guy."

"How are you feeling?" Kate asked.

"I have some pain. My vision is still a little blurry, and you can hear my voice," Mandy said, gesturing toward her throat again. "The doctor says he doesn't know what's going to be permanent yet." Her face darkened.

"Do you remember what happened?"

Mandy shifted uncomfortably. "No. I remember waking up a few times in the hospital, but there was so much pain they knocked me out pretty fast."

"Nothing about what happened before?"

"I remember staying with a friend for a few days after I left your house. Everything else is fuzzy." Mandy turned away from Kate, letting the silence between them hang like a curtain, cutting off communication. Kate wondered how far she could, or should, push Mandy. She had been hoping Mandy could point a finger or shed some light that would help Kate come to terms with everything, but not at the expense of Mandy's emotional well-being.

The silence was broken when David came back to the room. "I brought you a cup, too," he said. "Didn't know how you take it."

"Thank you," Kate said, accepting the offering. "How are you holding up?"

David sighed, taking a seat in the corner. "I'm better now that she's awake. Doc says she'll be able to come home in a few days."

"That's great," Kate said, turning back to Mandy. "Will you be staying with your dad?"

"Yeah," Mandy replied. "Actually, we're moving to Albuquerque. Dad got a job offer, and there are a lot more doctors to see while I recover." She paused. "It'll be a fresh start. I don't want anyone to see me like this anyway. I'll finish up my senior year at home and then start college up at UNM."

"Is your sister going with you?" Kate asked, thinking about what she'd said to Sarah Garcia in the lobby.

"Yeah. At least part of the year. She wants to be with my mom part of the year."

"Until my court petition goes through," he said, gritting his teeth. "I think they'll be more open to full-custody, given that Sarah had our girls living with a murderer."

Kate looked at Mandy, but the girl shook her head. It was clear that David didn't know the whole story and that Mandy wasn't going to tell him. More secrets. Unfortunate, but Kate could relate. Mandy had to come to terms with her trauma in her own time.

"Well, I'd better get going," Kate said, standing and moving toward the door. "If you need anything, Mandy, I'm here."

A tear slid down Mandy's cheek. "Thanks, Ms. Medina. For everything."

CHAPTER FORTY-ONE

The next morning, Kate headed to the county jail. She wasn't sure what she hoped to accomplish but after another sleepless night, she wanted answers—and there was really only one place she could think to look for them, even if it was a long shot.

When she arrived at the detention center, it was clear she wasn't going to get in. She appealed to the warden but was still denied her access. Feeling defeated, Kate walked back to the parking lot. There, parked beside her, was Allen Parks.

The elder Parks was leaning against the trunk of his car like he was waiting for someone. When Kate approached, he straightened up.

"Hello, Kate."

"Mr. Parks," Kate said. She kept walking but when he stepped between her and her vehicle, she felt a twinge of fear followed by a flood of anger. She stopped and looked him in the eye. "What do you want?"

Parks chuckled. "Feisty. Just like your sister."

Kate's fury grew. She moved forward, thinking she might punch the man; thinking it would feel so good to slam her fist into his face as hard as she could. But Parks frowned and raised his hand. "I wouldn't do that if I were you." His gaze flickered over her shoulder where two detention center officers were walking toward them. "I don't think you want to cause a scene, do you?"

The thing that made Kate angriest, the thing that pushed her over the top, was the confidence with which Allen Parks spoke. Kate didn't know who to trust, and Parks felt sure that the officers would be on his side. He was probably right, so she forced herself to relax.

"Is everything okay here, Miss?" The officer who'd spoken was young, maybe twenty years old. His expression was a mix of concern and confusion. He looked back and forth between Kate and Allen. "Mr. Parks?"

"Of course, Robert. I was having a word with Ms. Medina before I went in to see Benny."

The officer's gaze traveled to Kate. She tried to conjure up a neutral expression. "I'm sure we'll only be a second."

Both officers paused another moment, then the one who'd spoken nodded and they headed back into the building. Kate watched them go, but when she turned back to Allen Parks she felt like she'd been watching the scenery while the mountain lion readied himself to pounce. There wasn't a trace of civility left in his face. Instead his eyes were dark, his smile thin.

"Your father didn't give you a proper education, Kate."

"About what?" Kate's rage was barely contained, her teeth gritted.

"About how things work here." Allen leaned against his car door, still blocking Kate's path.

"Funny, your nephew said the same thing right before assaulting me." She stood her ground, holding his gaze.

"This is a small community, Kate. Close-knit. We take care of each other. There are consequences for bad behavior. Take my nephew, for instance. He never did learn to be discreet, and believe me, Kate, I gave him a lot of chances to figure it out."

"What are you saying?" Kate asked, but Allen ignored her, pressing on robotically. His lack of emotion was more terrifying than the words he spoke.

"Then look at you. How many have times have I suggested that your talents are wasted here? You've got a bright future somewhere else, but you don't listen, Kate. Now you've gotten Detective Aguilar involved, and look what's happened to him. I don't understand why you have to make it so difficult."

He looked at her and smiled. "But you're a smart woman, Kate. You understand now, don't you?"

Kate wanted to reach out and strangle this horrible man, so she kept her hands plastered at her sides when she leaned in and hissed. "Let me educate *you*, Mr. Parks. This is my home, and I'm not going anywhere." She took another small step forward, forcing Allen to lean back just a hair, and she smiled. "I promise you, I will not rest until every girl in this town is safe from you and your pedophile friends."

Allen frowned then shook his head. "Such a shame," he lamented, pushing himself off his car. Kate stepped back and braced herself, but Allen Parks walked right by her and into the detention center, leaving her alone in the parking lot.

All the arrogance and entitlement had left Benny Parks. He slumped next to his lawyer, looking gray and deflated. He pled guilty without comment, and as the judge affirmed that Benny would spend the rest of his life in prison, Kate could see the rise and fall of his shoulders, that only indication that he still drew breath.

The judge closed the proceedings and left the room. The criminal case against Benny Parks had taken less than a month, a fact that should have raised red flags. Instead the whole town seemed to be patting itself on the back. The courtroom was packed with men and women Kate recognized from outings with her father, a veritable who's who of the Alamogordo elite.

Benny's lawyer spoke to him in hushed tones as the bailiff approached to take him back to his holding cell, and then on to the Otero County Detention Center. Kate was glad this would be the last time she'd ever see Benny's face. But as he was exiting the courtroom he looked back at his uncle, whose face reflected the censure that a teacher might show an errant student. Benny hung his head and disappeared from sight.

Kate was watching the exchange when Allen's eyes met hers. He smiled and nodded, without a hint of malice, greeting those around him, his tone jovial as if he were at a social function rather than the sentencing hearing for his own flesh and blood. The sight made Kate's skin crawl.

"What was that about?" Roman asked. He'd been standing beside her, observing. Kate had given Roman a full report on her altercation with Allen Parks in the jail parking lot. Since that day, neither had left the house much outside of errands. Today's hearing was the first time Kate had seen Allen in public.

"I don't know. He looks pleased."

It was hard not to scrutinize every exchange as Parks shook hands with the men and leaned in to kiss women's cheeks. Did they think he was a hero for condemning the brutal acts of his deviant nephew? Or were they congratulating each other on another narrow escape? As Kate's eyes followed Parks's movement, they locked with another man's. Chief Gunnison was waiting in the receiving line, but his look was not carefree or kind. She could feel his eyes on her as she maneuvered Roman toward the furthest exit.

Her choice to stay in town was going to lead to more drama, but in the time since Benny's arrest things had settled down. Roman had begun applying for new jobs, though he was still hoping for a position with the State Police. Kate had been busy getting ready to move into her new house. Until this moment, it had been easy to imagine that this was an ordinary small town, and she was an ordinary woman. But Kate couldn't allow herself to become complacent.

"Thanks for coming in, Kate," Pete McIntyre said, offering her a chair. When Kate had walked into the high school, she was overcome by how normal everything seemed. The kids chatted in the hallways. Homecoming was approaching, and every surface overflowed with black and gold. Sitting in the principal's office, Kate was disappointed. It was human nature to seek normalcy and calm in the wake of disaster, but Kate couldn't help but think about Mandy, Gabby, and all the other girls who had been victimized but whose voices remained silent.

She hoped she could help them, no matter how long it took.

"What can I do for you, Pete?" Kate asked.

"I wanted to clear the air," Pete said. He was still standing, and now he started to pace. "I'm still not clear about what happened during these last months. I think everyone was so upset about Gabby Greene's death that emotions were high."

"It's understandable. A girl was brutally murdered," Kate said, annoyed at the way Pete's words sought to diminish the horror that Gabby had endured.

"I'm sorry, Kate. I really am. And we would like you to come back." When she started to shake her head, he added. "You're a great psychologist, Kate. These kids need you."

Kate stood, fighting to contain her fury. "You're right, Pete. These kids need someone who will listen to them, and someone who will stand up for them regardless of the pressure." Pete had the decency to look ashamed. "Your students are being stalked. They're being groomed, abused, and even killed. Right under your nose. And I tried to help, but the district made it clear that they weren't interested in my help. So no, I won't be coming back."

"Kate," Pete pleaded, taking a step toward her, "I know you're angry." But Kate held up her hand.

"I'm not angry, Pete. Angry is not a strong enough to describe how I feel." Her heart was beginning to race, but it wasn't anxiety causing her to lose her cool this time. "I knew you weren't going to back me up, but I hope you'll open your eyes to what's happening here. These kids need you to be stronger."

All the color drained from Pete's face, but he said nothing as Kate walked out the door.

CHAPTER FORTY-TWO

Kate drove to the realtor's office to finish some paperwork.

"Hi Kate," Janet said, bounding out of her chair to give Kate a hug. The unexpected show of affection and familiarity was a little unsettling given how professional the realtor had always presented herself. It also felt nice. "This process just got a lot easier," Janet said, leading Kate back to her desk.

"Why?" Kate said, quirking an eyebrow as she set her purse down and took a seat across from Janet.

"Well when I told the owner you were going to pay such a large down payment, he was ecstatic. So was our lender. The new balance will make the loan process a snap."

"Whoa, wait a minute," Kate said, thrown off-guard. "What large down payment? I was planning on paying the standard twenty percent from the sale of my dad's house, but I can't go much higher."

Janet gave Kate a look. "I'm surprised Tilly didn't want to tell you herself."

"Tilly? Tell me what?" Kate asked, now on high alert.

"That she's putting her part of the sale toward your down

payment. With your twenty and her cut, that puts the loan amount around forty percent."

Kate flushed. "No, she didn't tell me. Listen, Janet. I need to double check with her to make sure she's thought this through." Kate couldn't imagine what had come over her sister, or why she hadn't just told her what she was thinking.

Janet smiled. "She told me you'd say that, so she left this with me." She gave Kate a hand-written letter.

"When was she here?"

"A few days ago," Janet said. "Read it."

Dear Kate,

Thank you for your very generous offer to split the money from selling Dad's house with me. I feel unworthy—you've had to shoulder all the burden yourself. As sad as I am that Dad is gone, I am so thankful for the chance to have my sister back. And your safe house idea, crazy as it is, may be the most noble thing I've ever heard. I want my half of the house money to help you. I know what you're thinking, but I'm not going to take no for an answer. Those girls need you. And so do I. From this point on, there won't ever be a time when you have to doubt whether I have your back.

Love you forever,

Tilly

Kate was crying before she finished reading.

Kate had convinced herself that every day would be an uphill battle, but as soon as Benny Parks went to prison, everything went back to business as usual, at least as far as Kate could tell.

The holidays were approaching. Kate and Roman had fallen into a comfortable routine, as if the idea that they'd ever been separated was a bad dream.

It wasn't denial. Kate had spent too many years trying to pretend that she lived in a world of her making. Moving forward meant coming to terms with the fact that there were terrible, ugly things that she had no control over, but that there were wonderful things worth fighting for, too. Her relationship with Roman was one of them. The situation wasn't perfect, but Kate was no longer expecting it to be. Instead, she tried to live every moment to its fullest, having accepted the harsh reality that any moment might be her last.

"I got a call from Angela," Roman said, one morning over breakfast. Kate had gotten good at taming the jealousy she felt at the mention of Roman's former flame. Despite the present complications, Kate liked Angela Lopez and she still hoped they could work together in some capacity.

"How's she doing?"

"She seemed fine." His face darkened. "She called to let me know that the position I applied for had been filled."

"Ouch."

"It's okay." He reached for Kate's hand. "She sounded pretty relieved that we wouldn't be working together, and I can't say that I blame her. It would've been awkward. But she wasn't calling to rub it in."

"Why *did* she call?"

"She had news." Now Roman was frowning. "Gunnison painted a pretty unflattering picture when they called for a recommendation. It's going to be hard to get a job around here."

Kate's stomach churned. She was days away from closing on her new house, and for the first time in forever, she didn't want to leave. She watched as he sorted through his thoughts and feelings, wondering what they might be. As the minutes ticked by, her anxiety grew.

Finally he shook his head. "It'll be fine." He sounded like he was trying to convince himself.

"What's your plan?" she asked timidly. "Can you fight it?"

Roman looked at her and smiled. "I don't know, but right now I'm where I need to be."

Kate let go of the breath she'd been holding. "After I left home, I never felt that sense of being rooted to one place. My focus was on my work. It's strange how, despite all the things I've been through since coming home, that's always what this town has been to me. And no matter how hard I fought against it, I still ended up here."

"Any regrets?"

Kate blushed as he reached for her hand, lacing their fingers together and then raising her hand to his lips. "A few. I wish I'd figured so many things out sooner," she offered, using her free hand to caress his cheek. "That I hadn't been blind to what Tilly went through. It makes me so sad that she had no one to turn to."

Roman smiled at her reassuringly. "Hindsight is always 20/20, you know? And we can waste time dwelling on the things we could have done or should have known, but we can't change them. All we can do is move forward and try to make things better."

"Handsome *and* a philosopher," she teased, but the sentiment was exactly what she needed to hear. Coming back to Alamogordo had been an emotional rollercoaster but she was ready to put down roots, despite the danger. Ready to stay in one place and face the monsters, rather than running from them, both in her waking world and her sleeping one.

She still woke with anxiety, though the attacks had come less frequently in recent weeks. The visions of her attacker, the memories of Mandy Garcia's wounds, and the helplessness that followed haunted her. But this town was her home—the place she lived with her family, where her parents were buried, and where she hoped she might even raise a family of her own. It was a place worth fighting for.

AFTERWORD

"Sex trafficking: the recruitment, harboring, transportation, provision, obtaining, patronizing, or soliciting of a person for the purpose of a commercial sex act, in which the commercial sex act is induced by force, fraud, or coercion, or in which the person induced to perform such act has not attained 18 years of age;" - *United States Department of Health and Human Services, Trafficking Fact Sheet (2017)*

According to the US Department of Health and Human Services, an estimated 200,000 American youth are victims of sexual exploitation every year *within* the United States. When we think of human trafficking, we often think of humans being brought from one country into another, but the number of victims within the U.S. each year is staggering.

Let's be clear.

These are United States citizens.

These are our children.

To understand why this happens, we have to examine our

perceptions and assumptions. We need to look at behaviors and think about what they might mean beyond the obvious. Sexual predators are often not the people we expect. They're not necessary the dark lurking strangers. They might be a next-door neighbor or the shop owner down the street. *Complicit*, and the Kate Medina novels to follow, will explore what predation might look like in a small town, where everyone knows each other.

One of the first steps we can all take in preventing this kind of violence in our communities is to challenge the assumptions we hold and to learn about the signs and symptoms of sexual, interpersonal, and domestic violence. To educate ourselves, not only on how to spot signs of trafficking, but how to respond and how to intervene. To make our first instinct to believe so that all the heavy burden of proving abuse does not lie with the victim.

To be the change we want to see in the world.

Thank you for reading,
Amy

ACKNOWLEDGMENTS

Alamogordo, New Mexico is my hometown. It's not perfect, but it remains one of my favorite places in the world.

While living in Alamogordo, I was honored to serve as the Director for the Sexual Assault Nurse Examiners (SANE) of Otero & Lincoln Counties for several years. During that time, I worked with law enforcement officers from a variety of agencies including Alamogordo Police Department, Otero County Sheriff's Office, Lincoln County Sheriff's Office, New Mexico State Police and representatives of Holloman Air Force Base, the Mescalero Apache Tribe, the US Attorney's Office, and the Bureau of Indian Affairs.

I am very proud to have worked beside so many of you in our efforts to serve victims and prevent violence in our community.

And to the many SANE nurses who I had the honor of working with and knowing. Jennifer, Mandy, Celeste, Angie, Kay, and of course, my aunt Tina, without whom I would never have experienced the joys and the crushing pain so intertwined in the world of sexual assault service and prevention. Thank you for being the strongest people I've ever known.

I'd like to thank my editors Elizabeth Copps and Kim Huther, my book cover designer Carl Graves and all my beta readers for helping to birth this book. Ronda, Eleanor, and David—your feedback provided some serious AHA! moments and Kate's story is so much better for it.

To my critique partners Eleanor and Lynda, thank you for working with me even when my schedule is erratic and my life isa chaotic mess—which is pretty much all the time. I love reading your work and it makes me think outside my box. You inspire me!

Kate Medina began wiggling her way into my brain in 2019, but after I took the lead at Northern Colorado Writers, I knew she was going to have to wait. So grateful to all my friends and family who've been listening to me brainstorm despite the deadline being so far away.

To my best friend Jessica, who is so supportive and encouraging, despite all the crap you have to deal with in life. You're always my biggest cheerleader and I forgive you for the PTSD I suffered when you made me watch *The Human Centipede.* That's how much I love you.

To my parents, who taught me early on that I could do anything I set my mind to regardless of physical limitations and who meant it when they told me they'd love me and support me no matter what.

To Allen, my first reader, toughest critic, and accomplice in life. You put up with a lot.

And to my children. I am so proud of you and it is such a joy to be your mother. You make me laugh and keep me on my toes. You make me a better person. I love you.

ABOUT THE AUTHOR

Amy Rivers writes novels, short stories and personal essays. She is the Director of Northern Colorado Writers. Her novel *All The Broken People* was recently selected as the Colorado Author Project winner in the adult fiction category. She's been published in *We Got This: Solo Mom Stories of Grit, Heart, and Humor, Flash! A Celebration of Short Fiction, Chicken Soup for the Soul: Inspiration for Nurses*, and *Splice Today*, as well as *Novelty Bride Magazine* and ESME.com. She was raised in New Mexico and now lives in Colorado with her husband and children. She holds degrees in psychology and political science, two topics she loves to write about.

For more information, visit AmyRivers.com

ALSO BY AMY RIVERS

All The Broken People

The Cambria Series
Wallflower Blooming
Best Laid Plans & Other Disasters

CPSIA information can be obtained
at www.ICGtesting.com
Printed in the USA
FSHW011927230121
77949FS